DEBORAH RISING

A Novel

Avraham Azrieli

ISBN: 978-1-953648-01-3

BOOKS BY AVRAHAM AZRIELI

Fiction:

The Masada Complex
The Jerusalem Inception
The Jerusalem Assassin
Christmas for Joshua
The Mormon Candidate
The Bootstrap Ultimatum
Thump
Deborah Rising
Deborah Calling
Deborah Slaying
Deborah Leading
The Elixirist

Nonfiction:

Your Lawyer on a Short Leash – A Guide to Dealing with Lawyers
One Step Ahead – A Mother of Seven Escaping Hitler's Claws

Author Website:

www.AzrieliBooks.com

DEDICATION

For my brother-in-law, Avraham "Tsutsu" Davidovich (1959-2015), whose affection, wisdom and zest for life continue to illuminate my path.

DEBORAH RISING

1

The girls came early to the stoning. They emerged one by one from the gates of Emanuel, which the sentries opened at sunrise, and spread out over the barren slopes to collect rocks. There were more than seventy girls, all of the town's unmarried maidens, ten years and older. With their brown wool dresses and bent backs, they looked like an army of weary squirrels gathering nuts for the winter.

When the pile of rocks near the gates was high enough, one of the sentries whistled, and the girls gathered back. They sat on the ground, forming a wide circle around the Pit of Shame.

The sun had barely cleared the eastern ridges of the Samariah Hills, and the girls huddled together to keep warm. Most of them had dark skin and black hair. A few had a lighter complexion and wheat-colored hair. One girl, however, stood out from the rest with her white, freckled cheeks and braided orange locks—an unusual orange, brighter than ripe carrots and more radiant than the flame produced by the burning fat of a sacrificial lamb.

The girls didn't speak to each other and kept their eyes down, except for an occasional glance at the scavenger birds that circled above.

As the day warmed up, the hillside filled with spectators, not only from the town itself, but also from the neighboring villages and scattered homesteads. A public stoning was an infrequent spectacle, unlike the more common whipping of disobedient wives, defiant slaves, and thieves. The rumor that the accused was a family member of the town's ruler, Judge Zifron, drew an even larger crowd. Men, women, and children spread straw mats and settled down to wait, munching on dried figs, fresh dates, or carobs dipped in honey. Most of the men had full beards and wore wool caps in observance of the Hebrew tradition. They chatted and laughed in giddy anticipation, whereas the women sat quietly. Even a group of lepers showed up, coming down from the cave where they dwelled. Swathed in tattered rags and veils to hide their deformities, they shuffled to a rocky patch, apart from everyone else.

A short distance from the gates, along the main road, the fairgrounds served as a daytime market and an overnight campsite for trading caravans. Coins changed hands for jugs of wine or milk, baskets of apples or pears, or chunks of honey cake dipped in cinnamon. Fortune-tellers, charm healers, portrait painters, and even a hairdresser did brisk business while young boys ran around, chasing dogs, goats, and each other.

Despite the long wait and rowdy commotion, the young maidens didn't leave the circle around the Pit of Shame.

The sun reached a third of the way up in the clear, blue sky.

Obadiah of Levi emerged from the gates in his priestly robe—stark white and embroidered with blue threads that dangled from the bottom edges. His long beard was gray, his bejeweled breastplate glistened, and his oak staff had a silver handle.

The priest brought a ram's horn to his lips. It was long, with many serpentine loops. He inhaled deeply and blew. The sound was low and scratchy, more a growl than a roar, infused with sadness and dread that caused the crowd to quiet down until the only remaining noise came from the circling birds.

The seven elders of the town appeared next. Dressed in their white Sabbath robes, they followed each other solemnly in order of age and sat on a stone bench by the wall of the gatehouse.

Obadiah of Levi blew the ram's horn again, not continuously as before, but in a series of sharp toots. The audience rose to its feet, except for the maidens around the Pit of Shame, who would not be allowed to get up until the last stone had been cast.

A group of foot soldiers appeared, carrying the flag of the tribe of Ephraim—a white ox against a black background. They marched through the gatehouse, their boots pounding the road, and stood in attention.

The ruler of Emanuel, Judge Zifron of Ephraim, rode on a great black stallion. The aging sovereign wore a black coat embroidered with threads of gold and silver. The coat was unbuttoned in front to accommodate his bulging belly. His beard was closely cropped, and he wore no hat. Four of his young sons followed him on ponies.

Judge Zifron's stallion paused at the sight of the large crowd and reared up on its hind legs. The judge subdued his horse with an expert jab of the heels and leaned forward, whispering in its pricked ears until the horse calmed down.

A soldier stepped up and held the reins. Another helped Judge Zifron down from the saddle and supported him up the steps onto an elevated platform. The judge sat down in a large, padded chair and wiped his face with a rag while his young sons tied their ponies and sat at the foot of the platform. A third soldier carried onto the platform the black effigy of Mott, the Canaanite god of death. It had a human body, about a third of a grown man's height, and brandished the scepter of bereavement in one hand and the scepter of widowhood in the other. Its head was disproportionately large, with a protruding jaw and sharp teeth in its gaping mouth. The soldier handed Mott to Judge Zifron, who held it up for all to see.

The sight of the Canaanite effigy elicited murmured protests from the crowd. Obadiah of Levi turned his head and spat.

A group of mounted soldiers emerged from the gates, led by Seesya, Judge Zifron's first son and heir. At nineteen, he was tall and broad-shouldered. His clean-shaven face was square-jawed and handsome, except for a red scar that cut diagonally across his lips from the left cheek to his right jaw, endowing him with a permanent sneer. He wore a suit of leather armor and a matching leather helmet. A sword hung from his hip, and he carried a long spear.

As Seesya and the soldiers approached the crowd, his brown steed was also startled by the commotion and rose on its hind legs. Seesya cursed and punched it on the side of the head. The horse neighed and reared again. Seesya hit it twice more. The horse trotted sideways, stumbled on the uneven dirt road, and fell over, throwing Seesya to the ground. His spear dropped, and his helmet rolled away, exposing his shoulder-length black hair.

The crowd roared in laughter while the soldiers rushed to help Seesya. He sprang to his feet, collected his spear, and ran up the steps onto the platform, where his father sat stone-faced.

Obadiah then climbed the platform and stood at the opposite end from Judge Zifron and his son. The priest pounded his oak staff on the platform three times and announced: "Bring forth the accused!"

The large crowd watched the gates in rapt silence.

A lone figure emerged, dressed in a red robe, customarily worn by those accused of a capital offense, as well as by women during their monthly periods of impurity. A red scarf covered her head and most of her face, leaving a slit for her eyes. Two soldiers followed behind, making her seem even smaller. They nudged the accused through the gates, past the seven elders, to the elevated platform, where they made her kneel before Judge Zifron, his son, the priest, and the black effigy of Mott.

At the nearby circle around the Pit of Shame, the girl with the orange hair buried her face in her hands and began to sob.

Judge Zifron stomped his boot on the platform and called, "Who accuses this woman?"

His son stepped forward. "I, Seesya of Ephraim, son of Zifron, accuse this woman, Tamar, daughter of Harutz of Ephraim. She was betrothed to me with a ring, but on the first night that I came to possess her as my lawful wife, she no longer had her virginity." He pointed his spear at the red-clad figure at the foot of the platform. "She's a whore!"

Judge Zifron turned to the priest. "What is the law?"

Obadiah of Levi pulled a roll of parchment from under his white robe. "This is Yahweh's law, given to the prophet Moses on Mount Sinai."

He unfurled the scroll and read aloud: "If a man took a woman and came to her and disliked her and said, 'This woman I took and came to possess her as my wife but found her without virginity,' then the woman's father will bring to the town elders the bed cloth that shows the stains of her virginity and say, 'This man took our daughter and then he hated her and slandered her.' Then the elders will punish the man for slandering a Hebrew virgin. He will pay one hundred silver coins to her father and will keep her as his wife and may not divorce her all the days of his life."

Obadiah paused and glanced at Seesya, who gestured with his spear at the scroll, signaling the priest to continue.

"But if no stains are found," Obadiah read from the scroll, "you will take the woman outside, and the men of her town will stone her with rocks until she is dead, for she sinned among her people and disgraced the house of her father; you shall eradicate evil from among you."

The priest rolled up the parchment. "This is the law of Yahweh, the one and only God of the Hebrews." He pointedly looked at the effigy of Mott, and a twitch of disgust contorted his face.

"The law is clear," Judge Zifron said. "Let us hear from her father."

There was a long silence.

"Her father can't speak for her," Seesya said. "He's dead."

"Indeed." Judge Zifron turned to the priest. "Who may speak for a woman whose father is dead?"

Obadiah didn't answer.

"Tell us," the judge demanded. "What is Yahweh's law?"

The priest answered in a toneless voice. "Her husband may speak for her."

Seesya signaled to one of the soldiers, who ran to the platform and held forward a bunched-up cloth. Seesya picked it up with the tip of his spear and shook the cloth until it untangled. It was white, shaped like a woman's robe, but open in the front, with loops and buttons.

"Tell us," Judge Zifron said with a touch of impatience. "What is this?"

"It's her bed cloth from the night I possessed her as my wife for the first time." He waved it in the air to show that it was without stain.

Judge Zifron looked down at the accused. "Do you deny that this is your bed cloth?"

She shook her head.

The judge gestured at the crowd. "Is there a man here who wishes to speak in this whore's defense? Speak now."

No one stepped forward.

"I wish to speak," the accused said, her voice muffled by the veil over her face. "My defense is that—"

"Be quiet," the judge said.

"But I'm innocent!"

"Quiet!"

"No man has ever possessed me," she cried. "No one, not even when—"

Seesya threw his spear at her. The dull end of the spear hit her head, and she fell down.

The crowd laughed.

The soldiers pulled her up and held her arms.

Judge Zifron raised his hands to silence the crowd. He turned to Obadiah. "May a woman bear witness?"

"No," the priest said. "Only a man can give testimony."

After a brief consultation among the elders, they delivered the verdict in one voice. "Guilty!"

All over the hillside, hundreds of men applauded.

"Under the law," Judge Zifron announced, "Tamar, wife of Seesya, is guilty as charged. She has done evil, disgraced the house of her dead father, and dishonored our tribe. Therefore, she will be placed in the Pit of Shame and stoned by the men of her town until she is dead."

The men in the crowd cheered again.

Obadiah of Levi descended from the platform and led the way, followed by two soldiers, who held Tamar between them. They passed through the circle of maidens and stood at the Pit of Shame.

The priest pulled away the red scarf, exposing Tamar's face. She looked younger than her fourteen years. Her hair was orange—the same color as the girl seated in the circle, a dozen steps away. They looked at each other. Tamar was slightly older, her pale face fuller and her eyes a darker shade of green.

The younger girl cried out, but her voice was lost in the crowd's jeers and whistles. She started to get up, but Tamar shook her head, pointed up at the blue sky, and placed her hands under her chin, fingers interwoven. The girl sat back, pressed her interwoven fingers under her chin, and began to pray silently.

Obadiah raised his arms to silence the crowd and faced the condemned. "Repent now," he said. "Beg Yahweh for His forgiveness, for you have sinned."

"It's not true," Tamar protested. "I haven't sinned."

"He will receive your soul if you repent."

"He knows I'm innocent," she said. "You know it, too."

The crowd, which had quieted momentarily to listen, booed. Only the maidens seated nearby could hear the rest of the exchange.

"It's true." The priest hung his head, deflated. "I'm powerless to help you. Please forgive me."

"I'll forgive you on one condition." Tamar pulled a ring off her finger and gave it to the priest. "Make sure this ring doesn't go onto my sister's finger. Protect her from suffering the same injustice I've suffered."

Obadiah turned and walked away from the Pit of Shame. His gaze briefly met the eyes of the orange-haired girl, who was praying quietly for a miracle.

Tamar sat on the ground and eased herself, legs first, into the tight hole. Only her head and shoulders showed above ground level. A puff of wind blew at her hair, causing it to fan out around her head with a fiery brightness that contrasted with the brown earth and the somber occasion.

Seesya came down from the platform and blocked Obadiah's way. "Give me the ring."

The priest glanced at the ring resting in his open hand and looked up at the judge on the platform.

Seesya grunted, took the ring from Obadiah's hand, and marched over to the pile of rocks, just outside the circle of maidens.

The elders made their way over slowly and lined up behind Seesya. The rest of the men of Emanuel joined the queue behind the elders, starting with well-to-do merchants, then artisans, peddlers, and peasants. Men from the surrounding villages and homesteads, who were not allowed to participate in the stoning, watched the preparations in silence.

Reaching down for a rock, Seesya took his time to select one that fit nicely in his palm. He tossed it from hand to hand to get a measure of its weight and nodded with satisfaction.

Obadiah pounded his staff three times. "The condemned may plead for mercy now."

With difficulty, Judge Zifron rose from the padded chair. He lifted the effigy of Mott and held it so that its menacing face turned to the Pit of Shame.

The spectators grumbled. They hadn't come here to watch a whore win a pardon. A long moment passed. Everyone stared at the girl's head, sticking out of the Pit of Shame.

"I'm innocent," she said.

Sporadic booing came from the crowd.

"Spare me," she raised her voice. "For your own good, show mercy and save yourself from Yahweh's wrath."

Hundreds of eyes focused on Judge Zifron. He could either grant a pardon by putting Mott down, or refuse a pardon by raising Mott higher.

The girl continued to pray, her lips moving rapidly, her face creased in devotion.

For a long moment, it seemed that the judge was vacillating. He glanced at Seesya, who shook his head sharply.

With an audible sigh, Judge Zifron raised Mott high above his head.

The male spectators cheered. The women and girls lowered their eyes. At the circle of maidens, the girl with the orange hair stopped praying and looked up at the sky, her mouth open in midsentence.

The priest pounded his staff until calm was restored and said, "Let the accuser cast the first stone."

Seesya turned to face his young wife, who glared back at him from the hole in the ground. He raised his hand to throw the rock but changed his mind and walked over to the circle of maidens.

The girl was still staring at the sky in bewilderment over her unanswered prayers.

He poked her from behind with the tip of his boot.

Startled, the girl looked up over her shoulder.

"Give me your hand," he said.

"No," Tamar yelled from the Pit of Shame. "Leave her alone!"

Seesya reached down and grabbed the girl's hand.

"Don't do it!" Tamar's voice was desperate. "Not my sister!"

He slipped the ring on the girl's finger. "With this ring," he declared, "I betroth you to me, to be my wife."

"No," Tamar cried. "No! No! No!"

The girl tried to pull her hand away, but Seesya held on to it. "No more praying," he said. "Keep your eyes open."

She stared at him, her eyes large and green.

"Look there, little witch." He pointed at the Pit of Shame. "Watch your sister."

Still, she looked only at him.

Blowing air in frustration, he put his big hand on top of her head, clasped it, and made it turn so that the girl looked at Tamar. "Good," he said. "Watch and learn!"

With that, he threw the first stone at Tamar.

His aim was slightly off, and the rock passed beside Tamar's head, giving her a glancing blow.

The crowd sighed with disappointment.

"Seesya of Ephraim," Tamar shouted. "Son of Zifron! I curse you!"

Seesya ran back to the pile of stones.

"No more," the priest said. "One stone for each man."

The oldest among the elders, his hand shaking badly, tossed a stone, which missed completely.

"I curse you!" Tamar's screeching voice tore through the air. "I curse you, Seesya! May Yahweh condemn you to the same fate as I suffer today!"

The second elder bent slowly to pick up a stone.

Seesya grabbed one and gave it to him. "Throw it already!"

"I curse you," Tamar yelled. "I curse the house of your father!"

This time, the stone hit the ground near the Pit of Shame and bounced, striking her left cheek. Tamar yelled in pain but didn't stop. "I curse the house of Zifron, that a great fire will consume your sinful house and burn all your wealth to ashes!"

The third elder threw a rock, which went too far.

"I curse the town of Emanuel and all of you who watch this injustice and don't—"

"Enough!" Seesya picked up a stone and pitched it with all his power. It struck Tamar on the forehead, making a sound like the breaking of a clay jar.

At the circle around the Pit of Shame, the girl with the orange hair wailed, her voice shrill with sorrow.

The crowd didn't cheer Seesya's perfect strike, which snuffed out Tamar's cursing but not the fear it generated, for the curse of a dying person was known to be far more potent than even that of a wizard or a witch. And Tamar was clearly either dead or dying.

The snug walls of the Pit of Shame supported her body in the upright position, but her head slumped to one side. Her eyes had closed, and blood oozed from her forehead.

The spectators began to boo. A few men yelled, "One stone! One stone!"

"Go on!" Judge Zifron stomped the platform. "Continue!"

Seesya picked up a stone and handed it to the next elder, who dutifully tossed it, missing the target.

The stoning continued as required by the law. Each of the elders cast a stone, followed by the men of Emanuel—anyone thirteen or older. Many of them managed to hit Tamar's head, which gradually turned into bloody pulp. The spectators had recovered from the shock of Tamar's curses and cheered every successful strike.

The maidens remained seated around the Pit of Shame and watched the stoning as the law required them to do. They were all crying, except for the girl with the orange hair. After her initial heart-piercing wail, she shut her eyes and pressed her hands, fingers interwoven under her chin while her lips moved with words of prayer, as her sister had asked.

A pause in the stoning made the crowd protest.

The girl turned to look.

At the head of the line stood a boy of about fourteen, dark-skinned, stout, and muscular. His white cap was too small for his thick mane of black curls, and his adolescent goatee was short and sparse.

"Keep going," Judge Zifron called from the platform. "Cast the stone."

The boy had a stone in his hand, but he wouldn't throw it. "She's already dead."

The judge chuckled. "What's your name, boy?"

"I am Barac, son of Abinoam." He glanced at his father, who stood behind him.

"Abinoam the blacksmith," Judge Zifron said. "Better get your son to follow the law, or my son will make him."

Seesya leaned on his spear nonchalantly.

Abinoam pointed at the Pit of Shame. "Cast the stone, Son. You must."

The crowd taunted him. "Throw it! Throw it!"

"She's dead, Father." Barac's dark eyes found the green eyes of the girl with the orange hair, and they looked at each other for a long moment.

"Throw it, Son." Abinoam glanced around with an awkward smile. "You can't hurt her anymore."

"It's wrong, Father."

"It's the law. You must."

"Coward," someone shouted. "Stone the whore!"

Tamar's younger sister kept looking at Barac from the circle of maidens around the Pit of Shame.

Seesya stepped forward and tapped Barac's arm with the spear. "Do as you're told, boy!"

Barac pointed at Tamar's bloody head, sticking out from the ground. "It's a sin to desecrate the dead."

"A dead whore." Seesya pointed his spear. "Cast the stone, or you'll end up in the same place."

With a last glance at the girl with the orange hair, Barac dropped the stone back on the pile, which was half of what it had been when the stoning began. He turned and walked away.

Seesya grimaced and tilted his arm back to hurl the spear at the boy's back.

"No!" Abinoam rushed forward and rammed Seesya, who stumbled and fell.

The crowd groaned. No one had ever humiliated the eldest son of Judge Zifron and lived to talk about it.

Seesya got up quickly, drew his sword, and rushed at Abinoam, who was already retreating, his hands held up in surrender. Barac turned and ran back to help his father. As Seesya raised his sword to strike Abinoam, Barac grabbed his arm and hung from it, causing him to miss. Seesya shouted in rage and used his free hand to punch the boy in the face, but Barac wouldn't let go, and the sword dropped from Seesya's hand.

Abinoam pulled his son by the shirt and staggered backward as Seesya picked up his sword and lurched at his helpless prey, raising the sword for a deadly blow.

"Don't kill the blacksmith," Judge Zifron yelled. "We need him."

Taking advantage of Seesya's momentary hesitation, Abinoam and his son took flight.

"We'll punish them later," the judge said. "Continue with the stoning."

Seesya sheathed his sword and returned to the pile of stones, where a line of men waited for their shot at Tamar. Her sister resumed praying while her eyes followed the fleeing blacksmith and his son until they were gone.

2

As the sun descended on the western horizon, the soldiers pulled Tamar out of the Pit of Shame and carried her a short distance up the road to the Weeping Tree. They hung the corpse by the feet from a high branch where birds would pick at it until only dry bones remained.

Judge Zifron and Seesya mounted their horses and rode through the gates into the town, followed by the judge's younger sons, the priest, and the elders. Only then did the soldiers allow the crowd to leave. The people of Emanuel entered quickly before the gates were locked at sunset, whereas the rest of the people headed back to their villages and homesteads.

The girl with the orange hair slipped away and ran. She avoided the main road and followed goat trails through the low hills and dry streams. The sun was gone, and the moon, which was nearly full, appeared over the horizon. Coyotes howled in the distance, and she watched the ground for snakes, but after her sister's stoning, it was men she really feared.

Nearly two hours later, a lone palm tree appeared, its summit outlined against the moonlit sky above a small house. She stopped at the edge of a field and knelt, peering into the night, panting hard. Her brown wool dress came down to her sandals, the sleeves all the way to her wrists, but she began to tremble. She stayed put, gazing intently, searching for any sign of life.

The homestead was nestled in a valley, its fertile soil nourished by slow erosion from the gentle slopes. That soil was perfect, the girl knew, for growing wheat, barley, and flax. Up on the hillsides, the patches of arable soil supported apple, pear, pomegranate, and carob trees, while the rocky ledges sustained bountiful olive trees, their gnarled branches thick and ageless.

Looking back at the house, the girl saw no glow from a fire in the stove, nor yellow flickering from an oil lamp. She sniffed the air but detected no smoke, only the mixed fragrances of the crops in the fields, the wildflowers behind the house, and the trees heavy with ripe fruit. These were the scents of her lost childhood.

A sigh escaped her lips.

The bushes nearby rustled, and a dry stick broke.

She covered her mouth, paralyzed with fear.

Two shadows appeared. One was shorter than the other, with curly hair that glistened in the moonlight. "Deborah? Is that you?"

"Barac?"

He hurried to her. "I knew you'd come here!"

"I had to," she said, her voice breaking.

"I'm sorry about your sister."

She struggled not to weep, and he stepped forward, as if to hug her.

"Watch it, Son." Abinoam put his arm between them. "What's this familiarity?"

"Nothing, Father." The boy stepped back, his face glowing in the dark. "We only talk on the street, that's all."

"Keep your voice down." Abinoam glanced around. "You've caused enough trouble already."

"Your son helped me a few times." Deborah spoke softly, leaning close enough to notice the smoky smell of the blacksmith shop on their clothes. "With the haystacks, carrying them uphill to the basket factory—"

"You're not children anymore," Abinoam admonished.

She went to the doorway and peeked into the house. The main room had a brick stove in the center and enough floor space for people and livestock to spend the night. The thatched roof was mostly gone, letting in the moonlight.

Probing the doorjamb with her hand, about two-thirds of the way up her fingers found the small depression in the wood. It was empty. The sacred mezuzah scroll was gone. Its absence wasn't unexpected in an abandoned house, but she felt a pang of loss. Out of habit, she kissed the tips of her fingers before entering.

Deborah sat down on the dirt floor near the stone stove. Her former home was now cold and lonesome.

Abinoam put down the sack he'd been carrying. The clinking

indicated it contained his tools.

Barac walked around the large room, touching the broken table, the clay shards of bowls and jars, and what was left of a straw mattress in the corner. "What happened to your parents?"

She couldn't speak.

"They were killed last summer," Abinoam said. "Judge Zifron's son and his soldiers were chasing after some bandits in the area and found her parents' bodies in the field."

Kicking the soil with the toe of his sandal, Barac asked, "Who were the bandits?"

"Canaanite marauders, most likely," Abinoam said. "They were never caught."

Deborah cried softly.

Abinoam crouched next to her. "Don't cry, girl. You should be proud. Your father was a faithful man, God-fearing like his ancestors, who had received this good plot when the prophet Joshua divided the land between the tribes. He died defending it."

"Palm Homestead," she said, sniffling. "That's what Father called it."

"Why?" Barac asked, sitting down beside her. "There's only one palm tree outside."

"It's a special tree. I used to play with Tamar under it while our father finished his work in the fields and orchards." She paused, remembering. "At sunset, we'd see the lamps light up inside and peek through the windows to watch our mother prepare dinner. And now they're dead, and I'll never see them again." She broke down again, crying.

"You can see her in your memories," Barac said.

Deborah looked at him.

"My mother died when I was a baby," he explained, "before I could know her and remember how she looked."

His father took a deep breath, exhaling loudly.

"Your mother," Barac continued. "What was her name?"

"Raquellah." Deborah wiped her face on the sleeve of her dress. The fabric was coarse like the skin on the palms of her mother's hands. "She did everything—cleaning, cooking, helping Father in the fields—but she never got tired."

"They came to town," Abinoam said. "Picked up tools at my shop. Your mother was tall and beautiful, like a queen, with large green eyes."

"And long, wavy hair," Deborah said. "She would let it loose when there were no strangers around."

"Was it orange," Barac asked, "like yours?"

His father looked at him but said nothing.

"Yes," she said. "Mother came from the Judah tribe. Her family died when Edomite raiders attacked their village, which was called Tamar. She somehow made it to Shiloh, and it happened to be the fifteenth day of the month of Av."

"Ah, the Tu B'Av festival," Abinoam said. "It's the only time Hebrew girls are allowed to dance in view of men, once a year, at the vineyards in Shiloh—the Dance of the Maidens."

"She joined in," Deborah said. "My father saw her and chose her to be his wife. When my sister was born, Father named her for Mother's lost birthplace, Tamar. I came a year later—on the fifteenth of Av, the second anniversary of their meeting."

"That's a nice coincidence," Barac said. "Did he name you Deborah for the honeybee?"

"I also thought so, but one Sabbath, when I was about ten, Father sat with me under the palm tree." She looked up through the broken roof at the canopy of the palm tree, visible in the moonlight. "He told me the real reason he had named me Deborah."

Barac and his father listened eagerly.

"The night before I was born, Yahweh came to my father in his sleep and gave him two pieces of news—one bad, one good. The bad news was that this child—me—would be his last. Mother would bear him no more children."

"Poor man." Abinoam shook his head. "No sons to inherit his land and continue his name."

"And the good news?" Barac asked.

"Yahweh told him this: 'Your child will deliver my message to the Hebrews.' And in his sleep, my father saw a great crowd gathered around Palm Homestead, multitudes of Hebrew men and women on the surrounding slopes, watching me as I sat under the palm tree and delivered Yahweh's message. That's why he named me Deborah—a shortened combination of two words: *Deeboor* and *Yahweh*."

They nodded, impressed. The two Hebrew words stood for: *Speech* and *God*.

"That's why my father started calling the old palm tree Deborah's Palm."

As if in acknowledgment, the palm tree rustled high above—not in a scary way, but softly, swaying with the breeze. She got up, ran outside, and threw her arms around the trunk of Deborah's Palm, her cheek pressed against its rough texture. She wept for her father and mother, for the happy days that would never return, and for Tamar's bloody corpse that would remain hanging by the roadside until her bones dried up and crumbled in the wind. And she cried for herself, knowing that from this day on she would always be alone in the world.

When Deborah calmed down, her cheeks were wet, but her throat was dry. Motioning Barac and his father to follow her, she walked to the water cistern. Even at night, it was easy to find the round wall made of stone blocks, the top about as high as a man's waist. The old bucket was gone, replaced by a wooden frame on top, with a handle fixed to a crossbar that had a rope attached in the middle. The rest of the rope was down in the deep hole.

Abinoam patted the top of the circular wall and said reverently, "So this is the famous cistern of Palm Homestead!"

"Who built it?" Barac asked.

"The Egyptians did, generations ago, long before they left Canaan. It's the only remaining cistern in the Samariah Hills."

"It looks like a regular well."

"Looks can be deceiving," Abinoam said. "A well can go dry, because it's just a vertical tunnel into an underground pond. A cistern is much more. There's a huge reservoir under us, bigger than Judge Zifron's house." He stomped with his foot. "And it's full of water."

Barac glanced inside the hole, which was deep and dark. "How did they build such a thing?"

"With many slaves," Abinoam said. "No one knows exactly how they did it, but I assume there was an existing spring or an underground stream here. They must have worked for a long time to dig the reservoir underground and plaster it to keep water from seeping into the belly of the earth."

Deborah turned the handle. The rope tightened as it looped around the crossbar, and sounds of splashing water echoed from below. The handle resisted her with growing force, but she kept turning it with both hands until a bucket came up. Barac helped her place the bucket on top of the circular wall.

Abinoam drank first, then Barac and Deborah. The water was cold and sweet, and she felt grateful. The above-ground streams in the Samariah Hills had been dry for many weeks, the narrow crevices resembling wrinkles on an old man's face, yet the ancient cistern provided without hesitation, quenching her thirst as it had always done.

Stepping away from the cistern, Deborah stumbled in the dark and almost fell. Peering at the ground, she saw a narrow canal. It was dug recently and stood out with the pale color of the exposed bedrock under the topsoil. She stood in the canal. It was as wide as her side-by-side sandals and about as deep as her ankles.

"They're not wasting any time." Abinoam followed the canal for a dozen steps and pointed. In the moonlight, the pale canal meandered away. "It's well built, nice and even. Soon they'll be able to deliver water from the cistern to other fields, maybe even all the way to Emanuel."

"They?" Barac caught up with his father. "Who?"

"The judge and his sons. Why do you think they took in the two girls? This water is more precious than gold."

Tugging at the ring on her finger, Deborah remembered that terrible day last summer, when the priest had dropped her parents' corpses into the communal burial cave outside the walls of Emanuel. Afterward, Judge Zifron had decreed that the orphaned sisters would be brought into his household to work—Tamar in the flour mill and Deborah at the basket factory. His eldest son, Seesya, then betrothed Tamar with a copper ring.

"They might chase us tonight." Abinoam glanced back in the general direction of Emanuel. "Let's get my tools and continue on our way."

Walking back to the house, Deborah noticed an old bucket on the ground. It had been discarded with the original rope still attached. She touched the rope. It was dry and brittle, disintegrating in her hand into thin strands, the same way her life had disintegrated when her parents died a year earlier, and again today, with Tamar's execution.

Deborah couldn't comprehend it. When Tamar's first female bleeding had come the previous week, they had been excited about soon becoming part of the judge's family. As the law required, seven days after the bleeding stopped, Tamar immersed herself in purifying waters.

Dressed in white, she was taken on a celebratory wedding procession up the main street to Judge Zifron's house, where guests filled the courtyard. Obadiah of Levi slaughtered a goat and recited the words of the covenant between Yahweh and the Hebrew patriarch, Abraham: "If you keep my laws and do not stray after false gods, your seed will fill the earth like the sand upon the sea and the stars in the sky, and all your enemies will fall down before you."

After the priest left, a second goat was sacrificed—this time in front of the effigies of two Canaanite deities: Baal Ammon, the god of fertility, and its wife, Ashtoreth. Then, while the guests enjoyed food, drink, and music, Seesya took Tamar to his bed to possess her as his wife.

The women of Emanuel had envied Tamar for becoming the first wife of the first son of Judge Zifron, who ruled over Emanuel and its vicinity. The young woman would not have to work very hard, would live in comfort with the other women of the house of Zifron, and her sons would become rich and powerful like their father and grandfather. Deborah, as a member of Judge Zifron's family, was sure to win a good match in Emanuel and stay near her sister. A year after their parents' death, the marriage made the future seem hopeful again.

All that ended the morning after the wedding. For some reason, Yahweh had decided to toss them back into terrible misfortune.

Inside her family's abandoned house, Deborah sat on the dirt floor by the cold stove and tugged at the ring on her finger. She wanted to pull it off, but removing a ring of betrothal was a serious crime, punishable as harshly as thievery. She gathered a fistful of soil in her hand and sniffed it, craving the familiar smells of her mother's cooking and the good days with her family.

"You can't stay here," Abinoam said from the door, where he and Barac remained. "It's not your home anymore."

Deborah let the soil pour out of her hand. "This is my only home."

"Look at it," he said, waving his hand. "There's nothing left here for you."

"My memories are here," she said. "This stove always had a fire in it. Every evening, after a long day of hard work, my father would sit down to eat the food my mother had cooked. We sat by his side, my sister and I, and he told us stories about Abraham, Isaac, Jacob, and the tribes. He made everything seem so real. I could see the miracles Yahweh performed to free the Hebrews from Egypt and bring them to Canaan, which He gave us for all eternity—especially this place, Palm Homestead, where my family would live forever."

"You're talking nonsense, girl." Abinoam's voice sharpened with impatience. "You need to go back to Emanuel now. You'll never live here again."

"That's up to Yahweh," she said, closing her eyes and remembering an evening a couple of years earlier, when she'd sat at this very spot and listened to her father sing the words of an ancient hymn. When he finished, she asked whether he regretted that she was a girl and not a boy.

After a long silence, her father said, "How could I regret it? Yahweh chose you to speak for Him to our people."

"But Father," she said, "how could I possibly speak for God?"

"Why not? When you grow up, you'll become a prophet."

She laughed. "Girls don't become prophets!"

"Yahweh created the whole world. Don't you think He can create a prophet out of a girl?"

His argument made sense, but still, she thought the whole idea was outlandish. "Even if I receive a prophecy," she said, "who would listen to a girl?"

"To a special girl, they'll listen. You're a true Hebrew, the seed of glorious ancestors. One day, Yahweh will speak to you, and you will sit under your palm tree and deliver His message to the people—to us, the ancient Hebrews. I believe it with all my heart." He smiled. "I pray that I'm still alive to witness it."

Deborah remembered hugging her father tightly, for she knew he truly loved her. Otherwise, why would he believe that she, a girl, could become a prophet?

Fresh tears filled her eyes. How sweet her father's words had been— and how bitter this night was. She wasn't special at all. In fact, she was less than a common girl. She was an orphan, betrothed to a cruel man and disgraced by her sister's stoning!

The memory of Tamar's violent execution hit Deborah again—the sound of each stone thumping Tamar's skull, the bitter smell of blood spreading around the Pit of Shame. Deborah moaned and turned away from the imagined spectacle, covering her eyes. She pressed her forehead to the edge of the stone stove. Where was Yahweh now? Where was His message? How could He allow this terrible injustice to occur?

"Deborah," Barac said, "don't despair. Yahweh will show you kindness again. He will."

"No," she cried. "He won't "

In the dark, her hand found a pair of stones by the stove. She recognized them without looking—her father's fire-starters. One was a thin flint, about as long as a man's forefinger. The other was a coarse, veiny quartz rock, almost as big as her fist. She remembered its color of rusted iron, but also, under the sun, its curious glistening. Her father had called it "fool's gold," because fools mistook it for the real thing. The two stones always rested by the stove, except when he needed to start a fire in the fields to burn off weeds or shrubs to clear an area for farming. He had taught her how to use the fire-starters by hitting them against each other at an angle, producing sparks that ignited the dry grass and twigs he had prepared in advance, whether in the stove or outside.

She held the fire-starters, one in each hand, and pressed them to her wet cheeks, imagining that the stones were her father's warm hands, caressing her cheeks.

"We have to go," Abinoam said, hefting his sack of tools.

Deborah slipped the stones into her pocket and got up. "Where will you go?"

"South, far away from here."

She stepped out into the fresh night air and walked to the edge of the field. The wheat was dry, past its ripeness. She moved her hand back and forth between the shafts, bending them from side to side.

"My mother's village was in the south. Men from Edom destroyed it. Can't you hide somewhere nearby in the Samariah Hills?"

Abinoam shook his head. "We have to go south, as far as possible."

"Aren't you afraid?"

"Yes, but I fear Seesya more, and the people around here fear him, too, enough to put us in shackles and hand us over to Judge Zifron and his black Mott." Abinoam sighed. "Yahweh warned us about what would happen if we started to worship false gods and adopt the ways of the Canaanites."

"But isn't the north safer?" she asked.

"The Canaanites rule over our tribes in the north. They're even worse than the Edomites. Besides, my wife, may she rest in peace, was from the Simeon tribe."

"Will they take you in?"

"Everyone can use a good blacksmith."

"And a soldier, as well." Barac pulled back his shoulders. "That's what I'm going to be."

Abinoam adjusted the white cap over his son's unruly curls. "You'll become a blacksmith, like me and my father before me."

"Yes, Father, but in addition, I'll learn to be a soldier and a great warrior so that I can fight Canaanites and Edomites until we restore the glory days of Joshua!"

Abinoam chuckled.

"Won't you stay until morning?" Deborah gestured at the house.

"It's not safe." Abinoam turned to go.

"You should come with us," Barac urged.

She held up her hand, showing him the ring on her finger, which felt as heavy as a boulder.

"You aren't safe here," Barac insisted. "It's the first place Seesya will look for you."

"She can't come with us," Abinoam said. "She's betrothed to a man."

"A bad man, Father. She's in danger!"

"She's safe if she's never been with another man."

He didn't say this accusingly, but Deborah felt compelled to respond. "I haven't been with a man," she said. "And my sister hadn't, either."

"You can't be sure," Abinoam said.

Deborah was thankful for the darkness that hid her red face.

"Please, Father," Barac said. "We can't leave her here alone."

"Too risky." He pointed at her finger. "This ring means ownership. Taking her with us would be the same as taking a man's milk cow, his good horse, or his sheep that's ripe for shearing. And just as an owner will chase his stolen cow, horse, or sheep, Seesya would chase her."

"Your father is right," Deborah said to Barac. "I must follow in my sister's footsteps now. I have no father to defend me."

Abinoam passed his sack from one shoulder to the other. "Harutz of Ephraim was a good man, but even he couldn't have helped your sister today. The facts were clear."

"Tamar tried to explain," Deborah said. "Judge Zifron wouldn't let her."

"I noticed that," Barac said. "Why did the elders stay quiet?"

"That's our tradition," Abinoam explained. "The wealthiest man among us becomes our judge, the ruler of the community. He defends us from enemies and punishes criminals. Elders assist the judge with their collective wisdom by deciding an accused person's guilt or innocence, but the judge decides the punishment or issues a pardon. It's up to him to deliver justice."

"Stoning Tamar wasn't justice," Deborah said, her voice breaking again.

"When you're older," Abinoam said, "you'll understand that a man deserves certainty that his firstborn son, who will carry his name and inherit his land, is of his seed, not another man's."

Deborah pointed up at the dark sky. "Yahweh knows that Tamar was innocent. If I were a man, God would've helped me save my sister today. Oh, if I could turn into a man!"

"Maybe you could," Barac said.

"How?"

"I heard that the women of Edom turned into men and won a great battle against the Egyptians."

"That's a myth," Abinoam said.

"But Sallan told me that it really happened."

"Sallan? The judge's Edomite slave?" Abinoam scoffed. "He's a big talker."

Barac didn't argue with his father, but he didn't concede either.

"You have no choice, girl," Abinoam said. "You must accept who you are."

"Why?"

"God created men in His image, and then He created women to serve us and bear us children."

"He is merciful," she said. "He wouldn't mind if I—"

"There's no choice in this matter. You're a girl, and that's it." Abinoam looked up at the moon, trying to determine the time. "We must move on. Seesya is coming, I'm sure of it."

"Tell me more," she said to Barac. "How did they do it?"

"Sallan said that a young man prepared a powerful elixir for the women to drink. It turned them into men, and they beat the Egyptians and saved their king."

"What was his name?"

"King Esau the Eighteenth."

"Not the king. The young man who made the elixir. What was *his* name?"

"That's enough." Abinoam placed his hand across his son's mouth. "We don't speak of magic. God forbids it. Let's go!"

"She could follow us." Barac's brown eyes gleam in the darkness. "Stay a short distance behind us, hide if someone approached."

Deborah touched the wheat again. "I wish this was still my father's homestead, so that I could stay here forever."

"Technically, half of it still belongs to your father," Abinoam said. "When a man dies without a son, his land doesn't pass until his daughters marry and their husbands becomes owners of the dead man's land."

This was news to her. "What does it mean?"

"It means that Seesya became owner of half the land as soon as he possessed Tamar in his bed, and he'll own the rest of it when he marries you."

"But if I refuse to marry him—"

"Refuse?" Abinoam laughed. "Who do you think you are? With the ring he put on your finger, Seesya betrothed you to him. Only he can release you, and he'll never do it because he and his father want this homestead. The ancient cistern alone is worth more than the whole town of Emanuel."

"Still, if I own half—"

"You'll be his wife soon, together with your inheritance."

"I'll run away."

"Even if you ran all the way to Egypt, he'd chase you, find you, and possess you right there on the hot sand in the shade of the pyramids that our ancestors built. If you wish to live, go back to Emanuel and submit to Seesya. That's your only choice, girl. Obey the law!"

Deborah stepped back, shaken by his harsh words. "He'll do to me what he did to my sister."

"Don't be afraid." Abinoam's tone softened. "Tell me the truth. Have you been possessed by another man?"

Barac inhaled sharply and looked away.

"No," Deborah said. "I swear to you in the name of Yahweh. Never."

"Then you have nothing to worry about," Abinoam said. "Serve Seesya as a good wife would. Do whatever you can to please him. In time, you'll find comfort in your children and in the company of the other wives he'll marry."

"He has a dark heart."

"Even the most wretched young man grows up to love his children and respect his children's mothers."

The faint sound of approaching horses startled them. Abinoam grabbed his son's arm and pulled him to the bushes.

Barac slipped out of his father's grip. "Come with us," he urged Deborah again. "I'll protect you!"

She shook her head.

The horses were getting closer.

Abinoam ran to hide, but Barac lingered. "I can't leave you here."

"You can't protect me, either. Quick, tell me the name of the Edomite who turned women to men."

The ground shook with the horses' hooves, and voices of men could be heard over the crest of the hill.

Abinoam hissed from the bushes.

"The Elixirist," Barac said, walking backward. "That's what Sallan called him. The Elixirist."

Deborah turned and ran toward the approaching horses, waving her arms. "The Elixirist," she repeated quietly, committing it to memory. "The Elixirist."

3

A burning torch in one hand, the reins in the other, Seesya rode at the head of six soldiers, all of them heavily armed and hot for the hunt. He almost ran Deborah over, swerving his horse at the last moment. He handed the torch to one of the soldiers, leaned over, and pulled her up, planting her sideways on the saddle before him.

"I knew you'd run to Palm Homestead." He laughed. "Foolish girl!"

He stank of sweat, and his breath smelled of garlic. She wriggled to get away, but he grabbed her neck in one big hand. "Do you want to live," he asked, "or end up like your sister?"

In her mind, she saw Tamar's bloodied head sticking out of the ground.

"Did you see Abinoam, the blacksmith?"

She didn't answer.

He squeezed her neck harder. "Answer me, girl!"

"Yes," she managed to say. "I saw him."

"Where?"

"Near the gates." She struggled to breathe. "Running away from Emanuel."

"For a good reason," Seesya said, laughing. "Which direction?"

Deborah tried to jump off the horse. He held her for a moment, then let go. She dropped to the ground and run, but the soldiers rode around in a circle, fencing her in, hooting as if it was all a big joke. She tried to get through, but they were quick in repositioning, and she feared being crushed by the beasts. Finally she stood still.

"That's better." Seesya pulled a short horsewhip. "Now tell me where that cursed blacksmith and his ugly son went, or I'll flog you like a stray dog."

"North." Deborah coughed, her throat constricted by the discomfort of telling a lie. "To the Galilee Mountains."

"Through the land of Manasseh and the Canaanites?" He raised the horsewhip over her. "You're lying!"

"It's the truth." She held up her arms to shield herself. "They might be afraid of the Canaanites, but they're afraid of you even more."

"They're too far by now," one of the soldier said. "We won't catch them tonight."

"We won't," Seesya said, "but you will. Ride north and find them."

"Me alone?" The soldier wasn't happy. "The blacksmith is a big man."

"Tell him that Judge Zifron forgave him."

"Really?" Deborah was filled with hope. "Has he forgiven them?"

"The father, yes, but not the son." Seesya sneered as he reached down, seized Deborah, and pulled her back onto the horse. "A blacksmith is hard to replace, but that boy's neck will meet my sword."

Whatever guilt Deborah felt for the sin of lying, it went away now, for she believed Seesya really intended to kill Barac. Shutting her eyes, she prayed silently for him and his father as they travelled south, all the way to the distant desert, where the tribe of Simeon lived.

Holding the torch in one hand, Seesya led the group at a fast pace. Seated sideways on the hard saddle in front of Seesya, Deborah tried to lean away from him, but he held her tightly, his arm encircling her just below her small breasts, their bodies pressed against each other. His long hair tickled her neck, and she convulsed in disgust. She remembered Tamar's lush hair, soaked with bloody mud, and imagined various horrors that Yahweh should visit upon Seesya, his father, and the elders, and even upon Obadiah of Levi, the priest who knew Tamar was innocent yet participated in her trial and failed to stop her execution.

The howling of coyotes came from the surrounding hills. The sound made the horses go faster, their hooves pounding the dirt road. Deborah put her hand in her pocket, clasped her father's fire-starters, and submitted to the rhythm of the galloping horse and the cool wind on her face.

Out of the darkness, Emanuel appeared ahead as a cluster of lights from torches and cooking fires. As they rode by the Weeping Tree, Deborah looked away from her sister's dangling body and began to sob.

"What's wrong?" Seesya put his lips near her ear and yelled into the oncoming wind. "You miss the whore?"

"That's a lie," Deborah cried. "She was good!"

"A whore," he shouted. "Your sister was a whore, your mother was a whore, and maybe you're a whore, too!"

Deborah was still crying as they slowed down near the gates, which were locked for the night. The sentries recognized the group and opened the gates.

Inside Emanuel, the bitter stench of rotting garbage and human waste drifted from the hundreds of tents and shacks where the poor lived at the bottom of the hill, just inside the walls. She buried her face in her sleeve as the horses headed up the hill.

The houses along the main street were dark and quiet. Modest and simple at first, they grew larger and more elaborate higher up the street. The greatest of all, at the top, was the house of Judge Zifron. It was filled with his wives, concubines, children, and slaves. But Tamar was no longer there, and Deborah felt a terrible longing for her sister's happy laughter and loving embrace. How could life continue without Tamar?

Deborah tugged at the ring on her finger. She was thirteen, and her next birthday was coming up. How long did she have before her first blood arrived and, after purification, her first time in Seesya's bed?

She felt wetness between her legs. Was she imagining it?

At the top of the hill, they rode into the courtyard, which was lit with torches. The ground was covered with straw to soak up any animal waste. Stone columns supported the two-story house, which formed three sides of the courtyard.

Several stable boys ran over to take the horses. They were young slaves, easily recognized by their short-cropped hair, bare feet, and sleeveless wool shirts that came down to their knees. The soldiers dismounted and untied their spears and shields from the saddles.

Seesya grabbed Deborah at her hips, lifted her off the saddle, and lowered her to the ground. He prepared to get off the horse but paused and examined the saddle.

"What the hell is this? Did you piss on my saddle?"

Still dazed from the ride, Deborah realized that the warm wetness between her legs was real. Shame filled her, and her face flushed.

Seesya held a torch to the saddle, which was stained with red blood. "Look at this," he said. "From a stupid girl to a stupid woman!" He jumped off the horse, his soldiers laughing with him.

4

Seesya opened the door leading into the women's quarters. Deborah touched the mezuzah scroll on the doorjamb and kissed her fingers before entering.

Judge Zifron's wives and concubines shared a large room next to the basket factory. A small oil lamp burned in a wall recess. The women slept on straw mattresses beside each other, except for the one who had been summoned by the judge to his bed that night. Newborn babies slept in bassinets, and toddlers slept along the wall on the opposite side.

The only person not sleeping was Vardit, the judge's oldest wife, who stood at the window overlooking the courtyard. She hurried to the door. "Praise God, you're back safely!"

Seesya grunted.

"I was worried—"

"Don't wait in the window anymore. My men can see you standing there like a dumb cow eager to nurse her calf."

His mother bowed her head.

"And watch this little witch. If she runs away again, I'll hold you responsible."

He left, and Vardit shut the door behind him. At thirty-two, she was getting old. After Seesya, she had given birth to eleven more children, fulfilling Yahweh's command to the Hebrews to multiply and fill the land. Sadly, other than her first son and two girls, none had survived infancy. As the first wife and the mother of the judge's heir, Vardit was more important than the other women, even the young ones, whose company their husband now preferred. In the past year, since the two orphan girls had been brought from their dead father's homestead, Vardit had assumed responsibility for them.

Deborah felt a drop of blood run down the inside of her thigh. The room spun around, and her knees folded under her. She fell to the stone floor and began to shake. She panicked. What was happening to her? Was she falling ill? Was it the red fever, which took a week to kill a grown person with vomiting and incontinence until death was a relief? These possibilities made her shake even worse, and a film of cold sweat covered her face. She moaned.

"Poor thing." Vardit knelt, sighing from the pain in her joints. "You must feel completely alone in the world, but you are not. You're a daughter of the tribe of Ephraim. We're all your family now." She opened her arms for an embrace.

"I'm bleeding," Deborah said.

Vardit retreated. Impurity passed by touch from woman to woman, requiring seven days of waiting, and then, immersion in purifying water, before a woman was suitable for her husband's bed again. Touching Deborah would have made Vardit impure as if her own blood had come. An aging wife like her would not want to reduce her already diminished chances of being summoned by her husband to his bed.

"Let me see," Vardit said.

Deborah got up, fetched the oil lamp from the wall recess, and brought it over. At the spot where she had sat on the floor, the flickering flame illuminated a wet, red stain.

Vardit looked closely. "It looks like it."

"But I'm almost a year younger than my sister." Deborah tried to control her voice. "It's too early!"

"Sometimes a bad fright, a shock, or an illness makes it come sooner." She took the lamp from the girl's shaking hand. "Don't be afraid."

"I don't like blood."

"This isn't like blood from an injury or a wound. This is good blood."

"It's dirty blood."

"Not dirty. Impure, which is very different." Vardit put the lamp on the floor. "Every young woman is scared when her first blood comes, but when you grow old, its arrival makes you very happy, because it proves that you're still a complete woman."

"I don't want to be a woman."

"Shhh. Don't say that."

"It's the truth."

"Some truths should not be pronounced out loud. You can dislike being a woman as much as the sentry by the gate dislikes the night, but as the sentry cannot change the night into day, you can't change what you are."

"The night will change into day in a few hours."

"Yes, but you will still be a woman tomorrow and every day after that. Instead of worrying about whether you like it or not, you should give thanks to God for blessing you with fertility."

"What should I do?" She pointed at the blood on the floor. "About this, I mean."

"Are you in pain?"

"No."

"That's a good sign." Vardit rose to her feet with another sigh. She went to the trunk where they kept their clothes, pulled out a red robe and a set of undergarments, and tossed them to Deborah. The girl quickly changed. She rolled up her brown dress and undergarments for the next washday.

Vardit gave her a rag. "Press it between your legs inside your undergarments and go to sleep. The first time should be quick. The bleeding may be over tomorrow, and the seven-day count will begin. I'll check you every day to make sure." She dragged a straw mattress to the side of the room where women usually slept during their monthly impurity. "Here you go."

Deborah carefully lay down with the rag pressed between her legs. She was still shaking. "I miss Tamar," she whispered, tears flowing again.

"I'm sorry about your sister." Vardit covered her with a wool blanket. "It must have been terrible to watch her being punished—even though it's the law. Think of it as the will of God."

"It couldn't be His will. He is just."

"Try to forget what you saw and think about the happy times ahead."

"How can I forget Tamar?"

Gesturing at the line of sleeping children near the wall, Vardit took a deep breath and exhaled. "I lost many children. Do you think I didn't love each one of them? Do you think it didn't hurt? Let me tell you, losing a child is more painful than giving birth." The older woman's eyes filled with tears. "What God gives, He may take back. You have to let go. As soon as you feel the pain come back, tell yourself that it's in the past, that you must forget about it and think of the future."

"But Tamar didn't die of an illness. She was executed even though she hadn't done anything wrong! It's not fair!"

"Keep your voice down." Fixing the blanket over the girl, Vardit shook her head. "It's hard to understand the ways of the world. I was once as young as you, and I remember how confusing it was."

Deborah sat up. "I'm not confused."

"Then you know what it meant that Tamar was without her virginity."

"I know what it would mean for another girl, but Tamar had never been with a man." She hugged the blanket to her chest. "Why did he accuse her falsely?"

"Hush!" Vardit looked around the room, making sure no one was awake. "How dare you speak against my son?"

"I mean no disrespect. Forgive me." She wiped her tears with the sleeve of the red robe. "But why? Tamar would've been a good wife. She would've given him sons and daughters—"

"Hush!" Vardit took a deep breath. "Listen to good advice from a woman who has survived twenty years of marriage. Let it go. It's not a woman's place to ask questions."

"But I don't—"

"Our job is to serve a husband, to please him, to make him happy so that he'll provide for us and protect us and summon us to his bed even when we're no longer young and pretty. Nothing good ever came to a wife from questioning her husband."

"He's not my husband yet."

"You're betrothed. It's practically the same." The older woman glanced at the ring on the girl's finger, and her voice softened. "It's better that you accept what God planned for you. Be obedient and respectful, and your husband will be good to you."

"Tamar was obedient and respectful, and Seesya was not good to her."

"He's young, my son. Not even twenty yet. He doesn't stop to think deeply about things. He's aggressive, like a colt that thinks it's already a stallion."

"A colt doesn't think."

"The moment he was born, when I heard his first scream, I felt a divine presence in the room. That's why I named him Seesya, because I saw Yahweh right there. And Seesya is blessed. He's destined for greatness." Vardit's face glowed with pride. "Seesya's name will be known across the land as a great warrior and conqueror. He'll defeat the Canaanites, bring back the glory of Joshua's days, and lead our people with justice and goodness!"

Deborah lowered her eyes. Obviously, Vardit's love for her son had blinded her to his true nature. "Evil doesn't change," she said.

"My son is not evil. It's the horrible scar that makes him look bad, that's all."

Deborah knew that the older woman was wrong, but how could a mother admit that her son was evil?

"How did he get the scar?"

"Every man has scars. Unfortunately, Seesya's scar is on the face. Other than that, he's very handsome. Wasn't your sister happy to marry him?"

"Then why did he accuse her falsely?"

"Because she didn't please him," Vardit said. "That's all there is to it. She failed to please her master, and therefore she failed as a wife."

"He caused her to be stoned to death!"

"The way he got rid of her is not important. It's his right."

Several sleeping women shifted under their blankets. One of them murmured something about the noise.

"Get it into your head, girl." Vardit lowered her voice to a sharp whisper. "We're women! What does a man do with his lame horse? Or his lame donkey? Or his lame dog? It's the same thing with a lame wife. Let it be a lesson to you. To all of us!"

Deborah turned away, pulled the blanket over her head, and murmured, "Tamar wasn't lame."

5

Deborah woke up with her head still under the blanket. Around her was the usual bustle that followed sunrise, with babies crying, children running about, and women chattering. She expected to hear Tamar's voice. Her sister had always slept beside her, but was an early riser and an eager participant in the women's conversations, perhaps to make up for all the years of growing up at an isolated homestead. But Tamar's voice wasn't among them, and when Deborah remembered yesterday's stoning, she whimpered involuntarily and bit on her knuckles to keep silent. She remained covered up, hoping the others would leave her alone. Last night, Vardit had advised her to forget about Tamar, to let it go. But how could she forget her sister? And how could she stop crying?

Vardit pulled off the covers. "Good morning," she said.

Deborah sniffled and wiped her eyes.

"It'll get easier, I promise." Vardit handed her a bowl of cooked oats. "In the meantime, you must eat to regain your strength."

Deborah looked at the food and felt sick.

One of the women, a Canaanite concubine the judge had bought the previous year, carried a small bowl of oats and placed it before the knee-high wooden effigy that stood beside her baby's bassinet. Her deity had a human body, a hawk's head, and a polished copper disk for a crown. The young woman mumbled a few words and pulled aside the window curtain. The rays of the sun touched the copper disk, making it glisten like gold.

"Pretty, isn't it?" Vardit smiled. "Ra is the sun god. They say his powers are great, especially with new babies."

The concubine picked up her baby and held it before Ra. The baby began to cry. She pulled out a breast and sang quietly in her native Canaanite language while nursing her baby. One of the other women, a Hebrew wife, brought her young daughter over and helped her add food to the bowl before Ra.

"You heard my son's warning last night," Vardit said to Deborah. "If you escape again, he'll punish me."

Filling her wooden spoon, Deborah nibbled on the oats.

"You'd gain nothing from running away, because he'd catch you again. And this time, he'd whip you in front of everybody. Is that what you want?"

She shook her head and ate some more.

"Promise me you won't try to escape again."

Deborah looked away.

"Stubbornness is the worst disease." Vardit sighed. "There's no point in escaping. My husband controls the whole area. He owns more slaves, farms more fields, and collects more taxes than any other judge in this land. He is the master here."

"Yahweh is the only master."

Vardit laughed. "How long will you cling to the old faith? If you want to live well here, you must embrace the world of today. My husband is blessed by Yahweh and all the other gods—that's why he rules over everything here, including you."

"Yahweh alone rules over everything, including me and the land of my father."

"Silly girl. Your head is filled with foolishness." Vardit made to pat Deborah's head but withdrew her hand. "That old order is long gone. My husband says that land is owned by the man who can defend it. And who defends us from the Canaanites? Have you forgotten what happened to your parents?" Vardit clucked her tongue.

Deborah glanced at the Canaanite concubine feeding her baby next to the effigy of Ra. "Why does he allow idol worship in his house?"

"Again with the old faith." Vardit rolled her eyes. "Ra brings light into a new life—it's known. I used to put Ra in window above Seesya's cradle, and look how he's grown into a healthy and strong man. He's fearless, my son!"

Deborah pushed aside the bowl of oats. "My father told me what Yahweh said to Moses on Mount Sinai: 'If you follow my laws and observe my rules, I shall give you rains, the fields shall yield crops, and the trees fruit. Harvest shall precede vintage, and vintage shall precede seeding. You shall eat to satiation and sit safely on your land. But if you don't—'"

"This is silly. Why are we arguing about things that a woman's mind cannot comprehend in the first place?" Vardit handed Deborah a clay figurine. "It will make your bleeding pass more quickly and with less pain."

The figurine fit in the palm of Deborah's hand. The top part was formed as a naked woman with long hair, her arms folded under her full breasts. Below the hips, the shape blended into a column or a pillar, with the base flaring out like a dish. Deborah had never seen it before.

Vardit went to the window. "Come here. You must stand on one leg, look at the sky, and kiss her."

"Stand on one leg?" Deborah followed her to the window. "What is this? A Canaanite goddess?"

"Womanhood Charm. She's a collective mother that brings us good luck with our female challenges."

"She does," said one of the other women while rocking a baby over her shoulder. "Everybody knows it."

Other women voiced their agreement.

Deborah handed the figurine back. "I don't want it."

Vardit refused to take it. "What do you have to lose?"

Deborah hesitated.

"Lift your left foot off the floor." Vardit checked that Deborah was doing it. "Good. Now look up at the sky and kiss her head."

"I don't know—"

"I'm like your mother now, and she would have made you do it, too."

Deborah brought the Womanhood Charm near her lips but hesitated to kiss it.

"Do you prefer a lot of bleeding and bad pains in your abdomen? Three quick kisses while you look at the sky, or it doesn't work as well."

Deborah complied.

"Wonderful. Keep your foot up and count in your head to twelve—the ideal number of children you should bear."

In her head, Deborah repeated the number zero twelve times.

"You'll see how well it works." Vardit took the Womanhood Charm back and slipped it into her pocket. "Let's concentrate on what's important—your betrothal to my son."

"Your son scares me," Deborah said.

"We're all scared of our husbands sometimes."

"Really?"

"Why would I lie to you?" Vardit sighed. "You're a woman now, and the women in this house tell each other everything. How else could we serve our husband as good wives?"

Deborah nodded, though serving Seesya as a good wife was far from her mind.

"My Seesya was born good and sweet, but he was raised to cause fear. Before he even walked properly, his father taught him to fight with little swords and short spears, told him to attack, attack, attack, took him hunting, and made him slaughter animals. Whenever a slave needed whipping, my husband would bring Seesya along and make him take part, egging him on until the boy drew blood with the whip." Vardit lowered her voice almost to a whisper. "I wasn't happy about it, but my husband said that every ruler needs a powerful heir to scare the people and keep them in line—especially our people, the stiff-necked Hebrews, who are prone to questioning and complaining about everything, right?"

"I don't know."

"One day, my son will become the next Judge Zifron, but his dominion will be ten times greater than my husband's. He'll rule over the Samariah Hills, from Shiloh in the north to Ramah and Bethel in the south—all the land of Ephraim!"

Deborah saw the spark of ambition in Vardit's eyes and looked away.

"And you'll be his lucky wife!" Vardit added.

Deborah picked up the bowl and stirred the oats. "If I live that long."

"Of course you'll live. I promise you that everything will be all right."

"But—"

"I figured out why my son was not pleased with your sister. I should have thought about it before she went to him. It's the hair, you see."

Deborah put the spoon back in the bowl. "The hair?"

"The color." Vardit rubbed her hands. "Orange hair is not natural."

"But it is natural."

"On carrots, not on a girl's head."

"My mother had the same—"

"I don't mean that it's not real. I know you were born with it, but still, it's very ugly."

"Ugly?"

"Like your head is on fire. It's unsettling."

Suddenly self-conscious, the girl covered her head with the hood of her robe.

"Don't worry," Vardit said. "It's easy to fix. A cup of dye, and you'll be like a normal Hebrew girl with beautiful black hair. I'll also powder your face to hide those dreadful freckles."

Deborah touched her cheek.

"And you'll keep your eyes down. I think that also unnerved him about your sister."

"Her eyes?"

"Green isn't—"

"Natural?"

"It doesn't matter. It's in the past." Vardit gestured as if she were throwing something over her shoulder. "Forget about what happened. It's your wedding we must plan for. We'll dye your hair and do your makeup before the ceremony next week. When Seesya sees you, the new look will surprise him, and surprise is the secret to pleasing a man." She blushed, which made her look younger for a moment. "This is so exciting!"

"I don't understand."

"Of course not. You're too young to understand men. Trust me. With men, there are two ways it can go for a girl: either you excite your husband and please him, or you displease him and cease to be worthwhile."

"And my hair color—"

"It's the same as your sister's, and we know that Seesya didn't find her pleasing. You're going to look completely different—as beautiful as any Hebrew girl of good Ephraim ancestry. There's nothing like a dramatic change of appearance to entice a man, draw his interest, make his heart pound with excitement, and flood his body with passion."

Her face hot, the girl looked down.

"I guarantee that Seesya will be pleased with you, not like your poor sister."

"Thank you," Deborah managed to say. "I need to wash now." In her haste to leave, she knocked over what was left of her bowl of oats.

The courtyard was already busy with soldiers, slaves, and visitors who had come to bargain for Judge Zifron's various goods, pay their taxes,

or plead for his mercy—or for his harshness toward someone with
whom they had quarreled. A few of them congregated around the firepit
at the center of the courtyard.

Deborah crossed the courtyard quickly and took the three steps up
into the washroom, shutting the door behind her. Tears flowed down
her cheeks. Vardit was right. None of the other Hebrew girls had orange
hair and green eyes, not to mention pale skin with brown dots. Back at
Palm Homestead, with their loving parents, the sisters had never realized
how odd they looked. On the contrary, the resemblance to their mother
was a source of pride and joy. Oh, how she missed her mother now!
And her father! And Tamar! Why had Yahweh taken all three of them
and left her alone in a house full of strangers and false gods?

Despite her efforts to keep quiet, hard sobs burst out.

After a few minutes, she calmed down. Someone else might want to
use the washroom, and she was due at the basket factory soon. She
wiped her face.

The washroom was small, built against the outer wall of the side wing
of the house. A round hole was cut in the wood planks of the floor, right
above a waste pit. The floor was covered with a layer of straw. A barrel
of water stood in one corner, and a bucket of lime powder in another
corner. A small window in the wall above her head allowed odors to
escape to the street outside the judge's compound. She could hear
vendors proclaiming their merchandise, women washing clothes and
dishes at their front doors, and children squealing.

After she relieved herself into the hole, Deborah stood over it and
washed with cold water from the barrel, scrubbing the dried blood from
her thighs until the skin turned raw. She checked her undergarments and
the red robe but found no stains. The rag she had kept between her legs
overnight was sullied with blood. She replaced it with a clean one.

Fully dressed again, she scooped up a fistful of lime powder and
tossed it through the hole into the waste pit. Before leaving, she made
sure her father's fire starters were still in her pocket.

When Deborah exited the washroom, a group of soldiers were
pulling their horses out of the stable and getting their equipment ready
in the courtyard. She stood aside and watched. A moment later, Judge
Zifron appeared, dressed in his black coat with gold and silver
embroidery. He held a leather tube that was customarily used to keep

important scrolls. The people in the yard advanced toward him, some of them already pleading their case. The soldiers shoved everyone back.

Seesya came out next, dressed in battle gear. A young slave in a sleeveless long shirt carried his spear, shield, and helmet. The judge handed Seesya the leather tube, whispered a few words in his ear, and went back inside.

The soldiers mounted their horses and secured their spears and shields for the ride. Each horse carried a rolled-up straw mat and several waterskins. They were obviously planning to travel overnight.

Seesya got on his horse and trotted up and down the line, inspecting the soldiers. When he was satisfied, he yelled, "Let's go and collect some silver, boys!"

Riding to the courtyard exit, Seesya noticed Deborah. He pointed at her with the tip of his spear and made a few rapid jabs in the air. The soldiers laughed as they followed him out to the street.

She walked over to the firepit and dumped the soiled rag into the flames. Keeping her head down, she avoided people's eyes. Her red robe was impossible to miss, and people lowered their voices when they saw her. She couldn't hear the hushed words they were saying to each other, but she could guess: "There goes the orphan girl, the whore's sister. Has she also whored with another man? Will she also be stoned to death at the Pit of Shame?"

Their whispering became like a loud buzz in her head. Deborah pressed her hands to her ears and ran into the basket factory.

6

When Deborah entered the basket factory, all conversations ceased, and everyone stared at her. After what felt like an eternity, the foreman, Sallan, pointed at the dipping tub, which was Deborah's usual workstation. She hurried over.

Everyone resumed working, but she felt their eyes on her back.

The basket factory was adjacent to the women's quarters, sharing a wall with a door that allowed the women to pass through directly and avoid having to go out to the courtyard and walk among the leering men. The proximity was also useful for nursing mothers, who could hear when their babies cried.

The front of the factory, facing the courtyard, was lined with stone pillars. Straw mats hung between the pillars, which supported the ceiling and the second floor above their heads. More than sixty workers toiled in the factory. Judge Zifron's wives, concubines, and unmarried daughters preferred to work here, as the labor involved was easier than at the flour mill. The rest of the workers were female slaves. Like male slaves, the women wore sleeveless long shirts made of coarse wool and no shoes or sandals, but they were allowed to grow their hair, which they covered with a scarf. The only men allowed in the basket factory were the foreman and his two boy-servants, who occasionally came down from the foreman's private quarters upstairs.

Sallan was an Edomite slave who claimed to have been a free man before Moabite marauders abducted him many years earlier and sold him into slavery. He ruled the factory with an iron fist, and his light-blue eyes missed nothing.

Unlike other slaves, he wore a fine coat with sleeves down to his wrists, and good leather boots that helped with his heavy limping. His hair was white with remnants of red, growing long over his ears. He had the ruddy complexion and stocky figure of a gluttonous eater. His arms were thick and coated with golden fuzz, but his cheeks were smooth from daily shaving. His hands were large and meaty, yet nimble, manipulating the straw strands with ease. Deborah had heard the women say that Judge Zifron treated Sallan well because profits from the basket factory had soared under his management, filling the judge's coffers with silver coins.

The factory was divided into sections. Along one wall were rolls of hay, brought in after the wheat had been thrashed and winnowed to separate the kernels from the stalks. The rolls were stacked high and arranged by freshness, with the older, drier lots in front.

Deborah and five other girls unfurled rolls of hay and separated out single stalks of straw. They plucked any remaining whiskers, careful not to break the delicate stalks, and dipped each one in a tub filled with Reinforcing Liquid, which Sallan mixed once a week with his boy-servants. He did it at night, after everyone else had gone to sleep. No one, not even the judge himself, knew the secret formula for the Reinforcing Liquid, which Sallan kept in his head. According to him, it strengthened the straw stalks and in turn made the baskets produced at Judge Zifron's factory stronger and sturdier than all other competitors.

After dipping each stalk in the Reinforcing Liquid, Deborah and her fellow workers placed the stalks on one of several long tables in straight, parallel lines for braiding. Young slave girls, aged five to ten, sat at the tables shoulder to shoulder and braided three stalks each into a tight strand. Their small fingers were ideal for this work, which required dexterity and nimbleness. Besides, adult hands were too strong for working with the individual stalks, which were moist from the Reinforcing Liquid and thus prone to tearing. If torn, stalks were useless for anything but stuffing pillows and starting fires.

The slave girls draped the braided strands over a grid of ropes for drying overnight. Once dry, the braids were strong, yet as thin and as flexible as a single strand and easy to use in weaving the baskets.

The middle of the factory was taken up by three large, round tables where dozens of skilled women labored under Sallan's close supervision. Deborah had watched them furtively for months while doing her own work. She longed to leave the mundane, repetitive task at the dipping tub and learn to weave the strands into baskets. It fascinated her to see how all beginnings looked the same, but each final product was different.

Baskets were made for specific uses, each type distinct in shape, size, and strength. The most popular products were simple baskets that farmers bought for carrying lightweight produce, such as fruit and vegetables, some with curved bottoms that facilitated carrying on the head. Larger baskets with looped handles were made for stonemasons and builders to lug construction materials. Tall baskets with lids were popular for storing dates and wheat for extended periods of time. Some of these baskets had straps that allowed them to be hung from a tree or a ceiling out of reach for mice and moles.

The weaving patterns were simple, aimed to keep costs down while maximizing utility and strength. There were no decorations or colors, except for the insertion of black-dyed strands into the weaving to form a short horizontal line over a longer vertical line, resembling a tent peg, which stood for *zayin,* the first Hebrew letter in the name Zifron. It was a unique decorative design that represented the exceptional strength and superior durability of the baskets produced by the ruler of Emanuel.

In the corner of the factory was a structure of wood and ropes that Sallan had built and improved over the years to produce straw mats—a process more mechanical than basket weaving, which could be done only by hand. Operating the apparatus required more muscle than skill and was done by the strongest female slaves, whose exposed arms were as thick and as muscular as men's arms.

Deborah worked quickly, her hands doing the tasks in the right order by habit. She picked each stalk of straw, plucked off any whiskers carefully, dipped it in the Reinforcing Liquid, placed it flat on the long table in front of one of the braiding girls, and went back for another stalk. The monotony of the work calmed her down and freed her mind to enter a dreamy state, allowing her thoughts to wander back to happier days with her family at Palm Homestead.

Work continued for as long as sunlight was available. Bread and milk were brought in at midday and consumed without interrupting the work. As darkness began to descend, Sallan clapped his hands to signal the end of the workday.

Judge Zifron's wives, concubines, and daughters went through the door into the women's quarters, where they would soon prepare dinner and put the children down for the night. The slaves went out to the courtyard and then to the back of the compound, where they were locked up for the night in the slave quarters. Sallan, though a slave, lived with his two boy-servants in rooms above the factory.

None of the women had ever been upstairs, but they heard Judge Zifron complain often about the various luxuries that Sallan requested and received, including fine clothing and linen, various furnishings, a well-stocked kitchen with its own cooking stove, and even a private washroom.

This day, as Deborah left her workstation, she wished she could ask Sallan about the Elixirist, but she didn't dare look at him, let alone question him over a casual conversation he'd had with the blacksmith's son.

As she was walking to the door, her head down, she heard Sallan clear his throat. She looked up, and he curled his finger at her.

His servants were coming down the staircase from the second floor. They were about her age, with light, smooth faces. Their reddish hair was a shade lighter than hers and cut very short. Sallan signaled them to wait. They stood on the stairs, watching quietly.

"You'll work here tomorrow, girl." He pointed to one of the round tables in the middle of the factory.

"Thank you," she said.

"You're about to become the wife of my master's son. It's unwise for me to keep you doing a slave's work." Sallan collected a handful of strands, tied them together, and handed her the bundle. "Ask one of the women to teach you the basic weave."

She turned to leave.

"Shame about your sister," he said.

Pausing, she unconsciously touched her hair.

"The good lady Vardit asked me for a cup of black dye. She thinks it'll save you." He fluffed his long hair over his ears. "My master's wife is foolish. In my country, kings and their offspring have hair the color of orange, like yours. It is a sign of strength and nobility, not something to hide with dye."

Deborah wanted to tell him that this wasn't his country, but kept quiet.

"What's wrong? Lost your tongue?"

She swallowed hard, trying to remember what Vardit had said. "If

I'm more pleasing to Seesya, it will give me power over him."

"Black dye will give you power?" Sallan went to his workbench and picked up a braided length from a pile of strands that had been dyed black for the Zifron brand on the baskets. Holding it at each end, he pulled. The strand tore easily. "See? As weak as anything."

She didn't answer.

"A bit of color won't make a bull out of a cow."

"I'm not a cow."

He tossed the torn black straw away. "In the name of Kothar-wa-Khasis, I'm wasting my time on a stupid girl!" He turned to the servants, said something in the language of Edom, and the two boys came down the rest of the stairs to assist him.

"Wait—please," Deborah said. She picked up a few more black strands from the pile, arranged them together lengthwise, and grasped the ends in her hands, holding them horizontal.

"Try these," she said.

Sallan paused and looked at her with astonishment. She could tell that he was unsure whether to snap at her or comply.

He took the ends from her.

"Thank you," she said. "Now pull in opposite directions."

He pulled, but nothing happened.

"Harder," she said.

He complied with no result.

"Harder!"

Sallan tried until his arms trembled, but the combined strength of multiple strands was too great. He dropped the strands on the table.

Deborah glared at him. "Who's stupid now?"

Sallan threw his head back and laughed.

Shaken by her own audacity, Deborah grabbed the bundle of stalks he'd given her for practice and ran to the door leading to the women's quarters.

He was still laughing when she closed the door behind her.

7

The next morning, Deborah woke up in the middle of a dream, which she remembered as vividly as if it had actually happened. It started with an escape from Emanuel—not through the gates, but over the walls in a silent flight accompanied only by the sound of wings beating against the air. She looked up, saw no birds, and realized that the bird was below—she was sitting on it! It was a large bird whose body and wings were almost as dark as the night, except for the neck and head, which were ghostly white. The wings tilted, and she fell off. The ground was soft. She got up and ran. It was the road out of Emanuel. She passed by the Weeping Tree, where Tamar's body, suspended up side down, grinned with bared teeth. Deborah left the road for a rocky, dry stream, crossed it, and headed up the steep side of a crevice between giant black boulders. At the top she found a flat rock, serving as a natural threshing stone. She sprinted across, but it didn't end. It was larger than any threshing stone she'd ever seen. A layer of wheat stalks covered it, as if threshing had just been completed. The kernels were as big as almonds, and she felt them under the soles of her sandals. Behind her, horse hooves drummed the threshing stone, getting closer. She ran faster, but the straw got deeper, reaching her knees, slowing her down. The horse was very close, its breath hot on her neck. A hand clutched her hair and pulled her up. She screamed in pain and kicked the air with her legs. But when she looked down, she had no legs, because her body had turned into a human-size stalk of straw, except that it wasn't golden like wheat but flaming orange, the same color as her hair. A strong odor hit her nose, a mix of body odor, garlic breath, and horse sweat. The horse stopped with a neigh, and Seesya grabbed her, she realized, his right hand clenching her hair and his left holding her feet, which were not feet any longer, but the sliced ends of wheat stalks that had been dyed orange. He held her horizontally and began to pull in opposite directions. She begged him to stop, but her pleas only made Seesya laugh, and he pulled harder until the middle of her orange-straw body turned red with spots of blood, and the pain grew so intense that she woke up.

She must have screamed before waking up, because Vardit rushed over to her. "What's wrong, child?"

Trying to speak, she had to clear her throat. "I had a bad dream."

"It's not your fault. The other girls were also shaken by the stoning, but it's the law."

Deborah heard a moan from across the room and looked over.

The other women were clustered around Mazal, Judge Zifron's youngest wife, who was heavily pregnant. She was only a year older than Deborah.

Lying on her back, Mazal clasped the hands of two older women. Her face was white and her bare legs were bent at the knees. Between Mazal's open legs, Deborah saw dark blood pouring out, some of it congealed into small lumps.

Mazal moaned again, and the women looked at each other, their faces worried.

Alarmed by all the blood, Deborah stood. The rag that she had kept between her legs dropped.

"Let's see." Vardit bent down and peered at it. "As I expected, your bleeding is already over."

"That's it?"

"Youth is a wonderful thing, and the Womanhood Charm didn't hurt, did it?"

Deborah picked up the rag and stuffed it under her red robe.

"Mother," Mazal cried from across the room. "Help me!"

"Calm down," one of the women said. "It's almost over."

Mazal tried to sit up, but the women held her down.

"The baby is coming," another one said. "You'll have a beautiful baby."

"I don't want a baby," Mazal cried. "I want my mother. Please!"

"Come, Deborah." Vardit took out the Womanhood Charm and went to the window. "Let's do it again to make sure you're really done with the bleeding."

Holding the figurine, Deborah lifted her foot, looked at the sky, and kissed the tiny clay head three times. She pretended to count to twelve in her head, though in truth she didn't count at all but prayed for Yahweh's help in escaping Emanuel.

"It's hurting," Mazal cried. "Mother!"

"Your mother is far away," one woman said. "Now it's your turn to be a mother."

"No!" Mazal struggled in vain to sit up. "It hurts!"

"Very good." Vardit took the figurine from Deborah. "Are you feeling well?"

Deborah felt awful, not only for Mazal, but also for her own fate. With her bleeding over, the seven-day impurity countdown had started, and the prospect of coming under Seesya's possession had turned from a threat to complete certainty. She was sure that he would either find a way to get her killed as he had Tamar, or cause her to be like Mazal, lying on a her back with a huge belly, crying for her mother while lumpy blood poured out of her.

Deborah swallowed hard and said, "I'll go to wash now."

"Don't be late for work," Vardit said.

As she left the room, Deborah heard Mazal's thin, fearful voice. "I don't want a baby. Please make the pain go away!"

Deborah walked quickly. She thought about the dream and how it ended, with Seesya tearing her body apart, and wondered what it meant. Was it a reminder that she was a mere girl, as weak and as disposable as a stalk of straw? That if Seesya caught her running away, he would tear her apart?

At the washroom, the water in the barrel was cold. She splashed her face several times until she felt better. After relieving herself, she adjusted her robe, causing the fire-starters to clank in her pocket. She took the two stones out and pressed them to her cheeks. If only her father were alive to protect her with his big hands and quiet faith. She remembered how he had taught her to start a fire. Could she still do it?

Deborah knelt on the floor and formed a small mound of straw. It gave off an odor of urine but seemed dry enough. She held the flint in one hand and hit the fool's gold against it at an angle.

Nothing happened.

She remembered that it had been the same when her father was teaching her. He chuckled and said, "Place the flint closer to the straw, Daughter."

She tried again. This time, a single spark shot out from between the stones and hit the straw, but it fizzled, leaving a black speck and a small puff of smoke. She pressed the tip of the flint to the mound of straw, held the palm-size fool's gold higher, and hit the flint with more force.

The impact produced a burst of sparks, which sprayed on the straw and startled her. She fell backward and hit her head on the wall. Rubbing the back of her head, she smiled for the first time since Tamar's stoning.

The smile was short-lived, however, because when she got up, there was smoke rising from the straw, and flames crackled.

She blew on the mound, hoping to blow out the flame as one put out a candle. This caused the burning straw to disintegrate and fly in all directions, landing again on the floor of the washroom. The fire began to spread to the rest of the straw. She tried to stomp it out with her sandals, but as she extinguished one spot, another flared up. Worse yet, at the corner the flame was now licking the wooden wall.

The smoke burned her eyes, and she started to cough. Grabbing the water barrel with both hands, she pulled it over. The water spilled with a big splash, flooding the small washroom and putting out the fire. A moment later, the water had drained through the hole and the wood planks of the floor, leaving only wet, smoldering straw.

Deborah stood still and listened for alarmed voices outside, but apparently no one had noticed. Stepping out of the washroom, she paused at the sight of Seesya and his soldiers. They rode into the courtyard herding a group of women and children, bound together with ropes as a human chain. They were dirty and ragged, a few had open wounds on their arms and legs, and none wore shoes or sandals. Their feet left red prints on the ground. On the street, a herd of cows, sheep, and goats was being led to the corrals behind the house.

Obadiah of Levi appeared at the entrance to the courtyard. People moved aside to let him pass, bowing respectfully. The bearded priest walked slowly, leaning on his oak staff. His breastplate glistened with colored jewels, and his white robe was spotless.

One of the captive women saw him and pleaded, "Help us, priest. We are Hebrews, faithful to Yahweh."

One of the soldiers kicked the woman, who fell down, pulling on the rope, which yanked the prisoners on each side. They, too, fell down, crying in pain.

"Stop!" Obadiah stepped forward, raising his staff. "No need for violence!"

Still standing by the washroom, Deborah stepped back, flat against the wall, trying not to draw attention.

"Where's the slave warden?" Seesya turned his horse, circling the group. "Tell him to lock them up."

"Slaves?" Obadiah looked up at Seesya. "What's the meaning of this?"

"We're tired, priest. Go back to your temple. We'll send you a goat later."

"They attacked our village," one captive woman said. "Ein Zahav."

The soldier raised his horsewhip to strike her.

Obadiah came between him and the woman. "Ein Zahav? The one in the lower Samariah Hills, near the Yarkon Valley?"

"That's right," the woman said. "We are of the Manasseh tribe."

"Not anymore." Seesya advanced his horse, which stomped its front hooves and neighed. "Slaves don't belong to tribes. They belong to their master."

"Hold on," Obadiah said. "Taking fellow Hebrews for slavery is a violation of Yahweh's law."

"We went there to collect a debt," Seesya said. "My father sent me."

"Our village owed no debt," the captive woman said. "We've never taken anything from the house of Zifron."

Seesya held up the leather tube his father had given him. "This is an obligation, signed by three men from their village who received wheat and oil on credit from us and never paid. You can ask my father."

"I believe you," Obadiah said. "Nevertheless, a personal debt doesn't justify attacking their village or taking slaves."

Seesya put away the tube. "They attacked us with axes and pitchforks. The whole village took part in it. There was a fight, and we won."

"Not true," the woman said. "They came in the middle of the day, and when they didn't find the men they were looking for, they demanded that we all hand over our silver and animals. When we refused, this man and his soldiers killed all our men, raped the women, and took us in chains after stealing everything and setting the village on fire."

The other captives nodded, confirming her story.

"Son of Zifron," Obadiah said, "may I remind you what Yahweh's law says: You shall be merciful to strangers, for you were once a stranger in Egypt and they enslaved you for four hundred years."

The people in the courtyard recognized the sacred quote and murmured in support of the priest.

"Lies," Seesya said. "All lies. Their men attacked us."

"You killed them!" The woman pointed at him. "Murderer!"

Seesya rode over and, with a downward stab of his spear, pierced the woman's chest.

Deborah turned away and pressed her hands to her mouth, blocking a scream.

Obadiah stumbled back, steadying himself on his staff. "You shall not commit murder!"

Seesya glared down from his horse. "Are you siding with a slave who insults her master with false accusations?"

The priest took another step back.

"The people of Ein Zahav attacked us," Seesya yelled. "We won the battle. Yahweh's law gives us the right to take the women, children, and livestock as legal plunder." He made his horse turn in place as he stared at the other captives. "Does anyone else want to call me a liar?"

None of them dared to speak.

Obadiah of Levi knelt by the dead woman. He closed her eyes, pressed his hand to his bejeweled breastplate, and recited the blessing on the dead: "Blessed be Yahweh, God of Israel, king of the world, the true judge."

Many in the crowd answered, "Amen."

"The true judge," Deborah whispered. "Amen."

Above the noise, an agonized scream came from the women's quarters. Deborah recognized Mazal's voice.

Seesya pointed his spear at the sound. "There goes another goat." He jumped off his horse, which a stable boy took by the reins, and went into the house.

The soldiers dismounted and tended to their horses while the slave warden came to take possession of the new captives. The priest got up with difficulty and made his way through the crowd of spectators toward the exit.

Mazal screamed again.

Deborah pulled down the edge of her hood to hide her face and hurried along the side of the courtyard in the direction of the exit. People saw her red robe and moved aside to avoid contact. She intercepted Obadiah before he reached the doors to the street and blocked his way.

"Move aside," the priest said.

She didn't.

He tried to get around her.

"You must save me," she said quietly.

"What?"

Deborah was much shorter than Obadiah. She pulled up the edge of her hood and tilted her head backward to show him her face.

His eyes widened. He looked around at the people surrounding them, but the excitement of the confrontation and killing was over, and everyone had returned to their business.

"Foolish girl," he hissed. "How dare you speak to me!"

Mazal screamed again, but no one in the courtyard paid attention.

"You made a promise to my sister before she died."

He shook his head quickly, as if in fear. "I didn't make any promises, and you don't need help. You're in no danger, unless you have also whored with another man."

"I'm a maiden, pure and untouched, same as my sister was." She tugged at her red robe. "In seven days, I'll be ready for his bed—and he'll do to me what he did to her."

The priest tried to go around her. "You're impure. Stay away from me."

She stepped into his path, blocking him.

He stopped to avoid touching her.

Mazal wailed in a high pitch, filled with desperation. The courtyard quieted for a moment, and after brief break, another wail came, fraught with torment and despair.

Everyone waited for her to scream again, but Mazal didn't make another sound. It was over, and now one of the women was supposed to come to the window and announce whether it was a baby boy or only a girl.

No announcement came, which meant that the baby had been born dead.

After a long moment, the courtyard returned to its usual bustle as if nothing had happened. Deborah felt tears come to her eyes, for Mazal's pain had been in vain, and now she would have no baby to nurse and cuddle.

"Let me pass," Obadiah whispered. "Move aside."

"My sister's curse is upon you," Deborah said, "unless you save me."

He bent as if a heavy weight had been placed on his shoulders. "There's nothing I can do. Nothing at all."

"You can help me escape, give me food and money for the road, and pray for me."

"Pray?" The priest chuckled bitterly. "My prayers don't work very well these days."

"If you help me, perhaps Yahweh will listen to your prayers."

"Didn't you see Seesya kill that poor woman a moment ago? He's a vicious little boy in a big man's body. If he found out that I assisted in your escape, I'd need to hire another priest to handle my own burial."

Deborah gestured at his breastplate. "Yahweh will protect you."

At first he seemed offended, but then he exhaled and beckoned her to the side, where the wall curved, offering a measure of privacy. "Where would you go?"

Without thinking, she said, "To Shiloh."

He nodded in approval. "Smart. The Holy Tabernacle attracts many pilgrims and beggars. It would be easy to hide among so many people."

"I'll pray to Yahweh at His house," she said. "He will free me from my betrothal to Seesya."

"A girl's betrothal is final." He pointed at the ring on her finger. "There are only two ways for you to become a maiden again: either Seesya takes the ring back and releases you, or he dies before possessing you in bed."

There was a third way, Deborah knew: if she ceased to be a girl altogether and became a boy. But she wasn't ready to tell the priest about that.

"Yahweh created everything," she said. "The earth, the sun, the moon, and all the stars that fill our sky. I believe He can find a way to free me from Seesya's betrothal."

Obadiah looked at her at length. "You're a true believer, aren't you?"

She nodded.

He glanced back at the crowded courtyard to make sure no one was paying attention. "I need time to think about it."

"I don't have time."

Two men standing nearby looked at the priest and the girl curiously.

Obadiah turned away and spoke under his breath. "Go pray at the temple."

Deborah was about to argue, but the priest left her.

"Make way!" His voice roared over the noise of the crowd. "Make way!" He returned to the center of the courtyard, where the slave warden and his helpers were busy untying the captives and dressing their wounds. Obadiah pointed at the corpse. "Carry this Hebrew woman to the temple so that I can prepare her for burial in accordance with our sacred laws."

Four slaves in sleeveless long shirts lifted the dead woman by her arms and legs and followed the priest out of the courtyard. Deborah lowered the hood of the red robe over her face and trailed them.

The temple was located a small distance up the main street from Judge Zifron's house. It had an open plaza with seven stone columns lining up the front, benches on the right side, and an elevated platform with a large altar in the middle, as well as a stone basin filled with water for washing hands. On the left, under a canopy, open baskets awaited offerings. She could see a few olives, grapes, dates, pomegranates, and apples. A wooden barrel was marked for wheat, and another for barley. A small corral carried no sign. Its purpose—livestock offerings—was obvious. Deborah noticed that the baskets and barrels were almost empty, and the corral held only one small goat that looked back at her with sad eyes.

The slaves carried the dead woman across the plaza and put her in an open handcart with four wheels. Obadiah waved them off and covered the corpse with a sheet of red cloth. Deborah stood by one of the columns, drawing no attention from anyone. When the slaves were gone, the priest beckoned her.

Deborah glanced around to make sure no one was in the street and hurried over. His house was in the rear of the plaza. He led her into a room off to the side and closed the door.

A single oil lamp burned in the corner. A desk held a large parchment, which was about one-third filled with words, beautifully written along straight lines. Several writing feathers rested next to a bottle of ink. Behind the desk, wooden shelves were filled with dozens of scrolls.

Deborah peered at the parchment. "What are you writing?"

"Yahweh's laws." Obadiah pointed to the first line and quoted. "Honor your father and your mother, and your days shall be long upon the land that I give you."

"My father used to recite that when my sister and I misbehaved." Deborah paused as the memory of Tamar brought a new wave of grief.

"I still quote it to my sons, who are grown men already."

She took a deep breath, struggling not to cry. "My father said it was one of the Ten Commandments, written on the stone tablets that Yahweh gave to Moses on Mount Sinai."

"That's correct," the priest said. "Your father was a good man, a God-fearing man. He used to bring his offerings here every harvest time, one-tenth of all his crops and new livestock, without delay or deceit, unlike most other men."

His kind words about her father brought up the tears Deborah had been struggling to keep at bay. She wiped her eyes. "Most men don't bring offerings?"

He gestured at the door. "You saw the baskets out there. Did they look full to you?"

"No, but why?"

"Too many Hebrew men have turned their backs on the one and true God. Even our ruler, Judge Zifron, holds up the effigy of Mott at trials, while his women kneel before Ra when the sun rises." The priest's voice was bitter. "That's why God is punishing us, sending one tribe to fight against the other and allowing the Canaanites to oppress the northern tribes—and it will get worse unless the we repent and correct our ways!"

"Is that why you write down the laws?"

Obadiah sat down in a chair and sighed. "Since Moses threw down the tablets and broke them, Yahweh's laws have passed from father to son, each law recited repeatedly until it was etched in our minds. My father made me memorize Yahweh's laws, as did his father before him. I've always felt blessed to learn such a treasure, a whole system of laws that came down from the Creator to Moses to each one of us, guiding us on how to live righteously as Yahweh's chosen people. But now, many fathers fail to teach their sons, and my own sons are more interested in counting the offerings and complaining about our diminished revenues than studying the law."

"I'd like to memorize God's laws."

He laughed as if she'd told a joke.

Deborah reached out to touch the parchment.

"Don't!"

She recoiled.

"You're impure." He rolled up the parchment and put it on a shelf. "You asked that I help you escape. What's your plan?"

"I must leave tonight."

"That's not a plan. Zifron's courtyard is locked up every night. How will you get out?"

"There's a small window high up in the wall of the washroom. I'll use it to climb down to the street."

"When?"

"When the moon reaches the top of the sky."

He tugged on his beard. "What about the town walls?"

"I don't know, but if you want to be released from my sister's curse, you should find a way to get me out of Emanuel."

"How? The gates are closed at night and guarded by sentries."

"Pray to Yahweh." Deborah went to the door. "He'll provide you with a solution."

Out in the plaza, near the covered handcart bearing the dead woman, Deborah saw a group of young boys. There were over thirty of them, from about five to twelve years old, sitting cross-legged on the ground in the shade.

Deborah paused behind one of the columns and watched.

Obadiah of Levi appeared. One of the boys brought him a chair. The priest sat down and began to recite. "Moses came down from Mount Sinai and said to the Hebrews: God has spoken. I am the Lord, your God, who brought you out of the land of Egypt, the place of slavery."

The boys chorused in thin voices, "I am the Lord, your God, who brought you out of the land of Egypt, the place of slavery."

The priest continued, "You shall worship no other gods but me."

Deborah murmured with the boys, "You shall worship no other gods but me."

As she walked away, the priest continued his recitation. "You shall not make any statue or picture of what is in the sky above or in the water under—"

Halfway down the street, she could still hear the boys repeat after him, their voices young and full of enthusiasm.

8

When Deborah returned, the courtyard was quiet again. The captives had been taken to the slaves' quarters, and the puddle of blood was covered with straw. At the factory, Sallan told her to sit between Vardit and a young concubine at one of the round tables. The two women moved farther apart to avoid unintended contact with Deborah. She sat on the bench, her heart beating hard in her chest. One of the slave girls brought her a bundle of braided strands.

"Go ahead," Vardit said. "Start as I showed you last night."

From the neighboring women's quarters, Mazal could be heard crying for her mother.

Deborah looked at the connecting door.

"Don't worry," Vardit said. "She'll be with another child soon enough."

Deborah's hands shook as she started to weave the strands together, alternating over and under to interlace them in a checkerboard pattern, as she had practiced the night before. Her unstable hands made the task harder, and when Mazal cried out again, the weave collapsed and the strands fell from Deborah's hand.

Vardit got up. "I'll be right back," she said to Sallan and went to the women's quarters.

"Go on," Sallan said. "Back to work."

Deborah started a new weave. Her hands still shook, but she was determined to succeed. After all this time of doing mindless work at the dipping tub, she was finally being allowed to prove herself as a real basket maker. Even if this was her last day in the factory, she didn't want to fail.

Vardit came back and looked at the weave before taking her seat. "Very good," she said.

Deborah smiled. "Thank you."

A sense of accomplishment filled her. If only Tamar could see this. She would have clapped with joy, hugged her tightly, and told her how proud she was of this achievement.

As Deborah continued weaving, it occurred to her that she might have been hasty to make an escape plan with the priest for tonight. Perhaps Vardit was right about Seesya and his dislike of orange hair. After all, who knew him better than his own mother? Vardit had been certain that dyeing Deborah's hair black and applying a layer of makeup would surprise and please Seesya. If true, then Deborah would be no worse off than every other wife in the household. Their lives were hard, with frequent pregnancies and related illnesses, but the women lived and worked together, sharing the pains and joys of motherhood. She would become one of them, no longer alone in the world.

And, speaking of being alone, how could a solitary girl make the journey by foot through land she didn't know all the way to Shiloh—at least three days away? There was no doubt in her mind that Tamar would tell her to trust Vardit and stay.

The thought of Tamar led to recollection of the stoning. Images of that horror flashed before Deborah's eyes. Her hand slipped, and she lost grip of a strand.

"Careful, girl." Vardit reached over and pointed. "Put it through again, right here."

Deborah did, and it held. She glanced at the other women around the table. None of them looked up from their work. Their fingers moved much faster than hers, with confidence and accuracy that she could only hope to match one day.

As if reading her thoughts, Vardit said, "You'll get better, don't worry. By harvest time, you'll be as good—"

"No talking!" Sallan limped over. "That's all you've done so far?"

His words made Deborah's chest tighten. Her fingers grew stiff. She struggled to push one strand between two others.

"Not like that." He reached over her shoulder and touched the loose strand with his thick forefinger. "This one should go in from the bottom."

When Deborah tried to turn the piece over, the whole thing separated and fell apart, dropping to the floor.

"Stupid girl." Sallan nudged her from behind. "Clean up this mess."

The factory went quiet, and everyone watched.

Her face burning with embarrassment, Deborah bent and picked up the braided strands. She began to weave them again, but her hands trembled so badly that the strands separated as soon as she tried to interlace them.

Vardit put down her own work. "Here, let me help—"

"Leave her alone." Sallan's hand came between them. "I told her to practice last night."

Deborah looked up at him. "I practiced until the oil ran out."

"It's true," Vardit said. "She was still at it when I fell asleep."

"I don't care how long you practiced. Either you can do the work, or not."

Using more force, Deborah held the strands together with one hand while forcing each strand into the next interlock, but the pressure forced one strand to bend too far, causing the rest of the woven piece to bend.

Sallan reached down and snatched the piece out of her hand. He tossed a fresh bundle of strands on the table in front of her. "Try again."

This time, she arranged the strands on the tabletop and started to interlace them there, avoiding the complexity of holding the strands while weaving them. The women around the table watched her.

Sallan knuckled the table. "It's not a show."

They resumed working, but Deborah felt them glancing at her hands, expecting her to fail again. She breathed deeply, trying to ignore everyone and concentrate on weaving according to the pattern.

It went well for a while, and she was getting near the full length of her strands. At this point, Vardit had explained to her, she should tie new strands to the ends and continue the pattern. But the strands weren't all the same length, and when she tried to pull one of them slightly so that it would reach the same length as the others, the whole thing separated and fell apart. With Sallan hovering behind her, she groaned in frustration, and the women around the table giggled, except for Vardit, who seemed ready to cry.

"You're wasting my time." Sallan pointed. "Go back to the dipping tub!"

Barely able to see through the tears, Deborah walked across the factory to the dipping tub.

Behind her, Sallan said, "Stupid girl."

She stopped and turned. "I'm not stupid."

"I think you are." Sallan limped toward her. "I think you're totally stupid."

All her shame and distress combusted into anger. "If you think I'm stupid, then you're stupid."

The whole factory froze, the workers' hands suspended in midair, their eyes wide open.

The foreman himself seemed stunned. After a long moment, he limped to his work desk and picked up a parchment from a stack of scrolls. He came back, holding it in front of her.

"Read, girl." He pointed to a line of inked text. "What it says here?"

She couldn't read.

"How about this line?" He pointed. "It's in your language, the language of the Hebrews, the language of your prophet Moses."

Her eyes dropped.

"What's wrong? Can't you read it?"

She shook her head.

"Anyone else?" He waved the parchment at the rest of the factory workers. "Well?"

No one responded. Only men could read and write. The law forbade women from even trying to learn, a crime punishable by fifty lashes.

"I'll tell you what it says." Sallan read aloud: "We require twenty-four small baskets and eighteen medium-size baskets before the next apple harvest—"

Deborah turned and went to the dipping tub.

"Stupid! Stupid! Stupid!" Sallan's voice rose. "You're all stupid!"

9

Deborah spent the rest of the day without looking at anyone else. She dipped the stalks, pulled any remaining whiskers, and passed the stalks on for braiding. When sunlight finally dimmed, Sallan clapped to signal the end of the workday. She dried her hands on her red robe and headed for the door. In a few hours, she would slip away from the compound and leave Emanuel to begin a new life that, even if cut short by violence on the road to Shiloh, would be better than this life of worthlessness and humiliation.

Vardit was waiting for her at the door to the women's quarters, her face filled with pity.

"Hey, stupid girl!" Sallan called from behind her. "Where do you think you're going?"

She turned.

"Come back here."

"I'm tired," she said.

"Me too. Do you see me walking away?" Sallan pointed at the round table. "Sit down and practice your weaving."

Deborah glanced back over her shoulder, but Vardit was gone.

"That's it? Giving up?" His voice was sarcastic. "You want to remain stupid?"

His words stung. She went back to the table and sat down, determined to get it right this time. Sallan lighted several oil lamps and sat at his desk. The factory was quiet except for the rustling of his parchment and the scratching of his writing feather.

With the oil in the lamp almost gone, her stomach aching from hunger, Deborah finished a rectangle of woven stalks, interlaced in even checkerboard pattern, its size fitting the measurements Vardit had given her.

Sallan took it, examined the pattern, and used a ruler to measure the length and width. "Not bad," he said. "Not bad at all."

Bending it into a circular sidewall of a basket, he placed it over a flat, round base and used a thread and a long needle to stitch it together. The needle moved rapidly in his hands, the thread tight and evenly looped, binding the bottom of the sidewall around the edge of the base.

He handed her the small basket. "Maybe you're not as stupid as I thought."

Carrying the basket in her hand as if it were a treasured heirloom, she headed to the door, eager to show it to Vardit.

"Wait," Sallan said. "Aren't you hungry?"

Surprised by his question, she pointed toward the women's quarters. "There might be something left from the evening meal."

He sneered. "I've seen what the women eat. Worthy of cows and chickens. Come upstairs, and I'll show you what real food looks like."

He snapped his fingers, and the two servants appeared with a lamp at the top of the staircase. His limp made the climb slow.

His invitation was so unusual that Deborah was paralyzed by confusion.

"Are you coming, girl?"

She realized that this might be her only opportunity to ask him about the story he had told Barac. Did he know where she could find the Elixirist?

Entering Sallan's quarters, Deborah found herself in a dim, cozy foyer. Her eyes took a moment to adjust, and when her vision returned, she recoiled from the toddler-sized figure facing her. Its body was made of wood, and elaborate bronze pieces were attached to its hands.

"Let me introduce you," Sallan said. "This is Kothar-wa-Khasis, our god of craftsmanship." He held a lamp close to the deity's hands. Each finger was fitted with a miniature piece made of forged bronze. "Hammer and rod, for his metalworking. Measuring ruler for his engineering. Inkwell and feather for his inventions. Bowl and crusher for his potion-making. Wand for his spellcasting. Saw and chisel for his woodworking. And a key to open the window through which Baal Ammon sends rain to nourish the land that feeds us."

Deborah wanted to say that it was Yahweh who sent rain, nourished the land, and gave men the abilities to engage in crafts, but Sallan turned and left her in the near dark with Kothar-wa-Khasis. She quickly took off her sandals and followed him into a spacious living area, which was clean and opulent, in stark contrast to the basket factory below.

The floor was covered with straw mats that felt soft under her feet. Linen sheets in cream colors draped the walls. The roof was made of wood beams and thatch. Various ornaments hung from it—stuffed birds, ceramic figurines, and dried flowers. There were sofas along the walls, covered with cowhides and many pillows.

The boys helped Sallan take off his work clothes and wrapped him in a linen robe. He sat on a sofa and patted the cushion next to him.

Deborah sat down.

One of the boys knelt and massaged the foreman's right foot while the other removed the wooden piece that served for a left foot and rubbed olive oil on the stump.

"I trust you can keep a secret," Sallan said.

Her eyes glued to his stump, she nodded.

"Not that," he said, chuckling. "My limp isn't a secret." He gestured at their surroundings. "No one is ever invited here."

Deborah didn't know what to say. Why had he invited *her*?

"Sad business with your sister," he said. "In my country, a woman is protected as a person of value and wisdom. Our greatest god, Qoz, is both a man and a woman. And why would anyone destroy a fine young woman, even if she made an error?"

"My sister didn't do anything wrong."

The boys disappeared behind a partition.

"Men sometimes turn into a single-minded beast," he said. "Like a herd of bloodthirsty coyotes tearing up an antelope."

"Some men don't."

"I heard a boy stood up to Seesya in the middle of the stoning."

"Barac, the blacksmith's son. He is brave."

"I've seen you two on the street, talking, laughing. You like him, don't you?"

She blushed.

"Perhaps that's what happened to your sister."

Deborah opened her mouth to protest but changed her mind. She had never even touched Barac, or he her, but she was honest enough to remember that she had wanted to.

The boys returned with plates of warm food. There were three types of red meat, each prepared differently, a whole pigeon covered in spices she didn't recognize, as well as vegetables, including sugary carrots, and warm bread with honey.

Sallan surveyed the food and, apparently satisfied, dismissed the boys. Using his fingers, he scooped up small samples from the various dishes and filled a small copper plate. He placed it in front of a pedestal holding an effigy. The figure was made of copper, which had been polished until it glistened. Its large head sprouted three curved horns, and its sculpted face was human, through Deborah couldn't tell whether it was male or female. The eyes were large and blank, the chest hinting at breasts with shallow protrusions. It sat on a throne between a bull and a cow and wielded a multipronged thunderbolt in its left hand.

Bowing his head, Sallan said, "Thank you, mighty Qoz, supreme master of the world, for the food that you deign to share with us."

Deborah turned away, closed her eyes, and silently thanked Yahweh for the food.

Sallan took a plate and began to fill it.

She did the same.

"Have you ever seen our mighty Qoz before today?"

"No. I'm surprised it's made of copper, not clay or wood like all the other—" She wanted to say "false idols" but stopped herself in time.

"Qoz blessed Edom with an abundance of copper, the source of our national riches. We forge the image of Qoz in copper to show gratitude for this eternal blessing."

"Why does it carry a thunderbolt?"

"To control light and darkness, storms and rain. Qoz either blesses and anoints, or curses and avenges, and all such things the mighty Qoz delivers with strikes of the thunderbolt."

They ate in silence, except that Sallan often licked his fingers noisily and groaned with pleasure. Deborah ate slowly, savoring each bite. The tastes and textures were all new, and she concentrated on the food to such an extent that a loud burp from Sallan startled her. It was also a signal to the boys, who appeared from behind the partition and cleared the dishes, leaving only the yet-untouched plate of Qoz. They returned with cups of hot milk and bowls of dates, figs, and almonds.

After the meal, Sallan and Deborah relocated to a circle of cushions on the floor around the skin of a large tiger. A pungent smell hit her nose, and she sniffed the skin, confirming that it was the source.

"Magnificent, isn't it?" Sallan caressed the fur with pride. "I got it from a Moabite trader last week in exchange for a hefty discount on a large order of storage baskets. He was happy with the bargain, because the smell of this skin made his animals nervous. The tiger came from the mountains south of the Sea of Salt. My father once killed a male tiger like this one during one of his travels. For many years, its skin covered a wall at our home. I still remember how it smelled during the first year." He lifted the long tail and brought it to his nose. "Exactly like this." He brushed the tail against his cheek. "A ferocious cat, second only to a lion in striking the fear of death in all other creatures."

Sallan stuffed aromatic dry leaves into a pipe, lighted it with the oil lamp, and smoked in silence. The boys brushed his bushy hair, pinned it up, and applied oil the sides of his head, where his ears were missing. She wondered whether his leg and ears had been harmed at the same time.

He offered her the pipe.

She declined.

"It's good," he said. "Relaxing."

"I should leave now. Vardit must be concerned about me."

Sallan waved dismissively. "My master's wife is concerned only with herself and her vicious son."

His cutting words shocked Deborah. Was he right about Vardit? Was her kindness insincere? Until now, it had not occurred to Deborah that the older woman might be pretending to care, or that she had an ulterior motive for helping the girls.

"Did you enjoy the meal?" Sallan asked.

"Yes," Deborah said. "It was very good."

"The only thing missing was a roasted pig. I never understood why the Hebrew God forbade the best meat of all."

"I don't know," she said. "Thank you for the most luxurious meal I've ever had."

"Not bad for a crippled slave." He lifted the stump of his left leg.

She looked away.

"And not bad for you either. In the span of one day, you went from a worthless girl, humiliated in front of all the others, to eating a meal worthy of a king—or a queen." He grinned. "Do you want to know how it's possible for me to have all this?"

Deborah shook her head.

Taken aback, he asked, "Why not?"

"I already know the answer."

"You do?"

"People say you alone know the secret of making the Reinforcing Liquid that makes the baskets so strong and helps Judge Zifron get rich."

Sallan opened his arms wide. "From Egypt to the Hittite Kingdom, everyone has heard of the Zifron baskets."

She picked up the small basket he had given her. "Thank you again."

"They're right about the secret liquid." He drew from the pipe and blew rings of smoke. "But they are also wrong. Do you want to know why?"

"Actually, I'd like to ask you a different question."

He laughed, smoke shooting from his mouth, and his eyes glistened. "You remind me of a girl I knew a long time ago. What's your question?"

"Barac told me about a young Edomite man who turned women into men."

Sallan drew smoke and blew it out slowly.

"Is it true?" Deborah shifted forward, now at the edge of her seat. "Did he really win a battle against the Egyptians by turning women into men?"

The foreman smoked some more. "It was a long time ago."

"So it's true!"

"According to legend, yes, the Elixirist saved Edom, but the king locked him up, isolated from all human contact except for a single guard who was nearly deaf and almost mute."

"Why would the king do that? It's very unfair."

Chuckling made Sallan cough. "Young people expect the world to run on wheels of fairness and justice, but that's not how it works. In reality, powerful rulers and men of great wealth don't make decisions based on what's fair and just."

"Why not?"

"We have an old saying in Edom," he said. "The higher the rise, the steeper the fall."

Deborah shook her head.

"That's what they're afraid of, and it drives all their strategy decisions."

"What's that?"

"Strategy is what men of power and wealth use for self-preservation. When a situation comes up, they look at all the facts, figure out what they can use for their advantage, and come up with solutions that promote three things: their safety, their fortune, and their power. Strategy is the reason they rule the world, whereas everyone else submits to them, works hard for them, and pays them taxes."

She tried to digest what he was saying. "Did strategy make the king lock up the Elixirist?"

"A king cannot allow another man to win the people's admiration. It's a threat to his power. The king also cannot appear to be jealous or vengeful. That would be a threat to his image. What's the best strategy for these problems? Trumped-up accusations, a bogus trial, and a public execution, which the people always enjoy. But King Esau worried he might need the Elixirist to save the kingdom again. That's why he locked up the Elixirist and told everyone that Egyptian spies had abducted him and taken him to Pharaoh's palace on the Nile."

"That's terrible!"

"Strategy has nothing to do with justice or fairness. Its purpose is to protect the king's interests. Pure and simple, isn't it?"

"Now I understand why Yahweh forbade us from anointing a Hebrew king."

Sallan's eyebrows rose. "Is that right? No king ever?"

"My father told me." She paused to let a wave of longing pass. "Yahweh said, "Do not anoint yourself a king to reign over you, for I am your king, the Creator of the world." We may appoint priests for worship and local judges to rule by God's laws, but we may not have a king."

"People need a king they can see, a king whose right hand wields a shining sword to protect them while his left hand brandishes a knotted whip to subjugate them."

"And to lock them up."

"Exactly." Sallan chuckled. "The Elixirist, however, managed to escape."

"That's wonderful!"

"I thought so, too."

"How did he get out?"

"The guard assisted him."

"Why?"

"Gratitude, for being able to hear and speak."

Her eyes widened. "He cured the guard? How? With an elixir? Could he cure all the deaf and mute people in the world?"

Sallan smiled. "Cure is a big word. Let's just say that he helped the guard rediscover those innate human abilities of hearing and speaking."

"That's magic."

"Easier than turning all of Edom's women into men and commanding a battle."

"Do you know where I could find him?"

He drew from the pipe, not answering.

"Please tell me. I need his elixir to become a boy."

"A boy?" Sallan laughed. "You're far too pretty to pass for a boy."

He was toying with her again, telling her she was pretty while they both knew she was nothing of the sort. "I beg you, help me find the Elixirist."

"What I know is is from a long time ago."

His tone was neutral, but his words gave her new hope.

"Please tell me."

Sallan drew from the pipe, but the leaves had turned to ashes, and the flame had died. He put it aside. "It could be a long and dangerous journey."

"Life as a woman is a long and dangerous journey. I have nothing to lose."

"Even if you survive the journey and find him, you'll have to somehow convince him to make the elixir for you. And drinking it might be ineffective, or even harmful. I'm sure there are less hazardous ways to survive your first night with Seesya."

"For what?" Deborah's eyes suddenly welled up. "I don't want to live like the women here. No, I want to become a man."

"Are you willing to die trying?"

"I'd rather die than live as Seesya's wife."

"Why?"

"Because I want to be free!"

"What's so good about freedom?" He gestured at the opulence

surrounding them. "I live much better than most free men, don't I?"

"Material comforts are nice, but wouldn't you like to be free?"

"Answering a question with a question?" He sighed. "Of course I want to be free."

"Me too," she said. "As a man, I'd be free to choose my mate, or not to marry at all. Free to inherit Palm Homestead and grow my own crops. Free to buy and sell my own goods, to read and write, to speak up against evil—and to fight and do battle, if I had to!"

Sallan leaned back on the cushions and looked at her – not in condescension but with something close to fascination. "And if I tell you what I know about the Elixirist, what will my reward be?"

The girl gestured with her hands as if saying, "Whatever you want."

"I'll point you in the right direction," he said. "It's only a start, and the road will be long and hard, but if you win your freedom, then you must come back and help me win my freedom."

"Really?" She gestured at their surroundings. "You'd give all this up?"

"The curse of old age is that discomfort grows from within your own body." He patted his legs and arms. "Physical pains, which the softest bed no longer eases. And the pains in your heart." He patted his chest. "The longing for loved ones and the regrets for past errors – hurts more with every passing year. The only cure is to return to my homeland before I die and embrace whoever is still alive. And to see Bozra again. It's the most beautiful city in the world, with white walls and copper roofs, built on the north face of a red mountain, overlooking a fertile valley, rich with water and copper mines." His voice trailed off as he shut his eyes, remembering.

More than anything, Deborah wanted to agree, but she knew it would be dishonest, and therefore a sin. "I'm only a girl. How could I come back here, confront Seesya and Judge Zifron, who would surely punish me for escaping, obtain your freedom, and take you all the way to Edom? Keeping such a promise would require much more strength than I'll ever have."

"You're honest," Sallan said. "I like that. As to strength, I can help you."

He summoned one of the boy-servants and whispered in his ear. The boy fetched an empty goblet and ran to the door. Soon he returned with the goblet, now full, and gave it to Deborah.

"Drink it," Sallan said.

The goblet contained an opaque liquid that looked and smelled familiar. She hesitated. "Is this from the dipping tub?"

He put his hands over hers and brought the goblet to her lips, leaving her no choice. Expecting bitterness or an otherwise foul taste, she was surprised that the Reinforcing Liquid had the taste and texture of fresh water with only a trace of sourness, much like the tang that a few drops of lemon juice would give to a jar of well water.

He tilted the goblet all the way. "Finish every drop."

The boy took the empty goblet and left.

She put her hands in her lap. "You're not supposed to touch me. I'm impure for seven days."

"Hebrew superstitions." Sallan chuckled, shaking his head. "A woman's blood is as pure as pomegranate juice."

Deborah burped. "Excuse me. I think it's making me sick."

"You're fine. More than fine." He coughed and wiped his lips. "The truth is, my secret Reinforcing Liquid works not only on straw. It will gradually give you strength to keep even the most difficult promise."

Deborah looked at him doubtfully. "Are you sure? I don't feel any stronger."

With a thick finger, Sallan touched her forehead. "It's all here, in your head. That's where your strength begins to grow like yeast in fresh dough. Believe in it, and it will rise." He shifted his finger to her chest. "Your heart must not resist or doubt the magic of your strength but allow it to grow and make you mightier than the challenges facing you and taller than the barriers on your path." His hand dropped and squeezed her hand. "At times, you'll shake with fear and self-doubt, confronting a powerful man or a sudden danger, but you must steady your hand, banish your fear, and embrace your strength. If you do, by the time you find the Elixirist, the strength within you will be more than sufficient for you to return to Emanuel and help me."

The doubts he had referred to were already brewing in her heart, but Deborah pushed them aside. "If you're certain about it," she said, "then I'll give you my promise."

"Take an oath," Sallan said. "Invoke your Hebrew God."

"I swear in the name of Yahweh that I will come back here to obtain your freedom and take you to Edom, where you'll reunite with your people."

"Good," he said. "We have a deal."

Deborah could hardly breathe from the excitement that filled her. "The Elixirist—where will I find him?"

Sallan leaned back on the cushions. "His name is Kassite."

"Kassite?"

"It's an Edomite name, like mine, but we don't look alike. He's very tall and thin, and he speaks slowly. When you find him, tell him that I sent you. He won't believe you, but I'll tell you a code that will convince him."

"Why?"

"Because no one else in the world knows what it means, except for Kassite and me." Sallan took a deep breath. "Thirteen hundred and thirteen."

"Thirteen hundred and thirteen," Deborah repeated. "And where will I find him?"

"I'll tell you what I know." He paused, taking a deep breath. "We were travelling in the same caravan when Moabite marauders took us captive. We tried to escape after a few days. They caught us, maimed us, and sold us as slaves. He stood next to me on the dock. I was sold first, and Kassite was bought after I was taken down from the dock. I don't know who bought him, but they keep records at the slave market in Shiloh."

"Shiloh?"

"That's where the Moabites sold us. My first owner was a merchant from Mitzpah, a man of the tribe of Dan. He bought me in Shiloh in the first spring after the Great Famine, on the eve of the Passover holiday, eighteen years ago. Kassite was sold immediately after me to someone else. You'll find the answer there."

If Deborah had any doubts about Yahweh's all-powerful grace, none remained. Here she was, about to escape tonight and go to Shiloh to pray for her freedom at the Holy Tabernacle, and it turned out that Shiloh was also the place where she would find the way to the Elixirist! Deborah shut her eyes and thanked Him in silence.

10

"What happened to you?" Vardit was the only one awake. She was rocking a toddler, whose mother had fallen asleep. "It's been hours!"

"I know," Deborah said. "Sallan made me practice until I could weave perfectly."

"I was very worried about you."

Recalling Sallan's derision of Vardit's true concerns, Deborah searched her face for signs of pretense or insincerity, finding nothing but genuine care and exhaustion.

"Sallan is pleased with my work now," Deborah said.

"Then tomorrow will be a better day."

"I hope so." Deborah wondered where she would be this time tomorrow.

The toddler whimpered, disturbed by their talking. Vardit covered his head and whispered, "There's some bread left on the table."

Deborah took a few bites from the bread and drank some water. She crossed the room to check on Mazal. The girl had thrown off the covers. Her exposed skin was moist with sweat, and her long black hair was drenched and rumpled. She breathed heavily and tossed from side to side, groaning in her sleep.

Vardit put the toddler down and went to sleep.

After using the clay bucket in the corner to relieve herself, Deborah lay down. It was quiet, and she struggled to keep her eyes open. It was difficult to tell how much time had passed. She went to the window, moved aside the curtain, and looked up at the sky. The moon was not even halfway up to its apex.

Back under the blanket, she tried to remain awake by thinking of her escape. Once outside the town walls, she would face many dangers. There would be animals at night and people during the day, all threatening her survival. Hiding from people would be easier, because she'd be able to see and hear them from a distance. Animals, however, would be able to smell her from a great distance and sneak up on her in the dark. How would she keep them away?

Sweat covered her. She took off the blanket and sat up. What had Sallan said after making her drink the Reinforcing Liquid? "You'll shake with fear and self-doubt at times, confronting a powerful man or a sudden danger, but you must steady your hand, banish your fear, and embrace your strength." That's what she needed to do: think of the Reinforcing Liquid and banish her fear. But how? It was easier said than done. She had no chance of surviving against hungry coyotes, or even a single bear.

Thinking of Sallan gave her an idea. It was risky, yet not as risky as facing wild beasts on the road without any protection.

Deborah tiptoed across the women's quarters and through the door back into the basket factory. She stood still and listened. The ceiling, which was also the floor of Sallan's quarters, was made of wood and supported by stone columns. She was used to it squeaking and creaking whenever his servants walked around upstairs during the day. Now it was quiet, and after several more moments of waiting, she pulled off her sandals, picked up a knife from the toolbox, and climbed the steps.

The door to Sallan's living quarters was closed but not locked. She opened it very slowly. Inside, she saw the dark outline of Kothar-wa-Khasis with its raised hands and myriad tools.

With the knife clenched in her hand, Deborah moved slowly, staying along the walls to minimize the risk of squeaky wood planks under her bare feet. Moonlight came through the window, and she realized it would soon be time for her rendezvous with Obadiah of Levi. She moved faster, the floor creaked, and she heard someone sigh nearby.

The boys' light skin stood out in the dark. They slept with Sallan, one on each side, in a large bed at the other end of the living room, not in a separate bedroom as she had expected. One of the boys shifted in his sleep but didn't wake up.

Deborah crept toward the center of the room. She crouched by the cushions, moved them aside to expose the tiger skin, and found the tail.

The floor squeaked, and she froze. From its spot next to the sofa, Qoz watched her, its face lighter than the surrounding darkness. The copper plate remained at the foot of the small pedestal, but the food was gone. Had Qoz eaten it? For a moment, she imagined Qoz moving its three-pronged thunderbolt, aiming it at her, and striking her with a jolt of lightning as punishment for what she was about to do.

Nothing happened. The thunderbolt remained in the same position as before. There was only one true God, she reminded herself, and it wasn't Qoz or Kothar-wa-Khasis.

Deborah used the knife to cut a circle around the base of the tail, removing it with a portion of the skin that formerly covered the animal's lower back. It stank as before, but now she found the odor reassuring, because it would keep her safe from wild animals on the way to Shiloh. Surely this was Yahweh's blessed hand, coming to her aid again.

Back in the women's quarters, everyone was asleep as before. Deborah rearranged her mat and bunched up the blanket and pillow to make it look as if she was asleep under the covers. Her father's fire-starters were in the pocket of her red robe, and her new basket was stuffed with the tiger tail.

The night was silent. She paused before stepping into the courtyard. It was dimly lit by two torches, one at each end. To her right, the open horse stable gave off the stench of manure, but the horses were quiet. On the far left, the heavy doors that led out to the street were locked for the night. The soldiers slept in a room adjacent to the entry, ready for action at a moment's notice.

She ran to the firepit, which was glowing red with embers. As always, there was a pile of firewood next to it. She selected a large piece before continuing across the courtyard. The washroom was not occupied. She entered it and bolted the door from inside.

Propping the piece of wood against the wall, she stepped on it to reach the small window above. She was too short to look outside and see the street below. Was the priest waiting for her? Cupping her mouth, she whispered, "Are you there?"

There was no response.

"Anyone there?"

Again, there was no response. Had the priest changed his mind? Was he more afraid of Seesya than of Tamar's curse?

Deborah hesitated. Going back now would be easy. She could slip under her blanket and fall asleep as if nothing had happened. She would have to hide the tiger tail somewhere to avoid Sallan's suspicion. But if she didn't escape now, then when? And if not the priest, who else would help her?

No one would help her. No one. Either she escaped now, or she never would. That was the choice she had to make.

Sallan's words played in her mind again: "Banish your fear and embrace your strength!" He was right. It didn't matter that the old priest had failed to show up. She would find a way to get over the walls of Emanuel and begin her journey tonight.

Deborah pushed the basket out first, pulled herself up, and squeezed her head and shoulders through the tight opening, followed by her upper body. But in her nervous determination, she had failed to realize what would happen next, and found herself falling headfirst toward the hard ground below.

11

Dropping upside-down from the small washroom window, high in the outside wall of Judge Zifron's house, Deborah put her hands forward to protect her head from hitting the hard-packed dirt of the street. But sooner than she expected, her outstretched hands collided with something softer than the ground, covered in cloth. Her legs went over her head, and she fell backwards while grasping the cloth to stop her fall. She landed on her back, and the cloth-wrapped, bulky object fell on top of her.

Facing Deborah in the moonlight, nose to nose, was a woman's face, white as milk and expressionless. It was the captive Seesya had killed that morning. Her corpse pinned the girl down with morbid heaviness and stiff limbs. The mouth was slightly open, and the knock of the fall pushed out a gust of sour odor that puffed on Deborah's face, making her retch.

Had she any air left, Deborah would have screamed. But with her chest pressed down, all she could do was try to push the corpse off.

The woman's body barely gave.

Desperate, Deborah pushed harder, but she was no match for the lifeless, rigid corpse whose pale blank face fueled an overwhelming terror. Deborah's vision fogged up, and she wanted to surrender to the inevitable end, but a last burst of anger made her push one more time. With sudden ease, as if it had magically become weightless, the corpse rolled off, and Deborah was able to fill her lungs.

"For heaven's sake," Obadiah whispered, "are you trying to get us both killed?"

She tried to respond, but words wouldn't come out.

"I almost gave up on you, girl!"

Propping herself up on her elbows, Deborah looked around. Parked under the washroom window was the four-wheeled handcart used to transport indigent dead people for burial outside the walls. The more affluent townsmen carried their dead relatives on decorated wagons with flowers and various personal items to be buried with the bodies in individual graves. A few even paid for the fabrication of stone coffins to keep the deceased safe from worms and critters. But for most families, the living could spare nothing for their departed relatives. A body would be brought to the temple, sometimes with a small gift. The priest would conduct the appropriate rituals and dispose of the body in the community grave—a deep, bell-shaped cave with a small mouth, located downhill from the town's gates.

"I called you." Her voice was shaking. "You didn't answer."

"You were late. I had to hide." He gestured at a clump of bushes across the street. "I placed the cart under the window so that you could climb down, not jump headfirst like a mad goat."

"I didn't see—"

"Doesn't matter. Get up and lie on top!"

Deborah climbed onto the handcart. Its bed was sized to accommodate an adult male lying flat. Wide planks had been attached on all four sides to keep a body from rolling off, and tar had been applied to the bed and the sides to prevent bodily fluids from dripping. It gave off the same stench as the dead woman, only worse.

"I can't lie here," Deborah said. "I'm not dead."

"We'll both be dead soon if you don't do as I say!"

She lay down flat. The priest placed two short planks across the cart, one above her chest, another above her knees, the crosspieces resting on the raised side planks.

"Turn your head sideways," he said, "so you can breathe."

She obeyed.

Grunting with effort, he picked up the murdered woman and put her on top, legs pointing toward Deborah's head. The two cross-planks kept the weight off Deborah, except that one of the woman's heels pressed Deborah's skull into the bed of the cart. She wanted to shout in revulsion and pull out from under the corpse, but she clenched her teeth and edged her head to the side. At the other end of the cart, the woman's shoulders rested on Deborah's feet due to their difference in height. The arrangement was uncomfortable, but at least the head was further down, the sour stench all the way at the other end of the cart.

Unfurling a red sheet, the priest covered the whole cart. He placed a sack on top of the sheet. "Don't make a sound," he whispered. "Don't move. Don't even blink. Our lives depend on it."

The main street led at a moderate decline from Judge Zifron's great house, through the town, to the gates. Tradesmen and shopkeepers inhabited the houses along the street, but everyone was asleep now. The four wheels made the cart stable, but every bump rattled Deborah between the hard bed below and the stiff corpse above. Obadiah proceeded down the street slowly. In one of the houses, a baby cried. In another, a dog barked, and a man's voice yelled at it to stop.

The street flattened at the bottom of the hill. Deborah smelled the stench of poverty that drifted over from nearby tents and shacks.

The priest began to chant a mournful hymn, his voice rising as they neared the gates.

"Who goes there?" The sentry's voice was youthful and drowsy.

"It is I, Obadiah of Levi, servant of Yahweh."

Deborah held her breath.

The sentry's weapons rattled as he walked toward them. "What do you want?"

"What I want," Obadiah said, "is to be in my bed, warm and asleep."

"Me too."

"Unfortunately, my son, we both have jobs to do."

The sentry held a lamp over the cart. "What's this?"

"Eternal rest—even for a slave woman."

"In the middle of the night?"

"Seesya brought her today with a bunch of other captives. Preparing her for burial took me longer than expected. I'm getting old, my son. Please let me through."

"I can't. The gates stay locked at night. What's the urgency?"

"She stinks." The priest sniffed noisily. "It's worse than the usual smell of death, which I'm very familiar with. I fear she's carrying a sickness, perhaps the red fever. Better get her out of Emanuel before we all get sick."

The sentry kicked the cart, startling the girl. "I don't smell anything."

"Here, take a sniff." Obadiah uncovered the dead woman's face. "Go on, smell her."

The sentry stepped back. "I believe you."

"Then open the gates."

He hesitated. "We're not supposed to."

"Do you think I want to go out there at night? But I want even less to get sick with the red fever. Do you?"

"I don't know—"

"Fine." The priest pushed the cart to the side of the road. "I'll leave her here and come back in the morning. Try to hold your breath, will you? Maybe she's not carrying the deadly fever. Who knows?"

"Don't leave her here!"

"What do you want me to do? I'm an old man. I can't push her back uphill to the temple." The priest walked away. "Just to be safe," he added, raising his voice, "I suggest you pray for your soul."

"Wait!"

The sentry went back to the gatehouse and woke up the other sentry. They argued in hushed voices. A moment later, loud creaking indicated that the gates were opening.

Through the red sheet, Deborah could tell that the priest had lighted a torch.

"Beware of the wolves," a sentry said, making the other one laugh.

"What wolves?" The priest stopped the cart. "Did you hear any wolves tonight?"

"Hundreds of them!" The sentries laughed again.

"You are joking, yes?" The priest's voice was fearful, and the girl couldn't tell whether Obadiah was truly afraid, or faking it. "Maybe one of you boys want to accompany me? God would reward you for it."

Their laughter died down. Neither of them volunteered to go.

The passage through the gates was paved with cobblestones. The cart quivered and wobbled as it passed. The gates closed behind them, and the priest steered the cart to the right and down a dirt path.

Horses snorted nearby. Deborah peeked from under the red sheet. There were lights in the open field, probably a caravan of foreign merchants, camping for the night.

The cart rattled and shook on the rocky path, making her feel sick. Finally, the cart stopped. She heard Obadiah grunt as he rolled the heavy wooden cover from the mouth of the communal burial cave.

"Hold tight," he said, tilting the cart. The woman's corpse slipped through the mouth of the cave. "Blessed be Yahweh," the priest recited, "God of Israel, king of the world, the true judge."

"Amen," Deborah said, remembering her parents' burial a year earlier. She took a deep breath as a lump formed in her throat.

"Quick, I must get back." He rested the torch against a rock, removed the crosspieces, and helped her off the cart. "Here are a few things I prepared for you." He emptied a sack on the cart and showed her each item. "A purse with a bit of money. Don't show it to anyone, or they'll rob you."

She nodded.

"Bread, butter, salt, and this waterskin. It should suffice for two days, but if you take longer, you must find food and water by yourself."

That was something she had never done. How could she find food and water by herself?

"A wool blanket to keep you warm, and a letter to my cousin in Shiloh." He unrolled the parchment and pointed at the first line. "That's his name: Shatz Ha'Cohen."

"I can't read." Her face flushed. "But I'll remember. Shatz Ha'Cohen."

"That's correct." Obadiah rolled up the parchment and put it back in the sack. "Shatz is one of the seven elder priests officiating at the Holy Tabernacle. He's very rich and powerful, not like me. Our late mothers were sisters, but his mother married a Cohen—a descendant of Aaron, brother of Moses—while mine married a regular Levite. When you arrive in Shiloh, ask for him. This letter tells him what happened here and asks him to help you."

She could tell by the tone of Obadiah's voice that his cousin's help was less than certain. "Will he assist me?"

"At best, he'll give you shelter for a few days and consider your case. The betrothal of an orphan girl is usually up to the town's judge, but since Seesya is the judge's son, and you don't wish to marry him, perhaps the elders in Shiloh could find a way to obtain your release. I don't know. Meanwhile, you'll probably have to work for food and shelter until the issue is resolved."

"I'm a good worker," she said, more to reassure herself than to convince him.

"Only speak with Shatz. Don't tell anyone that I helped you escape."

"I won't."

"Here is a plain robe and a headscarf. Keep yourself covered up as a modest woman would—especially your hair. It's the first thing people would remember about you."

He turned, and she pulled off the red robe and put on the brown one. She braided her hair quickly, tied it in a knot, and covered her head with the scarf. "Thank you."

"Don't thank me. I do this in order to remove your sister's curse from over my head."

"I thank you all the same."

He pointed at the red robe. "Better get rid of this."

The girl took her father's fire-starters out of the pocket, bunched up the red robe, and tossed it aside.

"Not here," Obadiah said. "If Seesya found it here, he'd connect your escape with me."

She picked up the robe and put it in the sack, together with everything else, including her basket with the tiger tail. "Which direction is Shiloh?"

"Follow the road north for about one and a half days. The road will split, left to Tapuah and Aphek, right to Shiloh. From there, it's about a half-day's walk. When you get close, you'll see people on their way to the Holy Tabernacle with offerings of produce and livestock."

"Where is north?"

He sighed. "You really are a child. It's not too late for you to change your mind and go back. No one would know."

"I've made my choice. Show me where to go."

Obadiah nodded and looked up at the sky, searching. "Over there, the group of stars around the one that shines brighter than the others. Do you see?"

She followed the direction of his finger. "Yes. I see it."

"That's the North Star. At night you should follow it. During the day, go by the sun. Do you know how?"

"Yes. The sun rises in the east, so it'll be on my right, and in the afternoon, on my left."

The priest picked up the torch, got behind the cart, and started uphill.

"Will you give me a blessing?" Deborah asked.

He paused and looked back as if checking whether she was joking. "Please?"

Obadiah held his hands above her head, the four fingers in each hand spread in two pairs as was customary for the priestly blessing in the temple, and recited, "May Yahweh bless you and protect you. May He show you kindness and grace. May He illuminate your path and grant you peace."

Deborah watched him push the cart up the path toward the gates of Emanuel. His back was bent, and he breathed heavily. Darkness surrounded her. She reached into the sack, pulled out the tiger tail, and looped it around her neck. It took her some time to go around the town's walls in the opposite direction from the gates, but she managed to find the road without falling or stepping on a snake. She tossed the red robe into a ditch by the roadside and looked up at the sky, searching for the group of stars as the priest had taught her.

The North Star shone brightly.

Deborah began to walk as fast as she could, eager to put as much distance as possible between her and Seesya in the hours left until sunrise. She planned to hide and sleep during the day and continue walking at nightfall until she arrived at Shiloh. There, she would pray at the Holy Tabernacle and begin her search for the Elixirist.

She walked without stopping for the rest of the night. Coyotes howled nearby, and she swung the tiger tail to spread the odor into the air to scare them away. She passed by a few isolated homesteads, and dogs ran toward her, barking and growling, but soon scampered back to the safety of their owners' land.

At sunrise, she stopped to drink. Obadiah of Levi had filled the waterskin to capacity. It was made of a sheep's bladder with a bottleneck fashioned of a hollowed-out piece of bone, plugged with a cork. The water was cool and sweet, and she silently thanked the priest.

Proceeding along the meandering road through the low hills, she looked for a hiding place that would be invisible to travelers, allowing her to get some sleep during the day. She noticed a cluster of boulders and dry shrubs, about halfway up the hillside, and hiked up to check it out. A patch of soft soil between large boulders seemed perfect for lying down in the shade while remaining hidden from the road. With the sack as a pillow, the wool blanket wrapped around her, and the tiger tail resting on top to ward off animals, Deborah fell asleep immediately.

12

She was riding a giant eagle above the clouds when it suddenly veered to the right and dove, piercing the clouds, shooting down from the sky as if aiming to snatch an oblivious prey on the ground. Deborah grasped the white feathers at the back of the neck and struggled to breathe against the oncoming rush of air. The ground below was pale and arid, with no vegetation, only jagged rocks that approached rapidly as the eagle dove faster and faster, showing no sign of slowing down. She screamed, but the voice wasn't her own. It was a man's voice, which terrified her even more. She pulled on the eagle's neck in an effort to force the bird out of the dive before hitting the ground. The eagle didn't change direction, continuing downward at a terrifying speed. What was it after? Her eyes scanned the ground below but could see no prey on the harsh, rocky land. The prey, she suddenly understood, wasn't a rodent or a snake, or some other little animal scurrying for its life. The eagle's intent was to kill her! She was the prey! Desperately, Deborah shouted, "Stop! Stop! Stop!" The voice still wasn't hers but a man's voice. A second before they hit the ground, she let go of the eagle's neck and covered her face. The terrible collision she had expected didn't happen. Instead, Deborah woke up.

She was curled up on the ground, shaken and covered in sweat. The eagle was gone, yet a man continued shouting. She took off the coarse blanket, put aside the tiger tail, and peeked between the boulders at the road below.

There were several horses and donkeys loaded with goods and packages, as well as a few goats and sheep tied together. The animals were restless, and the travelers they belonged to were trying to pacify them. She counted three women and about ten children of all ages. They had dark skin and black hair. An older man in a multicolored striped coat stood at the edge of the road, facing away from her, his hands cupping his mouth to amplify his voice. Deborah looked in the direction he was yelling and saw a boy running after a horse. Large packages were strapped to the horse, bulky and ungainly, which made its galloping awkward and comical.

One of the other horses tried to break away as well. A girl of ten or eleven in a blue dress held on to the reins, and the horse dragged her along. The man hurried over, pulled a piece of carrot from his pocket, and offered it to the horse with soothing words. As if by magic, the horse calmed down, ate the treat, and allowed the man to rub its neck.

While he soothed the horse, the man's eyes searched the surrounding hills. Deborah crouched back down behind the boulder as his gaze shifted in her direction. After a brief wait, she peeked again at the scene below.

The man, judging by his gestures, instructed the women and children to bring the animals closer together. As they gathered in, he pulled a short sword from a sheath at his hip and paced along the edge of the road between his caravan and the hillside where Deborah was hiding, as if he expected an attack from that direction. She glanced over her shoulder at the hillside rising further behind her, but saw nothing. The man continued to pace along the edge of the road, watching, his sword ready. What was he worried about? Despite his gray beard and the thick midriff under the loose coat, he radiated a cunning vigor that caused her to lower her head again.

Meanwhile, the horse and the boy were lost from sight. She kept down and listened to the travelers' anxious voices. The language they spoke sounded familiar. They were Moabites, she decided. The women pleaded repeatedly with a phrase that, she guessed, was the man's name: Abu Zariz.

After some time, the drumming of horse hooves could be heard. Expecting to see the boy returning with the fugitive horse, Deborah took a peek and froze in fear. It was Seesya, galloping up the road from the direction of Emanuel with six mounted soldiers. A cloud of dust trailed them, and as they reached the caravan, the cloud caught up and surrounded everyone.

When the dust cleared, Seesya and his soldiers circled the caravan.

Abu Zariz came forward, his left hand raised in greeting, his right holding the short sword. "Shalom," he called in Hebrew. "Shalom!"

Seesya nodded. "We're looking for a girl. She ran away last night."

"We haven't seen any girl." The Moabite man's Hebrew pronunciation was accented, but he spoke clearly. "One of our horses ran away. There might be a bear or a wolf nearby. The scent is making the animals restless."

Confirming his words, Seesya's horse shifted around, as did the soldiers' horses.

"The girl has white skin and orange hair," Seesya said.

"Orange hair?"

"Like pealed carrots."

"An Edomite girl?"

"She's a Hebrew. Her mother came from the south. Maybe she whored with the Edomites." Seesya laughed, and his soldiers joined in.

On the hillside, Deborah hunkered behind the boulder, shaken by Seesya's insult of her dead mother, who was as righteous as the highest priest at the Holy Tabernacle.

Abu Zariz chuckled. "We didn't see her or any other girl."

"Are you sure?"

"Absolutely. Could she have gone in a different direction?"

"I've sent men in every direction." Seesya twirled his spear. "We'll find her and punish whoever's helping her."

The man took a step back but kept smiling. "I traded with your father yesterday, and every year before that. You can ask him about Abu Zariz from Moab, who sells him tools and arrowheads. Also Egyptian linen of excellent quality."

"My father trades with many men. Some are honest, others are crooks."

Abu Zariz laughed as if it were a joke. "I hope the baskets he sold me will not fall apart at first use." He pointed at one of the horses, loaded with baskets.

"How about your women and children?" Seesya pointed his spear at them. "Have they seen the girl?"

Abu Zariz took another piece of carrot from his pocket and spoke to the women, pointing at his hair and the carrot. They shook their heads, giggling into their hands.

"You wouldn't mind if we looked around, would you?" Seesya signaled to the soldiers, who dismounted and approached the Moabites.

"Go ahead," Abu Zariz said. "But please be careful with the merchandise. My family needs to eat."

Seesya remained on his horse but came closer to the group, causing the women and children to move aside. He stuck his spear into a large package.

"Don't do that!" Abu Zariz ran over. "You'll ruin my linen!"

Turning his horse, Seesya raised his spear.

The women screamed, and Deborah was about to stand up and yell to stop Seesya from killing the Moabite merchant, but she paused when Seesya lowered his spear and resumed stabbing into packages.

Following Seesya's example, the soldiers stabbed into every bundle and box, even those too small to hide a girl. They cut ropes that held things together and kicked the fallen goods around. Within a few minutes, all the merchandise was scattered on the ground.

Trotting back and forth, Seesya surveyed the destruction. "Looks like you spoke the truth."

"I always do," Abu Zariz said darkly. "Please give my regards to your father and tell him about the unnecessary damage you inflicted on his old friend for no good reason."

Seesya turned his horse away, ready to leave, but something drew his attention. He pointed with his spear. "What's this?"

One of the soldiers came over and picked it up. It was a red robe that looked like the one Deborah had thrown away by the roadside the night before.

"It's nothing," Abu Zariz said. "A cheap robe. You can have it if you want."

"Let me see it." Seesya took it from the soldier and looked at it carefully. He turned it inside out and used a finger and a thumb to remove something. "This looks familiar," he said.

Even from a distance, Deborah could tell that he was holding a strand of hair, though she could only guess at its color.

Abu Zariz looked closely and stepped back.

"Why aren't you laughing now," Seesya asked, "about this orange hair?"

"I swear to you in the name of Ra and in the name of your Yahweh that we found this robe on the way and took it. There was no girl. Only a robe."

The soldiers drew their swords and circled the group. Seesya made his horse move back a few steps to give him a commanding view over the whole situation. He grinned, still holding the strand of hair between a finger and a thumb.

"Your father will tell you," Abu Zariz said. "I always speak the truth. We will go with you back to—"

"She's here," Seesya said, turning his horse around in a full circle as he gazed at the area around them. "You're hiding her."

"I swear to you—"

"Tell me where she is." Seesya let go of the strand of hair, which drifted slowly to the ground. "Or your daughters will suffer, one after the other, and then your wives."

The women and children crowded behind Abu Zariz, who wiped sweat from his brow with his sleeve. "I beg you, son of Zifron. We did not see a girl, only the robe. She must have run into the hills, knowing that you'd be chasing her down this road."

"She's too foolish to plan ahead. Last time, she escaped to the place where everyone would know to look for her."

"Then you should go there!"

"I have. She's not there, but you already know that. I think you saw her run away last night and grabbed her. How much does a fertile virgin sell for in Moab these days?"

"We didn't see her! Please believe me!"

Seesya rubbed the scar on his face. "I don't believe you."

Two of the soldiers stepped forward, pushed the Moabite trader aside, and grabbed the girl with the blue dress.

"No!" Abu Zariz raised his sword and held it up at the soldiers. "Let her go!"

The other four soldiers aimed their spears at him.

"Don't kill him yet." Seesya moved his horse closer. "I need him to talk."

The soldiers circled the Moabite trader.

"If he doesn't drop his sword," Seesya said, "kill one of his wives."

In her hiding place, Deborah bit her knuckles, struggling not to scream. She had to reveal herself and stop Seesya before he hurt the Moabites! But giving herself up to Seesya would mean giving up her quest for the Elixirist and any hope of freedom.

"This is madness!" Abu Zariz dropped his sword. "Why are you doing this to us?"

Seesya sighed as if all this unpleasantness bored him. "You see, my deceitful friend, this is not just an ugly little witch we're after. The girl is my future wife, who comes with a highly valuable inheritance. It's not a question of if but of how soon I'll possess both her and her inheritance—which leaves us with another question." He grinned, again rubbing his scar. "How many of your lovely daughters and wives will I have to disfigure before you tell me where to find my betrothed witch?"

"Take me," Abu Zariz pleaded. "Let us go together before your father!"

Seesya beckoned the two soldiers holding the daughter, and they brought her forward.

"Please don't hurt my daughter." The Moabite trader stretched his arms wide. "She is only eleven!"

Seesya drew his sword, leaned down from the saddle, and rested the blade against her cheek. "What is your name, angel?"

"Orpah," she answered with a quiver.

"Stay still, Orpah," Seesya said. "Let's see if I can make your lovely face look like mine."

Deborah tried to stand, but her legs wouldn't obey her.

"Stop!" Abu Zariz fell to his knees. "Have you no fear of the gods?"

"The gods?" Seesya grinned. "Why should I fear the gods? Have they not given you into my hands?"

The Moabite trader was unable to respond.

"The gods," Seesya continued, "want you to tell me where you hid the girl with the orange hair."

Up on the hillside, Deborah held on to the boulder, pulling herself up, her legs wobbly, her body all but paralyzed with fear. Sallan had said, "Banish your fear and embrace your strength." How he would mock her when hearing that his inspiring words had caused her to surrender to Seesya less than a day after escaping Emanuel!

Embracing all her strength, she stood and stepped forward between the boulders.

The Moabite trader, who was the only one facing her way, shouted, "No!"

She opened her mouth to yell Seesya's name.

"No!" Abu Zariz waved his arms, turning away to divert attention from her. "It's no use! You will kill all of us!"

Realizing that he was talking to her, Deborah got back behind the boulders.

"I'm offended," Seesya said. "Why would I kill you if you give me what I want?"

"Because you are an evil man," the trader yelled. "A disgrace to your father's name!"

His face twisted in rage, Seesya told the two soldiers, "Hold her tight!"

They held the trader's daughter, whose dark face was lined with tears, and Seesya pursed his lips in concentration as he leaned over with the tip of the sword at the girl's cheek.

A long whistle sounded in the distance.

Everyone turned to look.

Coming slowly toward them was the boy, riding the loaded horse that had escaped earlier.

Seesya stood up on the stirrups and shaded his eyes from the sun. "Who is this?"

"My son," Abu Zariz said. "He's only fourteen."

"Is that so?" Seesya smiled. "Maybe he can tell us where the girl is."

"Perhaps," Abu Zariz said. "Perhaps."

This response surprised Seesya, and he looked at the Moabite trader, expecting an explanation, but none came.

The boy rode the tired horse without holding the reins. He steered it with his feet and knees while his hands remained behind his back. He came through the rough terrain, rising and dropping with the contours of the land, his path leading not directly at them, but slightly to the north. As he approached closer, Deborah's heartbeat sped up until her chest hurt. The Moabite boy, with his youthful masculinity and black hair, resembled Barac, son of Abinoam, except that his hair wasn't curly and he wore no cap.

When he reached the road, about fifty steps north of the standoff between Seesya's soldiers and his family, the boy stopped his horse, which shifted about, raising a swirl of dust.

One of the soldiers advanced up the road toward him.

The dust cleared away, revealing the boy, who was holding a bow. He threaded an arrow, aimed, and released it, all within the blink of an eye. The arrow made a *whish* sound and entered the soldier's right eye.

Before the dead soldier hit the ground, another arrow was at the ready, pointed at Seesya.

Everyone froze.

"That was not a fluke," Abu Zariz said. "My son can hit a coin from a hundred steps." With arms stretched sideways, he moved backward, leading his wives and children away from the soldiers.

"It's six of us," Seesya said. "He won't get us all. Tell him to stand down, and I'll be merciful."

"If you wish to live," Abu Zariz said, "drop your weapons and go in peace right now. I'll make sure that the weapons are returned to Judge Zifron."

The soldiers hesitated.

"Fine," Seesya said. "You win."

As the soldiers' weapons hit the ground, Seesya leaned over and swept Orpah up, pressing her against himself, using her as a shield between him and the boy.

"Kill them all," Seesya yelled. "Kill them all!"

The women and children scattered, running as fast as they could. The soldiers picked up their swords and split up. Two of them sprinted in the direction of the boy while the others chased the women on foot, swords held high.

Abu Zariz threw himself at one of the soldiers, the two men falling over together. Another soldier stepped over and raised his sword to stab the trader in the back, but a sharp *whish* sounded, and the soldier clasped the arrow that pierced his throat and dropped. Three more arrows flew in short succession, cutting down the pursuing soldiers before they managed to hurt any of the women and children. The last remaining soldier was on the ground, wrestling with Abu Zariz, whose older age and smaller size put him at a disadvantage. The soldier managed to get on top of the Moabite and pull a knife from a hip sheath, but before he could stab downward, the boy released his last arrow. It hit the soldier's forehead at the hairline, penetrating halfway into his brain.

By this time, Seesya had planted the trader's daughter on the saddle behind him, holding her against his back with one hand while he grasped the horse's reins with the other and sprinted south at full gallop. The soldiers' horses took off after him, making the ground shake.

Pushing the dead soldier off himself, Abu Zariz sat up, panting. His son galloped over, jumped off the horse, pulled an arrow out of one of the corpses, and got back on his horse to chase Seesya.

"Stop!" The trader got up with difficulty and blocked his son's way. "If you kill him, his father will kill us all."

Obeying his father, the boy watched helplessly as the trail of dust disappeared in the distance.

When it was gone, Abu Zariz turned to the boulders on the hillside and yelled, "You can come out now."

Deborah stuffed the blanket and the tiger tail in the sack, straightened the scarf over her hair, and clambered down to the road. The women and children were crying, and even Abu Zariz blinked rapidly as tears filled his eyes. The horses shifted fearfully as she came closer, and the donkeys brayed, their nostrils flaring.

The boy jumped off the horse and ran over. He grabbed her sack, reached inside, and pulled out the tiger tail, showing it to his father.

Abu Zariz took the tail, put it back in the sack, tied the strings, and returned it to her.

"My name is Deborah," she said, "daughter of Harutz of Ephraim."

"I am Abu Zariz." The man placed his hand on the boy's shoulder. "And this is Zariz, my son."

The boy looked at her intently but said nothing. Up close, she could see that he was skinnier than Barac, with darker eyes and a sparser goatee.

"I'm sorry for causing this disaster." She shouldered the sack. "I didn't expect the tiger tail to work so well."

"It's not your fault," Abu Zariz said. "The son of Zifron would have caught up with us even if we hadn't stopped. It was my error to pick up the red robe. I should have known not to touch what's intended for the Hebrews' impure and condemned."

"Which one are you?" the boy asked her.

Her face flushed.

"You'll stay with us for now," Abu Zariz said. "It's safer that way—for you and for us. We must gather our things and leave quickly."

"What about your daughter?"

Abu Zariz glanced in the direction of Emanuel. "They won't harm her."

Deborah wasn't sure how he knew that, but the time for talking was over. The women collected the goods from the ground and bundled everything up. Abu Zariz and his son dragged the dead soldiers off the road, stripped them of their weapons and body armor, and tied it all together. Zariz retrieved the rest of his arrows, cleaned off the blood, and packed the horses and donkeys, making sure the loads were well balanced. The Moabites were efficient and quick, as expected of a large family that lived on the road, set up camp every night, and packed up every morning.

Everyone mounted the horses and donkeys. Zariz waved Deborah over to get behind him on his horse, which she did, and the caravan moved off at a fast pace.

After a short time on the road, Abu Zariz turned right into the hills. He followed a dry stream for a while but turned away when they saw a small settlement up ahead, and headed into the sun for a while. After climbing over another hill, he found a goat path that took them over a ridge with the sun on the left. He changed direction several times between hills and giant boulders. By midafternoon, they were heading away from the sun.

Deborah understood that the maneuvers were intended to make it difficult for Seesya to follow them with a new company of soldiers, but the frequent changes in direction and topography confused and disoriented her, and she barely managed to stay awake.

As the sun was setting, Abu Zariz pointed to a patch of flat ground on a hillside. The surrounding area was steep and rocky, far from any settlement or road. They would be safe here.

Zariz slipped off his horse and helped Deborah get down. The women cleared rocks and unloaded food, blankets and a tent for shelter. Deborah put down her sack and walked back and forth along the hillside, collecting dry twigs, shrubs, and weeds for a fire. She selected a spot downwind from the camp and used her father's fire-starters to ignite a few dry leaves. Feeding the flame gently with more leaves, then weeds, and twigs, she built a nice fire.

Zariz untied a bundle of charcoal logs and added one to the fire, which embraced it with flames. They smiled at each other, and Zariz returned to help set up camp. The women prepared a small meal. Before anyone ate, Abu Zariz placed a bowl of food in front of clay figurines of Baal and Ashtoreth and bowed to them.

After the meal, Deborah found a small patch of sand beside a large boulder and lay down. The air was turning chilly. She pulled the blanket from her sack and wrapped it around her shoulders.

13

Under her feet was a bed of palm fronds, green and glossy with moisture from last night's dew. The wind blew at her back, nudging her forward, and her heart beat loudly. She was standing on top of the old palm tree. Far below, the thatched roof over her family's house seemed full and solid, the adjacent corral was alive with goats and sheep, and the garden bloomed with vegetables and flowers. The tree swayed, and she stretched her arms out for better balance. The wind pushed her another step forward, right to the serrated edge of the canopy of fronds, which bowed under her weight. She fell forward, her chest constricting with the same choking sensation she had experienced when falling from the washroom window outside the walls of Judge Zifron's great house. Her hands tried to grasp at something, anything, but she kept falling through the empty air, the earth below rising, growing, rushing at her. Then the wind changed direction and came from below, decelerating her fall. She moved her hands rapidly up and down as if trying to fly—and it worked! She was flying, her arms magically transformed into the wide wings of a giant eagle, flapping effortlessly in an exhilarating ascent. The top-down view of Palm Homestead widened again as she gained height, circling in the air above the summit of Deborah's Palm, and higher yet. Her father's fields were ripe with wheat and barley, the trees on the terraced slopes were heavy with fruit, and the old olive trees, in random clusters, rustled with silvery leaves and fat olives. Her lungs filled with cool, fresh air, and her heart swelled with a wonderful sensation of weightlessness and freedom. But as her view expanded beyond Palm Homestead, a column of smoke appeared in the distance. A town was burning, and another, farther yet, and more coming into view as she soared higher. Plumes of smoke rose in every direction, all across the Samariah Hills. Hebrew towns, villages, and homesteads were burning down to ashes. Her nostrils filled with the bitterness of smoke. The wings flapped harder and harder as thick, black smoke engulfed her in suffocating darkness. Her heart beat louder and louder until the noise became unbearable and she couldn't breathe anymore.

Deborah opened her eyes, sat up, and gulped air in quick, short breaths. The sound of flapping wings made her look up. An eagle flew above her, its wings wide against the ashen sky of dawn. She followed it with her eyes, then looked around for plumes of smoke and sights of destruction but saw only the fading trail of smoke from the fire she had started the night before, now reduced to embers.

Yet the dream had felt real—not only the falling and flying, but especially the joy of seeing Palm Homestead flourishing again, and the sorrow of the burning Hebrew towns.

Everyone in the camp was still asleep, except for Abu Zariz, who was feeding the animals from a sack of grains. When he finished, he gave them water in a flat ceramic bowl and spoke to them in a low voice. She couldn't hear the words, but the soothing tone made her feel better.

The frightening dream receded from reality, although it continued to puzzle her. Why was she flying above Palm Homestead? Why had it been spared the fury of the enemies who had burned down all the other Hebrew settlements? And why did she have wings? Was she an angel, rising to be with Yahweh, or an eagle, observing the plight of land-bound people below? She smiled at the idea of life as an eagle, soaring to limitless heights, flying through the clear sky, boundless and free from the harsh land of cruel men. That's what she would like to become—an eagle!

Abu Zariz saddled his horse and loaded the bundle containing the dead soldiers' weapons. He sheathed his short sword, put on a plain hooded robe over his multicolored coat, and woke his son up. They spoke quietly for a few minutes, embraced, and kissed on both cheeks.

Deborah joined Zariz, and they watched his father walk the horse to the bottom of the hill, where he mounted it and rode away. Zariz took a figurine out of his pocket and held it to his chest until the horse and rider went out of sight. He kissed the figurine and murmured a short prayer.

Sensing her curiosity, he showed it to her. Carved in wood, the figurine looked like a child with a ball on his head, sitting on a miniature horse with a single horn. "It is Khonsu," Zariz said, "the moon god, the protector of travelers. As Khonsu travels safely across the sky every night, so will my father travel safely on his journey."

"Is he going to Emanuel?"

Zariz nodded. "To get my sister back."

"Isn't he afraid of Seesya?"

"One can always find reasons to be afraid in the world." Zariz pointed at the patch of sand where she had slept. "Venomous snakes, for example."

Beside the depression left by her body, there were wriggly lines as if someone had drawn in the sand with a finger.

"An adder," he said. "They slither sideways sometimes. It's funny."

"Funny?" She felt the blood drain from her head, making her dizzy. "It could have bitten me!"

"A snake reserves its venom for things it can eat." He smiled. "A sleeping person is too big to eat."

"What if I rolled over it by mistake?"

Zariz made a striking motion with his hand.

The speed of his gesture reminded Deborah of his deadly archery skill. "Could you kill the snake with an arrow?"

"I could hit a snake in the open, yes, but this one is hiding."

"We have to tell the women!" She stepped backward. "We have to move the camp to another place!"

"The snake is gone. Why should we fear it?" He used the tip of one sandal to turn over a rock. His leg was very dark, but his foot was light with dust from the road. He kicked over a few more rocks. Underneath one of them was a scorpion, which scurried away and hid under another rock. "If you run away from danger," he said, "a worse danger will be waiting for you over there."

His words made no sense to her. How could one avoid injury, or even death, without feeling fear and taking flight? But then she remembered how he had returned with the lost horse yesterday, taking his time to observe the standoff, and rather than run away at the sight of Seesya and his men with their sharp spears and overwhelming advantage, he had shot the six soldiers in quick succession without missing a single target.

"You're brave," she said. "I'm just a girl."

He looked at her, surprised. "I'm with my family. You're alone.

That's harder."

"You don't feel fear, but I'm afraid all the time."

Zariz glanced at the women, making sure no one could hear. "I'm also afraid a lot, but I'm the oldest son. It's my duty to help my father defend the family."

"My fear is different," Deborah said. "It chokes and paralyzes me."

"I used to feel like that, but my father told me something that helped me become stronger." Zariz shut his eyes and recited from memory. "Fear is good if it makes you careful and watchful, but it's bad if it turns you into a coward who runs from hard duties and fails to pursue good opportunities."

His words confused her. She had just run away from Emanuel and all her duties there. Did it make her a coward?

"I asked my father," Zariz continued, "how I could tell the difference between situations in which duty requires staying and situations in which opportunity requires pursuing."

"What did he say?"

"He told me a simple rule: 'Listen to your fear, but don't let it control you.'"

She realized that it would take her some time to understand the way the men of Moab contended with the world. "Does your father have a plan for saving your sister?"

"My father is a good trader. He will make a deal."

"Today is our Sabbath. No trades are allowed on the Sabbath."

"But talking is allowed, yes?"

"It is," Deborah said.

"That's good. For a successful trade, there's always a lot of talking beforehand."

"Will he trade me for her?"

"You are not his property. He'll trade with what he owns, whatever the buyer desires. That is the way of the trader."

"Seesya won't give her back."

"He is the son. He must obey his father. Judge Zifron has traded with my father for many years."

"What about the dead soldiers?"

He shrugged. "Soldiers have no value."

"Six soldiers have no value?"

"Soldiers are not like slaves," Zariz said. "You can't buy or sell soldiers, and if you can't trade them, then they have no value. Any rich person can hire soldiers for pay and food, and when they die, he hires new ones. Only their weapons are valuable."

"What about their horses?"

"The horses are trained to stay together and follow the leader when the battle is lost. That's why they ran after Seesya yesterday. And when my father brings back the soldiers' belongings, Judge Zifron will be satisfied that he lost nothing."

"But you killed his soldiers. Won't he seek revenge?"

"They're not his family. My sister is family. Even a rich man who rules a town does not want to start a cycle of revenge." Zariz put away the figurine of Khonsu. "He will trade for Orpah."

"But your father didn't take any goods with him to trade for her."

"Whatever price they agree on, he will promise to bring the goods next year. There is a long tradition. My grandfather traded with Judge Zifron's father, and now my father trades with him. Your judge will make the trade on trust, and my father will bring Orpah back. We'll wait here until he returns."

Deborah looked at the surrounding hills, which were barren and without unique shapes or landmarks. "How will he find us?"

Zariz laughed. He had a rolling laughter that creased his eyes to narrow slits.

"What's so funny? All these hills and crevices look the same. We crisscrossed a hundred identical places yesterday, until my head was spinning."

He covered his mouth, unable to stop.

"You're laughing at me!"

"Because you argue all the time." He laughed even harder, which made it contagious. Despite herself, Deborah giggled, then let go and laughed outright.

14

When the sun had cleared the hills and everyone was busy with morning chores, Zariz and Deborah went for a ride on his horse. With the scarf tight over her hair, she sat in front of him, the wind cooling her face. She held the reins while he guided her hands, directing the horse to go slower or faster, left or right. She glanced down at their joined hands on the reins. His dark hands seemed much stronger and healthier than her pale hands, covered in brown freckles and red sunburns.

"Look straight ahead," Zariz said. "Always keep your eyes over the horse's head at the direction you want to go."

She did as he said, relieved that he couldn't see her flushed face.

"If you look down," he explained, "the horse will sense it and think you're unsure where to go."

"What if it's the truth—that I am unsure where to go?"

"Keep your doubts from showing. You must pretend to be confident, or the horse will not respect you."

They didn't descend the hill the way his father had gone, but stayed at the same elevation until they reached a dry stream. Zariz helped her make the horse turn by pulling the reins on one side while nudging the animal with her knees. The horse obeyed, stepping deliberately between the rocks. They made a few more turns, crossing from one dry stream to another, always ascending, until eventually they reached all the way to the crest of a hill.

They got off the horse and tied it to a clump of dry shrubs, which the horse began to nibble. Stepping up to the highest point, Zariz turned around in a full circle.

"Now," he said, "you can see how my father finds his way around. The land is arranged in a certain order, starting from this watershed line, where we are now." He pointed at the chain of hilltops extending north and south. "From the watershed line, everything goes down in either direction. That's east." He pointed in the direction of the rising sun. "From the watershed line, the hills get smaller, and all the crevices and streams that descend to the east drain to the long valley of the Jordan River."

"I've heard about the Jordan River. My father saw it once."

"I've crossed it several times," Zariz said proudly. "It runs from the Sea of Galilee in the north to Jericho and the Sea of Salt in the south." He pointed at the hazy valley far to the south.

"Have you seen the Sea of Salt?"

"Of course. Our homeland, Moab, borders the eastern shore of the Sea of Salt. I've traveled south, too, across the land of Edom and down to the Sea of Reeds, which is more blue than the sky."

"That's near Egypt!" Deborah was excited to share her knowledge. "Our Hebrew ancestors crossed the Sea of Reeds when they escaped from Pharaoh's bondage."

He smiled. "We tell that story, too. The Hebrews came from Egypt through Edom at Etzion Gaver, near Eilat. They passed near our land, but without fighting us, because Moab was descended from Lot, the nephew of your ancestor Abraham."

Deborah nodded, happy that they shared the same ancestry.

"But after that," Zariz said, "something bad happened between our nations. Nobody talks about it in Moab, but there's a saying, 'Beware of the Hebrews, for their tongue is oily and their sword is invisible.'"

The quote was insulting, and Deborah turned away to prevent him from seeing the hurt on her face.

"I didn't mean to offend you," he said. "My father talks to me all the time when we travel. He learned everything from his father, too."

"My father was also wise," she said. "And kind, too." Her hand reached for the fire-starters in her pocket. "He's dead now."

"Did he tell you about Moab?"

"Only one story."

"Tell me."

"A long time ago, in the time of my father's great-great-grandfather, the Hebrews sinned against God. He punished us by letting the king of Moab oppress us. Our suffering was great, and we repented and prayed. God forgave our sins and sent a brave man named Ehud, son of Gerah, who fought the Moabites and liberated the Hebrews."

Zariz nodded. "Maybe your story and our old saying relate in some way."

They stood in silence for a few minutes, looking at the view. Below them, the morning mist gradually faded, revealing ever more details of the land. A column of smoke rose from a valley far below, and patches of green could be seen between the slopes.

A bird came up from the valley, flying in circles, gaining elevation until it flew over their heads and began to descend to the west.

"She's going to the Great Sea," Zariz said. "It's a long journey, about two days of walking down the Samariah Hills, then another day or two across the Coastal Plain all the way to the shoreline."

"I get it," Deborah said. "The whole land is like a large field divided into sections for wheat, barley, and flax."

"Something like that." He smiled.

She crouched and used a dry branch to draw in the dirt. "Up is north, down is south, left is west, and right is east."

Zariz nodded.

"There are three parallel lines from north to south." She drew them. "On the left is the shoreline of the Great Sea. In the middle is the watershed line. And on the right, the Jordan River."

"That's correct," he said.

Deborah drew waves in the area to the left of the shoreline. "That's the Great Sea." She drew several horizontal lines perpendicular to the shoreline. "That's the Coastal Plain." She drew zigzag lines off the watershed in both directions. "That's the Samariah Hills to the west and east of the watershed line."

"And that's your town, Emanuel." He made a depression with his finger to the left of the watershed line. "And we are here." He made a depression on top of the watershed line, slightly northeast of Emanuel. "And here is your holy city, Shiloh." He marked a spot north of where they stood.

She looked around at the land, trying to compare the reality with the drawing, and used the stick to deepen the line on the right. "The Jordan River. Is it beautiful?"

"Yes, it is." Zariz took the stick from her hand and drew a round shape at the top of the line representing the Jordan River. "That's the Sea of Galilee." At the bottom of the Jordan River, he drew an oval shape with a depression in the middle. "That's the Sea of Salt." He marked an area east of it with many lines. "That's the land of Moab." Further down, he filled another area with dotted lines. "And that's the land of Edom, all the way south to the Sea of Reeds."

Deborah stared at the whole map for a long time, then closed her eyes and imagined it in her mind, from left, where the sun set every evening in the Great Sea, to the shoreline and the Coastal Plain, to the Samariah Hills that sloped down from the watershed line in both directions, and the long, straight depression that formed the path of the Jordan River. She imagined the river as a giant waterway of gushing blue, with swaths of fertile land on both sides, green with lush crops ready for harvest.

When she opened her eyes, she found Zariz watching her.

He turned away, embarrassed. "The women in Edom," he said, "many of them have hair like yours, and white skin, too, like ivory."

"Not so white anymore," she said, rubbing the sunburned top of her hand. "There is a slave in Emanuel who came from Edom many years ago. He runs Judge Zifron's basket factory."

"You speak of Sallan," Zariz said. "My father is wary of him."

"Why?"

Zariz kicked the dry earth. "When a slave is allowed to behave like a master, the world is out of balance. We believe that the gods disapprove of this and will show their anger."

"In what way?"

He struggled to recall the exact words of his father. "When the world is out of balance, a painful adjustment is bound to happen."

Deborah wondered if that was the reason Sallan wanted to leave Emanuel and return to his home. "What kind of place is Edom?" she asked.

"My father buys copper in Edom. The land is mostly desert and mountains, but I've traveled with him to their great city, Bozra, where all the roofs shine like gold. I haven't traveled beyond the Sea of Reeds, though." He pointed at the bottom of the map in the sand. "Maybe one day."

"Now I understand," she said, "how your father will find us. He knows this map, and after many years of travel, his memories have filled the map with countless details, so he can find his way not only between the Great Sea, the watershed line, and the Jordan River, but also through all the small places in between."

"And the people, too," Zariz said. "The map in my father's head also tells him the names of each town's ruler and the strongman in each village, what tribe they came from and what tribe they hate, what gods they worship and what goods they like to buy or sell. He told me that the same goods might fetch gold in one town and simple cloth in another. It's this knowledge that turns a poor trader into a rich trader."

The sun was directly above them now, and the heat was rising. They drank from a waterskin and got back on the horse, Deborah in front.

"Take us back," Zariz said. "If you can."

Deborah tightened the scarf, took the reins, and pressed her ankles inward to urge the horse forward. Her head held high, her gaze fixed above the horse's head, she steered it down the crevice through which they had come up. She pulled the reins to slow down, and pressed inward with her knees to direct the horse between boulders. When she made the first turn to cross over to another dry stream, she heard Zariz chuckle approvingly and felt his breath on the back of her neck.

15

They waited with the evening meal until sunset, but when his father did not return, Zariz placed a small bowl of food in front of Baal and Ashtoreth, murmured a prayer, and told the women they may eat.

Sitting on the ground around the small fire, the women fed the children and put them to sleep. Zariz and Deborah sat nearby on opposite ends of a large plate. Zariz scooped oats with raisins and almonds onto a flat piece of bread, sprinkled a few drops of olive oil, lemon, salt, and spices, and rolled it tightly. He handed it to Deborah, and she took a bite. It was delicious.

Zariz drank some water but ate nothing.

She stopped eating. "Aren't you hungry?"

"I'm very hungry," he said. "But my father is not back yet."

"Does he expect you to starve until he returns?"

"He taught me that a hole in the stomach keeps a man alert at night. I'll eat in the morning."

"You plan to stay awake all night?"

"I'll sleep lightly. The horses are the first to notice when danger is coming. They stomp around and snort. I'll hear them better if I'm sleeping lightly."

As everyone settled down for the night, Zariz fed the fire and checked on the animals. He tested the string on his bow and counted the arrows in his quiver. With a blanket around his shoulders, he selected a spot above the campsite, which gave him open view in all directions, and sat with his back to a boulder.

Deborah could not fall asleep. She took her sack and blanket and went to sit with Zariz. He said nothing, but she sensed that he was pleased. They sat in silence for a long time, looking at the starry sky.

"That's the North Star." She pointed. "It guided me when I escaped from Emanuel."

A coyote howled in the distance.

"Don't worry," Zariz said. "The fire will keep it away."

Moments passed, and the howl sounded again, but much closer. Zariz stood and put an arrow in his bow, aiming it in the direction of the sound.

Another howl, joined by a different one, and a third.

"It's a pack," she said, getting up.

"Not good," Zariz said. "They're more brazen together."

More howls sounded, closer yet.

Deborah found a fist-size rock, aimed toward the sound, and pitched it.

An animal whimpered, followed by the rustling of paws running away.

"Nice." Zariz sat down and put away the bow and arrow. "Lucky strike."

"It wasn't luck."

He laughed briefly and stopped when he realized she wasn't joking. "Really? In the dark?"

"Whenever my father went away to sell his crops, my mother, sister, and I stayed alone at Palm Homestead. We didn't have weapons, but we felt safe inside the house with the fire going. Our goats and sheep, however, were unprotected, and whenever coyotes approached, the goats would bump against the corral and the sheep would cry. The three of us used to go out and shout and shake jars with pebbles inside. If that didn't scare away the coyotes, we threw rocks by aiming at the sound."

"Like a blind person?" He stared at her, and his brown eyes gleamed in the glow from the fire. "It sounds silly."

"I'm telling the truth."

His white teeth flickered. "I know, but I've never heard of anyone trying to hit something without looking at it."

"Trying was easy, but actually hitting something was hard." Deborah paused, remembering. "The first time, my sister and I hit none of the coyotes, and had my mother not started pitching rocks, they would have taken one of our goats. The next morning, Mother blindfolded us and made sounds for us to aim and pitch at. We did it for hours." Deborah laughed at the memory. "It was fun."

"Will you teach me tomorrow?"

It was hard to see his expression in the dark, but from his tone she could tell that he wasn't mocking her.

"If you want," she said. "Will you teach me how to shoot an arrow?"

The bow was resting on the ground next to him. He picked it up and plucked at the string, producing a series of pings. Finally, he said, "Among my people, it's forbidden to teach girls the use of weapons."

"I'm not one of your people. I'm a Hebrew."

Zariz laughed. "Don't the Hebrews have the same rule?"

"I won't tell," Deborah said, smiling.

16

The next morning, Deborah woke up to the noise of children and their mothers starting the day. Zariz was asleep, his back to the boulder and his bow across his knees. She stood up slowly, not wanting to wake him, and joined the group.

One of the women, the youngest of Abu Zariz's three wives, appeared to be not much older than Deborah. She was nursing a baby girl whose skin was smooth and shiny, like a wooden doll painted dark brown and polished with linen pads to a glossy perfection. The baby suckled eagerly and, without pausing, passed gas and defecated a whole lot of green-yellow paste. Looking down at her soiled dress, the young mother sighed with tired resignation.

Deborah found a rag and cleaned both mother and baby. When the nursing was done, Deborah extended her arms, and the young woman gratefully handed her the baby. Deborah put the little girl over her shoulder, the way Vardit had done with the babies at Judge Zifron's house, and walked back and forth, humming a tune her own mother used to sing.

Zariz woke up when the sun cleared the ridges. Deborah brought him water and some bread. As he ate, his eyes kept turning to the path at the bottom of the hill, where they had last seen his father.

She asked, "Remember our trade?"

He stopped chewing. "What trade?"

"I'll teach you how to hit a target with a stone while blindfolded, and you'll teach me how to shoot arrows."

"There was no trade," he said with a slight grin.

"What was it, then?"

"It was bargaining. Until the parties agree on the terms of the exchange, there's no binding trade. And I didn't agree."

"You could agree now."

"I could, but I don't think I should."

"Why? Don't you want to learn how to hit a coyote at night? Or are you too afraid of failing at something a girl already knows how to do?"

"You're arguing again. When you get married, your poor husband will have to whip you every day."

"And I'll throw rocks at him every night."

"I believe it!"

Deborah grabbed his arm. "Come, I'll teach you to throw rocks like a blind man."

He followed her. "What about the trade?"

"No trade. It's a gift."

They walked until they were out of sight but within earshot of the campsite. The hillside was almost barren, with only scattered shrubs clinging to the dry soil.

"Right here is good." Deborah collected a few pebbles and put them in his hand. "Turn your back, shut your eyes, and count to thirty while I find a place to hide. When you hear me howl, keep your eyes closed, aim carefully, and throw a pebble—only one at a time."

He shut his eyes and turned, and she ran. There were several boulders of different sizes, and she chose one at least fifty steps away from him. She crouched, peeked over the top of the boulder, and did her best to imitate a coyote howling.

Zariz turned, his eyes shut. "Howl again," he yelled.

She howled.

He turned his head in her direction and threw a pebble. It hit the boulder and bounced over her head.

She stood up. "You peeked. Cheater!"

He laughed. "You chose the biggest boulder. I couldn't miss it even if I tried."

"We'll see." She ran over to him. "Turn around and stand still."

He did.

She removed her scarf, rolled it up, placed it over his eyes, and tied a knot behind his head. "Don't turn yet," she said.

Heading back toward the boulder, she changed direction and went downhill, treading carefully to minimize the noise of her sandals on the rocky ground. Her long hair fell loose, its thick locks heavy on her shoulders, down her back, and to the sides of her face, narrowing her vision like horse blinders. She collected it, separated its mass into three, and quickly braided it, tying the ends as best as she could.

This time, she hid behind a shrub, crouching low, and looked back. Zariz had turned around, but he was facing in the direction of the first boulder, where she had hidden before. The blindfold seemed undisturbed, and he was ready with a pebble in his right hand.

She howled.

He turned his head toward her, hesitating.

She howled again.

Zariz raised his arm and pitched the pebble. It hit the ground a few steps away from her.

Careful not to make a sound, Deborah made her way to another shrub, about ten steps away. She crouched and howled.

He turned his head this way and that. "Keep howling!"

She did.

The first pebble missed her by a wide margin. But he kept throwing, one pebble after another, while she went on howling like a mad coyote. Finally, a pebble hit her shoulder.

"Ouch!"

He pulled off the blindfold and waved it victoriously.

She picked up the pebble and threw it back at him, hitting the ground at his feet, making him jump.

"You howl well," he said. "Do you have any coyote blood in you?"

"Only lions and tigers."

He cupped his mouth with his hands and roared.

"Let's practice more," she said. "With the blindfold."

"You want me to plug my ears, too?"

"How about your mouth?" As Deborah approached him, her hair fell loose again, and she shook her head to release the remaining tangles.

The last few pebbles fell from Zariz's hand. He tried to say something, coughed dryly, and looked away, but his eyes returned to her.

"Why are you staring at me?" She took the scarf from him and unfurled it.

"Sorry." His gaze dropped to the ground. "You look different with your hair down."

"Maybe we should stop." Her face burning, she tied up her hair and covered it with the scarf.

"Wait here." He hurried toward the campsite. "I'll be right back."

Deborah sat on a rock and cradled her face in her hands. Was he repulsed by the sight of her orange hair? It had been stupid of her to take off the scarf. What had she been thinking? Would a leper remove the rags from her rotting flesh?

The sound of a baby crying came from the direction of the campsite. Was Zariz telling his father's wives about her hair, or confiding in his young sisters, who were all beautiful with their dark skin and black hair?

The memory of Seesya riding off with Orpah made Deborah shudder. There was no way Seesya would give the Moabite girl back—unless her father gave him what he really wanted. Perhaps Zariz's attention had meant more than she realized. She recalled Abu Zariz speaking quietly to his son before leaving for Emanuel. What had he told Zariz? "Watch the Hebrew girl and make sure she suspects nothing and goes nowhere before I make a trade with Judge Zifron"? The thought filled her with fear, but she remembered what Zariz had told her: "Listen to your fear, but don't let it control you." The urge to flee was strong, but she should wait and slip away when no one was looking. The map was still fresh in her mind. She would go uphill to the watershed and follow it north until she found the road heading east to Shiloh. Obadiah of Levi had said that the road to Shiloh would be busy with travelers on their way to the Holy Tabernacle, which meant she wouldn't stand out.

Relieved that she had a plan to save herself from the Moabite traders' betrayal, Deborah turned to go back to the campsite and wait for the opportunity to grab her sack and escape.

To her surprise, Zariz came toward her, holding the bow in one hand and the quiver of arrows in the other. "Ready for a lesson?"

Deborah hesitated. Was this yet another ruse to pacify her until Abu Zariz returned with Seesya to take her back to Emanuel? But if Zariz was supposed to prevent her from leaving, why had he taught her to ride a horse? And why had he showed her the lay of the land and where they were in relation to the watershed line and Shiloh?

"It'll be our secret," Zariz said. "Don't tell anyone. Promise?"

"I promise."

He looked around and selected a small bush about twenty paces away. Fitting an arrow in the bow, he took aim. "This is how you get ready. One foot forward, left hand holding the bow midway with your thumb hooked and elbow locked. The right hand pulls back the base of the arrow over the string, like this."

Deborah looked closely at his hands and nodded.

"Then, without moving your hands or the rest of your body, you let go of the base of the arrow." He did it, and the arrow shot out of the bow and hit the bush, sinking into the dirt.

She took the bow, and he handed her another arrow. It was made of wood, smooth and straight, with a pointy bronze head shaped as a triangle with its base pressed into a notch at the head of the stick.

"Pull, aim, and hold," he said.

Her first try was a failure as both the bow and the arrow fell from her hands.

"No worry," Zariz said. "That happened to me many times before I learned how to hold the bow. Here, let me show you."

He stood behind her and put his arms around her shoulders, placing his hands on top of hers to hold the weapon, as he had done with the horse's reins. But this was a more intricate task, and he had to bend her fingers in the right places to show her how to hold the bow, the string, and the arrow. The closeness made her feel hot and dazed.

"Now," he said, "let's pull the string back with the arrow until it's tight."

They did it together, his hands taking most of the pressure of the tightening string.

"That's good," he said. "Ready?"

Deborah had a hard time breathing, much less talking. She nodded.

"I'll count," he said. "One. Two. Three."

They released the arrow on three, and it flew halfway to the bush, landing flat on the ground.

"Nice," he said. "Let's do it again."

She felt his body press against her back, his arms lined up with hers as they pulled back the arrow on the string, balancing it together. His face was just behind her ear. He smelled of dust and sweat and something else, perhaps mint. She turned her head slightly and breathed in through her nose, taking in his scent.

"Look straight," he said. "Focus on the target. Your arrow will go where your eyes are looking."

"Sorry," she said and gazed straight. "Ready on three."

"One. Two. Three."

They let go, and the arrow shot out much faster than before, losing altitude only when it was about to reach the bush.

"Very good," Zariz said. "Now you do it."

He guided her hands as she placed the arrow across the bow. His fingers touched hers lightly, leading her as she began to tighten the string.

"Keep your aim," he said.

He slowly removed his hands, and she was holding the bow by herself, aiming the arrow at the bush.

"Don't move any part of your body." His hands descended and rested on her hips. "Steady now. One. Two. Three."

Deborah let go, and the arrow shot out, giving off a sharp *whish* as it cut through the air, the way his arrows had flown, killing Seesya's soldiers. The arrow flew straight and true, went through the bush, and stuck into the dirt beyond it, its rear pointing at her.

"You did it!" He turned her around, their faces very close. "Perfect shot!"

She laughed, looking up at his smiling face. "Not bad, is it?"

"Not bad? It was great!"

"Zariz!" A girl's voice sounded behind them. "Zariz!"

The sound jolted them apart.

Running up the hillside was his sister Orpah, wearing the same blue dress and holding her arms up for Zariz, who hugged her.

At the bottom of the hill, Abu Zariz sat on his horse, watching. Zariz ran to his father and kissed his hand.

Still holding the bow, Deborah went over to the bush, collected the spent arrows, and headed down the hill. Zariz took the bow and the quiver of arrows from her outstretched hand.

Abu Zariz's face and his clothes were coated with a film of dust, and he seemed very tired. His gaze went from Deborah to his son. He wasn't smiling.

"Welcome back," she said.

He nodded, turned his horse, and nudged it toward the campsite. Zariz held his sister's hand as they followed their father. Deborah walked behind them, the joy of her time with Zariz replaced by worries over his father's silent disapproval. She found consolation, however, in the fact that he had returned without Seesya.

17

That night, after the evening meal, while everyone prepared for sleep, Abu Zariz sat by the small fire and beckoned Deborah to sit next to him. He stuffed dry mint leaves into a pipe and smoked in silence. She waited for him to speak first.

"The tiger tail," he said. "Did you carry it to keep wild animals away?"

Deborah nodded.

"Was that your idea?"

"Yes."

"It's a good idea, but a tiger tail isn't cheap. Where did you buy it?"

"It belonged to a friend."

He drew from the pipe and blew smoke. "Did you steal it?"

Deborah looked down, ashamed.

"Better to steal than to die," he said.

"I'll return it when I go back."

Abu Zariz smoked some more. "The owner's precious tiger skin will remain mutilated even if you return the tail."

"I had no choice."

Abu Zariz fiddled with the pipe. "The slave from Edom is not a man you want to cross."

"Did you tell him that I'm with your family?"

"He didn't need telling."

"But how did he know?"

Abu Zariz shrugged. "He heard about the confrontation between the judge's son and us, made the connection with his missing tiger tail, and drew the correct conclusion. He's very clever, and his cleverness is dedicated completely to his self-interest, which makes me wonder why he didn't share his insight with his master."

"Judge Zifron didn't figure it out, did he?"

"He must have suspected, but he acted as if he believed me that we hadn't seen you, and that our horses had been spooked for some unknown reason."

"Why would the judge pretend to believe you?"

"It's bad for business to explicitly accuse another of dishonesty," Abu Zariz said with a wry chuckle. "But I heard that Seesya suspects the priest of helping you escape."

"Who told you that?"

"Sallan, who else? It's only a matter of time before the priest is forced to tell Seesya where you're going."

Deborah's hands began to shake. She clutched them together. Despite her efforts at controlling it, the shaking spread to her lips and knees.

Abu Zariz drew deeply and blew the smoke out slowly.

"Thank you for not betraying me to Judge Zifron." The quiver in her voice made Deborah ashamed. She hugged her knees, pressing them to her chest.

"Don't thank me. Had I admitted that Seesya was right and you were with us, things would have become very complicated, even violent, for me and my family."

"I don't understand," she said. "Didn't you say that the judge suspected you were lying?"

"Lying is a crude concept," Abu Zariz said. "A successful trade is always based on a fair balance of mutually assured exaggerations and overstatements."

"But you made his son look bad, as if his attack had been unjustified and he'd lost the soldiers for no good reason."

"And what's wrong with that? I think my wise friend, the judge of Emanuel, was pleased with the opportunity to deflate his son's arrogance and teach him a lesson in humility."

All this circuitous talk did nothing to calm her anxiety. "Why would the judge want to humiliate his son?" she asked. "Seesya is his right hand, his enforcer, his heir—"

"And his biggest threat."

"What?"

Abu Zariz shook his head, smiling. "You are very innocent. It's charming. But along my travels I've heard countless stories about kings and chieftains who died a violent death, and many of them died not in battles with enemies, but at the hands of their impatient heirs."

Deborah inhaled deeply. The idea of a son killing his father was inconceivable. She pushed the thought aside, because the tension between Seesya and his father didn't concern her. They were both her enemies. The only news that mattered was that Seesya might soon know her plans. She must reach Shiloh as soon as possible, find out who had bought an Edomite man named Kassite eighteen years earlier, and leave Shiloh before Seesya caught up with her.

Pointing the smoking pipe at her, Abu Zariz said, "I sense that there's more to your journey than the desperate flight of an unwilling bride."

He drew again, and the glowing pipe illuminated his eyes. She knew that it was time to be cautious and reveal as little as possible.

She asked, "What did Sallan tell you?"

He chuckled, smoke escaping his mouth. "Just like that shrewd Edomite slave, I'm also capable of looking at the facts and drawing some conclusions."

His cryptic response made her realize that she should do the same— look at the facts and draw conclusions. The fact was, Sallan had helped her search for the Elixirist in exchange for her promise to go back and free him. Conclusion: Sallan would do nothing to jeopardize her quest, which meant that he'd told nothing to Abu Zariz.

"The purpose of my journey," she said, "is to reach Shiloh and pray to Yahweh at the Holy Tabernacle."

His quick, appraising glance told her that he was hoping to learn more. "Pray? That's what you'll do in Shiloh?"

"Yes." It was the truth, though not all of it, which made her uncomfortable. She tugged at the ring on her finger. "I'll pray to Yahweh for help in obtaining my freedom from Seesya."

Abu Zariz looked at her for a long moment. "You hope to beat that cunning, violent son of Zifron by praying to a Hebrew god that nobody can see, hear, or touch?"

"Yahweh is the Almighty Creator of the earth, the sun, the moon, and the stars." Her voice filled with indignation, she added, "He is the only God!"

"Fine. Fine. Fine." Abu Zariz held up his hand. "It's your faith. It's your life. All I can do is wish you luck."

Deborah got up. "I'll leave at sunset. Thank you for your hospitality."

"You're welcome." He rose with effort, sighing. "As it happens, we're also traveling to Shiloh tomorrow."

She looked at him suspiciously.

"Your people celebrate the Dance of the Maidens this week," he said. "It's a good time to trade with the priests. I carry white Egyptian linen for them, and they are flush with silver. You can travel with us, if you wish."

She bowed her head in gratitude and turned to leave. Her sack was with Zariz, who had settled back at the same spot as the previous night to watch over the campsite.

"One more thing," Abu Zariz said.

Deborah paused.

"It's our way of life for a father to prepare his son to take over one day—to travel along his father's trade routes, frequent the distant places his father frequented, trade with the sons of those his father traded with, and worship the gods his father worshipped." The leaves in Abu Zariz's pipe no longer glowed. He stuffed it with new leaves and relit it. "When I'm old, I'll settle back at our family home in Moab, and my son, Zariz, will travel with his wives, children, and gods as I do now, and as my father and grandfather did before me. Do you want to become one of my son's wives?"

Her face burning, Deborah shook her head.

"I didn't think so." Abu Zariz pointed at the tent where his wives and children had already gone down for the night. "You should sleep with the women over there."

18

They left early in the morning, heading north through the hills and valleys. Zariz and his father rode up front, navigating along narrow paths that were barely noticeable. Deborah rode with Orpah on a donkey, the younger girl sitting in front and holding the reins. They sat on a rough blanket tied over the donkey's back. The monotonous back-and-forth rocking made Deborah feel sick. She would have liked to ride with Zariz on his horse, holding the reins while his arms supported her on each side and his hands rested on top of hers. Abu Zariz, however, had told her to ride with Orpah.

Orpah drank from a waterskin and offered it to Deborah, turning with a bright smile that made her resemble Zariz.

"Thank you." Deborah took a few sips and recorked it. "The sun is getting hot."

"Yes," Orpah said. "It's always hot in Canaan."

Deborah was curious about what had happened to Orpah at Emanuel. "It's good that you're back with your family."

The girl's smile faded.

"Do you miss your home in Moab?"

Orpah nodded.

"Will you be going home soon?"

"In the winter." She smiled again. "My grandfather's house is only a two-days' ride from the Sea of Salt."

The path descended a hillside, and the donkey tripped, regaining his footing with a jolt that almost tossed them both off. They held on, and when the danger had passed, they giggled.

"Is your home in a town?" Deborah asked.

"It's in Dibon." Orpah moved one hand in a wide circle. "A big town."

"Do you have a king?"

"King Bin-Lot of Moab. His palace is in Dibon, not far from our home. I wish we were going home now." Orpah leaned forward, rested her head on the donkey's neck, and shut her eyes.

When the sun reached its apex, their path intersected the main road to Shiloh. As Obadiah of Levi had predicted, the road was busy with travelers. They rode on horses or donkeys, or walked while pulling handcarts loaded with produce, young lambs, or baby goats for the priests. Many had a daughter or two with them, young maidens who seemed ready for betrothal and marriage. The Moabite caravan joined in, heading east into the higher peaks of the Samariah Hills.

It was late in the afternoon when Deborah first saw the vineyards—rows upon rows of grapevines, vividly green and lined up perfectly, stretching across the vast valley and over the slopes like long strands of freshly combed hair. As the caravan got closer, the individual grapevines came into view—lush, leafy coils over wooden frames, with meaty bunches of red or green grapes hanging from the vines.

Soon Shiloh itself came into view. Built on a hillside, it was bigger than Deborah had imagined, with fortified walls that seemed twice as tall and as thick as the walls of Emanuel. The top of the hill was dominated by a large structure painted turquoise. From a distance, it appeared many times bigger than a house, with heavy columns evenly spaced along the sides and front. It was the Holy Tabernacle, Deborah knew, and the sight made her heart beat faster.

The fairgrounds near the city gates served as a marketplace and campground for visitors. It was crowded, but Abu Zariz found a spot near the road. Everyone got off the horses and donkeys, and the family began to set up camp for the night.

As the sun touched the horizon, drums began to beat, trumpets sounded, and various string instruments came to life. Hundreds of girls in white dresses and loose hair emerged from tents in the fairgrounds and from the city gates. Like a river of milk, they filled the road and flowed down into the valley, where they danced their way into the vineyards. Hundreds of torches were fixed to poles along the lines of vines, turning night into day. Music filled the air, and the girls sang as they danced in long white chains between the rows of vines.

Deborah stood with Zariz and his father, watching the event from the edge of the fairgrounds.

"A beautiful sight," Abu Zariz said. "I have seen it several times before, and it always amazes me. No other people I know allow this."

"Why not?" she asked.

"It's a mating ritual," he said. "Bees and birds do it, but even the poorest Moabite man wouldn't allow his daughter to dance around for strangers. Marriage is a serious business to be arranged in advance between fathers, who bargain and agree upon proper terms before marriage, not a game of matching left to the whims of foolish girls or the lust of precocious boys."

Young men, fourteen and up, soon emerged from the tents and the city. They stayed in groups and ventured to the slopes around the vineyards, talking to each other, pointing, and laughing with feigned swagger. Once in a while, one of the boys would leave the group and approach a girl, who would either decline and continue dancing, which would cause his friends to laugh, or leave the dancing to speak with him, which would earn him cheers from his friends. The couple would step aside and chat by themselves for a few minutes, and then return to their respective friends.

"It's nice," Zariz said. "They find someone they like, and then their fathers can arrange the marriage terms."

His father waved in dismissal. "A girl should like the man her father chose for her. This kind of foolishness leads to bad marriages."

"My parents met at this dance," Deborah said. "And their marriage was good and happy."

"Really?" Zariz's eyes widened. "Did their fathers approve?"

"My mother was an orphan with no family. She'd heard about the Dance of the Maidens and traveled here all the way from the land of Judah. And my father was here to sacrifice a lamb in memory of his parents, who had died of the fever. He said that, of the hundreds of maidens that night, my mother was the most beautiful."

"I believe it," Zariz said, his voice scratchy. "I do."

Deborah turned to him, dismayed.

Abu Zariz cleared his throat. "It's time to say goodbye."

She shouldered her sack. "I'll pray to Yahweh at the Holy Tabernacle tomorrow for your safety and prosperity, and for good husbands for your daughters."

"I appreciate that." The Moabite trader smiled. "And I'll pray to

Khonsu that the journey taken by the girl with orange hair leads to the place where her dreams come true."

Deborah touched her scarf, making sure it was tied properly. "Thank you."

"I'll walk with you," Zariz said, gesturing toward the gates.

His father put a hand on his shoulder.

"Please, Father," Zariz said. "I'd like to say goodbye."

Abu Zariz lowered his hand. "Make it quick."

Zariz and Deborah walked together. Guards in leather armor and long spears stood along the access road, and others watched from atop the gatehouse and adjoining towers that overlooked the whole area.

"Your father disapproves of me," she said.

"He says you're a hardheaded Hebrew." Zariz smiled. "Can't argue with that."

Deborah didn't think of herself as hardheaded, but she realized that arguing would only reinforce Abu Zariz's characterization. "I'm a Hebrew—that much is true—but my tongue isn't oily and I don't carry an invisible sword."

Zariz laughed. "My father actually likes you very much. That's why he's worried."

"About me?"

"He is a wise man, experienced in the way of people. He explained to me that a young man like me is bound to become enamored of a girl occasionally—caught by a glint in an eye, a shy smile, a lock of hair catching a slight wind. He said that a girl can steal a boy's heart with her scent alone, draw him to her like the swirl of spinning water in the river until he drowns."

Anger filled Deborah. She wanted to tell Zariz that his father's clever words were mean and that the only reason she had liked him in the first place was his likeness to Barac, who would never accuse her of trying to steal his heart or trick him with her scent.

Zariz stopped before they reached the gates. "I can go no further. Only Hebrews are allowed inside your holy city." He glanced at the soldiers.

Deborah was still upset. "Better check your chest, make sure I didn't filch your heart."

"It's too late," he said, looking down.

She regretted her harsh words. "Don't be sad. It's my birthday today."

He looked up, surprised. "Really?"

"The fifteenth of Av in the Hebrew calendar. I was born exactly two years after my parents met."

"How old are you today?"

"Fourteen."

He stepped off the road and pulled two trumpet-shaped orange flowers from a honeysuckle bush. "Look, the same color as your hair."

She took one from his hand and placed its stem between his lips. He did the same, inserting the second stem between her lips. Their eyes locked. They sucked the drops of sweet liquid from the flowers and let the flowers fall to the ground.

"Zariz!" His father called, beckoning him to return.

Pulling the Khonsu figurine from his pocket, Zariz kissed the single horn on the miniature horse and the ball on top of the childlike god's head. "Keep her safe, Khonsu. Keep her safe from danger and evil men."

He held it forward for Deborah to kiss.

She hesitated.

"Zariz!" The Moabite trader was now walking briskly in their direction. "Zariz!"

"Please," Zariz said. "If your Yahweh really created the whole world, then He created Khonsu, too."

The argument was easy to counter, because Yahweh was the only God and would not create other gods, but she saw the distress on his face and relented, touching her lips to the figurine.

His father was getting closer.

Replacing the figurine in his pocket, Zariz stepped backward, smiling, his dark eyes glistening with tears. "Goodbye, Deborah," he said. "I'll see you in my dreams."

Deborah wanted to say goodbye but was too choked up to speak.

19

With the scarf pulled low over her eyes, Deborah approached the gates. On the right, the twelve flags of the Hebrew tribes flapped in the wind from tall poles. The soldiers were watching the Dance of the Maidens. She hoped they wouldn't notice her.

"Hey, you," one of the soldiers yelled. "Girl!"

"Yes?"

"Do you live here?"

Deborah shook her head.

"What's your name?"

"Deborah, daughter of Harutz." There was a tremor in her voice, though she tried to mask it. "Harutz of Ephraim," she clarified, pointing at the black flag with the white ox, which flew next to Manasseh's flag, also black, but with a picture of a white antelope, its horns long and straight like arrows.

"Where are you from?"

"Emanuel."

"Who's that boy you were talking to?"

"He and his family are Moabite traders, friends of our judge."

"A girl alone shouldn't be cavorting with Moabites." The soldier stuck a finger in her face. "If I see you again, I'll tell your father."

She lowered her head. "Yes, sir."

"Go on," he said.

Deborah passed through the great gates into Shiloh. Aware that the soldier might still be watching her, she kept walking as if she knew where to go.

The poor lived at the bottom of the hill in a dense mass of tents and huts, which gave off the same stench of poverty as in Emanuel.

She continued up the main street. It gradually widened, and the packed dirt gave way to cobblestones as it ascended the hillside. The houses and shops grew in size and apparent affluence. The sewage, which in Emanuel ran down the street in an open ditch, was covered with a wooden grate. The houses weren't the hodgepodge of wood, mud, and rough-hewn stone dwellings of Emanuel, but well-built structures of clay bricks and blocks of limestone. The front facades were plastered, and flowers bloomed in small gardens between the houses and along the street. Alleys branched out on both sides, with houses that seemed more modest, but still tidy and comfortable.

With the sun gone, most of the shops were closed, but the blacksmith's door was open. It reminded her of Abinoam's shop in Emanuel, where she had often watched Barac help his father work on bronze and iron tools. Inside the shop, the owner bent over a workbench, his hammer landing repeatedly on the red-hot piece of iron that he was forging into a tool.

He noticed her and frowned. "What do you want, girl?"

Resisting the urge to turn and go, Deborah stepped in through the door.

He reached into his pocket, drew out a coin, and tossed it to her. Raising his hammer, he struck the iron with a deafening bang.

Deborah picked the coin up from the floor and placed it on his workbench.

His hammer paused in midair, and he looked up.

She pointed at the tool he was forming. "A sickle, is it?"

"Correct." His expression softened.

"My friend in Emanuel worked in his father's shop." She looked around. "Just like this one."

The blacksmith put down the hammer. "You come from Emanuel?"

She nodded. "Do you know Abinoam?"

"I know of him. My grandfather, a bronze smelter, learned the work from his grandfather, whose name was also Abinoam." He put the piece of iron back in the fire. "My name is Nehoshtan of Ephraim. My grandfather moved to this holy city during the Great Famine, when most of the Samariah Hills emptied out."

She was relieved that he was also from the tribe of Ephraim. "I am Deborah, daughter of Harutz."

"Harutz of Ephraim? Owner of Palm Homestead?"

"Yes," she said eagerly. "Did you know my father?"

"No." He moved the piece of iron around in the fire, disturbing the embers to reignite them. "My grandfather told me about Palm Homestead and the ancient cistern that had been given to the family of Harutz. Many among the tribe of Ephraim were envious of it, especially during the Great Famine."

"It's a good homestead, but my father is dead now, and he left no sons."

"A pretty name, Deborah. Did your father keep bees?"

"There was no need. We had enough wild bees."

"It figures," Nehoshtan said. "Where there's water, life blossoms."

Deborah looked around more carefully, now that her eyes had grown accustomed to the dark interior. She saw no figurines of false gods and decided she could trust this man, Nehoshtan. "Abinoam and his son had to escape from Emanuel."

He watched her, waiting for more.

"Our judge is onerous and unjust."

"Unfortunately, many of the judges today rule over their people not with Yahweh's justice, but with Baal Ammon's greed." Nehoshtan again reshuffled the embers. "Here in Shiloh, we have no judge. The priests rule here with their strict laws and heavy taxes."

Deborah put down her sack. "I just arrived here, and—"

"I'm sorry." He gestured vaguely. "It's not possible for me to host you. My wife is pregnant and works too hard as it is, with the children and all."

His eyes went to her hand, and he noticed the ring on her finger. "You didn't mention a husband," he said.

"I'm betrothed." She adjusted the scarf over her head. "To a very bad man. There is a priest here who will help me, I hope."

"Who?"

"His name is Shatz Ha'Cohen."

"Shatz?" Nehoshtan's eyebrows rose. "Why would he bother to help you?"

"I have a note from our priest." She patted her sack. "They are cousins. Can you direct me to his house?"

Nehoshtan went out to the street with her and pointed uphill. "Go almost to the top. You will see the large houses of the elder priests. Shatz's house is on the right side of the street. It's at least ten times bigger than my house, with a horse stable on the right and livestock pens on the left. Above the front gate you'll see a menorah made of silver."

"Real silver?"

"As real as the shekels I pay the priests in taxes every new moon." He shook his apron, jangling coins. "Go into the courtyard and ask for Shatz. At this time, he'll be adding up his take for the day."

"Thank you." Deborah shouldered her sack. "I have another question. When they sell slaves here, in Shiloh, is there a list of who bought each slave?"

"That's a strange question. Why do you ask?"

Deborah took a deep breath. She didn't want to tell him about the Elixirist, but lying would be almost as bad. "One of the judge's slaves," she said, "asked me to find out who bought his friend many years ago."

"The slave warden keeps the records of sales, but that nasty old man won't give you any information."

His warning hit her hard, but she didn't want him to see her disappointment. "Thank you," she said. "Good night."

Nehoshtan watched her walk up the hill. "Listen," he called after her, "if you need anything, come back here."

Deborah waved. "Yahweh's blessing upon you."

"Amen," Nehoshtan said. "And upon you, too."

Near the top of the hill, the houses grew to sizes that awed Deborah. They were like palaces, easily dwarfing Judge Zifron's house, which she had naively imagined to be the greatest in the land. With stone columns and elaborate carved-wood doors, they exuded wealth and luxury. Each was set back from the street to accommodate a large courtyard. Mint bushes and flower boxes gave off pleasant scents, and a soft breeze carried away the day's heat.

Deborah recognized the house of Shatz Ha'Cohen by the large silver menorah mounted over the courtyard entrance. The horse stable on the right had a separate gate and enough space for twenty or thirty horses. The livestock pen on the left housed cows, sheep, and goats, fenced in sections and filled to capacity.

She entered the large courtyard. A healthy flame burned in the firepit at the center, producing a thick column of smoke. Two slaves worked by the well on the right, raising bucket after bucket and pouring the water into a barrel. Near them, a group of women sorted fruit and vegetables from hefty baskets. They arranged the produce by type and quality, tossing the bad ones onto a heap of trash. In a corner to her left Deborah saw an open workshop, similar to the basket factory at Judge Zifron's house, but more odorous. Shirtless men worked under the glow of torches, cleaning large pieces of cowhide and goatskin with heavy brushes. The workshop didn't have a roof. She saw tall piles of skins on top of open carts, sorted by the type of animal they came from.

A man in a dark coat approached her. "What do you want here, girl?"

"I'm looking for Shatz Ha'Cohen." She searched inside her sack and found the note. "I have a letter from his cousin, Obadiah of Levi."

The man took it. "Wait here."

He went into the house.

A few minutes later he reappeared and beckoned her to follow him into the house.

The difference between Obadiah of Levi and his cousin was like the difference between Emanuel and Shiloh. Where Obadiah was thin and soft-spoken, Shatz Ha'Cohen was large and boisterous. He had a massive gut, and multiple chins supported his round face. His traditional priestly white robe, with blue threads dangling from the edges, was further adorned with threads of gold.

Shatz Ha'Cohen sat in a large leather chair and ate grapes from a clay bowl that rested in his lap. His breastplate was far more elaborate than Obadiah's, made of solid silver with many jewels set in a pattern of tiny stars surrounding two columns of words.

Three men sat cross-legged on the carpeted floor at Shatz Ha'Cohen's knees. One was counting coins, passing them from one basket to another. A second man was writing with ink and feather on a long parchment. A third was tending to the priest's toenails.

Holding Obadiah's note, Shatz asked, "Are you Deborah, daughter of Harutz?"

"Yes," she said.

"Take off the scarf, girl." He had a booming voice that left no room for argument.

She pulled off her scarf. The knot in her hair came undone, and her thick tresses dropped over her shoulders.

"Look at that hair!" The priest laughed. "Just as my cousin wrote: 'A head like an abundant orange tree that's ripe for the picking.' How entertaining!"

The men on the carpet sniggered.

Her face burning, Deborah quickly tied up her hair and fixed the scarf to cover it. There was that fear again, tightening her chest, and the pressure in her eyes as tears threatened to erupt. "Banish your fear and embrace your strength!" she recalled. She forced her gaze away from the priest's grinning face and focused on the one item that represented Yahweh—the breastplate. She inhaled deeply and focused on the pattern of jewels.

"Do you like my breastplate?" Shatz patted it. "Shiny, isn't it?"

She nodded and wondered what the two columns of six words each symbolized.

"You love pretty things?" He smacked his wet lips, leaning forward, his beady eyes staring at her. "Do you? I can show you more pretty things in my private quarters, because I also love pretty things—"

"I love Yahweh," she said.

The grin froze on his face. He sat back, ate a grape, and spat out the seeds. "Tell me, girl, do you know what 'Ha'Cohen' means?" He didn't wait for her to answer. "It means that I'm not just another small-town priest like my poor cousin Obadiah. Rather, I'm a direct descendent of Aaron, the wise brother of the prophet Moses. Only we, the sons of Aaron, the first High Priest, are allowed inside the Holy Tabernacle, where the Ark of the Covenant resides."

He patted his breastplate. "Do you recognize these words on my breastplate?"

Deborah shook her head.

His finger pointed at each of the words. "Reuben, Simeon, Levi, Judah, Issachar, Zebulon, Joseph, Benjamin, Dan, Naphtali, Gad, Asher."

"Yes," she said. "I know these names. They are the twelve Hebrew tribes."

"Wrong! Wrong! Wrong!" His booming voice hurt her ears. "These are the names of the twelve sons of Jacob, not the tribes! Do you know the difference?"

She shook her head, her face turning red.

"I didn't think so. Have you heard of Jacob?"

"He was the son of Isaac and the grandson of Abraham."

"And who were they?"

"Our ancestors," Deborah said. "The three Hebrew patriarchs: Abraham, Isaac, and Jacob, who was called Jacob only for a while, until he scuffled with a seraph and Yahweh changed his name to Israel."

"Very good." Shatz seemed surprised that she knew all this. "And what tribe do you belong to?"

"Ephraim," she said.

"Ephraim?" He pointed at his breastplate. "Do you see the name Ephraim here?"

"I can't read."

"Trust me, girl. It's not here. Do you know why?"

"Ephraim and Manasseh were the sons of Joseph, son of Jacob. When Joshua brought the tribes into Canaan to conquer it, he gave Joseph's share of the land to his two sons, Ephraim and Manasseh."

"And they're still fighting over it!" The priest laughed, which caused his chins to shake. "I'm impressed. An illiterate runaway knows our people's history."

The men laughed again, as if on cue.

"My father taught me," she said. "He is dead now."

"Apparently." Shatz glanced at Obadiah's letter. "Harutz, owner of Palm Homestead."

Hearing her father's name pained Deborah. She took another deep breath.

"Dead and gone," the priest said. "And no son to continue his name and inherit his family's valuable homestead—the worst punishment for a man, isn't it?"

The three men grunted in agreement.

"I wonder," Shatz continued, "what reasons Yahweh had to punish your father so harshly."

Deborah bowed her head. It was true that her father's death had deprived him of succession, which was all a man could hope for after life on this earth. And there was no doubt that Yahweh was the true judge. But she could think of no sin her righteous father had committed that would have justified such severe punishment. Dread came over her. She had been only twelve when he died, a young girl who knew little and understood even less. The priest must be right that her father had sinned gravely and earned Yahweh's wrath. There was no other explanation.

She could no longer suppress her tears.

"We must humbly accept His judgment," Shatz announced, resting his right hand on the breastplate, "as we joyously embrace His many generous blessings."

"Amen," the men at his feet mumbled.

She wiped her tears on her sleeve.

"And now my cousin sent you here." The priest picked a grape from the bowl and tossed it in his mouth. "It's not like him to take such risk. How did you convince Obadiah to engage in this subversion?"

"He's afraid of my sister's curse."

"Ah." Shatz made a dismissive gesture. "If women's curses had any power, all men would turn into lepers."

The men at his feet laughed again.

"Now, tell me, have you taken off the betrothal ring?"

She showed him her hand with Seesya's ring still on her finger.

"That's good." He spat the grape seeds aside. "Violating a betrothal is a deadly sin."

"I know," she said. "That's why I came to you. He's a very bad man."

"Not even twenty, that boy, is he? Youthful mistakes may be forgiven."

The priest's words shocked her. "Seesya is evil!"

"The son of a powerful judge has to act with a heavy hand sometimes." Shatz ate another grape. "I'll think about your case. Meanwhile, you'll be given food and shelter tonight."

"I can't go back to Emanuel. In the name of Yahweh, please help me!"

"Yahweh is everywhere, even in Emanuel." Shatz waved his hand. "Go now. Tomorrow, we'll decide what to do about you."

The man in the black coat showed her to the door.

"Wait a minute." The priest curled his finger at her. "Obadiah wrote something about you being due for a marriage ceremony in a few days."

She nodded.

"Then you're still within the seven days of impurity, yes?"

Again, she nodded.

"Where is your red robe?"

Deborah hesitated. Should she tell him that Obadiah of Levi had told her to throw away the red robe?

"Doesn't matter," Shatz said. "This is Shiloh, the city of the Holy Tabernacle. Here you must obey the sacred law of our forefathers. I'll have a robe brought to you."

Deborah was shown to the women's quarters, where she stayed with Shatz's four wives and three concubines, who among them had three babies and many children. The youngest wife was only a year or two older than Deborah. The women had their own washroom with a water basin and a bath that, she was told, was filled every night with warm water. She was given a clean red robe and undergarments and assigned her own cot for the night.

To help the children fall asleep, one of the wives played a harp, and another sang softly in a clear, beautiful voice. Deborah lay down, closed her eyes, and listened to them until sleep came.

In the morning, she wanted to go to the Holy Tabernacle to pray, but the women told her there was work to do. Due to the Dance of the Maidens, there were many pilgrims in Shiloh. All the members of Shatz Ha'Cohen's household were required to help with the pilgrims' offerings down by the gates. Deborah joined them.

The priest himself came on a horse-drawn cart a little later. He was dressed the way she had seen him the night before, but with the addition of a white cap, which like his robe was threaded with gold.

A large, level field across from the fairgrounds was divided among the seven elder priests, who each carried the title "Ha'Cohen" and were the rulers of Shiloh and the leaders of all the rituals at the Holy Tabernacle. Each of the seven families set up a receiving table with many workers to process the various categories of offerings: fruit, vegetables, wheat, barley, oil, wine, sheep, goats, and cattle, as well as copper and silver coins. The pilgrims lined up along the road, and a group of Levite ushers directed each one to the next available table.

Order was maintained by groups of soldiers, who marched back and forth in leather armor and long spears. Their commanders bowed to the elder priests every time they passed by. The soldiers' demeanor made it clear that they would not tolerate even the slightest misbehavior.

Deborah was assigned to pack fruit in tall baskets. She watched her surroundings with great interest. Shatz Ha'Cohen had a well-run system that processed the offerings quickly and efficiently, which increased the number of pilgrims and offerings his family received, compared to the slower neighboring tables. As each pilgrim approached with a handcart and livestock, workers quickly collected the offerings, counted them, and yelled to the scribe, who wrote the information down on parchment. Live animals were checked and probed for any malady or lameness, and when cleared were pulled into a holding pen behind the table. Shatz's two eldest sons counted money offerings and wrote down the amounts before dropping the coins in a tall basket.

Like the other elder priests, Shatz Ha'Cohen sat on a high chair at the end of his family's long receiving table and oversaw the operation. Every pilgrim announced his name and tribe. Most were from Ephraim or Manasseh, but a few came from the neighboring tribes to the south—Judah, Dan, and Benjamin. The priest raised his hands, parting his fingers in pairs, and conferred Yahweh's gratitude and grace upon the pilgrim and his family.

Once received, the various offerings of produce and livestock were sorted out in the back. Except the very best, everything that was sellable was taken to the fairgrounds and sold to the throngs of pilgrims and caravans of foreign traders. Whatever remained of the offerings, such as unripe or overripe produce, or scrawny livestock that was unlikely to attract buyers in the market, was given to the poor.

Every hour or so, a goat or a sheep was taken to a communal altar on a small hill overlooking the fairgrounds, slaughtered, cleaned, and burned on the altar. The smell of roasting meat drifted over the whole area, and pilgrims lined up before the altar to purchase edible parts of the sacrificial animals, which they ate with their hands while facing the Holy Tabernacle at the top of the hill.

Deborah remembered her father explaining that every Hebrew must give offerings to the priests. Tithing required one-tenth of all produce and income. In addition, the priests were entitled to the first crop of all fields and orchards, and the firstborn of every farm animal. But now, witnessing the actual process up close, she heard some of the pilgrims announce that their offerings exceeded the mandatory obligation. They did it as a way to express gratitude for good things that had come to them since their last pilgrimage, or to ask for special blessings to improve their future lot. Others, in lower voices, confessed egregious sins they had committed and begged forgiveness in exchange for the additional offerings, pledging to be righteous from this day on. Without exception,

Shatz Ha'Cohen granted blessings and pardons in the name of Yahweh while praising the pilgrims for their generosity.

In the early afternoon, while sorting apples from a basket of offerings, Deborah noticed that everyone around her suddenly grew quiet. Looking up, she saw a group approaching—not to join the long queue of pilgrims along the road, but directly through the nearby field. They wore dark robes with hoods, sheer veils over their faces, and rags over their hands.

Everyone turned away, for it was common knowledge that staring at a leper would cause a healthy person to become afflicted with the dreaded curse. None of the pilgrims, who had waited in line for hours, protested when the lepers bypassed the line.

Deborah turned away as well, but curiosity soon drew her eyes back to the group. They seemed pitiful and sad, not scary or threatening. Their suffering was obviously a punishment from Yahweh for sins they had committed, and she wasn't committing any sin by looking at them with compassion.

The group of about twenty might have been a family, or merely a collection of unrelated lepers who had joined together after their families had cast them off. It was hard to tell anyone's age, or even their gender. Each one brought an offering—a basket of fruit or vegetables, a bale of sheep's wool, or a newborn goat.

The ushers, whose job was to direct pilgrims from the head of the line to one of the tables, said nothing as the lepers came closer and stopped, unsure which table to choose for their offerings. The silence lingered as hundreds of pilgrims and dozens of priests and workers gazed at the ground and said nothing.

"They should come here," Deborah said quietly to no one in particular. She dropped the apples into a basket, stepped forward, and yelled, "Come over here!"

The lepers' masked faces turned in her direction and she shuddered, seeing that some of their eyes were gone, leaving empty black holes.

Raising her hand, she waved them over. "Right here."

Shatz Ha'Cohen hissed, "Shut up, girl!"

The lepers walked over slowly, carrying their gifts.

He rose from his comfortable chair and, without looking at them, declared, "Step up, brothers and sisters, and make your offerings to merciful Yahweh."

The lepers put down the offerings on the ground before the table and tied the rope of the baby goat to the leg of the table.

"Repent your sins," Shatz proclaimed. "Renounce your depravities. Throw away your turpitudes for which Yahweh punished you with the curse of affliction and disfigurement."

The lepers stood before the elder priest and bowed. Extending his hands forward with the fingers parted in pairs, he looked up at the sky and recited the blessing: "May Yahweh bless you and protect you. May He show you kindness and grace. May He illuminate your path and grant you peace."

As they walked away, Deborah noticed that some of the lepers had to lean on each other for support.

When they were out of earshot, Shatz sat down, sighed loudly, and pointed at Deborah. "You, big mouth, take all of this away. Burn all of it. The goat, too."

She heard a few people laugh as the activity resumed at all the tables. One of the women gave Deborah a straw mat in which to pack up the fruit, vegetables, and wool. The young goat followed her to the garbage dump near the gates, where a fire was kept burning all day. She tossed the lepers' offerings onto the fire, followed by the straw mat. Making sure no one was looking, she released the young goat near a clump of bushes, where it began to nibble as Deborah ran back to work.

About an hour before sunset, a priest blew a ram's horn to signal that no more offerings would be received that day. The pilgrims still waiting along the road to deliver their offerings went across the road to the fairgrounds, where they would spend the night. Merchants conducted the last business of the day while their women cooked the evening meal and fed the children and animals.

When cleanup was complete and no one was paying attention to her, Deborah slipped away. She ran across the road and over to the other side of the fairgrounds, where Zariz and his family had set up camp the day before, eager to tell him what had happened at Shatz's house and to beg his father to shelter her again if Shatz decided in favor of Seesya.

The Moabite family was no longer there. A Canaanite caravan selling figurines and trinkets now occupied the spot.

She crisscrossed the whole fairgrounds from end to end, back and forth, searching in vain until the sun went down and the first music came from the vineyards. It was the evening following the Dance of the Maidens, and young men were going to dance while the maidens watched from the hillside.

The realization hit her hard. Zariz was gone!

Back on the road near the gates, Deborah stood in the dark, filled with a sense of loss and disappointment. The music and cheers from the vineyards mixed with the hum of countless people talking in various languages. The air was filled with smells of cooking and animal waste, and the flames of hundreds of torches painted the city walls with a red glow. In the midst of all this human activity, she felt completely alone.

A burst of lights drew her eyes to the top of the hill, above the dense houses of Shiloh, where fires ignited simultaneously around the Holy Tabernacle in a spectacle that drew a collective groan of surprise and elation from everyone in the valley below. Lit up against the night sky, the columned edifice with its turquoise walls appeared to float in the air above the city. It was a breathtaking sight, and the pilgrims and merchants watched in awe.

Deborah knelt on the dirt road, interwove her fingers, and pressed them under her chin, as Tamar had used to do. Looking up at the radiant Holy Tabernacle, she prayed to Yahweh.

"I am Deborah," she cried, "daughter of Harutz from Palm Homestead. Please help me find Kassite and convince him to give me the elixir that will turn me into a boy. I will be your servant forever."

Her tears clouded the glorious view at the hilltop. In desperation to be heard by Yahweh over the surrounding noise, she raised her voice.

"If you still want me to be your prophet," she cried, "I will, I swear to you! As a man, I will deliver your message to the Hebrews! I will serve you all my life!"

With the last few words uttered at the top of her voice, Deborah collapsed to the ground. She curled up by the roadside, pressing her knees to her chest. Her whole body shook—slightly at first, but worsening quickly until her teeth chattered and involuntary moans escaped from her mouth. Then there was darkness.

20

When Deborah came to, she was lying on a soft bed of straw, a wet cloth resting on her forehead. She pulled it off and saw a cover above, like a tent, but with one side open, facing the fairgrounds and its many campfires. The city of Shiloh sparkled with torches and firepits, but the Holy Tabernacle was dark now.

"You are safe, child," a woman said.

Deborah sat up. "Who's there?"

"My name is Miriam." The woman stood outside the small tent, barely visible in the dark. She wore a robe with a hood.

Trying to stand up, Deborah became dizzy.

"You should take it easy," the woman said.

Lying back down, Deborah saw that the woman's hands were wrapped in rags and her eyes glistened above a sheer veil that covered most of her face.

"Why am I here?"

"We saw you faint by the roadside and brought you here to recover."

Deborah noticed several other tents nearby, dark figures sitting in front, also covered from head to toe like Miriam.

The lepers!

"Don't be afraid," Miriam said. "We won't hurt you."

Deborah got up—more slowly this time. There was a slight breeze from outside the tent, and it cooled her face, making her feel better. She cleared her throat. "Yahweh's blessings on you for helping me."

"We only returned a favor. When we brought our offerings this morning, you spoke up when everyone else wouldn't even look at us. What is your name?"

"Deborah, daughter of Harutz."

"Pray for us, Deborah." Miriam bowed as if before a priest or a judge. "Pray the way you did earlier by the roadside. Ask God to lift our curse and heal us."

Deborah was relieved to find the gates still open for workers cleaning up after the day. A sentry stopped her, extending his spear across her way. "Where are you going, girl?"

"I'm a guest at the house of Shatz Ha'Cohen."

"Are you from Emanuel?"

She was surprised he knew. "Yes."

"Go ahead," he said, pointing the spear up the hill.

As she turned to go, a large group approached the gate. Deborah stepped aside and watched as armed men on horses led a few dozen slaves into the city. The men and women, wearing soiled sleeveless shirts and no shoes, were tied to each other in a long column. They entered Shiloh and turned left, away from the main street.

Remembering what Nehoshtan had said about the slave warden who recorded all sales, Deborah decided to follow them. She stayed in the dark as the slaves were led down a street along the tents and shacks of the poor, right under the perimeter wall. The sentries patrolling along the top of the wall whistled, and one of them yelled, "Send up a slave girl, will you? We'll throw her back down in the morning."

The armed men laughed and kept going.

A few minutes later, the slaves were pushed into large wooden cages—one for the men, one for the women. The cages, which already held other slaves, were backed up to the walls. A smaller cage held children, both boys and girls together. Unlike the adult slaves, who were uniformly quiet, some of the children were crying.

Having secured the slaves, the armed men tied their horses and entered a house nearby. Deborah peeked in through the open doorway and saw them speaking with an old man, who sat at a table covered with parchments. He gave them a purse of coins.

Turning to go, one of the men saw her and yelled, "What do you want here, girl?"

Pushing away her fear, Deborah said, "Nothing from you."

The men laughed at her audacity, and the old man beckoned her inside.

Deborah entered and asked, "Are you the slave warden?"

The old man nodded and waited as the armed men walked away. He scrutinized her up and down, his eyes pausing briefly on the ring. "This isn't a safe neighborhood for a respectable woman."

"I heard the children crying out there. Perhaps they need food."

"Or toys, maybe?" He grinned, his red gums missing most of the teeth. "Bedtime stories?"

"They're only children."

"They're merchandise to be sold for profit." He gestured dismissively. "Tomorrow they'll go on the dock, and their new owners can fatten them up and sacrifice them to Baal, for all I care."

His callous words silenced her.

"Who are you?" the old man asked.

"I live at the house of Shatz Ha'Cohen."

"Oh, I see." The slave warden fumbled with his parchments. "How may I assist the elder priest at this time?"

Deborah gulped to stop herself from correcting him. She realized that this coincidence—her finding the slave warden and his thinking that Shatz had sent her—was Yahweh's doing, the answer to her prayers.

"Only a small matter," she said. "A question came up—"

"I paid my taxes in full." The old man raised his hands as if in surrender. "I have nothing to hide."

"It's not about your business, sir. It's about a small piece of information."

"What information?"

"The name of the buyer of a certain slave."

"That's all? You had me worried for a moment. Which slave exactly?"

"Let me make sure I remember it correctly." Deborah looked up at the ceiling as if trying to recall the priest's instructions. "The slave's name was Sallan. He was from Edom."

"Sallan? I don't remember this name. When was that?"

"He was sold during the first spring after the Great Famine, on the eve of the Passover holiday, eighteen years ago."

"Eighteen years ago?" The slave warden sat back, shaking his head. "How am I to remember such information?"

"It must be in the records." She gestured at the parchments.

"I'll have to look through many records to find information that old. It's already late, and I haven't eaten the evening meal yet. Come back tomorrow."

"I'm sorry," she said. "It can't wait. There's one more fact to help you search. Sallan was sold right before another Edomite slave, a man named Kassite. One of them was bought by a merchant from Mitzpah."

"Wait here, girl." Mumbling under his breath, he carried a small lamp down a short hallway to another room.

The minutes passed, and she could hear him unrolling parchments, muttering to himself. She began to worry that he wouldn't find it, that the records didn't go so far back. Through the open front door, she heard men yelling outside, and the unmistakable sound of whipping, followed by shouts of pain.

"Tell me," the slave warden yelled from the other room, "why did he send you and not one of his Levite minions?"

Deborah froze, her mind racing, and then she had an idea. "Probably because this must remain a secret. No one but me knows about it."

"And no one shall hear it from me. You can tell him that, too." The slave warden reappeared, carrying a parchment, which he flattened on the desk. He pointed at a line written in faded ink. "First on the dock was Sallan. And then Kassite. Each one was sold for eight silver shekels and three goats. Sallan was the one who went to Mitzpah." The old man squinted at the writing. "His new owner was Karam of Ephraim."

"Karam of Ephraim from Mitzpah," Deborah repeated. "And just in case Shatz asks me, what about the other one, Kassite?"

"He was sold to someone else." He peered at the parchment. "Orran of Manasseh from Aphek."

Deborah struggled to control her excitement. She had to remember what he'd said, or all this would be for naught. "Can you repeat that?"

He groaned. "Orran of Manasseh from Aphek. Haven't you heard of him?"

"Orran of Manasseh from Aphek? It sounds familiar." A question occurred to her. "Isn't Aphek a city of Ephraim?"

"It is, but the land around it belongs to Manasseh, which is another source of trouble between these tribes." The slave warden rolled up the parchment. "Shatz does a lot of business with Orran." He shook his head, chuckling. "And in business, good information is like silver shekels."

"But I came to ask about Sallan," Deborah said, desperate to maintain the ruse. "The other slave is not important."

"That's what you think." He ambled out of the room with the

parchment. "Foolish girl."

The discovery of the information she had sought filled Deborah with joy. She retraced her steps, hurrying down the street between the massive outer wall and the tents and shacks of the poor. The gates had been shut for the night. Halfway up the main street, Nehoshtan's door was still open, letting out the heat of his oven and the pounding of his hammer. As she came to the door, he looked up.

"It's you again." He put down the hammer, slipped the piece of iron back into the fire, and yelled, "Wife, come out for a moment."

A woman appeared from a back door connected to the rest of the house. She was short and round, her hair was covered with a scarf, and her face was red and sweaty.

Nehoshtan pointed at Deborah. "This is the girl I was telling you about—Deborah, daughter of Harutz from Palm Homestead."

The woman wiped the sweat off her face. "Shalom," she said. "I am Michal."

Deborah smiled.

"My husband told me about you. Did Shatz Ha'Cohen help you?"

"He gave me shelter until he decides what to do. I trust in Yahweh that all will be made right and just."

Nehoshtan smoothed his beard, exchanging a brief smile with his wife. A toddler came out from behind her and grabbed the bottom of her dress. He was naked except for a loincloth, and his large, dark eyes went from Deborah to his father. He grinned, showing little teeth.

Nehoshtan swept the boy up in his arms and kissed him. "This is my youngest son, Tsoreph."

The boy buried his face in his father's shirt.

Michal laughed and patted the boy's back. "Shall I add another plate to the dinner table?"

"Thank you," Deborah said, "but I cannot stay. I just stopped by to ask your husband something."

"Another time, then." Michal took the boy and went back into the house.

Nehoshtan glanced after them and turned to Deborah. "What is it?"

Deborah pressed her interwoven fingers under her chin. "Yahweh heard my prayers and helped me find the information I was seeking. Blessed be He!"

"Amen." The blacksmith scratched his head. "I once heard Shatz Ha'Cohen's father—who was truly righteous, unlike his son—preach at the Holy Tabernacle on the Day of Atonement. It was the last year of the Great Famine, though we didn't know at the time that relief was near. I was a boy of eight or nine, but what he said stuck in my mind: 'When you pursue your True Calling, God provides the shortcuts.'"

"Yes!" Deborah clapped excitedly. "It's happening to me!"

He shifted the iron in the fire, producing a burst of sparks and smoke, giving her a moment to compose herself. "And what is it that I can provide?" he asked.

"Do you know of Orran of Manasseh from Aphek?"

"The tanner?"

"What's a tanner?" Deborah blushed. "I don't know this trade."

"Why should you? It used to be a Philistine art. Only they knew how to turn butchered skins into fine leather. But a few Hebrews learned it, too. You'd find a tanner only in a big city near a river—a city like Aphek or Megiddo. Tanning isn't something one can do in a small shop." He gestured at his own work area.

"Why?"

"A tannery needs lots of water to feed the soaking tubs and wash the skins, and it has to be downwind from the town because the feces smell terribly."

"Feces?"

Nehoshtan laughed. "I'm not explaining it well. Part of the process in a tannery involves soaking animal skins in tubs filled with water and rotting waste to soften the skins. By varying the length and harshness of the soaking, and by using certain types of chalk and sharp liquids, a tanner can turn the skins into different kinds of leather, depending on the intended use—thick and hard for armor, supple and pliable for chairs, or even thin as a leaf for writing, like parchment or really fine vellum."

"Now I understand," Deborah said, and she meant not only that she understood what a tanner did, but also how Kassite, a man who knew how to mix potent elixirs, would be helpful to a tanner. "Have you met Orran of Manasseh?"

"Who hasn't? Orran owns the biggest tannery between the Great Sea and the Jordan River. The priests sell him animal skins from all the offerings and sacrifices. Once he turns the skins into leather and parchment, the priests buy those products from him for ten times over."

It occurred to Deborah that Orran's tannery success might be due to Kassite, the way Judge Zifron's basket business owed its success to Sallan. There was no doubt left in her mind that the slave warden's information was correct. She wanted to jump up and down with joy, but she controlled herself and asked, "How far is Aphek from here?"

"It's two days due west, right above the source of the Yarkon River. Do you plan to go there?"

"At first light tomorrow morning!"

"Be careful," Nehoshtan said. "The roads are dangerous, even for a man."

Deborah smiled and waved. "Yahweh's blessings upon you and your family."

21

Her chest bursting with excitement, Deborah ran uphill. She would spend the night in the women's quarters, keeping to herself, and leave in the morning. Her prayers had been answered, and there was no doubt that Yahweh wanted her to succeed in becoming a boy. Otherwise, why would He bother to help her find the Elixirist? "When you pursue your True Calling, God provides the shortcuts." She felt a rush of gratitude. As eager as she was to reach Aphek, before departing in the morning she would go to the top of the hill and give thanks at the Holy Tabernacle.

Approaching Shatz Ha'Cohen's house, she slowed down and shielded her eyes from the bright glow. Dozens of burning torches turned night into day. Men filled the courtyard as if it were a market. Over their heads, at the opposite end, she saw Shatz Ha'Cohen sitting on a black stallion with a silver bridle.

"A magnificent beast," Shatz announced. "Please give your father my sincere gratitude for a generous gift!"

"You're most welcome," said a familiar voice.

Only then did Deborah notice the man standing beside Shatz, holding the silver bridle, a red scar cutting across his face.

She screamed, drawing everyone's attention.

"What do you know," Shatz said. "Here's your lovely bride."

"In all her glory," Seesya said with a crooked grin.

Deborah turned to run, but she was too late. Two soldiers blocked the courtyard's exit.

"Come, girl." Shatz climbed down from the stallion, aided by his servants. "Step over here. Don't be afraid."

The crowd of men parted as she slowly walked across the courtyard.

Seesya was dressed in armor and held a horsewhip in his hand. Vardit, her face dour, stood behind him in a dark robe. Obadiah of Levi, a travel coat over his white robe, leaned on his wooden staff, his eyes downcast. She recognized some of the servants and soldiers from the judge's household in Emanuel. A whole sheep was roasting over the firepit, and servants walked around with trays of fruit and cheese, as well as wine jugs to top off the guests' goblets.

Shatz Ha'Cohen smiled as he patted the horse's neck. "Look what Judge Zifron sent me. A magnificent stallion, isn't it?"

Deborah couldn't respond. She was rigid with shock.

Seesya twirled the horsewhip and touched the end of the whip to his forehead in a gesture of mock greeting, his dark eyes half-hidden by his oily hair.

"Did you lose your tongue, girl?" Shatz waved over a servant. "Give her a drink!"

The servant filled a goblet and offered it to her.

Deborah had to make a concerted effort to move her hand, take the goblet, and bring it to her lips. She took a sip, aspirated some of the wine, and coughed.

"Don't spill my good wine," Shatz protested good-naturedly. "Drink it. It'll make you feel happy like the rest of us."

Everybody laughed, and Seesya stepped forward and pushed the bottom of the goblet up without touching Deborah's hand, forcing her to drink until the goblet was empty. She coughed some more, bending over. When the coughing spell was over, the priest clapped, and all the men joined him.

Deborah fell to her knees and held her hands up to Shatz. "Please help me! I don't want to marry him!"

The laughter around her died down.

"I beg you," she cried. "In the name of Yahweh, save me!"

"No need for that," Shatz Ha'Cohen said. "Come, girl, stand up."

Deborah wiped her tears. "Please release me from Seesya's betrothal." Her voice quivered. "I'm an orphan, with no father or brother to defend me. You can protect me. Only you."

There was a rapt silence around them, and the priest's round face softened. "Who am I to protect you, poor child? The Almighty, the Creator, the God of the Hebrews is our protector. The one and only."

She opened her mouth to protest, but he silenced her with a raised finger.

"Do you remember, girl, what Yahweh said to Eve after she lured Adam to eat the forbidden fruit in the Garden of Eden?"

Deborah could not remember.

"Anyone else?" Shatz turned to Obadiah of Levi. "Cousin?"

The old priest raised his head, met Deborah's eyes, and cleared his throat. "'And to the woman God said: I shall multiply your pain and agony; in anguish you shall bear children; always you shall lust after your husband, and he shall reign over you.'"

The men murmured in agreement, but Deborah struggled not to break down in tears again.

"Those are divine words," Shatz said. "A clear and precise law for Eve and all women until eternity: 'Always you shall lust after your husband, and he shall reign over you.' God ordained that women belong down here." He put his hand down near the ground. "And men reign over you from up here." He held his hand at eye level. "Do you wish to argue with Yahweh, our Creator, the Almighty?"

Deborah shook her head. "I'll submit to a husband, but not this one."

Everyone burst out laughing, especially Shatz, who pounded Seesya's shoulder several times, bellowing, "She doesn't like you, young man. She wants someone else!"

When they calmed down, the priest wiped his face and smiled at her. "Do you want to choose a husband for yourself? Is that it?"

"Yes!"

He sighed and looked up in contemplation. "Tell me, girl, did your father grow wheat at Palm Homestead?"

The question surprised her. Why did he want to know?

"Yes," she said. "A great field of wheat still grows there. I saw it recently."

"Imagine how the wheat looks when it's ripe." Shatz put his arm out and moved it from side to side as if caressing shafts of wheat. "Like a thick, golden carpet, perfectly flat, yes?"

She nodded.

"And if you look across the field and see a stalk rising above the beautiful expanse of ripe wheat, what is it?"

"A weed."

"Correct. It's a weed. And what did your father do when he saw a weed rising above his good wheat?"

"He pulled it out."

"Exactly," Shatz said. "And the same goes for a girl who demands to choose her own husband. She is like a weed, rising above the field of good women. We can't have it, can we?"

The men in the courtyard voiced their agreement.

"It's settled, then," the priest said. "Tomorrow night, after sunset, we will hold a wedding procession to celebrate this blessed union, and the bride will ride on my new stallion!"

Seesya bowed to Shatz. "Thank you."

Everyone applauded, and the horse neighed, swaying its head.

"In honor of our esteemed guests," Shatz said, "I'd like to name this stallion Emanuel. What do you think of this name, girl?"

Again, she was the center of attention, but she felt paralyzed by dread and sorrow. The warmth of the wine in her belly made Deborah remember the Reinforcing Liquid she had ingested. What was Sallan's advice? "Banish your fear and embrace your strength." But with all these faces looking at her, expecting her to respond, fear clung to her with a hawk's clutches, whispering words of discouragement in her ear.

"Go on," Shatz said, "don't be afraid, child. What do you think of naming this gorgeous animal Emanuel in honor—"

"It's a bad idea," she blurted out.

Everyone groaned at her rudeness, but Shatz laughed again, his chins shaking. "Why do you think my idea is bad?"

Deborah's fear spiked again, muting her.

"Speak up, girl." Shatz clapped. "Tell us—"

"I think your idea is bad," she said, "because Emanuel means 'God is with us,' and Yahweh wouldn't be happy to have a horse named for this sacred declaration of faith in Him. The name you propose is a mockery of God."

The priest stopped laughing.

Everyone quieted down.

The silence lingered.

Turning to Seesya, Shatz said, "My young friend, considering that this girl will soon become your wife, let me say this: I feel sorry for you!"

Everyone laughed, and Shatz Ha'Cohen waved the tail of his white robe and walked into the house, followed by Seesya and the rest of the men.

Deborah followed Vardit up the stairs to the women's quarters on the second floor, where a separate room had been prepared for Judge Zifron's wife. Once inside, Vardit handed her a small clay bottle.

"Sallan prepared this," she said.

Deborah took the bottle. "What is it?"

"A potion with olive oil and herbs to soothe the pain and heal the wounds."

"I'm not injured," Deborah said, confused.

"It's not for you."

Vardit pulled off her dress and lay down on one of the straw mats, face down. Her exposed back was crisscrossed with angry red welts.

"Yahweh's mercy!" Deborah cried. "What happened to you?"

"You escaped, and I got punished. That's what happened."

Barely able to speak, Deborah whispered, "I'm sorry. It's terrible."

"You should be sorry. And yes, it's terrible. Now rub the potion in, but do it gently."

Deborah knelt and poured some of the potion into the palm of her hand. She hesitated to touch Vardit. "I'm still impure," she said.

"Why should I care about impurity?" Vardit laughed bitterly. "My husband won't summon me to his bed any time soon."

As lightly as she could, Deborah spread the potion on the wounds. The older woman groaned. When it was done, Deborah put away the bottle and fanned Vardit's back with a cloth until her breathing slowed and she appeared to be asleep. But when Deborah put out the lamp and lay down next to her, Vardit spoke quietly.

"I don't blame you for trying to escape," she said.

"Really?"

Changing position, Vardit groaned in pain. "If he can do this to his mother, what will he do to his wife?"

Deborah was shocked. Husbands had the right to beat their wives, and most did it, though rarely with such severity, and almost never a mature wife with grown sons. But for a son to have his mother flogged was unheard of—even with his father's permission, which she assumed Seesya had received prior to committing this sordid act.

"He's a wicked boy," Vardit said.

"Yes," Deborah said softly. "He is."

"But I'm his mother, and you'll soon be his wife." Vardit began to weep. "I don't have a choice, and neither do you."

In the dark, Deborah reached over and held her hand.

22

Deborah woke up at dawn. She went to the window, which overlooked the courtyard. Shirtless slaves were already cleaning animal skins on the opposite side, and others were loading empty baskets and cloth sacks onto a wagon in preparation for another long day of accepting pilgrims' offerings down by the gates. She leaned forward through the window and looked down. Two soldiers sat on wine barrels by the entry to the stairs. They watched the slaves work, but Deborah knew why they were stationed there.

"You're up already," Vardit said.

Deborah turned, saw the welts on the exposed back, and felt a pang of guilt. "I'm sorry to have caused your punishment. And it was all for nothing. The calamity I tried to escape from is about to happen anyway."

Vardit sighed. "Marriage is not a calamity. It's the way of the world."

"Then why do I feel like a sheep going to slaughter?"

"There won't be any slaughter." Vardit eased herself up, her face twisting in pain. "I'm going to make you beautiful. Seesya will find you attractive, and all will be well."

Deborah touched her hair. The thought of being in a room alone with Seesya terrified her, but even worse was the idea of having physical contact with him.

"I promise you. He'll be happy with you."

"How can you be so sure?"

"Men are all the same," Vardit said. "A new wife excites them, at least for a while. Let's wash and begin to—"

"I want to pray at the Holy Tabernacle."

"Now?"

"Yes. Now."

A nervous smile crossed Vardit's face. "I'll take you there, but first you have to do something for me." She took the Womanhood Charm from her bag and held it out. "For good luck with your wedding and all future childbearing," she said.

Deborah didn't bother to argue. She held the naked female figurine by its concave base and went to the window. Lifting her left foot, she looked up at the sky, kissed the tiny head three times, and pretended to count in her head while thinking of the Elixirist and how only he could free her from the curse of womanhood.

"Very good." Vardit put it away.

"Will you take me to the Holy Tabernacle now?"

"Today is your wedding day, and it's a sacred duty to make a bride happy on her last day as a maiden." Vardit slipped on a dress, careful not to disturb the fresh scabs over her back, and tied a scarf over her head. "Let's go."

They went downstairs, and Vardit spoke with the two soldiers, who followed them out of the courtyard. At the exit, Deborah touched the mezuzah scroll, fitted in a rectangular cavity in the doorjamb. It reminded her of the missing mezuzah at Palm Homestead.

Heading up the street, they passed a few more houses, as large and as opulent as Shatz's, and a square building with no windows.

"That's the bathhouse," Vardit said. "The elder priests immerse here before every ritual."

"Is this where I'll immerse tonight?"

Vardit pointed downhill. "Women use a purifying bath near the slave cages. That's where you'll immerse before the procession."

The hilltop was flat, cleared of stones, and at least five hundred steps across. The Holy Tabernacle, a large structure painted in pale turquoise, occupied the center and was surrounded by a fence made of wood pillars and turquoise cloth. The fence had two tall wooden doors, carved with intricate designs. Both doors were closed.

The rest of the hilltop clearing was taken by a great stone altar, much larger than the modest altar at the temple in Emanuel, with two stone work surfaces off to the side. Thick smoke rose from the altar.

Many priests in white robes were busy around the altar area. Some of the priests held a live goat or a sheep for sacrificing, and others helped with cleaning carcasses of slaughtered animals.

A group of musicians played various instruments, including a gold harp, a silver trumpet, a mahogany flute, a pair of copper tambourines, and several hand drums. A choir of Levite boys sang in thin voices that pierced the air and touched the heart.

Deborah noticed how efficient the sacrifice process was. A priest would place an animal on a stone surface next to the altar and cut its neck with a single slice. The gushing blood drained into a receptacle connected to a channel that went downhill. The intestines were removed and thrown away, the internal organs were placed on the burning altar, and the fleshy parts went on a bed of embers for slow cooking.

Most of the priests were young men, but the one standing over the altar had a long white beard and a breastplate that rivaled Shatz's in its elaborate ornaments.

"That's Mankaliahu Ha'Cohen," Vardit said. "He's the High Priest, the most senior of the elder priests."

Deborah craned her neck to see him better. "Is he the one who enters the Holiest of Holies on the Day of Atonement?"

"That's him. He leads the sacrifices and decides all the affairs of the Holy Tabernacle."

Deborah was filled with awe. "What about the offerings? Doesn't he collect from the pilgrims at the gates?"

"His family takes care of that," Vardit said. "In addition, the other elder priests must give him one-tenth of everything they collect, and he alone receives all the gifts the people give during the ten days between New Year and the Day of Atonement. Besides, every household inside the walls of Shiloh pays taxes, which the elder priests share equally except for the High Priest, who receives a double share."

"You know a lot," Deborah said.

Vardit smiled. "My husband is an ambitious man. He often entertains important visitors, and I'm a good listener."

"You eavesdrop on their conversations?"

"A wise woman keeps her mouth shut but her ears wide open."

Vardit's tone hinted of criticism, which Deborah understood, considering how much trouble she had caused. But the advice made her realize that she would have to learn a lot more if she wanted to survive as a woman in a world run by men. Listening helped a woman gain knowledge and gather information that could be useful, or even lifesaving. Deborah committed Vardit's advice to memory, determined to listen more and speak less.

The smell of burning flesh sickened Deborah. Skirting the altar area, she approached the tall doors in the fence around the Holy Tabernacle and peeked through the crack between the doors. Inside, the structure itself was built with wooden columns and turquoise walls that appeared to be made of fine linen. She could barely breathe, in awe at being so close to the house of God. Her father had once described to her the ornate top of the ancient Ark of the Covenant, with its arching gold seraphs and elaborate adornments. She imagined it resting inside the Holy Tabernacle, only a stone's throw away from where she stood, its splendor glowing with divine holiness.

She knelt and pressed her interwoven fingers under her chin. "Yahweh, God of Israel, I am your servant Deborah, daughter of Harutz. I was going to come here to thank you for helping me discover information about the Elixirist, but instead I must pray for more help. Please deliver me from evil, help me regain my—"

Shouts interrupted her, and the music and singing stopped. She turned to look.

A herd of young Levites in white robes ran toward her, wielding red sticks, yelling, "Impure! Impure! Impure!"

Before Deborah could move, they were upon her, beating her with the red sticks, which were actually bones of sheep and goats that they had picked up from the refuse pile. She cowered and covered her head as they kept yelling, "Impure!" and raining blows on her back.

The two soldiers ran over and pulled Deborah and Vardit away from the irate Levites, who followed them from the Holy Tabernacle to the edge of the hilltop, hurling the bloody bones and yelling, "Impure! Impure! Impure!"

23

When they entered the courtyard, Seesya was standing by the firepit with a few men, chewing on a roasted leg of lamb. The men paused and stared at the two women, who were disheveled and covered in bloodstains.

"It was my mistake," Vardit said. "We went to the Holy Tabernacle. The priests saw her red robe and shooed us away."

"Looks worse than shooing," Seesya said, making the men around him grin. He gestured at Deborah. "Better clean her up before tonight. I don't want my bed getting more filthy than necessary."

This threw the other men into a fit of laughter.

Vardit waited for them to quiet down and said, "Please, Son, may we have a word in private?"

He grunted.

Walking ahead of them, Deborah crossed the courtyard, took the stairwell halfway up to the women's quarters, and stopped to listen.

They reached the bottom of the stairs, just outside the doorway, and stopped.

Seesya cleared his throat and spat.

"I wasn't much older," Vardit said, "when your father possessed me as a wife in his bed. I carried you in my womb for nine month, gave birth in agony, and nursed—"

"Every cow, goat, and sheep does all that."

"It's true." Vardit spoke in a voice so low that Deborah could barely hear her. "But their offspring doesn't have them flogged and humiliated."

He spat again.

"Son, listen to me. She's practically a child, and you should—"

"Is that why you helped her escape from Emanuel?"

"She slipped away while I was asleep. Why don't you believe me?"

Seesya sneered. "You think I'm still a naive little boy, don't you?"

"Sometimes I wish you were still a boy, it's true. I do miss those old, innocent days." Vardit sighed. "You're a grown man now, but you're still my son, about to marry a girl, and I know about—"

"You know nothing. There's a lot riding on that ugly little witch. When I possess her and make her my wife—only then!—we'll have full ownership of Palm Homestead and the endless supply of water from its cistern. All those men of power who kiss my father's ass—the elders in Emanuel, the rich priests of Shiloh—all of them would like nothing better than to use the law against us and tell the people that we don't own Palm Homestead. So hear this, Mother. If the girl escapes again, it'll be the end of you. The end!"

"Son, please, listen to me—"

"If you betray me again," he said, "the flogging will take place in public, for everyone to see, until all the skin peels off your back."

"No! Your father won't allow it!"

"He didn't interfere the first time."

"He will!"

"You think he's still the big man, the judge, the all-powerful ruler? Not anymore. Behind all the pomp and ceremony, Father is an old man who knows I control the soldiers—and the future."

"How dare you?" Her voice broke. "Have you forgotten Yahweh's commandment? 'Honor your father and mother, and your life shall be long on this land that your God gave you.'"

"Don't preach—you of all people. I've seen your manipulations and trickery, how you've gotten Father to do what you wanted."

"I'm your mother," she cried. "Yahweh will punish you!"

"Enough with your Yahweh. I have plenty of gods on my side— better gods, stronger gods."

"Why won't you listen to me? All I do, all my efforts, everything is for your success and happiness. Everything!"

"That's your duty." He spat again. "Make sure she doesn't escape again, that's all."

"If you don't have compassion for me, at least have some for this girl. She'll make a good wife."

"She's a whore like her sister and her mother. I'll prove it tonight and, tomorrow, we'll go back to Emanuel and summon another trial. The tribesmen of Ephraim will enjoy another stoning—a better stoning, not like the last one. I'll make sure that this one goes as it should, that she dies slowly, little by little, one stone at a time, screaming and wailing and suffering like she deserves! And then, I won't have to look at those ugly freckles and orange hair ever again!"

Stunned by the naked venom in Seesya's voice, Deborah ran up the rest of the stairs and went into their room. With shaking hands she reached into her sack, pulled out the waterskin, removed the cork, and gulped water.

Vardit entered the room and closed the door. She pulled off her dress, lay facedown on the mat, and wept into the crook of her arm.

The conversation she had overheard left Deborah with no hope, but seeing Vardit's agony, compassion overtook her own helplessness. She poured Sallan's potion from the clay bottle on her hand and gently rubbed it on Vardit's back. All the welts had developed scabs and appeared to be healing well. She was careful not to disturb the scabs.

Gradually, Vardit calmed down, her breathing slowed, and she fell asleep.

In the late afternoon, Vardit got up and announced with forced cheerfulness, "It's time to get ready!"

She mixed black dye with water in a clay bowl until it was smooth and even. Deborah sat in a chair, removed her scarf, and untied her hair. Vardit applied the dye, starting at the roots.

Surrendering to Vardit's capable hands, Deborah thought about Zariz—his large, warm eyes, which looked at her with fervent longing, his face, bright and sad at the same time. She remembered a similar expression on the face of Barac, son of Abinoam. Both boys had black hair and a dark, handsome complexion. While in reality there were many differences between them, in her mind the two merged, and she wasn't sure who was who. And yet, the orange honeysuckle flowers and their sweet taste would forever be associated with Zariz.

"That's it," Vardit said, stepping back to look at the results of her labor. "We must let the dye dry slowly by itself, or it won't take."

Deborah held up a lock of her hair, now completely black. "I don't have my mother's hair anymore."

"In less than a year, you'll be a mother yourself. But in the meantime, since your mother is no longer alive, it's my responsibility to tell you what to expect tonight."

A shudder went through Deborah. "I don't want to talk about it."

"I understand how you feel, but unfortunately, you really need to know."

"I know what to expect. I've seen animals do it."

Vardit caressed her cheek. "You're not an animal."

But Seesya is, Deborah wanted to say, yet she didn't. Having overheard the conversation between Vardit and her son earlier, she felt sorry for the older woman.

"I want to know only one thing," she said. "Will it hurt?"

"For a short time," Vardit said. "Until he's done. Usually new husbands get very excited, finish quickly, and let you go back to the women's quarters to dry your tears and clean up." Vardit hesitated. "Blood comes out, but not thick and gooey like your female blood. When a girl loses her virginity, the blood is bright red and thin, as if blood from a fresh cut had been mixed with a bit of water."

A film of sweat covered Deborah's face.

Vardit handed her the waterskin. "Drink. You'll feel better."

Taking a few sips, she tried to calm down.

"All this talk of blood," Vardit said, "can make even a hardy girl scared. Think of it as spilled pomegranate juice, because that's how it will look on your bed cloth."

"What if there is no blood?"

"Have you—?"

"I've never been with a man, but neither had Tamar, and look what happened to her."

Vardit went to the window. She looked out for a few minutes, her breathing belabored, as if she was struggling not to cry.

"Please," Deborah said. "Tell me what to do."

"Some virgin girls don't bleed," Vardit finally said. "It's how they're made down there, or how the man is doing it. No one can tell."

"How can a bride know beforehand if she's going to bleed or not?"

"It doesn't matter, as long as she makes sure her new husband thinks she bled—the more the better. I've heard men brag about how much their wives bled on the first night, as if it were proof of their virility. Oddly childish, isn't it?"

Deborah looked at her, confused.

"You're not the first bride to worry about it," Vardit said. "Every girl is taught by her mother to produce blood, just to be safe."

"You mean—"

"As soon as the man is done, while he's busy catching his breath, cleaning himself, or getting dressed, the bride checks herself for blood. If there's none, she puts in a finger and gets it going."

Deborah sucked air in shock, covering her mouth.

"Show me your hands." Vardit pointed at the right-hand forefinger. "This one has the longest nail. Put it in and scratch really hard until you feel blood."

"Hurt myself?"

"That's the whole point."

"I could get sick, or lose the ability to bear children!"

"Would you rather have your new husband complain you're not a virgin? Besides, usually it heals just fine."

"Oh, dear Yahweh!" Deborah hugged herself, rocking back and forth. "This is terrible!"

"It's not as terrible as other pains we suffer—like childbirth, for example."

"No, I mean it's terrible that Tamar didn't know what to do."

"She did know," Vardit said. "I told her. But some girls aren't capable of doing what's necessary. They're afraid of the pain, or think it's wrong to start marriage with a lie."

"Is that what Tamar said to you?"

"She said she'd do it. That's why I was shocked when her bed cloth was clean and Seesya accused her."

"Did you ask her afterward?"

"She was locked away, guarded by Seesya's soldiers until the trial. I'll always wonder why she didn't scratch like I told her." Vardit touched Deborah's hair. "The dye isn't dry yet. Stand in the window to let the breeze through your hair. I'll go wash and change in the meantime."

Alone in the room, Deborah stood at the window and watched the preparations below. Slaves used brooms and water from the well to clean the courtyard. They replaced the torches on the walls and piled fresh wood by the firepit. Across the courtyard, they hung sheets of cloth to hide the workshop, where bare-chested slaves continued to clean the bloody cowhides. Along the inner part of the courtyard, where steps led into the main house, servants arranged tables and covered them with linen.

All these preparations for her wedding to Seesya felt unreal to Deborah, as if some other girl would be getting married tonight—a happy girl, a girl filled with gratitude for marrying a judge's first son, a girl who didn't know Seesya's dark heart and wasn't aware of what he had done to Tamar.

Vardit's latest revelation haunted Deborah. Why had Tamar failed to make herself bleed? Had she been reluctant to self-inflict an injury on her most intimate parts, or unwilling to perpetuate deceit at the outset of her marriage? It occurred to Deborah that her own reaction to Vardit's advice might be instructive. She was terrified of actually doing it, and Tamar had probably felt the same, but whatever the reason, she had paid dearly for failing to make herself bleed.

Now, knowing what she had to do in Seesya's bed, Deborah doubted whether she could actually do it. Should she try to escape again? If only she could find a way to sneak out of Shiloh. And then? She would travel to Aphek, find Kassite and convince him to help her become a boy before Seesya hunted her down. Her chances were slim, at best. It had been eighteen years since Oran bought the slave. Kassite could be serving a second owner, or a third, or be dead and buried for years with no one to tell her one way or the other. But still, he was the Elixirist, a man of great wisdom and abilities. Surely he had survived and could help her. And then—no more girl, no more betrothal, no more marriage to the evil Seesya!

Her hopes quickly faded under the weight of reality. She was a prisoner. There was no way to get away from here, and no chance of avoiding tonight's marriage. Could she bring herself to draw blood? And even if she produced enough blood to soak her bed cloth, would Seesya let her live much longer? A husband who didn't fear Yahweh could find a hundred ways to cause his wife's death, and no one would hold him accountable.

Her hands were shaking, and she clasped them together. Zariz had said: "Listen to your fear, but don't let it control you." Why was she unable to assert control? Why was she yielding to her fear? Sallan had promised that the Reinforcing Liquid would grow more effective with time and make her increasingly stronger. Why was she feeling weaker?

Deborah inhaled and blew air through pursed lips. She had to think as a strong person would. Her immediate survival depended on proving her virginity beyond doubt so that Seesya wouldn't be able to put her on trial. But what about the future? Abinoam had said, "Even the most wretched young man grows up to love his children and respect his children's mothers." Did the prediction apply to Seesya? Was he capable of change? Deborah didn't think so. Hadn't he subjected his own mother to flogging? Hadn't he threatened Vardit with even worse punishment? If he could be so vicious and cruel to his own mother, wouldn't he be worse to a wife he'd openly hated from the start? Deborah had no doubt that, once he won full ownership of Palm Homestead, Seesya would find a way to end her life.

Her conclusion was simple, born not out of fear, but out of facts. Seesya would never change, and she would never be safe as his wife. This conclusion made Vardit's advice impractical. Injuring herself in the most tender and sensitive part of her body could make Deborah bedridden for days, or even weeks. No. She had to survive the first night while remaining healthy and strong in order to run away as soon as possible.

Still at the window, Deborah returned her attention to the scene below. She watched as one of the soldiers guarding the stairwell hurled a piece of fruit across the courtyard, hitting a slave. Startled, the slave dropped a bucket of water on his bare feet and screamed in pain, which made the soldiers laugh.

After a moment of anger and disgust at this cruelty, Deborah had an idea. She tied a scarf over her head, took her waterskin, and left the room. Halfway down the stairs, she ran into Vardit.

"I'll be right back," Deborah said. "I'm going to fill my waterskin with clean water from the well."

"Don't do anything stupid."

"I won't."

When Deborah came out, the two soldiers got up. She held up her waterskin and pointed at the well.

They nodded and watched her go.

The bucket was at the bottom of the well. She turned the handle on the pulley to raise the full bucket, uncorked the waterskin, and dipped it in the water until it swelled about halfway. Taking a sip, she swirled the cold water in her mouth before swallowing, and glanced at the soldiers furtively. They were sitting on empty wine barrels, chatting again.

Making her way slowly across the courtyard, Deborah watched the slaves hanging sheets over the open wall of the workshop. On the right side were several open carts with piles of cowhides and other animal skins, ready for shipment. A large wooden container held discarded clumps of bloody flesh and fur that had been removed from the skins.

She leaned against the container, her back to it, and watched the courtyard. Up close, the stench of blood and rotting flesh was nauseating. The workers glanced at her, but she took her time, looking around with feigned interest. She took another sip from the waterskin and left it open. When no one was looking, she put the cork in her pocket, reached behind with her free hand into the waste container, and felt around for a small piece of meat. It was slippery, but she managed to grasp it with her fingers and push it in through the narrow neck of her waterskin.

Glancing around to make sure no one was paying attention to her, Deborah reached back into the waste container for another piece.

In all, Deborah got four bits of bloody animal meat into her waterskin before the soldiers started to eye her curiously. She pretended to sip from the waterskin one last time, corked it, and crossed the courtyard at a leisurely pace. Once inside, on the way upstairs, she pressed the waterskin to her chest to squeeze the blood out of the pieces of meat inside, pressing as hard as she could. Her life would depend on it tonight.

24

The sun had set, and its afterglow painted the sky red. The purifying bath, located near the slave cages at the bottom of the hill, was a rectangular hole in the ground, three steps by six steps, plastered thickly to keep the water from seeping into the ground. Yahweh's law required impure women to immerse in fresh water. A system of channels from several nearby roofs brought in rainwater a few times a year, and a wooden cover kept the water from evaporating during the hot days. A straw canopy and side curtains provided privacy. Every woman in Shiloh came here at the end of her seven days of impurity. Because the water was replaced only when rain came, the purifying bath was far from clean.

Under Vardit's watchful eye, Deborah put aside her waterskin, took off the red robe and scarf, as well as her undergarments, and entered the murky pool. The water felt warm against her naked skin. She knew that nothing could be lurking beneath the dark surface of the water, but her imagination was fueled by her anxiety, and she expected a rat or a snake to bite her. Quickly, she pinched her nose and immersed completely once, twice, and a third time. As she climbed out, Vardit poured clean water over her from a bowl, waited while Deborah rubbed her body with a rag, and poured another bowl over her.

Drying herself with clean cloth, Deborah said, "At least this part is over."

"It's the first time of many—every month or so for the rest of your days, except when you're pregnant, or if you live to the old age of fifty or more, when your monthly blood dries out."

"I don't know if I'll live until tomorrow, let alone to age fifty."

"Don't say that. You'll live for many years and have many babies." Vardit handed her clean undergarments and a white dress. "It's the best thing about being pregnant—no bleeding, and therefore no impurity and no immersion in the dirty purifying bath."

"People are waiting," Obadiah of Levi said from outside the curtains. "Is it done?"

"Almost." Vardit helped Deborah put on the dress and tie a scarf over her hair. "Ready now."

The priest came into the enclosure. "Did she immerse completely three times?"

"I witnessed it," Vardit said.

"Was there any sign of blood?"

"No."

"Very well," he said. "She is ready for her husband."

Vardit fixed a sheer white veil over Deborah's face and pinned it to the scarf.

"We'll start the procession now," Obadiah said, turning to leave.

"And then what?" Deborah ignored Vardit's restraining hand. "We go back to Emanuel, where you'll pronounce me a whore and let them stone me like Tamar?"

The priest paused. He leaned on his staff and sighed. "For your sake, girl, and for my sake as well, I pray that the bed cloth is stained tonight. Otherwise, even Yahweh in all His glory won't be able to save you."

The street outside was filled with people. While most marriages started with a simple blessing by a priest and a consummation in the husband's bed, wealthy families held more elaborate celebrations in their homes, with food and music to entertain guests. Yet only powerful judges and rich priests celebrated their sons' weddings with large processions and animal sacrifices. Tamar had also been taken by a procession from the purifying bath in Emanuel to the house of Judge Zifron. However, this procession was even larger than Tamar's, reminding Deborah of the Edomite proverb that Sallan had quoted: "The higher the rise, the steeper the fall."

Right in front of the exit from the bath was the huge black stallion, Seesya's gift to Shatz. Two stable boys held the silver bridle, and two female servants helped Deborah climb onto the elaborate leather saddle. The white dress was loose, so Deborah sat sideways on the saddle. She began to slide off, but Vardit noticed what was happening and supported Deborah's legs until the two servants could push her back up. Once her weight was balanced, she held steady with a firm grip on the saddle horn.

Shaken up, Deborah had a nagging feeling that she'd forgotten something, but the procession began to move forward. At the front was Obadiah of Levi, walking with his oak staff. Behind him were a dozen Levites, also in white robes, tapping on tambourines and hand drums. She recognized some of their faces from the group that had beaten her with bloody bones at the Holy Tabernacle that morning.

Suddenly she remembered. "My waterskin!" She looked around, spotting Vardit close by. "I forgot my waterskin—it's still in there!"

Vardit hurried back and soon returned with the waterskin. Deborah hung it from her neck by the strap.

A choir of boys commenced singing the traditional wedding hymn, whose lyrics described the marriages of Jacob and his two wives—the older and wiser Leah and the younger and prettier Rachel. The boys sang with the same angelic, thin voices that had touched her heart in the morning, though now she felt nothing but dread.

The procession turned onto the main street and headed up the hill. People came out of the houses along the street to watch. Some of them joined the singing, as the words were familiar to all. The blacksmith, Nehoshtan, came out with his wife and children, and they watched her go by.

The slow rocking made her queasy. She shut her eyes and tried to calm down. A memory came to her of riding the giant eagle in her sleep as it dropped through the clouds like a bird of prey on the attack. The vision was so vivid that she opened her eyes to make it go away. Had it been a forewarning about her helpless fall into a forced marriage, which would cut her life short as if she fell from the sky to the hard ground?

The procession reached Shatz Ha'Cohen's house and entered through the tall wooden doors under the great silver menorah. The Levites divided into two groups, creating a passage in the middle of the courtyard, and continued to tap the drums. The stable boys led the horse by the silver bridle to the firepit, and the servants helped her down.

A modest wood-and-stone altar had been set up for the occasion. Obadiah stood beside the altar, leaning on his staff, breathing heavily from the hike.

The singing stopped, and Shatz appeared at the doors to the main house, his arm interlocked with Seesya's. Through the sheer veil, Deborah saw that Seesya had put on a clean black coat, embroidered with gold like the coat she'd seen his father wear, and had oiled his shoulder-length hair, combing it back from his scarred face.

A servant brought over a white goat, its front and back legs bound together, and placed it on the altar. Lying on its side, the goat bleated and moved its legs back and forth in a futile attempt to run away.

"We're gathered here," Shatz announced, "on this seventeenth night in the month of Av, to bind in marriage under Yahweh's laws this man, Seesya, son of Zifron of Ephraim, to his betrothed bride, Deborah, daughter of Harutz of Ephraim.

Seesya tugged at the lapels of his coat and shifted his shoulders as if he were uncomfortable in this non-militant outfit.

"With this offering," Shatz continued, "we ask Yahweh to sanctify this marriage, make the bride's womb fertile, and give her many sons to continue her husband's name."

Everyone chorused, "Amen."

Raising a knife over the goat's neck, Shatz recited the traditional marriage blessing: "Blessed be Yahweh, our God, king of the world, who created man in His own image and made the woman to lust after her husband and obey him in all matters until death."

The goat bleated desperately as the servant lifted its tied legs so that its neck faced up. The knife came down and, with a single slice, opened the goat's neck from side to side. The bleating ceased as blood burst from the severed neck, but the goat continued to jerk its legs back and forth rapidly while the servant struggled to hold the dying animal in place.

A squirt of blood darted off in the struggle and stained Seesya's cheek. He laughed, wiping it on his sleeve.

Deborah groaned and looked away. The courtyard began to spin around her, and the numerous burning torches gradually gave way to darkness as she collapsed to the ground.

25

When Deborah regained consciousness, she found herself in Seesya's arms, her head on his shoulder, her veiled face in his oily hair.

She convulsed and turned her face away. "Put me down!"

"Look happy," he said quietly, maintaining a wide smile while people showered them with seeds of wheat and barley.

"Let me go!"

"Shut up, or I'll break your back on my knee."

Up three steps, he paused in front of the main entrance to the house and turned to face the full courtyard. A final volley of seeds flew at them, everyone clapped, the music grew louder, and the choir sang, "You, you shall be fruitful and multiply, you shall swarm the earth and procreate, you shall fill the land."

The singing continued in the courtyard while Seesya carried her into the main part of Shatz's house. The floors were paved in blocks of limestone and the walls were smoothly plastered. Seesya's steps echoed as he marched across the main room and down a hallway. Behind them, Obadiah walked more slowly, his oak staff tapping the hard floor.

They entered a room. Seesya set her down on her feet. Vardit and two girl-servants were waiting. They took her behind a partition, removed her veil and scarf, and helped her out of the white dress and undergarments. They held up an oversize gown that was open in front, like a linen sheet with sleeves. This was her bed cloth, and it was stark white and clear of any blemish. She turned, put her arms through the sleeves, and closed the front lapels over one another to cover her nakedness.

Seesya clapped. "Get on with it, women."

"She's ready," Vardit said, adjusting Deborah's black-dyed hair around her shoulders so that it framed her face.

They stepped out from behind the partition.

"Look, Son," Vardit said. "Look how beautiful she is."

Seeing Deborah without the veil and scarf for the first time, Seesya's eyes widened and he burst out laughing. "In the name of Mott, what have you done to her? Wasn't she ugly enough already?"

Vardit's face turned red.

Deborah took her waterskin from Vardit's hand. "I'll be fine. You can leave now."

"Yes," Seesya said. "Leave us."

Vardit and the two servant girls left the room and joined Obadiah outside. They would wait behind the closed door, as tradition dictated.

"Look at this." Seesya held up a lock of her hair, peering at it closely, shaking his head, still chuckling. "I was born of a stupid woman."

"Your mother's only trying to help," Deborah said.

He slapped her across the face, throwing her to the floor.

Dazed with shock, Deborah touched her burning cheek.

Standing over her, he raised his hand for another strike. "Did I ask you a question?"

"No," she said. "You didn't."

"Never speak unless I ask you a question. Understood?"

"Yes."

"That's a start." Seesya grabbed her arm, pulled her up, and pushed her toward the bed. "Let's get it over with."

The large bed had been made with soft linen sheets, oversized pillows, and wool covers. At the head of the bed, staring at her with beady eyes, were effigies of the Canaanite deities—Baal Ammon, the god of fertility, and his wife Ashtoreth, whose naked breasts and exposed genitals made Deborah look away.

She sat on the bed, clutching the waterskin. "May I ask you a question?"

He frowned but nodded.

"We're in Shiloh, the home of the Holy Tabernacle of Yahweh, who gave us the Ten Commandments, which include 'You shall have no other gods before me,' and 'make any graven image or likeness—'"

Seesya raised his hand over her, and Deborah scooted back on the bed.

"That's better," he said. "No more talking."

She slipped the waterskin under the pillows, lay back, and closed her eyes. Her cheek hurt and her heart pounded, but she felt no fear. Heeding Sallan's advice, she had come here with a strategy for survival, for living another day. She would escape again, renew her search for the Elixirist, and win real freedom.

The sounds of Seesya taking off his clothes were followed by splashing water. She opened her eyes and saw him urinating into a clay bucket in the corner of the room, facing away from her. His back was white where it was usually covered with clothes and armor, though his buttocks were red, perhaps from spending so much time in the saddle.

Seesya glanced over his shoulder and saw her looking. "What? Never seen a man urinate?"

"Is this a question?"

"Yes, it is." He shook himself over the bucket. "You may answer."

"I saw a dog do it once. He did it while lifting his leg, but the sound was the same."

"Feisty, aren't we?" He grimaced. "Turn away. I don't want to see your face."

She looked at the wall while he paced around the room and put out the lamps, leaving only a small one near the bed.

Without warning, he grasped her legs and twisted her over, face down. "Get on all fours," he said hoarsely. "Same as a dog."

She obeyed, and felt him lift the bottom of her bed cloth, exposing her rear.

"Your skin's like spoiled cheese," he said, "with dots like heads of maggots." He smacked her buttocks a few times.

Deborah gritted her teeth at the pain but made no sound.

He pressed his crotch against her, slapped her some more, and rubbed against her. His body odor made her sick, and she breathed deeply through her mouth, telling herself that the worst would soon be over. She could feel that he was limp, unable to penetrate her. She felt satisfaction, but also sadness, thinking of Tamar.

"Little witch." He smacked her buttocks some more. "You're doing this to me on purpose, aren't you?"

"I'm doing nothing," she said.

"Get on your back!"

Deborah turned, adjusted the bed cloth under her, and opened her legs while looking aside at the white wall.

Seesya pinched her breasts.

She yelped in pain.

"Flat as unleavened bread. What are you, a boy?"

"I wish."

He slapped her. "That was a question that didn't need an answer."

"You're hurting me," she said.

Slapping her again, harder, back and forth across her face, he yelled, "I told you to shut up!"

Deborah clenched her teeth and pressed her lips together, determined not to give him the pleasure of her crying.

"Moan!" He slapped her some more. "Moan!"

She wouldn't.

"Moan, witch!" He hit her harder, switching hands, left and right across her face. "Moan!"

It hurt like fire, and despite her best efforts, she began to cry.

"That's it! Cry!" He dropped on top of her, his crotch pressing down, and moved forcefully against her. Despite these exertions, he remained limp.

Turning her face away from the stench of garlic his mouth exuded, she tried to imagine herself in a better place.

"Cry, witch!" He grabbed a fistful of her hair and pulled hard. "Scream!"

She did, and as the middle of his body kept colliding against her, her screams sounded like broken bleats, as if she were a goat. He kept pulling her hair and pounding his midriff against her for what seemed like eternity, yet through all of it he remained limp and did not enter her.

All of a sudden, he stopped moving, rolled off her, and howled like a man in great pain.

Excited voices filtered through the closed door.

Seesya got off the bed and started putting on his clothes.

"That's why Tamar didn't bleed." Deborah pulled the lapels of the bed cloth over to cover her nakedness. "You couldn't perform."

He leaned over and whacked her on the face. "Keep your mouth shut!"

"I'm as good as dead," she said. "At least you can indulge me with answers."

"It's all your fault," he said. "I have no problem performing with ten whores in a single night, but the way you and your sister look, the same white, freckled face as your mother—"

"My mother? You knew my mother?"

He clenched a fist near her face. "One more word out of you, and your teeth will be scattered all over the floor."

Deborah cupped her mouth and yelled toward the door, "I discovered the reason why there's—"

Seesya punched her on the side of the head, and while she was momentarily stunned, he pulled a knife from a hip sheath and spoke in a low voice into her ear. "If you say anything, I'll kill you, my mother, Obadiah, and the two servant girls. And then I'll go outside and blame it on a couple of slaves, and kill them, too. Do you want all that blood on your hands?"

Shaking her head, she whispered, "Don't you fear Yahweh?"

"Why should I?" Seesya grinned, tapping the blade on his forearm. "Yahweh loves me. All the gods love me. Otherwise, why would they give me power, wealth, and the future of a king?" He was about to sheath the knife, but held it out and showed it to her. "Do you recognize this knife?"

She looked at the knife, which had a simple bronze blade and a wooden handle with carved lines running across it. She shook her head.

"You don't?" He laughed, putting it away. "My soldiers took it from your friend, Abinoam's boy, before we chopped off his head and kicked it around like a ball."

The image of Barac's head rolling in the dust was too terrible to bear. Deborah gripped her hands together, bit on her knuckles, and groaned.

A knock came from the door, and Deborah started to rise.

"Stay down!" Seesya pushed her back on the bed, turned her over roughly, pressed her wrists together behind her back, and tied them with a strap.

"What are you doing?"

"You think I was born yesterday?" He pulled on the strap to make sure it was tight. "We all know about those old women's tricks, busy fingers with long nails going where they shouldn't."

"Untie me!"

He turned her over so that she was sitting with her bound wrists out of sight. "That's a good girl—as good as your sister."

Deborah was crushed by the realization—that's why Tamar hadn't been able to follow Vardit's advice!

Seesya headed to the door, pausing to straighten his coat.

As overwhelmed as she was by the double shock of Barac's death and Tamar's tragedy, the smugness in Seesya's voice ignited a fiery rage in Deborah. She was determined not to let him win again!

Deborah slid her hips further back in the bed until her tied hands found the pillows. She slipped her fingers underneath and felt around for the waterskin.

Seesya reached the door and prepared to unlock it.

"Your hair," Deborah said as her fingers touched the waterskin. "It looks like a horse tail soaked in piss."

He brushed his hair with his hands. "When I cast the first stone at you, I'll aim at your mouth—that's a promise."

By feel, she grasped the neck of the waterskin and pulled out the cork. Seesya unlocked the door.

She tilted the waterskin and let it drain on the bed behind her buttocks.

Pulling open the door, Seesya announced to those outside, "What did I tell you?"

Deborah recorked the waterskin behind her back.

"Same as her sister," he said.

She shoved the waterskin as far as she could under the pillows and scooted backward to sit on the wet area.

Obadiah of Levi and Vardit entered the room.

Seesya pointed at Deborah. "My new wife, the whore."

Deborah felt the wetness spread under her, soaking the bed cloth and the sheets. She leaned back, reclining on the pillows.

Pushing past Seesya, Vardit approached the bed, followed by Obadiah. The servant girls lighted all the lamps.

"I'm hurting badly," Deborah said, tears flowing down her cheeks, which still burned from his beating. "Everything hurts."

"Look!" Vardit pointed, a smile spreading across her face. "There's blood under her!"

"What are you talking about?" Seesya hurried over.

Deborah sat up with effort, shifting about to make sure the blood stuck to her private parts.

"That's impossible," Seesya said.

Deborah tilted her body sideways, lifting her bottom to reveal the sheets underneath.

Obadiah bent and gazed closely. "This is the way a healthy maiden bleeds on her wedding night. Very good."

"I'm in pain," Deborah said, which wasn't a lie, though her pain wasn't where they assumed it was. "All over," she added.

"That's normal," Vardit said.

"Impossible!" Seesya was beside himself. "She did something to herself!"

"How could I?" Deborah turned to show them her bound wrists. "He tied me up."

Vardit groaned and released the knots.

"A virgin," Obadiah said. "No doubt about it."

"That's right," Vardit said. "A good girl."

"Very well." The priest pounded his staff on the floor three times. "May Yahweh bless this marriage with many sons." As he turned to leave, the figurines of the Canaanite deities caught his eye. He raised his cane and pushed them off the shelf.

Vardit leaped forward and caught the effigies before they hit the floor. She wrapped them in a rag and put them away.

Obadiah shook his head and left the room, followed by Seesya, who paused at the door and turned to glare at Deborah.

"Good night, husband," she said.

He spat on the floor and left the room.

"Come, my child." Vardit helped her off the bed. "Let's clean you up."

Reaching back, Deborah pulled the waterskin from under the pillows. Going behind the partition, she dipped a rag in a bowl of fresh water, washed the blood from her crotch and thighs, and put on the undergarments and dress.

"He had tied Tamar's hands, too," she said. "That's why she couldn't scratch herself."

Vardit sighed. "The past is the past. Today, the gods helped my son perform his duty, and you bled as a healthy virgin. Praised be the gods."

Deborah hung the waterskin around her neck, pressing it to her chest in silent gratitude. She could feel the small chunks inside.

As they prepared to leave the room, the door flew open and Seesya reappeared. "It's a trick," he yelled. "The witch did it!"

"You tied her hands," Vardit said. "How could she?"

"Maybe you helped her again."

"How could I do such a thing? It's madness."

"You left something here. I know it!" He pulled the pillows and covers off the bed, shaking them, then did the same with the stained sheets and the bed cloth. "Where is it?"

Vardit took Deborah's arm and pulled her toward the door.

"Stay here!" Seesya put his hand on the handle of the knife. "I'll cut your heads off! Both of you!"

"I don't understand," Vardit said. "Why are you upset? Everything is fine. It's the way things are supposed to be."

Finding nothing on the bed, he looked under it, then pushed aside the mattress. "It's somewhere here, I know it!"

Obadiah reappeared in the doorway, together with Shatz. The two priests watched Seesya with concern.

"That blood wasn't hers!" Seesya pointed at Deborah. "She brought it in here somehow!" He went around the room, knocked down the partition, and sifted through the pile of clothes on the floor—her white wedding dress, sheer veil, and the wet rag she had used to clean up. "Where is it?"

"Young man," Shatz said, "what exactly are you looking for?"

Seesya groaned in frustration. "I don't know. A bottle, a jar, something that held the blood."

"That's a false accusation." Obadiah rested his hand on his breastplate. "The blood came from the girl. I saw it."

"It didn't come from her," Seesya shouted. He went back to the bed and ruffled the sheets and covers. "It's in this room."

With her waterskin in plain view, Deborah knew what she had to do to save her life.

Seesya picked up the sodden bed cloth and sniffed it. "It smells rotten," he said.

She uncorked the waterskin and brought it to her lips. Her cheeks and jaws hurt from the beating, but she ignored the pain.

"Let me smell the cloth," Obadiah said.

Taking a sip from the waterskin, Deborah swallowed, shuddering at the sour taste and sticky consistency of the bloody water.

The priest took the bed cloth and raised it to his nose.

Steeling herself, Deborah drank the remaining liquid.

"There's always an odor," Obadiah said. "It's normal. Some girls smell worse than others."

"Smell?" Seesya shook the bed cloth. "It stinks!"

"My young friend," Shatz said, "you don't smell like pomegranate flowers, either."

Obadiah laughed.

Tilting the waterskin straight up, Deborah pressed on it to expel the pieces of meat through the narrow neck and into her mouth.

"Let me," Vardit said, taking the bed cloth from Seesya and smelling it. She twisted her face. "It's sharp, but I've smelled worse."

Deborah held her breath and swallowed the mushy lumps whole, afraid that any chewing would give her away. Her stomach heaved, but she kept it down.

Seesya drew his sword and cut through the mattress. "I'll find it—even if I have to tear this room apart."

"I assume," Shatz said, "that you're going to pay for the damage."

Obadiah pounded his staff on the floor. "Seesya, son of Zifron! I've witnessed the bed cloth, and I'll testify that you have possessed her, and that she was a virgin."

"There you go," Shatz said. "You own Palm Homestead free and clear now. There's no need for this craziness."

Deborah again tilted the waterskin over her mouth to make sure it was drained completely, forcing the last few drops down her throat. Immediately, bile came up, and she swallowed, forcing it down, struggling not to vomit.

"It's a trick!" Seesya shouted, pointing at her. "How did you do it, witch?"

She didn't answer.

His eyes focused on the waterskin, and he stepped over, tearing it out of her hands. He held it upside down and shook it, but nothing came out.

"This smell is normal." Vardit dropped the bed cloth on the floor. "We women smell different during each part of the cycle of our female—"

"Shut up, Mother!" He threw away the waterskin and roamed around the room, kicking at things. "Damn witch!"

"That's enough," Shatz said. "Your father will disapprove of this behavior."

Deborah picked up the waterskin with a shaking hand and plugged it.

"Let's go." Vardit led her to the door and out of the room, leaving the two priests with her son.

Halfway down the hallway, a belch caused bile to shoot up into Deborah's mouth. The urge to vomit was overwhelming, but she resisted, trembling in disgust.

"Easy now." Vardit patted her on the back. "The worst is over."

Deborah managed to say, "Thank you."

"No reason to thank me." Holding the door open, Vardit smiled. "You're my daughter now."

Out in the courtyard, music was playing and the guests were having a good time, eating, drinking, and talking. Vardit stopped to hand the rag with the two Canaanite gods to one of the servants. Deborah's stomach heaved again, worse than before. She looked around desperately for a place to vomit. Guests stared at her, probably because her face was bruised from Seesya's slaps. She hurried to the well.

The bucket was full, resting next to the well. Deborah knelt beside it, splashed water on her face while bending forward over the drain channel, and vomited. Everything came up with painful spasms until her stomach emptied up. She splashed her face again and tipped the bucket over. The water washed away the red liquid and lumps down the drain channel along the wall of the courtyard, mixing up with the accumulated waste.

A servant took the bucket from her hand and lowered it into the well, drawing fresh water. When the bucket came up full, she filled her waterskin, shook it, and emptied it into the drain channel. She filled it up again and plugged it.

The three men emerged from the house. Seesya's eyes found Deborah. Staring back at him, she scooped fresh water from the bucket, rinsed her mouth, and spat on the ground. She was feeling much better.

26

After the guests had left, the slaves began to clean the courtyard. They dragged tables back to storage, poured buckets of water all over the courtyard, and used brooms and brushes to push the litter out to the street. Deborah stood at the window of the room she shared with Vardit and watched through a crack between the curtains. When the slaves were done, they snuffed out most of the torches and went to the slaves' quarters in the back of the house. A soldier came out of a guardroom next to the courtyard's exit and locked the heavy doors under the silver menorah. She hoped to see where he placed the key, but there wasn't enough light.

"Finally, it's quiet," Vardit said. "We can go to sleep now."

Deborah sat next to Vardit and rubbed Sallan's potion on her back, which continued to improve.

"You're a good girl," Vardit said. "I've always hoped to live long enough to have grandchildren, and now it'll finally happen."

Deborah's hand paused.

"What's wrong?" Vardit asked.

"You've been good to me," Deborah said. "I want you to know the truth."

"What truth?"

"Your grandchildren will not come from my womb."

"How do you know?" Vardit sat up. "You bled while your hands were tied, which means that Seesya possessed you. Some girls get pregnant after the first time."

Deborah wiped her hands. "Or get stoned to death."

"Tamar didn't bleed. She was lying back on the pillows with her hands behind her back. That's why we didn't see her bound wrists when we checked for blood. He's a clever boy, my son."

Deborah took a deep breath. "He didn't do it," she said.

"Do what?"

Deborah blushed. "Tamar didn't bleed because Seesya didn't possess her."

"Don't say such a thing!"

"It's true. He admitted it to me."

Vardit inhaled sharply and burst into tears.

"I'm sorry," Deborah said. "It's the truth. His false accusation caused Tamar's stoning, and he would have done the same to me."

"Not to you." Vardit wiped her eyes. "I saw your blood with my own eyes."

"It wasn't my blood."

Vardit took a moment to digest the news. "How did you do it?"

"That's not important. He'll find another way to kill me. You must help me escape."

Vardit got up and went to the window, where she pushed the curtains aside and breathed in the night air. "If you escape, he'll punish me. At my age, a bad flogging could mean death."

"Then come with me." Deborah joined her at the window and looked below. The soldiers were gone from the stairwell entry. "They're not guarding me anymore. We could leave now. No one would notice until tomorrow, and by that time we'd be far away."

Vardit grasped her arm. "Listen to me, child. Some young men are too nervous the first night. My son is strong and fearless in battle, but he's only nineteen. This isn't his home, and with everything that's happened with your sister, and you running away—it put a lot of pressure on him. Tomorrow we'll go back to Emanuel, and you'll be able to find a way to his heart."

"How?"

"Be nice to him."

"Nice?"

"Smile a lot, take him food, show him he can be comfortable with you. One night, when he feels the need, he'll summon you to his bed and be able to do it."

The possibility of another bedroom encounter with Seesya sickened Deborah. "I must escape," she said. "I have no choice."

"Escaping is useless. It's a miracle you made it to Shiloh. A girl traveling alone with no protection is in a worse situation than one in a difficult marriage."

"Worse than death?"

"Death is easy. It's the things men do to you before death that you should fear." Vardit held Deborah's shoulders and shook her. "Don't even think of escaping. Give Seesya a chance to know you, and he will give you a chance to be a good wife."

"And if he remains evil?"

"Then I'll go to my husband and beg him to order Seesya to divorce you and let you go. My son may be stubborn and immature, but my husband is still in charge."

Deborah realized that the threat of more flogging terrified Vardit too much for her to consider anything other than submission. "I'll wait," she said. "But not for long."

"That's a wise choice."

"On one condition," Deborah said. "If he tries to kill me, you'll help me escape, whatever the risk to yourself."

"He won't try to kill you. You're his wife now. Hurting you would be like hurting himself."

"But if he does, will you help me?"

"I will." Vardit took Deborah in her arms. "You have my word."

The embrace took Deborah by surprise, especially because it wasn't perfunctory, as between distant relatives, but as tight and as lasting as a mother's hug, which Deborah hadn't felt since the year before. Her arms rose to encircle Vardit and hug her back, but made it only halfway before dropping limply by her sides. As much as Deborah longed for the comforting warmth of a mother's love again, she knew without a doubt that at the moment of truth Vardit wouldn't be able to keep her promise. She was Seesya's mother, and no matter what new and worse evil he did, her love would always belong to him.

27

Deborah woke up from deep sleep, opened her eyes, and saw a figure holding a burning torch. She couldn't see who it was, but recognized the voice when Seesya said, "I know how you did it, witch."

Vardit sat up. "Who's there?"

"Your beloved son," Seesya said, handing the torch to his mother. "Hold this steady."

She took the torch. "What's wrong?"

Seesya went around the room, throwing things around, until he found Deborah's waterskin. He picked it up, drew a knife, and cut through the waterskin. Water spilled on the floor.

He held the waterskin under the light of the torch, pulled it apart, and examined the inside.

"Damn you," he said. "You washed it clean."

Deborah got up and stepped to the door.

"Stay where you are!"

She stood still.

"Looks like we'll have to do it the hard way." Seesya tossed the mutilated waterskin aside and pointed his knife at her, approaching slowly. "Confess now, or I'll rearrange your face to make you look like your sister and mother—after they died!"

"Please, Son." Vardit moved closer, the torch shaking in her hand. "She's only a child."

He grabbed Deborah by the neck and put the knife to her cheek. "Speak up!"

"Leave her alone," Vardit pleaded. "The women in the next room will wake up and call the soldiers. You must go now."

He let go of Deborah's neck and hit his mother, who cried out and almost dropped the torch.

Taking advantage of that distraction, Deborah ran from him to the other side of the room, grabbed her sack from the floor, and raced to the window. She'd gotten one leg over the sill before he caught her, threw her to the floor, and placed his boot on her chest, pressing down.

"That's better." He sheathed the knife. "Raise a hand when you're ready to tell me how you got all that blood on the bed cloth."

With the weight of his rough sole on her chest, Deborah couldn't breathe. Her sack rested on the floor by her head. She reached up with both hands and tried to open it.

Now on her knees, Vardit grasped his wrist. "In the name of your father, my husband, I ask you to leave."

"Don't interfere!"

"Do you want everyone to know what really happened on your wedding night, that you couldn't—"

Without moving his boot from Deborah's chest, he grabbed the front of Vardit's robe, clenched his free fist, and punched her between the eyes. As she swayed, he took the torch from her hand, raised it, and landed its hard base on her head.

Vardit collapsed, unconscious.

Deborah's vision blurred for lack of air, but she managed to open the sack by feel alone.

"Finally, she's quiet." Seesya lifted his boot from Deborah, kicked his senseless mother onto her side, and propped the torch upright against her back. "And useful."

With his boot off her chest, Deborah filled her lungs with air while slipping her hands into the sack above her head.

Her relief was short-lived.

Seesya dropped down to sit on her, straddling her hips, clenched her throat with both hands, and squeezed. "Air is sweet, isn't it?"

The hard floor hurt her back under his weight, and her lungs burned from lack of air. Struggling to keep her mind focused, Deborah reached deeper into her sack, ever so slowly.

"Your neck is as soft as butter." He eased the pressure. "Tell me how you did it."

"Did what?" Her voice came out squeaky through her constricted throat.

He laughed. "You sound like a mouse. Squeak the truth, and I might let you live a bit longer."

"The truth?" She felt around inside the sack, avoiding sudden movements that would draw his attention. "I love cheese."

"Don't play games with me, witch!" He leaned forward, his hands tightening on her throat, his face above her, lit by the dancing flame of the torch.

Her hands touched the cold flint, then the fool's gold.

"Tell me where that blood came from, or your blood will stop running in your veins."

Her fingers clenched the fire-starters, one stone in each hand.

"Tell me!"

Deborah managed to nod.

Seesya eased the pressure.

"Here, my husband." Her voice barely sounded. "I'll show you."

"Show me? Show me what?"

"The magic of witches."

He looked at her suspiciously.

"Look into my eyes," Deborah said.

Keeping both hands on her throat, he gazed into her eyes.

"Closer." She started to pull her hands out of her sack. "Deeper in my eyes."

He brought his face lower until his nose nearly touched hers. "I don't see anything in your eyes."

"Deeper. In the back of my eyes."

He peered into her eyes, creasing his forehead, while her hands slowly emerged from the sack, each holding one of the fire-starters.

"You see it now?"

"See what?"

"Look more closely." Keeping her eyes locked on his, she extended her arms sideways.

He blinked. "Green," he said. "I see green, like green vomit."

The garlic odor of his breath sickened her. "It's right there," she said.

"What?"

She clenched the stones tightly and imagined Barac's head, rolling in the dirt. "His head," she said.

"Whose head?"

With the image of her murdered friend conjured up in her mind, Deborah brought the stones together as hard as she could, hitting both sides of Seesya's head at the same time.

His eyes opened wide.

"And now?" She did it again—hands out and back in, pounding the stones at his ears. "Do you see Barac?"

Seesya gulped, his hands tightening on her neck.

"Here!" She hit Seesya a third time with all the force she had left. "For him!"

Seesya's face twisted in a horrifying grimace, lips pulled back, teeth bared, the scar flushing red. But still his grip did not loosen, as if all his remaining consciousness were directed toward sustaining a deadly vice on her airway.

Her vision began to blur. Deborah clenched the fire-starters, gathered her last bit of willpower, and brought her arms up, banging the stones at his ears a final time.

A low growl came from Seesya's mouth as he exhaled while his eyes rolled up and he slumped on top of her, his hands dropping from her neck.

Air forced its way in through her compressed windpipe with a whispered shriek.

28

Pinned down under Seesya's heavy bulk, Deborah took quick, shallow breaths. She felt his chest rise and sink while blood dripped from his ears. Was he dying? Had she committed the sin of murder? He deserved to die after what he had done to Tamar, but his punishment should come through a trial and judgment under God's laws.

Should she call for help? If he recovered, Seesya's version of events would be the only one that mattered. As a rebellious wife, guilty of trying to kill her husband, her punishment would be stoning. And if Seesya died, her account of what had happened would likewise be of no use. Either way, she would pay with her life. No, she couldn't call for help.

With great effort, Deborah pushed him off, took a few breaths, and got up. How long did she have before he recovered, or someone came looking for him?

She knelt over Vardit, who was breathing normally as if she were asleep. Deborah was relieved. She collected her sack, put in the fire-starters, and ran out of the room.

Halfway down the stairs, she turned and went back up. The torch, leaning against Vardit's back, still burned, its flame dangerously close to her hair. Deborah picked it up. In its flickering light, she saw that the blood had stopped oozing from Seesya's ears and was starting to congeal. He snorted, but didn't move.

Deborah grabbed Vardit's scarf and travel robe and put them on. She snuffed the torch by stomping on it, and ran out, her sack over her shoulder.

The courtyard was empty and dark, except for two torches, one at each end. The sky, however, had begun to brighten with first light. The city gates would open at sunrise, which was coming soon. She wanted to go immediately, but paused to think. The sentries at the gates would pay no attention to her as long as she blended in with the first rush of workers and merchants exiting the city at the start of the day.

First, she went to the well, scooped up wet dirt from the ground, and smeared it on her face, covering her light skin thoroughly. Second, from the piles of empty baskets resting against the wall of the storage room, she took five baskets, packed one inside the other, and carried them against her chest.

Under the great silver menorah, the heavy doors to the street were locked. After a moment of panic, she found the large bronze key hanging on the wall. Careful not to make noise, she unlocked the doors and exited the courtyard, pausing to touch the mezuzah scroll and kiss her fingertips.

Walking down the hill, Deborah passed Nehoshtan's closed door. Near the gates, she joined a group of workers, using the baskets to partially hide her face.

As she passed through the gates, Deborah heard distant shouting from behind. Ignoring it, she hurried to the fairgrounds and melted into the dense mass of pilgrims' tents and merchants' caravans. Everyone was getting up to start the day. Men added wood to the fires and cared for the animals, women fetched water and prepared food, and babies cried, eager for their morning meal.

The shouting had reached the gates, but Deborah didn't look back. Keeping her head low, she made her way through the fairgrounds to the very back. The lepers' camp was still there. She ran across the empty strip of land separating it from the fairgrounds and found Miriam sitting by her tent, drinking from a clay mug.

"I need to hide," Deborah said.

Miriam lifted the flap of the tent.

It was dark inside and smelled of incense. A pair of yellow eyes blinked at Deborah, and she recoiled before recognizing a cat. She put down the baskets and adjusted her scarf over her face. From her sack, she pulled out the wool blanket and covered herself with it as she curled up in the corner. The cat sniffed her blanket and pawed at her sack, probably smelling the tiger tail.

Not a minute later, Deborah heard horses ride by, men shouting as they searched around the fairgrounds and among the campsites. The other lepers came out of their tents and exchanged hushed words with Miriam.

Seesya's voice sounded nearby, hoarsely commanding his soldiers. They went back and forth across the fairgrounds, searching each caravan, wagon, and tent. She heard the soldiers ride near the lepers' camp several times, but they didn't stop. Moments later, they were off to search the surrounding hills and dry ravines.

Only then, when Deborah's pursuers were gone and the hundreds of people at the fairgrounds resumed their noisy morning activities, did her body begin to shake. The shaking grew worse and her throat constricted, making it hard to breathe. Choked sobs forced their way out. Seesya's attack replayed in her mind, his torch in her face, his hands clenching her throat. She hugged her knees tightly, shaking and crying, her face buried in her sack to silence her sobs.

The cat rubbed against her arm, and she caressed it. Up close, she could see its colors—patches of black and white. It purred, and she remembered the odd sound Seesya had made when she hit his ears with the fire-starters the first time, the way his eyes widened when she hit him a second time, and how, when she hit him a third time, his face twisted, his lips pulled back, and his teeth showed the way an old man would clown around to make children laugh. Deborah smiled at the memory of that comical expression on Seesya's face, the way he glared at her and how, after the final ear pounding, he uttered that strange moan while his eyes rolled up in his head.

Through her tears, Deborah giggled. She turned her face away from her sack, filled her lungs with the fresh morning air, and laughed openly and loudly until exhaustion took over and she fell asleep.

29

The cat woke Deborah up by pawing at her sack, which served as her pillow. She reached into the sack and pulled out the tiger tail. The cat meowed and ran out of the tent. She adjusted her scarf to make sure it covered her hair and most of her face, and stepped out. She was surprised to see the sun setting, which meant she had slept the whole day.

Miriam was cooking over a small fire. In the fairgrounds, merchants closed the last deals of the day while their women prepared the evening meal and got the children ready for the night. Many of the pilgrims had left, and she saw no soldiers.

Miriam offered her a bowl of meat and barley.

Deborah hesitated.

"Don't be afraid," Miriam said. "It's our curse. You won't become afflicted merely by looking at us or by eating with us."

Deborah felt very hungry. She took the bowl and ate, emptying it quickly.

Miriam stirred the pot over the fire. She noticed Deborah staring at her bandaged hands. Putting down the wooden spoon, Miriam unwrapped the cloth from her right hand. Three fingers were missing, and tumors dangled from her forearm, stretching the skin.

Deborah flinched at the sight. "Yahweh's mercy," she murmured. "I'm sorry."

"God makes us in His image, and then afflicts us with a curse that mutilates the divine image." Miriam wrapped her hand with the cloth. "Worse yet, He also gives the curse to those we love, and we must watch them suffer and die for our sins. Difficult to understand, isn't it?"

Recalling her own suffering and the loss of her parents and Tamar, Deborah nodded. "His decisions don't always seem merciful, but I think there are reasons we don't know about. I hope to find out one day."

"How will you find out?" Miriam chuckled. "You expect Yahweh to give you an explanation?"

"I will hear His voice."

"Really? When?"

Deborah couldn't tell whether the leper woman was mocking her or was genuinely interested. "I don't know," she said. "When I'm ready."

The other lepers sat around the fire and ate. It was hard to guess their gender or age under the heavy black clothing and veils, except for a young man of twenty or so, whose exposed face wasn't deformed. He was small and wiry and ate quickly with a spoon, while the others held their bowls with their bandaged hands and slurped the food directly into their mouths.

"This is Deborah," Miriam told them. "She'll be our guest for a little while."

A mix of dark eyes and empty eye sockets turned to her.

"I'm Ramrod," the young man said. "What happened? Was the fat priest angry that you called us over with our offerings? Was he going to whip you? Is that why you ran away?"

Taken aback by his intense questioning, Deborah only shook her head.

"This is my sister's son," Miriam said. "She died of the curse, as did her husband and other children. Ramrod was still a baby when—"

"I can tell her about myself," he said. "I'm not a child."

"Then act like an adult," Miriam said, "and stop pestering our guest with questions."

He smiled at Deborah and continued eating.

When darkness descended, the lepers returned to their tents, some of them limping heavily. Ramrod added wood to the fire while Miriam cleaned the bowls and the pot before rejoining Deborah.

"Thank you for taking me in," Deborah said. "You saved me from a certain death."

"Was it the young man with the scar?"

"Yes."

"I could see his rage when he was searching for you. Our old priest used to quote the scriptures: 'Evil dominates man's heart from his youth.' I've witnessed many proofs of that sad truth."

"I'm sorry to put you at risk."

"Risk?" Miriam chuckled. "We're not afraid."

"Why?"

"Killing ourselves would be a sin, but otherwise, death would be a welcome release."

Deborah was shocked. People usually dedicated every effort to survival. "I don't want to have your blood on my hands. I'll leave tonight." She reached into her sack and found the small purse Obadiah had given her in Emanuel. She poured the coins into her palm and held them out. "Please take as much as you want."

"Keep your money. You'll need it, and what we need from you is something different." Miriam leaned forward. "Have you prayed for us yet?"

The guilt almost made Deborah lie, but she couldn't. "Not yet."

"Why?"

The question was simple, but the answer wasn't, considering all that had happened to her since Miriam had seen her praying by the roadside the night before last. Deborah cringed at the memory of running up the hill, giddy with excitement at the prospect of following the information she had discovered about Kassite's sale to Orran, the tanner in Aphek, only to enter Shatz's courtyard and find Seesya there. The elder priest's quote of Yahweh's words still rankled in her mind: "And to the woman God said: I shall multiply your pain and agony; in anguish you shall bear children; always you shall lust after your husband, and he shall reign over you." Had it really been only two days? It seemed much longer.

"Tell me, Deborah. Why haven't you prayed for us yet?"

With sudden clarity, the answer came to her. "Because Yahweh has forsaken me!"

And with those five simple words, all the disappointment and sorrow that had built up inside Deborah erupted in a torrent of sobs that made her sway back and forth. She cried bitterly for her wise father and loving mother, for beautiful Tamar and brave Barac, for the loss of Palm Homestead and the home she had loved, for Zariz, who had left her, and for Vardit, who had been powerless to help her, for the ugliness of her false marriage and the terrible loneliness that was her lot now.

The cat came over and rubbed against Deborah's leg. Its pointy face, divided down the middle between white and black, was like an image of good and evil. She scratched its back while her sobs subsided and her tears dried up.

"Your pain is great," Miriam said.

Deborah nodded. She noticed Ramrod, who sat on the far side of the fire, watching her.

"Do you know why we keep a cat?" Miriam held up the bandaged hand. "It protects us from mice, like the ones that chewed my fingers off while I slept."

"What? How can that be?"

"It's the worst aspect of our curse," Miriam said. "We lose the ability to feel pain."

"You don't feel pain?" Deborah found that hard to comprehend. "A life without pain would be a wonderful gift!"

"A gift? Mice chew our fingers and toes, fires burn our feet and hands, and boiling water peels our skin away—all before we notice anything." Miriam shook her head. "Pain is the real gift from Yahweh, for without pain, there is no life. You should thank Him for this gift, for your ability to feel pain. And when you understand it, you will pray for us, for me and my fellow lepers, that we shall regain the gift of pain."

Deborah spent much of that night swathed in her blanket behind Miriam's tent, looking up at the night sky and thinking about the gift of pain. The cat curled up on her legs, and sleep didn't come until the early morning hours.

She woke up when the sun was already up. The fairgrounds buzzed with morning activity. Miriam was cooking breakfast, and Ramrod was feeding the animals. The lepers had already packed up their tents and loaded everything on several carts. Each two-wheeled cart was hitched to a donkey. The goats and sheep were tied up with a rope behind one of the carts.

Miriam gave Deborah a cup of milk and a ball of goat cheese and sat beside her while she ate.

"Who was that young man with the scar?" Miriam asked.

"Seesya, son of Zifron."

"The judge who rules Emanuel?"

"Yes."

"I've heard of him. People say Judge Zifron wants to become king of all Ephraim and rule over the Samariah Hills."

"I don't know about these things." Deborah nibbled at her cheese.

"He left Shiloh this morning. I saw him ride off at sunrise." Miriam pointed west. "In that direction."

"Was he alone?"

"With a few soldiers, as well as an old priest and a woman."

"Did the woman seem in good health?"

Miriam thought for a moment. "She sat straight on the horse, nothing unusual. Who is she?"

"His mother." Deborah was relieved to learn that Vardit was well. She finished the milk, put away the cup, and stuffed the wool blanket into her sack. She gave the empty baskets to Miriam. "It's time for me to go."

"You're going?" Ramrod stopped what he was doing. "By yourself? Where to?"

"Aphek."

"All the way to Aphek? Do you think the roads are safe for a girl by herself?"

"I have no choice. I must go to Aphek."

"Why Aphek? Do you have family there?"

"There's a man in Aphek who can help me gain my freedom."

"A man?" Ramrod tilted his head curiously. "Is he a judge? A priest?"

Deborah laughed. "The opposite. He's a slave."

"A slave?" Ramrod tightened the rope securing the load to one of the carts. "How could a slave help you?"

It was a fair question, but she didn't want to give away any more information. "He might not be able to. I'm not sure, but I have to try. It's my only option. Can you tell me which direction to go?"

Raising her wrapped hand, Miriam pointed. "The same road the son of Judge Zifron took, but he's going to Emanuel, so he'll turn left after half a day and go south."

"Or not," Ramrod said. "What if he sets an ambush for you? What if he knows where you're going?"

"He doesn't know where I'm going."

"Are you certain?"

Deborah wanted to say yes, but the truth was, Shatz could find out about her inquiries from the slave warden and pass the information to Seesya, whose vengeful nature and doggedness could not be underestimated.

On the other hand, she remembered what Obadiah of Levi had told Seesya in the bedroom at Shatz's house: "I'll testify that you have possessed her, and that she was a virgin." To which Shatz had added, "There you go. You own Palm Homestead free and clear now. There's no need for this craziness." As angry as Seesya might be, he and his father had achieved their goal Chasing her down wouldn't serve any purpose, and catching her could lead to a trial that might expose the embarrassing truth about Seesya's failure to perform on their wedding night. Perhaps he would cool down and realize that he was better off letting her escape and having her gone from his life. He might feel differently if he knew about her quest to find the Elixirist, become a man, and return to Emanuel to fight for Palm Homestead. But for now, there was a good chance that Seesya had resigned himself to never seeing her again.

"I'm not certain," she said. "He might be able to find out about my intent to go to Aphek, but even then, he might just forget about me."

"Forget you?" Ramrod laughed nervously. "You really think that's possible?"

"My nephew is right," Miriam said. "You're not easy to forget."

"We could take you," Ramrod said, glancing at his aunt, who nodded.

"Seesya is a murderer," Deborah said. "If he found me with you—"

"Smear some ashes from the fire on your face, and make sure to cover most of it, as well as your hands. You'll look like one of us." Miriam signaled to the other lepers to get ready. "We won't follow the main roads, especially with all the fighting between the tribes of Manasseh and Ephraim."

"Is Aphek involved in the fighting?"

"Perhaps. I heard that Aphek itself belongs to the tribe of Ephraim, but the area around it belongs to Manasseh." Miriam picked up the cat and got into one of the carts. "Yahweh brought you to us for a reason. Come, sit with me. We're taking you to Aphek."

Filled with gratitude, Deborah remembered Nehoshtan quoting Shatz's father: "When you pursue your True Calling, God provides the shortcuts."

They took narrow paths, goat trails, and dry streambeds. The two-wheeled carts were surprisingly sturdy under the weight of tents, food, and two or three people each. The donkeys kept their heads down and their legs moving. Ramrod steered the leading cart with the help of another leper, a short, one-legged man who occasionally pointed the way with a wrapped hand.

Deborah rode with Miriam, who held the cat in her lap. Most of the hills they passed through were barren and uninhabited, and when they saw an occasional homestead, Ramrod found a way around it.

By evening, they saw a town in the distance, sitting low in a valley under a heavy cloud of smoke.

As they set up camp for the night, Deborah noticed two women climbing the hillside not far away. One was young and held a baby in her arms. The other was older, her back stooped, her hands grasping one cane each for support. Their clothes were torn and bloody, and their faces were blank, almost like wooden masks. When they saw the group of lepers, they came closer and sat on the ground some twenty steps away.

Miriam filled a waterskin, put apples and bread in a basket, and asked Deborah to take it over. As Deborah approached, however, the women got up and stepped backward.

"I don't have the curse." Deborah showed them her hands and face. She put the food and water on the ground, moved backward, and sat on a rock.

The women ate and drank quickly.

"What happened to you?" Deborah asked.

The old woman raised one of her canes and pointed at the cloud of smoke over the valley. "They attacked our town."

"We have no town," the one with the baby said in a toneless voice. "Tapuah is no more."

"What happened?"

"It was too quick," the old woman said. "The sun was up and the heat made our few soldiers sleepy. Now everyone is dead."

Deborah glanced at the baby, whose eyes remained close, his face peaceful, oblivious to the world. "Who were the invaders?"

The old woman pointed to the north. "Manasseh."

"Men from the tribe of Manasseh?" Deborah couldn't believe it. "Did they carry the black flag with the white antelope?"

"No. They carried the banner of King Javin of Hazor and the effigy of Ra, the sun god of the Canaanites, but when they thought we were all dead, they cheered, 'Manasseh's birthright is redeemed!' That's how we knew their true identity."

"Why would they do that?"

"We are of Ephraim, and the men of Manasseh believe that all of Joseph's share of Canaan should have gone to them as descendants of Joseph's eldest son, rather than being divided with descendants of Ephraim, the younger son."

The woman with the baby looked at the smoke-filled valley and murmured, "Evil always finds excuses."

"Would you like to stay the night?" Deborah gestured at the lepers' camp. "We could arrange a tent for you."

They glanced at the lepers, got up and walked away without a word.

"Wait!" Deborah called, following them. "Where will you go?"

"To Shiloh," the older woman said. "We heard that the holy city is safe from Hebrew strife."

They disappeared into the twilight with the silent baby, who might have been dead already, it was hard to tell.

30

Riding the eagle felt familiar. Its broad back and wide wings made the flight stable and smooth, but suddenly it swerved to the right and plunged through the clouds toward the earth. She grabbed its white neck, the feathers thick and soft in her hands. The rushing air stung her face, and the speed was exhilarating. When the people below came into view, she saw that they had flat noses and hollow eyes. They pointed up at her with fingerless hands on arms swollen with tumors. She pulled on the eagle's neck to steer it away from the lepers. It veered left and flew between olive trees. Its wings hit the branches, separated the olives from their stems, and popped them open, spraying her with oil. She leaned forward and pulled on the feathers to direct the eagle out of the olive grove. Only then, as the eagle soared up to the cloudy sky, did she notice that the lepers had somehow joined her. They sat on the wings, shoulder to shoulder, drenched in olive oil, and gazed ahead with dark eyes or empty sockets. One of them, who with his thin face resembled Ramrod, pointed at her with a finger that was whole and straight, yet black as coal. The finger that touched her forehead was cold and moist. She shuddered and woke up, finding the cat licking her forehead.

Outside, Miriam was making breakfast on a small fire. The others were busy taking down their tents and packing the carts.

"Good morning, Deborah." Miriam handed her a cup of warm goat milk.

"Thank you." Deborah held it with both hands, comforted by its warmth.

"You were tossing and turning," Miriam said. "Are we giving you nightmares?"

Taking a sip, Deborah smiled. "It wasn't a nightmare, but yes, you were in it. I'm not sure what the dream meant. I think I'm supposed to help you somehow, but in reality you're helping me. It's confusing."

"All in good time." Miriam gave her a bowl with bread and cheese. "The answers will come to you when you're ready."

Deborah ate quickly, stuffed her few belongings into her sack, and got into Miriam's cart. The small caravan traveled around the smoldering ruins of Tapuah at a safe distance and continued down the Samariah Hills.

When Miriam seemed tired, Deborah took the reins. The ring on her finger glistened in the sun. She tugged on her sleeve to cover it.

"A ring like that feels much heavier than its actual weight," Miriam said. "Doesn't it?"

"Yes, but I'll be free soon. I'm sure of it."

"Is there another man you like better than the one with the scar?"

Deborah shook her head, but her mind went to Zariz and his smiling face. "During my escape," she said, "a caravan from Moab saved me. There was a boy, about my age, who was nice to me."

"The Moabites are not our friends."

"Yes, he told me what they say of us in Moab: 'Beware of the Hebrews, for their tongue is oily and their sword is invisible.' Do you know why they say it?"

Miriam nodded. "A long time ago, there was a king in Moab named Eglon, who oppressed our people until a Hebrew warrior managed to kill him."

"Ehud, son of Gerah?"

"Yes. The story I heard was that Ehud made a small, double-edged sword, hid it under his robe, and convinced King Eglon to give him an audience in private, with no guards or soldiers in the room."

"How did he manage that?"

"He told Eglon that he was bringing him a secret message directly from God. When they were alone, Ehud drew the sword and sank it into the fat king's belly until the handle disappeared inside. The king died, and Ehud left, locking the door behind him. He told the courtiers that the king was asleep and left. By the time they discovered the truth, Ehud had already crossed the Jordan River. He called up the tribesmen of Ephraim, and together they vanquished the dispirited army of Moab, liberating the Hebrews tribes."

"Now I understand," Deborah said. "God helped Ehud defeat Moab with an oily tongue and an invisible sword."

In the late afternoon, with the sun in their eyes, low over the western horizon, they came over the crest of the last hill. The Coastal Plain stretched before them as far as the eye could see, lush with trees, pasture, and cultivated fields. The air was heavy with humidity, and thick flocks of birds soared over the trees. The abundance of water, trees, and life was almost magical, reminding Deborah of the stories her father had used to tell about the Garden of Eden.

"This is Aphek," Miriam said, pointing at the city below the cliffs.

Deborah shielded her eyes and looked down at Aphek, her destination. It seemed larger than Shiloh and Emanuel combined, and was strategically built above a narrow gorge where gushing springs launched the Yarkon River. The meandering river cut a natural barrier across the Coastal Plain between the cliffs of the Samariah Hills and the Great Sea. From their vantage point, Deborah could see how any traveler heading north or south had to pass through the narrow gorge at the head of the river under the control of the rulers of Aphek, who no doubt charged everyone a tribute for free passage. It was no wonder that the city radiated wealth and prosperity.

"It's an old city," Miriam said. "The Egyptians used it to rule the whole region, from the Sinai Desert in the south to Assyria and Aram in the north. Do you see the road?" She pointed. "It's called the Sea Highway."

"I see it," Deborah said. "Does it come from the sea?"

"It starts down in Egypt and goes along the shore of the Great Sea through Gaza, then around the Philistine cities of Ashdod and Ashkelon up to Jaffa, and then east around the Yarkon River through this narrow gorge." Miriam finger traced the road below. "From here, it goes to Megiddo and Hazor, and then splits for Sidon and Damascus, as well as all the great cities of Assyria and Aram, which used to be under Egyptian rule. There are also smaller roads that branch out just north of here toward Shiloh, Bet She'an, the Sea of Galilee, and many other places."

"The Sea Highway," Deborah repeated the name, which sounded so grand and adventurous to her ears. "But it doesn't look much bigger than the road that passes by Emanuel."

"It's very different," Miriam said. "Pharaohs and kings have traveled through here—whole armies with tens of thousands of soldiers and chariots painted with gold. They had to come through here, unless they wanted to swim across the river or climb the Samariah Hills."

"And now?"

"These days, the Egyptians, Philistines, and Canaanites must pay the Hebrew rulers of Aphek for passage. Aphek is one of the greatest cities in all the land of Canaan."

Deborah was impressed by the leper woman's knowledge. "Have you been here before?"

"We used to come here often. My family had beehives at our homestead near Bethel. Honey sold at a premium here, especially to the Egyptians." Miriam paused, taking a deep breath. "Life was good, but I didn't appreciate how blessed we were until the curse fell upon us and the happy days ended."

They set up camp for the night on the hill overlooking Aphek. Deborah was too excited to fall asleep. Tomorrow she would go down to the city and look for Orran's house. It shouldn't be hard to find the house of such a rich man, but then what? It had been eighteen years since Orran bought Kassite in Shiloh. What if Orran had sold him to someone else? Or set him free to return home to Edom? Kassite would be at least fifty, an old man like Sallan. He could have died, become sick, or grown feebleminded. And even if she found him, would Kassite admit that he was the Edomite known as the Elixirist? Would he agree to help her?

In the quiet of the night, with the dark city lying below, Deborah dreaded the setbacks tomorrow might bring. She felt small, weak, and fearful of finding her quest at a dead end. Had she made a terrible mistake? Should she have stayed in Emanuel? She recalled the last night at Judge Zifron's house, enjoying a dinner fit for a king in the foreman's plush quarters above the basket factory, drinking the dull-colored Reinforcing Liquid, which had tasted sour, but not repugnant. She remembered Sallan's thick finger touching her forehead as he'd said, "It's all here, in your head. That's where your strength begins to grow like yeast in fresh dough. Believe in it, and it will rise." Lowering his finger to her chest, he'd said, "Your heart must not resist or doubt the magic of your strength, but allow it to grow and make you mightier than the challenges facing you and taller than the barriers on your path." His hand had dropped and squeezed her hand. "You'll shake with fear and self-doubt at times, confronting a powerful man or a sudden danger, but you must steady your hand, banish your fear, and embrace your strength. If you do, by the time you find the Elixirist, the strength within you will be more than sufficient to return to Emanuel and help me."

The memory calmed her, because his words had proved true so far. She had felt her strength grow since drinking the Reinforcing Liquid. It had given her the fortitude to escape from Emanuel and overcome one harrowing setback after another, until she reached this point. Tomorrow she would overcome another challenge, break through another barrier, and grow stronger yet. If Kassite no longer lived here, she would find out where he had gone and follow him. She wouldn't surrender to despair or give up the search for Kassite, because she wasn't alone in her quest: "When you pursue your True Calling, God provides the shortcuts."

Wrapping herself in her wool blanket, Deborah pulled the tiger tail from the sack and bunched it up as a pillow. Its odor was no longer unpleasant, but comforting. She heard the goats shift about restlessly and smiled at the irony: the cause of their nervousness was the very thing that kept them safe.

31

The flight resumed where it had paused the previous morning. Deborah knew she was dreaming, yet the sting of air rushing at her face, the thick feathers in her clenched hands and the upward pressure under her body were all too real to dismiss as imagination. She slapped the moist black finger away from her forehead, and Ramrod smiled like a disciplined child and put the finger in his mouth, sucking on it. The other lepers, lined up on each wing, grinned toothlessly, holding on as the giant eagle soared high above a mountainous desert, passed over jagged peaks, and abruptly descended near a body of water. It was not the Great Sea, but a very large lake, its shoreline marked with a white crust forming the shape of an elongated oval with narrow hips. Remembering the shape from the map Zariz had drawn in the sand, she realized that this was the Sea of Salt. The eagle made a wide turn, flew straight along a river, which she knew must be the Jordan River, and leveled off over a field of green stalks with white and pink flowers. The wings were barely above ground level and, like a knife peeling the skin off a fruit, sheared off the green stalks and the attached bulbs from the field. At first she thought the bulbs were onions, but soon recognized the unique shape of garlic. From the front edge of the wings, the rushing air swept up the bulbs, which hit the seated lepers, bursting and covering them with a layer of ivory-colored mush. Suddenly, the lepers were gone from the wings. She glanced over her shoulder and saw them in the slick water of the Sea of Salt, near the white-crusted shore, submerged to their necks, surrounded by rings of garlic paste and olive oil that had washed off their skin. Only now the smell struck her, conjuring the memory of Seesya's bad breath, and she woke up to see the early sun of a new day.

Miriam was still asleep, and the fire had died overnight. Deborah took out her father's fire-starters, collected dry leaves, twigs, and a few bigger branches, and got a nice fire burning. She noticed Ramrod sitting up at the open side of his tent, watching her. She pointed at the goats and pantomimed milking with her hands. He smiled and did what she asked.

A short time later, the two of them sat together on a rock, drinking warm milk, and watched the city below come to life. Chimneys spewed smoke, wagons and horses raised swirls of dust, and herds of livestock ventured out to graze along the Yarkon River.

The cat joined them, and Ramrod scratched its back, making it purr with pleasure. Deborah glanced at his hands. They were bony, small, and coated with dirt, but he didn't miss any fingers.

He spat on his left hand, rubbed it on his shirt, and held up his forefinger. It was black. "I got the curse when I was little, but it stopped and stayed like this."

Deborah stared at his black forefinger, startled. It looked the same as in her dream.

He curled it, flicked it, and pulled on it. "It's working fine, and if I keep my hands dirty, no one notices."

"Do you feel pain?"

He looked the other way. "Go ahead, touch it."

She used the edge of her cup to touch the top of his forefinger.

"Topside, near my fingernail."

"Correct," she said. "How about your other fingers?"

He kept his head turned away. "Try me."

Again, with the edge of the cup, Deborah touched his thumb.

"Thumb," he said.

She tried again, and he said, "Forefinger," which was correct. She touched the other fingers, out of order, then those of his other hand, and some of his toes, which protruded from his sandals. He could feel each one of them without looking.

"That's wonderful," Deborah said.

"I'm lucky compared to the others, but I'm still cursed, banished from normal society for the rest of my life." He tugged on the black forefinger. "I'm marked forever, same as Cain, even though I didn't kill my brother, or anyone else."

She felt sorry for him. "At least you know that God forgave your sins, that He loves you."

"More than He loves them?" Ramrod gestured toward the other tents. "But less than He loves you?"

Deborah didn't know what to say.

"I've always wondered," he said. "Were my parents' sins so terrible that they deserved the curse? Why did God give me the curse, together with my parents and siblings, then stop my curse from progressing but keep theirs going until they died? Were my sins not as serious as those of the rest of my family?"

"Yes," she said. "That must be it."

"Really? Then how do you explain why God gave my younger sister the curse at birth, which killed her at five months? How could her sins at birth be more serious than the sins committed by me—older by a year? How could either of us, babies not yet walking or talking, commit any sins at all?"

"I don't know," she said quietly.

Ramrod tossed the rest of the milk from his cup and looked away.

Everyone was soon up and ready to go. Taking a steep path down from the hills, the caravan reached the Sea Highway when the sun was halfway up in the east. After the rough terrain of the prior two days, the carts rolled smoothly on the road, and even the donkeys seemed happier.

Advancing toward Aphek from the north, the road passed by a pond. A group of boys bathed in the shallows, splashing each other and laughing. When they saw the donkey carts with the lepers, the boys came out of the water. They huddled together, pointing and laughing. One boy threw a fistful of mud. The others joined in. The lepers cowered low in the carts and held their arms over their heads while the mud balls rained on them. The donkeys brayed and reared up, causing the two-wheeled carts to turn sideways and roll off the road. One cart overturned, and the boys rejoiced and intensified their attack.

Deborah jumped off the cart and was immediately hit by three mud balls in quick succession. Undeterred, she collected pebbles from the ground and pitched them at the boys, hitting them every time, eliciting shouts of pain. While causing no injuries, the pebbles were enough to drive the boys back into the water. They waded away as fast as they could, came out at the other side of the pond and ran in the direction of Aphek.

The lepers didn't look at Deborah as they straightened the carts and pushed them back onto the road, pointing in the opposite direction from Aphek. Ramrod fed the donkeys bits of carrot to pacify them. He glanced at Deborah and smiled, but looked away when Miriam gave him a stern glance.

"We don't fight back," Miriam said. "Yahweh wants us to bear our curse, and being taunted by people is part of our punishment."

Deborah took her sack from the cart and shouldered it. "Isn't your physical suffering enough of a punishment?"

"Perhaps, but in our experience, fighting back causes bigger problems." Miriam pointed in the direction the boys had run. "They'll go to the city, tell their friends what happened, and come back with clubs and stones."

"Why?" Deborah was shocked. "It's a sin to attack the weak and powerless!"

Miriam chuckled sadly. "Nothing excites the righteous more than an opportunity to torment sinners, and we, with our curse visible to all, make for an excellent target."

"I'm sorry," Deborah said. "It didn't occur to me."

"Why should it? You're not a leper." Miriam spoke harshly, but immediately her bandaged hands came together in a gesture of apology. "It's not your fault, Deborah. Please forgive me."

"There's nothing to forgive. It's the truth."

"We must get going," Ramrod said. "Once we're off the main road, they won't find us."

"Thank you for bringing me here," Deborah said. "I'll never forget you."

"Before we go," Miriam said, "will you give us your blessing?"

Deborah didn't think her blessing was any good, but the leper woman was pleading for a gift of hope, not humble excuses. Raising her hands forward with the fingers parted in pairs in the manner of priests, Deborah recited the blessing: "May Yahweh bless you and protect you. May He show you kindness and grace. May He illuminate your path and grant you peace."

Miriam bowed to her, as did the other lepers. They climbed into the carts.

"One more thing," Deborah said. "In the last couple of nights, I had dreams. I think they mean something."

"What?"

"That you should go to the Sea of Salt."

Ramrod jumped off the lead cart and confronted her. "The Sea of Salt? There's nothing there. It's a place of death!"

Miriam glared at him. "Where are your manners?"

"He's right," Deborah said. "It makes no sense to me either, but I saw it clearly in my dreams. Take olive oil and garlic with you, and when you get there, cover yourselves in olive oil and garlic paste."

Ramrod made a face. "Sticky and stinky at the same time."

"I'm sorry, but that's what I saw in my dreams. Smear it all over, as if you were dipping an apple in honey. To wash it off, submerge in the Sea of Salt. Do it again and again until you are cured."

Ramrod turned to Miriam. "Is this girl crazy?"

"Hush!" Miriam pointed at his cart. "Take your place and lead the way!"

He complied without arguing. As the carts took off down the road, the cat leaped out of Miriam's cart and ran back to Deborah. She picked it up in her arms and held it to her chest, kissing its snout on the line where white and black met. It meowed, jumped down, and raced back to Miriam. A moment later, the lepers were gone.

32

Deborah decided to hide in case Miriam's fears were justified. She stepped off the road, crouched among bushes of mint and honeysuckle, and waited. Sure enough, a group of boys and young men arrived from the direction of Aphek, brandishing wooden sticks and leather slings. They reached the spot where the previous attack had taken place and stopped. Looking around in all directions, they waved their sticks and shouted obscenities, before heading back to Aphek.

With the immediate danger over, Deborah considered her next step. A direct approach to Kassite's owner, Orran of Manasseh, would be too risky. A girl traveling alone in search of an Edomite slave would raise suspicion. Orran would ask probing questions, which she wouldn't want to answer truthfully, leading to more questions. Rather, she would approach his servants or slaves and make indirect inquiries about Kassite without drawing too much attention.

Kneeling at the water's edge, she washed her face and hands, patted down her robe, and retied her scarf.

A group of about twenty travelers appeared on the road, heading in the direction of Aphek. Some were on foot, carrying sacks and baskets or pushing handcarts. A few men rode on donkeys while their women paced behind. Deborah couldn't tell whether they were pilgrims coming back from Shiloh, travelers from cities to the north and east, or local farmers taking produce to the market. They seemed unrelated, traveling together for safety.

Deborah put up her hood, adjusted her scarf so that it covered the lower half of her face, and followed them.

Approaching the city, the group broke up. Most turned toward the fairgrounds, a few continued down to the guarded checkpoint at the narrow pass by the gushing springs, where the river started, and one man on a donkey headed to the city gates. Deborah followed him.

Several sentries stood by a tall pole just outside the open gates. The flag was black with a white ox, proclaiming that the city belonged to the tribe of Ephraim. The man on the donkey greeted the sentries, who replied in a familiar manner and waved him through. Deborah lowered her eyes and stayed close, hoping that the sentries would assume she was traveling with him.

A pair of boots appeared on the road before her, and she almost bumped into a sentry.

He laughed. "What's the hurry, girl?"

Deborah kept her head down. "I'm a visitor here."

"From where?"

"Shiloh."

"What's in the sack?" He took it from her, reached inside, and pulled out the tiger tail, letting it unfurl to its full length. "Look at this!"

The other sentries came over to see.

"It keeps wild animals away," she said.

"Clever." He gave her the sack back, but held on to the tiger tail. "Look up at me, girl. Show us your face."

Deborah loosened the scarf, revealing her face.

"Green eyes," he said, "and lots of freckles. Not of Manasseh, are you?"

"Looks like a girl of Judah," another sentry said. "Or even an Edomite."

"Maybe she's a spy," a third one said.

Fear tightened her chest, and she had to force the words out of her mouth. "I'm a daughter of Ephraim." She pointed to the flag on the pole. "That's my tribe. I swear to you in the name of Yahweh!"

The mention of God's name seemed to make little impression.

"You don't look like a daughter of Ephraim." The sentry sniffed the tiger tail and crinkled his nose. "If you're lying to us—"

"Do you know Shatz Ha'Cohen?"

"Who?"

"He's one of the seven elder priests at the Holy Tabernacle in Shiloh." Deborah kept eye contact with him to show she wasn't afraid. "Have you heard of the Holy Tabernacle?"

"Of course." The sentry glanced at his colleagues. "What about it?"

"I left Shatz's house two days ago to get here as quickly as possible. Do you want me to go back to Shiloh and tell him that you stood in my way? Do you want him to pray for your damnation at the Holy Tabernacle?"

The sentry shrugged. "I'm only doing my job."

"Shatz conducts trade with Orran of Manasseh, the tanner. I need to find him. Can you tell me where his house is?"

"Didn't you hear what I said?" The sentry tossed the tiger tail at her. "This city belongs to Ephraim."

It dawned on her that Orran's name meant that he was a member of the tribe of Manasseh, which made it impossible for him to reside inside Aphek at a time of fighting among the tribes.

"Go to the fairgrounds," said one of the other sentries. "The marketplace is always neutral—everyone is allowed there. Ask for Orran's shop. It's big. You can't miss it."

"Thank you." She stuffed the tiger tail back in her sack and shouldered it. "Yahweh's blessing upon you."

Entering the fairgrounds, Deborah blended in with the shoppers, many of them women and girls. Some of the vendors spoke languages she didn't know and wore strange headdresses or necklaces with charms or miniature gods. Pacing between the rows of stalls and tents, she marveled at the merchandise. There were dresses made of fine wool and soft linen in vivid colors, silk scarves with exotic patterns, and sandals and shoes made of supple leather. Jewelry pieces forged of brass, silver, and even gold were offered in open cases for all to see and touch. Glistening gems were displayed on trays of white linen. Miniature ivory figurines dangled on strings attached to wooden beams at eye level, swaying gently in the air.

One vendor offered live snakes and lizards, kept in wooden cages. He summoned a small crowd and dropped a mouse into a cage. A brown snake struck it with a rapid jolt. The mouse ran around the cage a few times and dropped. Its tiny paws twitched while the snake swallowed it, starting from the head.

The deadly snake terrified her, yet fascination kept her watching. The vendor took another snake out of a cage and held it out to her. Deborah stepped back so quickly that she fell, making everyone laugh. The vendor turned and held the snake out to one of the men, who stopped laughing and, in his haste to get away, tripped over two other men, and all three collapsed on top of each other. Now it was Deborah's turn to laugh.

The sentry had been right. She couldn't miss Orran's shop. It was much larger than the other shops, which ranged from simple stalls to makeshift tents and temporary shacks with cloth sides and straw roofs. This shop was made of animal skins nailed to a solid frame. The hides were dyed in shades of brown, forming solid walls on three sides and a pitched roof above. Even the wooden columns and horizontal beams were wrapped, giving the place a lush, luxurious atmosphere. She touched the leather wall and was surprised by how hard it was, almost like leather armor or boots. Deborah was in awe. She had never seen a structure made of leather.

The large space was filled with tidy piles of leather hides, arranged by the type of animal each had come from. The piles were lined up in rows, with enough space between the rows for all the customers who crowded the shop. A sharp smell permeated the place despite the open front, which allowed fresh air to circulate.

Keeping her eyes mostly on the various leathers, Deborah glanced around surreptitiously. She expected Orran of Manasseh to look like Judge Zifron—aging, portly, and dressed according to his high position. No one in the shop fit the description. The salesmen were young men in identical vests made of black-dyed leather—the same color Vardit had applied to Deborah's orange hair in a futile attempt to mollify Seesya. When not assisting customers, the salesmen reported to a supervisor seated at a desk on a platform in the corner. He was slightly older than the rest and never smiled.

One of the salesmen approached her. "Can I help you?"

"I was married two days ago." Deborah showed him her ring. "My husband is the son of a rich man."

He glanced at the dusty sack on her shoulder. "Congratulations."

"Where is Orran of Manasseh?"

"He's not here. What do you need?"

"My husband is the type of man who prefers to deal with the owner. When will Orran come here?"

"I don't know. He usually stays at his homestead, north of here, in the land of Manasseh."

"Near his tannery?"

He laughed. "You can't run a tannery on dry land."

The conversation wasn't leading her any closer to finding Kassite, and Deborah knew she had stretched the truth quite far already. She pointed to a pile of hides. "How much for one of these?"

"An excellent choice." He lifted the corner of the one on top. "Cowhide, whole skin, no seams. It takes the tannery a great deal of work to accomplish this high quality. The result is as supple as Egyptian linen, but a hundred times stronger. Here, feel it. Can you tell how good this is?"

Deborah touched the leather. "Very nice. You seem to know a lot about it."

He shrugged. "I've been working here for eight years."

Deborah tried to conceal her excitement. After eight years with Orran's business, surely this salesman knew Kassite! "How expensive is this piece?"

"Surprisingly reasonable—only three silver shekels."

"That's good," she said. "We'll need a few dozen."

"Excuse me?" His eyebrows arched. "A few dozen?"

She cursed herself silently for the foolish exaggeration. "My husband's family has a very large house."

He smiled warily. "I see."

"This is a big shop." She looked around. "It must require a lot of slaves to make all these leathers. Does Orran own many slaves?"

The salesman gave her an odd look, nodding.

"Do you know a slave named Kassite?"

"Gassike?"

"Kassite. He's an Edomite slave that Orran bought in Shiloh many years ago, and someone told me—"

"Never heard of him."

"I was just wondering—"

"When is your husband coming?"

"Soon. Very soon. I'll look for you when he arrives."

He nodded and left her.

Moving on to the next pile, Deborah felt the leather with her hand as if considering a purchase. She sensed that the salesman had answered honestly. There had been no hesitation in his voice when he said he'd never heard of Kassite. Even though Orran had many slaves, a person of high skills such as Kassite would have stood out and become known among Orran's workers. If a longtime salesman at Orran's shop had never heard of Kassite, what chance was there that he still worked for Orran? Either Kassite was dead, or he'd been sold off a long time ago.

Out of the corner of her eye, Deborah saw the salesman talking with the man at the desk, both of them looking at her. She walked out of the shop and beat a hasty retreat between two stalls across the way and down another row of shops. She glanced back to make sure the men weren't following her.

A large tree provided shade at the edge of the fairgrounds. Deborah watched the traffic of shoppers and reflected on what had happened. The disappointment of her futile visit to Orran's shop was crushing. Where would she go from here? Out of ideas, she decided to quell her hunger first, and then think again.

Using a coin from the purse Obadiah had given her in Emanuel, Deborah bought bread, dry meat, and a few dates. She went to the rear of the fairgrounds and sat on the grass at the top of a steep slope overlooking the river. She ate slowly, watching the water below. When the food was finished, she felt thirsty, but Seesya had destroyed her waterskin. She climbed down the embankment to the river, wary not to lose her footing, and knelt at the water's edge. The river was narrow here, the water deep, and the current swift. The noise drowned out all other sounds. Careful not to fall in, Deborah scooped water in her hands and slurped it.

She climbed back up the slope, sat down, and contemplated her situation. She needed a new strategy.

The facts were simple. She had no chance of obtaining any more information at Orran's shop. Going to the tanner's homestead was similarly pointless. The homestead was somewhere north of Aphek in the land of Manasseh. The trip would be hazardous, and even if she made it there safely, her arrival would raise suspicion, rewarding her with trouble rather than information. But what if she had been wrong to conclude that the salesman's unfamiliarity with Kassite was proof that he was gone? What if the Edomite slave had concealed his special skills and had been toiling in the tannery as a lowly worker ever since arriving there eighteen years earlier? It wasn't very likely, but it was possible. Her only choice was to find the tannery and ask for Kassite there. But where was the tannery?

The rushing river reminded Deborah what Nehoshtan had explained.

A tannery needed to be near a river in order to feed the soaking tubs, and it would be located downwind from the town because of the bad odors.

Closing her eyes, Deborah recalled the view from their overnight campsite above Aphek. The Yarkon River started in the gorge and flowed west. The road that Miriam had called the Sea Highway ran parallel to the river for a while. Was Orran's tannery located somewhere downstream on the riverbank?

Walking back through the fairgrounds, Deborah circled around to the main road and approached the checkpoint at the narrow gorge. Two sentries were busy inspecting a wagon loaded with sacks of wheat while the owner stood by, ready with a purse of coins. She expected the sentries to stop her, but they didn't, and she continued through to the other side.

A short distance down the road, she found a large rock in the shade and sat down to wait. She ignored the travelers arriving from the west but took notice of those heading away from Aphek. Most of them were farmers or peasants, a few were well-to-do homestead owners, and one caravan had the appearance of foreign merchants, reminding her of Abu Zariz and his family. None of them seemed associated with a tannery.

33

As time passed, Deborah was losing hope. Passing travelers looked at her curiously, and she knew it was only a matter of time before someone questioned her. She started to contemplate going back to Aphek and looking for a place to spend the night. But then, an oxcart passed by, heading downriver, that was loaded with gory cowhides.

Shouldering her sack, Deborah followed.

The oxcart moved slowly, and the two men who drove it never looked back. A couple of hours later, as they came around a curve high above the river, she gagged at the sudden onslaught of an awful stench. The oxcart turned off the road onto a path that went down to a large, busy compound at the riverbank. Deborah followed it, but stopped halfway down. She found a shaded spot behind a clump of bushes off the path and sat on a tree stump to acclimate to the offensive odors and observe the activity below.

At the bottom of the path, armed guards opened a gate to let the oxcart in through the tall wooden fence. Next to the gate, attached to a tree branch, a flag hung limp in the still air, bearing a white antelope against a black background. It was the flag of Manasseh, Orran's tribe.

The wooden fence surrounded the whole area, which was bustling with workers in and around two large open pavilions, one at each end, and a few other structures. The river here was much wider than it was up near Aphek.

The oxcart rolled through the gate and stopped near the pavilion on the right, at the upriver direction. A group of slaves, identified by their cropped hair, sleeveless long shirts, and bare feet, ran over to unload the cart. They sorted the hides into several piles under the large pavilion, which she estimated to measure at least fifty steps long and twenty wide. It had a thatched roof that rested on stone pillars. A manager in a fine coat and a wide-brimmed hat sat in a chair and counted the skins as they were taken off the oxcart. He used a scribe's feather to record the information on a parchment.

Deborah exhaled in relief. She had found the tannery. Now she would have to figure out a way to discover if Kassite still worked here.

A large part of the fenced area, starting near the upriver pavilion, was taken up by rows of square in-ground tubs, each about six steps across. The tubs were filled with various liquids in dull shades of gray and brown, in which animal skins were soaking. Male slaves stepped on the skins to keep them submerged. Another area held worktables and flat rocks, where slaves worked on skins with tools and brushes. At the river's edge, other slaves washed skins in the water, beat them in the mud, and rubbed them with stones.

The second pavilion dominated the left side of the tannery, at the downriver direction, and seemed to be assigned to female slaves only. They were dressed in the same long, sleeveless shirts and wore no sandals, but unlike the men, the women covered their heads with scarves.

Deborah remembered Sallan's description of Kassite: "He is very tall and thin, and he speaks slowly." She watched the male slaves, seeking one who matched the physical aspects of the description. Most of them were short, and the few tall ones were too young to be Kassite. She tried again, focusing on each area of the tannery in turn, peering at individual slaves one at a time, paying particular attention to the tall ones. Still, she couldn't find even one who was remotely old enough. Worse yet, seeing how grueling the tannery work was, she realized that the absence of old slaves made perfect sense. Who could survive to an old age in a place like this?

A fog of despair descended on her. Was this the end of her quest? Was she destined to remain in the confines of womanhood? Was she wrong to believe that delivering God's message from Palm Homestead was her True Calling?

The slaves finished unloading the skins. The manager got up from his chair and walked over to speak with the two oxcart drivers. Now that he was on his feet, she could see that the manager was very tall and thin. Despite his fine leather boots, he walked with a pronounced limp. It reminded Deborah of Sallan, who limped due to losing a foot after trying to escape the Moabite marauders with Kassite, who had suffered the same punishment. And this manager also looked as old as Sallan. Was this a coincidence, or could she be looking at Kassite?

Studying him carefully from her discreet spot on the hillside, Deborah noticed that his manner radiated an authority and confidence that befitted a prosperous free man, not a slave. Besides, wouldn't the salesman at Orran's shop in Aphek have recognized Kassite's name if the Edomite slave had risen to become the manager of the tannery?

No, this man couldn't be Kassite. She had to keep looking at the slaves and try to identify one whose appearance came close to Sallan's description.

At the upriver part of the tannery, behind the pavilion, Deborah could see a large stone oven emitting a column of smoke. A few women were preparing food on a wooden table near the oven. Through the stench of the tannery, she caught a whiff of meat roasting.

Tired of watching the men, Deborah turned her attention to the woman area on the downriver side of the tannery. Their pavilion was of similar size and had the same rectangular thatched roof, but the open sides were equipped with sheets of cloth that hung from the crossbeams, blocking her view of the activity inside. Female slaves worked near the curtained pavilion, stitching, sewing, and applying dye with brushes. The women went in and out of the pavilion through the curtains, carrying skins or buckets of water from the river.

The third prominent structure, near the upriver end of the tannery, was a wood-and-straw house built on stilts over the slow-moving water. It was connected to land with a short wooden bridge. The perimeter fence, which was twice the height of a grown man and made of wooden planks and cross beams, created a solid wall that encircled the whole tannery and reached into the river at both ends. Anyone wishing to enter or exit the tannery, other than through the gate, would have to wade a good distance into the water and back to land. On the inside, the fence was covered with skins. Deborah assumed they'd been hung up to dry. On the outside, all around the fence, the ground was cleared of vegetation to create a wide path. The guards patrolled it on foot. Altogether, she saw eight guards outside, and none inside. While not on patrol, they sat under a tree near the gate and appeared bored. Further back, a corral held eight horses, as well as several cows and goats.

Having watched the activity below for a long while, Deborah noticed that there were no supervisors walking around with whips, yet the slaves—who numbered well over one hundred men and almost as many women—worked diligently and seemed to know exactly what was expected of them.

The manager rang a bell.

The male slaves left their work and lined up in front of the oven near the east pavilion. The women pulled several heavy pots out of the oven and began doling out food into wooden bowls. Each man received a piece of meat and a chunk of bread, bowed before the manager, and sat on the ground under the pavilion to eat. One of the guards came in through the gate and collected food for all of them. He also bowed before the manager, though not as deeply as the slaves had.

Deborah's mouth watered. She hadn't eaten or drunk for hours.

The male slaves finished eating and returned to work. A few of them went behind the pavilion to use the latrines, which were partitioned by waist-high wooden grates. The slaves' upper bodies could be seen as they relieved themselves before returning to work.

Once the male slaves had finished eating, women came out of the curtained pavilion and, together with the women who had been working outside, lined up to collect their food. They bowed to the manager and returned to the west side of the tannery to eat their meal. The women also had a set of latrines behind their pavilion, similarly partitioned at waist level.

When all the slaves had finished eating, one of the women tending to the oven filled a bowl and took it to the manager. He ate quickly, seated in his chair under the pavilion, and returned the bowl to the women by the oven. From there, he walked down the length of the tannery, stopping at various points to inspect the work of the slaves and provide instructions. Deborah was too far away to hear what he said, but she could tell that he spoke calmly and enjoyed the total obedience of the slaves, who seemed eager to please him. His limp, which didn't interfere with his mobility, appeared to be the result of an injury to his left foot. She wondered whether it was missing altogether, as Sallan's was.

The manager entered the curtained pavilion and spent a long time inside.

Meanwhile, several male slaves went to both sets of latrines and carried out open barrels. Judging by their strained faces and bulging muscles, Deborah guessed that the barrels were filled with human waste. The slaves emptied the barrels into some of the open tubs. The yellow urine and chunks of feces were visible on top of the soaking skins in the tubs. Deborah was shocked to see several of the slaves step into the tubs and stomp repeatedly to beat the feces into the skins.

"You, woman!" It was one of the guards, and he was pointing up at her from the gate. "What are you doing there?"

Deborah felt a chill. She should have hidden better.

"Come down here!"

She considering making a run for it, but the guards had horses—and besides, she hadn't given up on finding Kassite here.

"Right now, woman!"

Her hands shaking, Deborah collected her sack and made sure the scarf was tied properly, covering her face. Whatever happened, she told herself, Yahweh would protect her until she found the Elixirist.

Two other guards joined the first one, and they watched her coming down the path toward the gate.

34

The three guards waited for Deborah at the bottom of the path. The others watched from where they sat under the tree. She tried to walk with poise, feigning purposeful certainty, though her legs barely obeyed her, and she had to clench her fists to hide the shaking.

"What're you doing up there?" The guard rested his hand on the handle of his sword. "Spying on us?"

Deborah shook her head.

"Who sent you? The Canaanites? The men of Ephraim?"

She tried to speak, but fear muted her.

The guard picked up a stick and poked her in the chest. "Answer, woman!"

Deborah cleared her throat. "I'm looking for a man."

The guards looked at each other and burst out laughing. One of those sitting under the tree yelled, "I'm ready! Come here!"

"Kassite." Deborah coughed to hide the tremor in her voice. "That's his name. Kassite. Do you know him?"

"You can call me Kassite." The guard holding the stick pulled at her scarf, exposing her face. "Ah, you're a young one."

"Look at her cheesy skin," another said. "What are you? An Edomite?"

"No, I'm from—"

"Show us more skin, girl."

"Make her," the others goaded him. "Make her!"

He grabbed the lapel of her robe. "You heard them. Let's see what you've got."

Deborah pulled away, stepped back, and stumbled, falling down.

The guard came after her, smirking.

She got up quickly and raised her hand, displaying the ring on her finger. "My husband is coming!"

The guard paused and glanced back at his friends.

"He's coming," she said, "with his soldiers!"

"She's lying," a guard yelled from under the tree. "No husband would let a young wife run around alone like this."

"Cheating little mouse." The guard waved his stick. "Get back here."

Resisting the urge to flee, Deborah remembered Zariz's advice when he'd taught her how to ride: "You must pretend to be confident, or the horse will not respect you." These guards were animals, she decided, like horses.

"My husband will flog you," she said, "until the skin is gone from your back. And then he'll demand compensation from Orran of Manasseh for your attack on me. Would you like to be sold off as slaves to pay my husband? Would you?"

Her audacity worked. The grins faded, and the guards looked at each other, unsure what to do.

Before they had time to recover, she said, "I wish to see Kassite. Call him out."

They didn't respond, and she couldn't tell whether they'd recognized the name. It was the longest moment of her life, because if Kassite couldn't be found here, she would truly need a message from Yahweh to tell her where to go next.

Finally, one of them said, "We don't know this name."

It was the response she'd dreaded, but Deborah wasn't ready to give up. She steadied her voice. "Do you know all the slaves' names?"

The guard shook his head.

That was a ray of hope. "Then call the manager over," she said. "I'll speak with him."

He opened the gate and went inside. A few minutes later, he returned with the manager, who was even taller than he had seemed from a distance. The brim of his hat sheltered his face from the sun, but she could see his eyes, alight with a bright-gray hue that radiated youthfulness in stark contrast to his weathered skin.

"What is the problem, girl?" He spoke in the Edomite language.

Her heartbeat quickened. Not only his age, height, and limp matched Sallan's description, but he spoke Sallan's language, too. Slave or not, either the manager was Kassite, or this was a cruel coincidence.

She glanced at the guards.

The manager turned to them and said in Hebrew, "Leave us."

They bowed and stepped away.

"I bring you personal regards," she said. "From an old friend."

"A friend?" The manager spoke slowly. "I do not have any friends."

"Sallan."

His expression remained blank. "What did you say?"

"Sallan," she repeated. "Your old friend sends his regards."

Had Deborah not been watching him keenly, she would have missed the slight widening of his eyes and the slow, barely perceptible exhalation that caused his posture to lose a tad of its erectness.

The manager shook his head.

"But he said—"

"Go away, girl."

Deborah couldn't believe it. "Sallan sent me! It's the truth!"

The manager turned to the guards. "You may do with her as you wish."

Without giving her another look, he went back into the tannery.

The guards advanced at her, grinning.

Deborah grabbed her sack and ran. Halfway up the path, she glanced back and saw the guards still at the bottom of the path, laughing. One of them dashed uphill after her. She sped up and, at the top, turned onto the Sea Highway and ran as fast as she could. Rounding the bend in the road, she heard boots pounding the dirt behind her and plunged into the bushes, wading through the dense vegetation down the embankment. At a small clearing, she collapsed and curled up on the ground, panting and shaking, her sack pressed to her chest.

35

The sounds of birds woke Deborah up. She didn't remember falling asleep, but here she was, curled on the ground in a small clearing on the hillside above the river. The birds flew here and there through the bushes, squealing urgently.

A large shadow passed above, and she heard thrashing in the branches a few steps away, followed by a sharp shriek. Rising to her feet, she saw a hawk take off, its wide wings flapping, a gray rodent clutched in its talons. She watched the hawk fly out over the river and swing around, heading downstream, past the jutting edge of the tannery fence, and land on the thatched roof of the stilts-supported house. The hawk pinned down its prey, belly up, and tore into it, pulling out strings of bloody intestines and yellow-tinged internal organs while the rodent continued to paw the air as if trying to run away. The rapid assault made for a nauseating spectacle, but she couldn't look away. The hawk's speed and precision in executing the attack, transporting its catch to a safe location, and devouring it with such shocking efficiency, mesmerized her.

Its meal consumed, the hawk flew away, leaving behind a red blotch and a circle of bloody tufts of fur on the thatched roof. Deborah watched the hawk grow smaller until it disappeared in the hazy western horizon, where the sun was setting. She wished to be powerful and fearless like that hawk, to find what she needed, take it without hesitation or remorse, and fly away, out of sight and out of reach, free and safe. Why had Yahweh endowed this hawk with such gifts while leaving her weak and vulnerable, an easy prey to wicked men?

The injustice of it all enraged Deborah. She recalled the manager telling the guards, "If she's not gone in one minute, you may do with her as you wish." His words had been vicious, but his eyes weren't. In fact, when he heard Sallan's name, his indifference briefly lifted, replaced not by surprise or joy, but by something else. Reflecting on it now, she realized that the manager's reaction, while subtle, had consisted of shock and apprehension. Why?

She must find out!

Collecting her sack, Deborah pushed through the thicket, slowly making her way downhill to the riverbank. Yahweh might have deprived her of the ability to fly over the water and reach her destination easily, but she could still get there the hard way, confront the manager, and force him to admit that he knew Sallan. Either the manager was Kassite, or he had learned Sallan's name from Kassite and could tell her where to find him.

Twilight was getting bleaker when Deborah reached the water's edge. A few hundred steps south, she saw the tannery fence jutting into the river. She began to advance slowly, hunched over to avoid being seen.

Near the fence, she ducked, made sure the guards weren't on patrol, and waded into the river. She held her sack above the water, which reached above her hips before the bottom flattened out. It wasn't cold, and the current was slow. She hoped there were no dangerous animals or snakes under the surface. Coming around the end of the fence, she stayed low in the water so that only her head showed as she advanced toward shore.

The stench inside the fence was even worse. She breathed through her mouth. Edging along the inside of the fence, she approached the riverbank. The short bridge connecting the house to the shore concealed her from the rest of the tannery. She pulled the hood of her robe over her hair, adjusted the scarf across her face, and stepped out of the water.

The tannery buzzed with activity, and the approaching darkness shielded her from attention. She was now at the east end of the tannery, in the upriver direction, where the men worked. The manger was siting in the pavilion, sipping from a wooden cup, examining a parchment against a small lamp. Deborah walked over and stood before him. He rolled up the parchment and put it aside, his pale eyes peering at her from under the rim of his hat.

"You are persistent," he said. "How did you get in?"

She put down her sack and squeezed water from the front of her robe.

"Through the river?" He chuckled. "Clever girl. The guards did not see you come back, did they?"

"Are you afraid of them?"

"I am in charge here."

"When I mentioned Sallan's name, your expression showed fear."

"Caution is not the same as fear. I do not want any trouble here."

"What kind of trouble?"

"The trouble one should expect when a Hebrew girl with a ring on her finger shows up alone and starts asking questions about long-forgotten names, and the trouble of an angry husband, who must be close behind."

"Does it justify telling the guards to ravage me?"

"They are too lazy for that, but when your husband shows up, they will remember that I sent you away. Now, what do want from me?"

"Sallan warned me you'd be suspicious."

"Sallan is dead," he said. "I know that for a fact."

His manner of speaking was deliberate, like someone overcoming a stutter. His pronunciation of the Hebrew words was halting, yet easily understood. And best of all, he had just admitted that he knew Sallan!

"Sallan is alive," she said.

"He was killed in Mitzpah by Canaanite raiders many years ago. I have inquired with several travelers, and they all said that everyone was killed that day. There were no survivors. You are lying. What do you really want?"

"It's true that his owner died, but Sallan didn't. He's now owned by Judge Zifron in Emanuel, where he runs the basket factory."

"The Zifron baskets?"

Deborah pulled the basket she'd made from her sack.

He examined it, feeling the weave with his fingers, which were long and delicate. "Triple stalks," he said. "Subtle, but very effective."

"Is your name Kassite?" She held her breath.

He looked up from the basket. "What did you say?"

"Are you Kassite?"

He grunted and turned his attention back to the basket. He sniffed it, turned it around, and sniffed again. "A tiger from the desert. What a marvelous scent."

Impressed that he could smell anything in this odorous place, she pulled the tiger tail from the sack. "Sallan has the rest of the skin in his quarters. We sat on it together the night I left Emanuel."

Slowly moving the long tail near his nostrils, he inhaled, taking the scent in with total concentration, his expression bordering on awe. When he put the tiger tail down in his lap, his eyes were moist. "The smell of home," he said hoarsely.

"That's what Sallan said."

His eyes narrowed and he shook his head. "Sallan is dead. You want to trick me."

"No."

"What is your scheme? What do you hope to steal?"

"Nothing. I have no scheme."

"Are you scouting the place for your husband? Is he an enemy of Orran? Is this another tribal skirmish in the making?" The manager groaned with frustration. "These Hebrew tribesmen never stop bickering."

"Sallan predicted your doubts. He gave me a secret code."

"A code?"

"He said it would convince you, because no one else in the world knows what it means."

The manager waved in dismissal. "Enough with the tricks, girl. Go away before I call the guards."

"Thirteen hundred and thirteen."

His hand froze in midair, and he whispered, "What did you say?"

"Thirteen hundred and thirteen."

He pulled off his hat, revealing a thick mane of white hair, and turned his face up, blinking rapidly. The corners of his mouth curled downward, his lips trembled, and tears began to flow down his cheeks. Pressing the tiger tail to his chest, he sobbed quietly.

Deborah lowered her eyes, looked at her hands, and waited for him to calm down.

Finally, his sobs subsided.

She reached over and pressed his hand. "I hope these are tears of joy."

"Yes." He cleared his throat. "Joy and disbelief."

The slaves lighted torches and continued to work all around the tannery, none of them staring or standing idle even for a moment.

He sniffled. "Tell me everything you know."

"Sallan was a free man," Deborah said. "He lived in a beautiful city with his parents and sisters, but on one of his travels, marauders captured him and his friend Kassite. The two of them tried to escape, but the marauders caught them and cut off each man's left foot and both ears."

"Yes, yes," the manager said quietly. "The harsh men of Moab did that."

"It happened about eighteen years ago. Sallan was sold to a merchant from Mitzpah, whereas Kassite was sold to Orran of Manasseh."

"What has happened to Sallan since then?"

"As I said, he runs a basket factory for Judge Zifron, the ruler of Emanuel."

The manager wiped more tears.

"Please tell me," she said. "Are you Kassite?"

He knocked his left foot against the leg of the chair, producing the hollow sound of wood against wood. He slipped his fingers under his long, white hair on both sides of his head and pushed the hair up, exposing his ears—or what was left of his ears after they had been cut off.

"It's you," she said, her voice choking.

"Yes," he said. "I am Kassite."

Even though Deborah had already guessed it, hearing him say his name out loud flooded her with delight and relief. She had succeeded! She had found the Elixirist!

"No one," he said, "has called me Kassite in many years."

"What do they call you here?"

"Master."

"Master," she repeated. "I like it."

He gestured at the gate and the path that went up to the main road. "You came here from Emanuel?"

Deborah nodded.

"By yourself?"

"It's a long story. Today I walked down from Aphek."

He signaled to one of the women, who brought a piece of cheese, a chunk of bread, and a wooden cup of water. Deborah ate quickly while Kassite watched in silence. When she was done, they walked to the water's edge.

Kassite looked out at the dark river. "On that day in Shiloh, when they sold Sallan and me to different owners, I lost my only friend in the world."

The gravity of emotion in his voice made her shudder. "He'll be happy beyond belief to know you're alive."

Kassite turned to her. "What was that?"

"When Sallan hears that you're alive, he'll be happy beyond belief."

Kassite smiled. "When will you go back to tell him?"

"Going back isn't so simple," she said. "My journey from Emanuel, searching for you, has been filled with horrors and disasters. I barely made it here alive."

"I am surprised you've survived."

"Yahweh's grace," she said.

"The Hebrew God?"

"He saw that I was pursuing my True Calling and paved my way to you."

"What is your name?"

"I'm Deborah, daughter of Harutz of Ephraim."

"And what is your True Calling, Deborah, which I am supposed to help you realize?"

After all that had happened during her search for the Elixirist, now that she faced the man in the flesh, her words had to be chosen carefully to ensure that he would agree to help her.

"Speak up," he said. "Do not be afraid."

"I don't want to be a woman anymore."

"Is that so?" He sighed. "You expect a lot from me."

"Not more than what you did with the women of Edom in order to defeat an Egyptian army and save your king."

He picked up a smooth stone and tossed it far into the water, where it skipped a few times before sinking. "Sallan told you that I had been responsible for that famous event?"

"A friend told me the story. A boy my age." She paused, letting the pain of Barac's loss pass. "He's dead now, murdered by Judge Zifron's son. At first, I thought the story was a myth, an exaggeration, but Sallan confirmed it. He said that you are the Elixirist, the man who saved Edom from the Egyptians."

"Sallan said that?"

"Yes."

"What else did he say?"

"He told me of the injustice you had suffered when King Esau the Eighteenth rewarded you for saving his throne by locking you up deep underground in isolation."

"Anything else?"

"Sallan also told me how you helped the guard recover his ability to hear and speak, and in return the guard let you go, though you soon lost your freedom again when the marauders captured you—the same marauders who also enslaved Sallan, punished both of you after your failed escape, and later sold you at Shiloh."

Kassite tossed another small stone across the water, making it skip six times before it sank. "I do not remember Sallan to be so carelessly loose with his tongue."

Deborah searched the ground and found a flat stone that the river had rubbed smooth. She pitched it in a course parallel to the water. It hit once, leaped over a great distance, and then skipped several times in decreasing gaps until it sank.

"Impressive. Can you do it again?"

She found another flat stone and managed to make it skip even more times, far enough that it disappeared in the dark while still skipping.

Kassite smiled. "You already have a boy's arm."

"I grew up throwing rocks, though not over water." Deborah picked up another small stone, but didn't throw it. "Will you help me?"

Turning his back to the water, Kassite surveyed the tannery, where the slaves continued to work without interruption. "There was nothing here," he said. "Orran bought the land, sent me here with ten Philistine slaves and a pile of bloody cowhides, and told everyone to call me Master. That was eighteen years ago. Now, look at this place."

"It's a big operation," she said.

"The largest tannery in the land. Only the Philistines in Ashkelon have a larger one, but even they don't make as many products as us." He adjusted his hat. "This tannery has been my life for a long time—a very good life, actually."

"Except for the stench."

Kassite chuckled. "There is an old saying among pig growers in Edom: 'One man's stench is another man's perfume.'"

Deborah had never seen a pig, and it was hard for her to imagine anyone mistaking the tannery stench for perfume, but she understood what he meant.

"Look at all my workers, everything they do." He waved his hand across the tannery. "Each one of these men and women, every job they do and every task they complete are planned by me, directed by me, and produce the results I expect."

"And Orran rewarded you with freedom?"

A cloud crossed Kassite's face. "No. I am still a slave, and the profits from my tannery go into Orran's pockets, not mine." He paused, taking a deep breath. "In every other respect, though, I am very content. No one tells me what to do, and I am in charge of all these men and women, who bow to me as if I were their owner. It is almost as good as being a free man. Do you understand?"

She nodded. If he was trying to impress her, it was working, but she hadn't come here to learn about the production of leather or to admire his skills in running a tannery. She'd come here because he was the Elixirist.

"I understand," she said. "Can you help me?"

He tilted his head doubtfully. "How did you know to look for me here?"

"Sallan told me about the records of slave trading in Shiloh. I went there and managed to discover that you'd been sold to Orran."

"Why did Sallan help you?"

"We made a bargain. I promised that, after I found you and won your help, I'd return to Emanuel and free Sallan from Judge Zifron's bondage."

"Now it makes sense." He looked up at the dark sky for a long moment before turning back to face her. "Sallan must be terribly anxious to go home, taking such a risk with your life, and with mine."

"Your life won't be at risk. I'm only asking that you make for me the same elixir you made for the women of Edom, so that I can be free. Helping Sallan gain his freedom in Emanuel is my promise to keep, my risk to take, not yours."

Kassite sighed. "When you are young, the world gives you the illusion that it is a simple place. But the world is not simple at all. You see, Sallan was not relying on you to obtain his freedom. He was relying on me."

Finally, Deborah understood why Kassite had boasted of the tannery he'd built here and the good life he enjoyed while running it. Her arrival today, and the news she had brought that Sallan was alive, meant that Kassite might have to give up everything for his old friend's freedom.

"Give me the elixir, and off I go." She gestured at the gate. "By turning me into a man, you'll empower me to free Sallan, while you can stay here to enjoy your luxuries and forget about him."

"How dense are you, girl?" He leaned over her, glaring, his finger in her face. "I'm talking with you only because Sallan needs my help. You're nothing but a mindless messenger."

Deborah stepped back, shocked by his sudden fury, and watched him limp back to the pavilion, where he rang the bell several times.

The slaves stopped working and lined up for the evening meal. They received bread and meat again, as well as cups of hot drink. Every slave went before Kassite, who was sitting in his chair, and bowed. Kassite responded with a nod and an occasional word or two. As far as Deborah could tell, no one noticed her, standing alone in the dark at the water's edge in her hooded robe, the sack at her feet.

The men settled down under the pavilion, talking quietly to each other while they ate and drank. The female slaves took their food back to the downriver side of the tannery. They raised the curtains at their pavilion to let in the evening breeze from the river.

After dinner, two torches were left burning in front of each pavilion. The slaves put down straw mats and went to sleep in long rows. A woman brought Kassite a cup. He remained in his chair and took small sips while the tannery quieted down.

Deborah waited, battling anxious thoughts and festering doubts. Had his fury subsided? Had he made a decision, or was he still enraged by the choice she had forced on him? Would he throw her out, as his parting words had threatened, or would he help her? After all she had gone through to find Kassite, it was maddening to find that he could be so cruel as to contemplate discarding her to be brutally abused by the guards. Had he really meant it? She stared at him, but his face was inscrutable in the flickering flames of the torches, and then her tears blurred the view altogether.

36

When all the slaves were asleep, Kassite left the pavilion. Deborah expected him to walk over to where she waited, but he went straight to the short bridge connecting the riverbank to the house. A servant appeared at the door, holding a lamp. Kassite paused and looked in Deborah's direction. She shouldered her sack, barely able to restrain herself from running to him and begging for his help.

A long moment passed.

Kassite raised his hand and beckoned her.

Deborah hurried along the riverbank, her sandals sloshing in the soft mud. She stopped at the foot of the bridge, facing him. "Will you help me?"

"I am of two minds," he said. "Send you out the gate into the guards' hands, or toss you in the water to feed the fish."

His tone was impassive, but the glow of the lamp on his face revealed bemusement.

"Difficult choice," she said. "Do you want my opinion?"

He chuckled. "Shall we discuss it inside?"

Deborah hesitated. She was unnerved by his earlier fury and even more by his joking about the two ways he could dispose of her. Kassite tilted his head at the door, which the servant held open. She relented and entered, half-expecting to be grabbed, tied up, and thrown to her death, one way or the other.

A table was set for two with plates, knives, and a burning lamp. Another servant waited inside. The two resembled Sallan's light-skinned boy-servants but were at least ten years older.

Closing the door, Kassite said, "You may remove your scarf and lower your hood now."

She did, making sure her hair was tied properly.

An effigy of Qoz, like the one in Sallan's quarters, stood on a pedestal near the table. Its buffed copper was shining, and its open eyes were blank. The servants stood aside, their heads bowed, and Kassite placed a bowl of food in front of Qoz.

"We thank you," he said, "the mighty Qoz, supreme master of the world, for the food you deigned to share with us, as well as for guarding us from illness and injury. May you keep us safe until it is our time to join the gods in eternity."

Sitting down at the table, Kassite pointed at the other chair.

"Me?" Deborah felt her face flush. "I'm not hungry."

"A proper meal is more than a way to quench hunger." Kassite poured wine into both cups. "With good food, you open a guest's mouth, and with good wine, you untie his tongue."

She sat down and moved the chair closer to the table. "Thank you."

"I should thank you. I rarely have the opportunity to entertain company here."

Why was he suddenly nice to her? Where had his anger gone? Deborah tried to read his face, but saw nothing alarming. He raised his cup, she did the same, and they drank. The wine was stronger than she was used to, but also sweet. She felt warmth spread inside her.

The servants began to bring the food. The first dish looked like a slice of meat, but it was white and flaky. Something stung her tongue and she pulled it out. It was a small bone, almost as thin as a hair.

"River fish," he said. "They are skinny and full of bones."

"I had fish at Sallan's quarters. It had no bones and tasted sweeter than this."

"Lemon and salt," he said. "That is all we use. They don't serve fish regularly in Emanuel?"

"Not in the women's quarters."

Kassite took another bite and chewed slowly, washing it down with a sip of wine. "Tell me more about Judge Zifron."

"He's the ruler of Emanuel, rich and powerful, with several wives and concubines, many slaves, and soldiers."

"Is he a warrior?"

"Not anymore. He's getting old and fat. His first son commands the soldiers." She cleared her throat, which was suddenly dry. "His name is Seesya."

"How old is he?"

She glanced at the ring on her finger. "About nineteen."

Kassite reached across the table and tapped the ring. "Did Seesya put this on your finger?"

She nodded.

"Will you ever agree to serve him as a good wife?"

"No."

"What is wrong with him?"

"An evil heart." She took a deep breath. "He had my sister stoned to death one day after he married her."

"That must be hard to forgive." Kassite watched her thoughtfully. "Yet you have kept his ring on."

"Men hesitate to abuse a woman whose husband might be close behind."

He nodded.

Deborah tried to pull off the ring, but it was too tight. She picked a flake of fish from her plate, rubbed it against her finger to make it oily, and tried again, but the ring remained stuck.

Kassite signaled one of the slaves, who brought a cup of water. She dipped her finger. The water was surprisingly cold.

"The springs that feed the river near Aphek are very cold," Kassite said. "When the sun goes down and no longer beats down on the river, the flow brings the cold water of the springs down to us."

A few moments later, she took her finger out. The cold water had shrunk it, and the ring came off. She put it in her sack.

"Your husband might not be so easy to put away. Does he know where you went?"

"I don't think so."

"How many soldiers does he have?"

"Judge Zifron has fifty or sixty soldiers with horses and weapons, but Seesya travels with only five or six at a time."

"Does Emanuel have walls?"

"Yes, it has strong walls. The gates are locked from sunset to sunrise. There are always sentries there. Visitors must camp outside at night."

"And Sallan, where does he live?"

"Above the basket factory, which is in a wing of Judge Zifron's house, along the courtyard. Sallan has nice living quarters and two boy-servants."

Kassite smiled. "In our country, keeping two personal servants is a sign of wealth and status."

"The judge provides Sallan with many comforts."

"Does Sallan deal directly with the traders who order baskets?"

"Yes, and he keeps the accounts on parchments, the way you do."

"You're observant," Kassite said. "That's good. Do you know if he's allowed to go outside?"

"The traders go up to the judge's house to deal with Sallan. I've seen him walk up and down the main street, but never outside the walls."

"That is unfortunate." Kassite sat back, his arms folded on his chest. "Does he have a second-in-command? Someone who is ready to take over at the basket factory?"

"I don't think so. He's the foreman. No one else gives orders in the basket factory. Also, he's the only one who knows the secret formula for the Reinforcing Liquid."

Kassite's hand, holding a chunk of fish, paused on the way to his mouth. "What did you say?"

"The strands of straw are dipped in the Reinforcing Liquid before weaving. That's why the Zifron baskets are so strong."

Kassite put the food down, threw his head back, and laughed out loud.

"What's so funny?" Deborah was insulted. "He gave me some of it to drink before I escaped."

"Did he?"

"Yes, and it worked. It reinforced me."

"Is that right?"

"I'm sure of it. I wouldn't have had the strength to keep going, to overcome the terrible things that happened to me, to persist until I found you, if not for Sallan's Reinforcing Liquid."

"Probably not," Kassite said, still laughing. "Probably not."

Confused by his laughter, Deborah pushed aside her plate.

Kassite snapped his fingers, and the servants cleared the dishes away.

"Show me that basket again," he said.

She pulled it out of her sack and gave it to him.

"Look at the strands." He pointed, holding the basket close to the lamp. "Most basket weavers use individual stalks of straw or flax, or even twigs or weeds. But here the weaving is done with strands made of three stalks that were braided together tightly."

"That's correct. We first dipped the stalks in the Reinforcing Liquid, and then every three stalks were braided and left to dry."

"My wise friend, Sallan. How I miss him!" Kassite held up his wine cup. "To all the reinforcing liquids under the sun!"

They drank the wine. Deborah felt her belly warm up again and her hopes rise. Kassite's questions about Emanuel, its defenses, and the daily life of Sallan could only mean that he was considering how to overcome the challenges of freeing his old friend. Or, she realized with dread, he could be looking for excuses to do nothing and dismiss her as a foolish girl in pursuit of a lost cause.

Taking another sip of wine, she asked, "Are you still angry at me?"

Kassite picked up the knife, which had rested next to his plate, and examined the blade at length. "Life is like a knife," he said. "It has a dull side, which is safe and predictable, posing no risk of pain and suffering, and a sharp side, which is scary and dangerous, but also makes the whole thing worthwhile."

His words were cryptic. Was he still angry or not? Deborah wasn't sure. Was he trying to explain his initial anger, when his dull life had been interrupted by her arrival? She kept quiet, sensing that it was better to respect his silence and wait for him to speak again.

The servants brought in two roasted pigeons on clay plates. Kassite carved the meat from the bones with his knife and ate slowly. Deborah tried to do the same, but her knife kept slipping off and she gave up. Instead, she pulled the pigeon apart with her fingers and bit the meat off.

For dessert, the servants brought sweet cakes and apples for both of them, as well as a hot drink for Kassite.

He slurped from the cup. "The transformation you seek, from a girl to a boy, do you wish it to be temporary or permanent?"

"Permanent," she said. "For the rest of my life."

"Are you sure?"

"Yes."

"What if a boy came along, someone nice, not like the son of Zifron, and you suddenly want to marry?"

The face of Zariz came to her mind, his smile, his glistening eyes, the honeysuckle flower in his mouth, and his father's stern voice in the back, calling him back.

"No," she said. "Never."

"Think carefully of the past," Kassite said. "What happened before might happen again. Has there ever been a young man who warmed your heart? Perhaps he still causes you to feel warm all over when you think of him?"

Deborah drove the image of Zariz away and shook her head.

"Not a single nice boy in Emanuel?"

Another image came to her—Barac, his severed head rolling in the dirt, his black curls white with dust. She groaned, shaking her head again.

"I find it hard to believe," Kassite said. "There must be someone you imagined, even for a moment, as your future husband—marrying him, bearing his children, being his wife."

"There's no one," Deborah said. "Not now, not ever. I want to become a boy, mature into a man, and grow old as a man."

"How about trying it for a short duration, a few days, as with the women of Edom, or even a month or two, to see how you like it?"

"I never want to be a girl again. I'd rather die."

Kassite nodded thoughtfully. "It is understandable, considering your experience of true misfortune, but life may bring good fortune, too. A painful past does not always foretell a painful future. With foresight, the lessons of the past could help create a happy future."

"Not for a woman. My future will be happy only if I'm a man. I'll reclaim my inheritance, plow my father's land, and serve my God."

"Serve in what way?" He leaned forward, curious.

She hesitated, afraid he would laugh at her. "My father had a dream that I would grow up to serve as Yahweh's prophet. I believe that's what I'm supposed to do with my life."

Kassite didn't laugh. "Now I understand. Becoming a prophet—is that what you meant earlier when you spoke of your True Calling?"

"Yes."

"Then you should consider the consequences carefully. What do you expect to change if you become a boy?"

"Isn't it obvious?"

He slurped from his cup. "Indulge me with an answer."

"I'd become a real person, free to own land, to carry a sword, to read and write, to study holy scriptures—"

"Yes, yes, yes. I know what men may do and women may not." Kassite waved his hand, exasperated. "A hundred men sleep under that pavilion, and not one of them owns land, carries a weapon, or reads and writes. My question is about substance. What would really change if you become a boy?"

"Everything would change. Everything!"

"Suppose I could do this," he said, snapping his fingers, "and produce the Male Elixir in one second."

Deborah's chest tightened with excitement. It had a name—the Male Elixir! It existed!

"And let us assume," Kassite continued, "that you drank it and became a boy. What specific changes would take place in you?"

"I don't know. I've never been a boy."

"Try to imagine," Kassite said. "How would you change?"

Deborah finally understood his question. It wasn't difficult, only awkward. "I'd have a different body. Do you want me to specify the male parts? Do you want to embarrass me until I give up?"

"I would be wasting my time," Kassite said. "You are obviously not one to give up, which is admirable. I have great respect for a True Calling."

"Why?"

"The pursuit of a True Calling is the highest human endeavor, because it springs directly from the soul and raises us above all other living creatures."

"Then why are you mocking me with these questions? Don't you know the differences between a girl and a boy?"

Kassite chuckled. "Yes, I know the differences, but it is not I who seeks transformation to the opposite sex. It is you, and before you actually go through with it, I want to make sure you understand what it would mean to become a boy."

"It would mean freedom!" She stood up, raising her voice. "It would mean everything!"

"No need to yell," he said. "You are among friends here."

She sat down. "I'm sorry, but being a girl has made my life miserable. I know what I want, and Sallan told me you could help me."

"Sallan, yes." Kassite sighed. "What Sallan wants, Sallan gets."

"Really? Will you give me the Male Elixir? Will you?"

Kassite put his cup down near the lamp, and the steam drifted above the small flame.

"Could you do it tonight?" She held her hands together as if in prayer. "Could you? Please?"

"It is not a simple yes or no. The question I asked you—how is a boy different from a girl?—has an answer in three parts. First, his physical strength is greater. Second, his character is masculine. Third, his private parts are male. To transform someone fully and permanently, a careful process must be followed, with each phase completed before the next one is tackled."

"But if I drink the elixir tonight—"

"The Male Elixir is not easy to make, and drinking it would only begin a long process comprising the three phases of transformation."

"Yes! I'm ready!"

"The first phase alone is very hard. Building the physical strength of a boy means not only growing muscles, but also developing resilience, tolerance for pain, and capacity for hard labor."

Deborah clenched her fists. "I can do all that."

"It could take weeks before you're ready to start the second phase, when you will have to change your character from the passive, temperamental, small-minded, and anxious female to the superior male character, which is proactive, even-tempered, adventurous, and logical."

She nodded, not in agreement with his description of the female character, which didn't fit her, but out of eagerness to please him.

"If you manage to complete the first two phases," Kassite continued, "then you will be ready for the third—changing your body to that of a real male. Do you understand the three phases?"

"Yes."

"It will be a long and difficult process that might be too hard for you to accomplish, being a weak girl."

"I'm not weak," she said.

He took a deep breath and exhaled. "Were you listening to me?"

"Yes."

"Did you hear what I just said about the female character?"

"Passive, temperamental, small-minded, and anxious."

"Each one is a weakness. Correct?"

Deborah didn't think of herself as passive, temperamental, or small-minded, but she was definitely anxious right now – anxious to convince him to help her, which would be more likely if she didn't argue with him.

"Yes," she said, "but maybe I'm different from other girls."

Kassite looked at her at length, as if trying to decide whether she really was different.

"I'm ready to take on the challenge," she said. "I won't disappoint you."

"I may be the one to disappoint you," he said. "Before I make up my mind, there is a condition. You must swear to obey me in all matters from now until the process is complete. Total obedience—no questions, no arguments, no hesitation."

"I'll swear to it right now."

"Consider it carefully before you agree," Kassite said. "The process will be long, hard, and painful. I might instruct you to do things that you find wrong, or even sinful. Worse yet, if you break your oath and disobey me, I might stop the process in the middle, leaving you in limbo, neither a girl nor a boy. You could end up an outcast, like a leper."

"I'm already an outcast." Deborah pressed her hand to her chest. "I swear in the name of Yahweh that I will obey you in all matters totally and without question until the process is complete and I become a boy."

"Very well," Kassite said. "I will make my decision by tomorrow morning. Now you may join me for quiet time on the river. No more talking tonight."

She followed him to a terrace at the back of the house. They lounged on soft cushions and looked out at the river. The current splashed gently against the stilts under the house. The servants stood behind them and fanned away the flies.

When it was time to sleep, Deborah lay on a straw mat at the foot of the table where they had eaten dinner. Kassite and his two servants retired to a bedroom off to the side. Within a few minutes, intermittent snoring sounded over the soft rustling of water under the house. She stretched out on her back and thought about her journey, starting with Tamar's stoning and all that had happened since. It had been a dangerous, painful, and at times hopeless journey, but she had succeeded in finding the Elixirist—he was sleeping in the next room! Would he decide to give her the Male Elixir? The morning seemed so far away. She glanced at the window. How long until first light? And what if Kassite refused? No, he couldn't refuse, because it made no sense. Why would Yahweh provide all the shortcuts that had brought her to this point, and then allow Kassite to deny her the Male Elixir? No, Yahweh would sway Kassite's heart in her favor to help her transform into a boy, a young man, and a free Hebrew. She would return to Emanuel, help Sallan gain his freedom, and win back Palm Homestead.

And then? How did one prepare to be a prophet? Was that also a process with three phases? She smiled at the idea. Whether or not there was a prescribed way to prepare, at least she knew where to begin: Obadiah of Levi's scrolls at the temple in Emanuel. She would learn to read and write in order to study the parchments containing the divine laws and prepare herself to fulfill her father's dream.

Closing her eyes, Deborah recalled standing with Obadiah in the dark by the communal burial cave outside the walls on the night she escaped Emanuel. The priest held his hands over her head, his fingers parted in pairs, and recited: "May Yahweh bless you and protect you. May He show you kindness and grace. May He illuminate your path and grant you peace."

37

The last words of the priest's blessing echoed in Deborah's mind when a hand tapped her shoulder, waking her up.

"Time to get up, girl."

It was the voice of Kassite—the Elixirist himself—and his words were not in her dream, but spoken by him right there in the room.

The previous day's events came rushing back—her futile inquiries at the Fairground in Aphek, trailing the loaded oxcart of butchered skins along the river, spying on the tannery in search of a tall, old slave, running away from the guards, watching the hawk ravage the helpless rodent, and coming around through the river to confront the only man who fit the description of the Elixirist.

"Still dreaming?" Kassite lighted an oil lamp. "The sun will be up soon."

Deborah sat up. "Have you reached a decision?"

"I decided there is no choice to be made. I must do what the gods of Edom expect me to do." He held up a long knife.

She yelped and crawled backward until her back hit the wall.

He chuckled. "It's not your flesh I'm about to cut."

"I don't understand."

"Do you want to become a boy?"

"Yes."

"This is the first step." Kassite turned one of the chairs away from the table. "Sit here."

Deborah sat quietly while he chopped off her hair with the sharp blade. In the window, the patch of visible sky was gray with a new dawn. From its pedestal by the wall, the three-horned effigy of Qoz watched in silence, its oversized eyes blank as those of a blind person. It wielded its three-pronged thunderbolt, not horizontally, as one would aim a spear, but upward, as if warning of an impending storm.

When Kassite was done, the floor around her feet was covered with her black-dyed hair.

"Clean it up," he said.

She collected the thick locks of hair from the floor and tossed them out the window, where the slow current took everything downriver. She wanted to touch her scalp but was afraid to.

He gave her a sleeveless shirt. "Put this on."

Deborah pulled off her robe and sandals, placing them in her sack, and put on the shirt, which reached down to her knees and left her arms exposed. It was made of coarse wool that chafed her skin. She straightened the front, checked whether her small breasts showed, and was relieved to find that the rough material and loose fit concealed her body's mild contours.

"You're tall and lean for a girl," he said. "Even if your feminine body showed, people see only what they expect to see, which in your case is a young man among many other slaves. Your skin color is a little too light for someone working out in the sun." He pointed at the stove, where the servants had cooked last night's dinner. "Smear ashes on your face, arms, and legs, and keep it up for a few days until you get dirty and sunburned."

She did as he said, quickly rubbing soot all over. "Is this good?"

Kassite checked her up and down, front and back. "Good enough, but remember that appearance will take you only so far. It's up to you to actually change."

"How?"

"From this moment on, focus your mind on your goal and make sure all your actions advance you toward that goal. Think of yourself as a young man and behave like one." He grabbed her arms and made her stand straight. "Start with your posture—shoulders back, head up, arms loose—ready to act, to work, to fight."

Deborah finally dared to touch her shorn hair. There was little left of it, but the absence of her long hair suddenly made her feel liberated as if she had become someone else.

"I can do that," she said. "I can pretend to be a boy."

"Pretending is only the beginning. The goal you have set for yourself—to become a boy, a man—will require much more than pretending."

She stood straight and shook her arms, which felt odd without the customary long sleeves. "More than pretending?"

"When it comes to achieving transformation, there is a secret method: imitate until you mutate."

"Imitate to mutate?"

"Exactly," Kassite said. "Imitate to mutate."

Deborah shouldered her sack. "I'm ready."

"Leave it here. Slaves have no belongings."

She hesitated, puzzled by his words. Was she a slave now?

"Let's go." Kassite was already at the door, and his voice left no room for argument. "Hurry up."

Leaving her sack on the floor, she followed him out of the house. Despite his limp, Kassite walked fast across the bridge and to the pavilion where the men were sleeping. Her head, exposed for the first time in her life without hair, a hood, or a scarf, felt cold in the early morning air. Sharp pebbles hurt her bare feet.

Kassite rang the bell, and the slaves began to rise. They folded the straw mats, piled them in the corner of the pavilion, and went to the river to wash.

"Petro!" Kassite waved one of the slaves over and pointed at Deborah. "This is a new boy. His name is Borah. He's part of your group now."

"Yes, Master." Petro bowed. He was short and stocky, with rust-colored hair and missing teeth.

"Borah needs to learn the work," Kassite said. "You are responsible for him."

Petro bowed again and walked away.

"Go with him," Kassite told Deborah. "Observe the men and act like one. Keep your voice down, stay calm, and work hard."

"Imitate to mutate," she said.

"Exactly."

"When will you give me the Male Elixir?"

"When I manage to obtain the necessary ingredients. Now get to work."

She lifted one foot and brushed off a pointy pebble that had become embedded in her sole. "How long will I have to work with—"

He stopped her with a hand. "Do you remember the oath you took last night?"

She nodded.

"Repeat it."

"I swear in the name of Yahweh that I will obey you in all matters totally and without question until the process is complete and I am a boy."

"Total obedience," he said. "Nothing less. You are one of my slaves now, one among many, same as every other slave."

"I have only one question."

"Has Yahweh ever answered one of your questions?"

Deborah shook her head.

"In this tannery, I'm your god. Don't speak to me unless I address you first, and when I do, there's only one acceptable response. Do you know what it is?"

"Yes, Master."

"Correct," Kassite said.

Barely holding her tongue, Deborah turned and followed Petro.

38

Petro's group numbered eight slaves, including Deborah. The men ranged in age from about fifteen to thirty and had the bronze complexion and sharp features of Philistines. Glancing around at the other groups working nearby, she saw that most of the slaves looked Philistine, with only a few exceptions of light skin or hair. The group's first task was to move the newly arrived skins from the pavilion to the riverbank. There were over a hundred cowhides, thick with yellow fat, rotting flesh, and globs of coagulated blood.

On her first run, Deborah was unprepared for the weight, which not only challenged her arms and shoulders, but also put pressure on her thin legs and bare feet, whose soles were soon punctured by multiple pebbles. Halfway down to the riverbank, she lost her grip and the skins dropped. One of the other slaves in her group came over and assisted her. He was missing his right eye, and his arms were badly scarred.

"Thank you," Deborah said, smiling. "I didn't realize they were so heavy."

The man's single eye focused on her for a long moment. He murmured a few Philistine words and left. Deborah realized that her smile, apology, and gratitude all befitted a fourteen-year-old Hebrew girl, not a rough slave boy. She glanced at the back of the one-eyed man, hoping he hadn't thought too much of it, and reminded herself: Imitate to mutate!

On the next run, she took a lighter load and transferred it without incident.

Once all the skins had been piled up on the riverbank, each man took one from the pile, stepped into the river up to his knees, and pushed the skin into the water, hairy side up. Forcing it all the way down to the bottom, they stepped onto their hide to keep it submerged.

Deborah followed their example. She stepped on the hide, pressing it to the muddy bottom. Through the bottoms of her feet she felt the rocks underneath. After a few minutes, Petro clapped, and everyone pulled their skins out of the water, turned them upside down, and repeated the action.

Next, they placed the hides flat on the shore near the water's edge, scooped mud onto them, and used fist-size stones to grind the mud in with circular motions. By grinding like this on both sides for a while, much of the coagulated blood and thick gore came off, though a layer remained attached to the underside.

Soon, Deborah's arms could barely move, the muscles burning painfully. She switched hands often to give each arm a rest.

Petro clapped, and they started the process again with new hides.

By the end of he second cycle, Deborah was near collapse, but she continued working, especially after she caught One Eye glancing at her several times.

At one point, Petro left the group and beckoned her to follow. He went to the first row of five tubs, which were filled with cloudy water but no skins, knelt at the corner of the first tub and pulled out a piece of wood that served as a stopper. The connected tubs slowly drained into a channel that led to the river.

When the tubs were empty, Petro replaced the stopper and went to an open storage area near the tannery gate. There were mounds of limestone rocks, stacks of wooden planks, as well as jars of oil and baskets of fruit, vegetables, and flour.

Petro pointed to a handcart. It had four wheels, a long handle, and two open-top wooden barrels. Near the bottom of each barrel was a hole with a cork plug.

"I get it." She pointed at the plugs. "Pull these out. Go into the river, fill the barrels, plug the holes, and use the water to fill the tubs."

He grinned. "Smart boy, Borah."

She felt her face flush, but rather than thank him for the compliment, she shrugged and kicked the dirt, as she imagined a boy her age would do. Imitate to mutate!

Before she could start the task, the bell rang. Happy to take a break, Deborah lined up with Petro and the rest of the group, along with the other slaves. She felt One Eye staring at her, but ignored him.

The morning meal consisted of bread, yellow cheese, and carob. Like the others, she bowed to Kassite, who gave her no sign of recognition, and sat down under the pavilion to eat. The bread was soft and tasty, the cheese neither moldy nor stale, and the carob sweet and chewy.

When mealtime was over, her bladder felt ready to burst. Deborah glanced furtively at the men's latrines. Only one slave was there at the moment. She walked slowly at first, then faster when she saw him leave.

Peeing while standing was something she had never tried, and her first attempt was messy. Thankfully, her long shirt and undergarments were already wet from working in the river earlier. From now on, she decided, every visit to the latrines would have to involve pretending to do more than peeing.

As she headed to get the handcart with the barrels, she noticed Kassite walking out through the gate. One of the guards, standing just outside, held a horse by the reins. Kassite mounted it and rode up the path alone. He paused at the top, turned his horse around to survey the tannery below, and rode east on the Sea Highway toward Aphek. Deborah was surprised to see him leave as a free man, without shackles or guards. It was hard to believe that an owner would allow a slave such freedom. No wonder Kassite was reluctant to give it all up for a risky attempt to liberate Sallan from Judge Zifron in Emanuel.

While Petro and the rest of her group worked on the skins by the river, she pulled the handcart into the water, waited until the barrels filled up, and reached down to replace the plugs. She had to do it by feel, and it took a while.

Pulling the handcart out of the river with the barrels full to the rim required all her strength. The mucky bottom stuck to the wheels, and rocks blocked them. Once the handcart was out of the water, she paused to rest and noticed that the soot and ashes were mostly gone from her wet arms and legs, exposing her white skin and freckles. She glanced at the group and saw One Eye watching her. She stared back at him, and he looked away. She quickly smeared fresh mud on her arms, legs, and face.

The soil of the riverbank was soggy, and Deborah had to get behind the handcart and push it all the way to the tubs. However, because the holes at the bottom of the barrels were small, she enjoyed a few moments of rest while the water drained slowly into the tubs.

Deborah managed to complete five trips when the bell rang for the midday meal. Her arms and legs hurt badly, the soles of her feet were lacerated, and the palms of her hands bubbled with blisters. After rubbing fresh mud on her arms, legs, and face, she skipped the line, went directly to the pavilion, and collapsed on the ground.

Petro came over, shaking his head. He pointed at the line of men. "You must eat, Borah."

"I'm not hungry."

"Everyone must eat," he said. "Master expects it."

"Master isn't here."

Petro grinned, showing his broken teeth. "Master always knows everything."

Back on her feet, the pain was a hundred times worse, but she clenched her teeth and made no sound while following Petro to the back of the line.

This time the meal consisted of bread, meat, and apples. She trod carefully on her sore feet and held the food with the tips of her fingers to avoid irritating the blisters. Following the other slaves' example, she bowed before Kassite's empty chair.

While they were eating, a commotion arose at the gate. Deborah's first thought was that Kassite had returned with the ingredients for the Male Elixir. She got up, filled with excitement, and stepped out from the crowded pavilion to welcome him.

It wasn't Kassite at the gate. Rather, a group of armed men on horses forced their way in, facing little resistance from the guards. Once inside the tannery, they moved aside, making way for their leader.

Seesya!

39

Despite the blast of shock and fear that hit her, Deborah had the presence of mind to retreat back into the pavilion before Seesya noticed her. His initial attention was on the west part of the tannery, where all the female slaves had stopped working and were about to come over to get their food.

Sitting back next to Petro, Deborah saw One Eye staring at her. He must have noticed her excitement, followed by her hasty retreat.

Advancing his stallion into the middle of the tannery, holding his nose, Seesya looked around, getting the lay of the land. He wasn't wearing a helmet, and his oily black hair hung loose around his head, down to his shoulders, covering his ears, which Deborah hoped were still bloody.

"Who runs this place?" Seesya looked toward the gate, where the guards stood. When they didn't respond, his soldiers dragged one of the guards over, and Seesya asked again, "Who's the boss here?"

"Master is in charge." The guard pointed at the house on the river. "He lives there."

Two of the soldiers rode over, dismounted, and entered the house. They reemerged a moment later, shoving the two servants while shaking their heads. The servants ran over to join the male slaves under the pavilion.

Seesya twirled his horsewhip. "Where is he?"

"Master isn't here right now," the guard said.

"I can see that, but where is he?"

"I don't know." The guard tried to step back, but the soldiers held him. "He left this morning."

Seesya whipped the guard across the face. He screamed and fell down.

The soldiers brought over another guard. Deborah recognized him as the guard who had pulled off her scarf and taunted her with a stick.

"Master went east," the guard said hurriedly, shielding his face with his hands. "Maybe to the shop in Aphek, or to see the owner at his homestead in the land of Manasseh. He doesn't tell us where he goes. I swear!"

"Thank you," Seesya said with mock politeness. "That's better. And who is in charge in the meantime?"

"No one," the guard said.

Seesya raised the horsewhip.

"The group leaders!" The guard cowered. "They know what to do—that's how it is, really!"

Whipping the guard back and forth across the face, Seesya cursed. He pointed his whip in the direction of the female slaves. The soldiers sprinted over to that side. The woman scattered to avoid being trampled and screamed in panic. The soldiers galloped back and forth, shouting and waving their spears to herd the women like goats to the back of the tannery, where they stood single file with their backs to the wooden fence.

A few of the male slaves got up and yelled in protest. Two of Seesya's soldiers rode over and scared them back under the east pavilion.

Strutting up and down on his stallion before the terrified women, Seesya ordered them to remove their scarves. He peered at them, examining one face after another as he advanced along the long line.

Deborah sat among the male slaves, watching the events unfold. Her chest was tight, making it hard to breathe. One Eye kept glancing at her.

Seesya finished inspecting the women and signaled to his soldiers, who rode over and ordered the men out of their pavilion. Deborah followed close behind Petro and stood with the group in the middle of the tight cluster of about one hundred slaves. The mounted soldiers surrounded them with ready spears.

"I'm looking for my wife," Seesya yelled. Mounted on his great stallion, dressed in armor, hand resting on the handle of his sword, he looked quite formidable. "She came here yesterday, looking for a man in this tannery—I'm not sure who, or why. She's fourteen, taller than most girls that age, and as thin as a dry twig. Her hair is orange, but it was dyed black a couple of days ago. She has chalky skin with brown spots all over, like maggots on goat cheese, and a big mouth."

Some slaves laughed and translated his words to those who had not yet mastered the language of the Hebrews. Her face burning, Deborah felt weak. Her knees threatened to buckle. To her left, standing next to Petro, One Eye bent forward and turned his head to look at her.

"I am a rich Hebrew," Seesya said. "Tell me where she is, and I'll buy your freedom."

Petro noticed that One Eye was looking at Deborah and spoke to him in a low voice. One Eye reached over, grabbed Deborah's arm, and rubbed off a bit of the mud, exposing the freckled skin underneath.

"Who wants to go free?" Seesya looked at them, searching for a response. "Don't be afraid!"

One Eye began to raise his arm, but Petro pushed it down and whispered urgently in his ear. They were surrounded by many other slaves, which was the reason Seesya and his soldiers hadn't noticed the argument, but Deborah knew it was only a matter of time before One Eye defied Petro and gave her away.

"I'm waiting!" Seesya pulled the reins, making his horse step sideways and neigh. "Don't you want to get away from this foul stench?"

Pulling his arm free from Petro, One Eye again tried to raise it, but Petro grabbed him in a bear hug and spoke into his ear. It was a brief sentence, only a few words, but One Eye suddenly relented. His arm went slack, his shoulders slumped, and he lowered his head in surrender.

Seesya cursed and bolted forward, straight into the slaves, his horse trampling some men as everyone ran out of the way, roaring in fear. Deborah barely managed to stumble away. As he rode by, Seesya kicked her in the back, causing her to fall facedown in the mud. Certain that he had noticed her, she expected him to circle around and cheer triumphantly while snaring her with a rope, but Seesya continued to ride back and forth, reveling in the slaves' fright and oblivious to how close he came to capturing her.

A moment later, after kicking a few more slaves and grabbing fistfuls of meat and bread from the serving area, Seesya and his men left through the gate, raising a cloud of dust as they sprinted up the path and onto the Sea Highway, heading east toward Aphek.

With the attackers gone and the gate locked again, the slaves seemed dazed with shock. They gathered back into working groups, and the leaders took charge, returning to work. The few injured slaves were carried to a small canopy near Kassite's home, where women slaves tended to them.

Saying nothing about what had happened, Petro told Deborah to resume ferrying water with the handcart from the river to the tubs. The rest of the group resumed work on the hides at the riverbank. One Eye didn't look at her again. He kept his head down as he worked with the others. She wondered what Petro had told him.

By the time she'd finished filling all five tubs with fresh water, Deborah's hands were bleeding, and the sun was touching the western horizon. Petro and the others finished washing the hides, brought them over to the tubs, and pushed them underwater by standing on top. Deborah dragged the handcart back to the storage area near the gate. Every part of her body was in agony. The ringing of the bell brought tears of gratitude to her eyes, which she quickly wiped away.

Besides bread, meat, and apples, the evening meal included cups of hot water spiced with mint leaves and honey. Only Petro's watchful gaze made her finish the food and drink. She glanced at the gate often, hoping to see Kassite come back alone. If Seesya had captured him and forced him to talk, she was doomed.

After the meal, Petro lighted a torch and led her to the small canopy near Kassite's house. Two slave women were tending to four male slaves—three with broken legs splinted to wood planks, and a fourth who appeared feverish.

"They'll dress your feet and hands," Petro told her, turning to leave.

"Wait," Deborah said. "What did you say to him?"

"That I'd poke out his other eye."

Deborah could tell by Petro's tone that he meant it. She was filled with gratitude, but the contradiction didn't escape her. How could blinding one person be an act of charity to another? And why had Petro defended her against One Eye, a fellow-Philistine whom he had surely known for much longer?

He answered her unspoken question without prompting. "Master said you are Borah, a new boy for my group. Master made me responsible for you."

She watched him leave while the meaning of what he said sank in. For him, Kassite's words—that she was a boy, not a girl—were sacrosanct.

The women helped Deborah sit on the ground. They smeared green paste on the bottoms of her feet and purple ointment on her blistered hands. The pain spiked at first, making her grimace, but it gradually subsided as the herbs took effect. The women tied linen bandages over her hands and feet and told her to go back to the men's pavilion.

By now, the tannery was completely quiet, with all the other slaves fast asleep and only a handful of torches left alight. Making her way slowly, she heard a horse whinny outside the gate.

Deborah paused and stood still, listening. Men spoke in hushed voices. Was it Seesya and his soldiers, coming back to get her?

More voices sounded, and the gate creaked.

She glanced over her shoulder. The river was only fifteen or twenty steps away. She could run for it, wade through the water, and sneak out around the jutting fence the way she had come in the day before.

Ready to flee, she gazed in the direction of gate.

A lone figure approached—tall, thin, and limping. He crossed the tannery toward her, carrying a sack, his face lit by the single torch that burned near the east pavilion.

Relief filled Deborah. She raised her hand in greeting. Kassite nodded and continued past her and toward his house. The small bridge squeaked under his boots. A slave opened the door, bowed, and took the sack, holding the door open for him.

Deborah expected Kassite to turn back and invite her in, but he entered the house, and the servant closed the door.

The disappointment made her feel sick. She sat down on the ground and extended her legs to take the weight off her bandaged feet. The night began to spin around her. She lay back, rested her head on the soft ground, and closed her eyes.

Her breathing slowed down and her dizziness eased. She opened her eyes to check whether the world was still spinning. It wasn't. The sky was clear, not a single cloud to blot the clear canopy of sparkling stars. The night was quiet except for the sound of her breathing and the subtle swoosh of shallow waves lapping at the riverbank. She imagined being truly alone with nothing around her—no people, no tannery, no ground—only her own body, floating in a dark space among the countless specks of glittering stars.

The burning was gone from her hands and feet, which throbbed with a distant, dull pain. A cool breeze came from the river, caressing her face and drying off the film of sweat. Was it Yahweh, comforting her at this moment of complete isolation, sending a silent message that she wasn't alone in the world, even now, when she had no family or friends to lean on?

Suddenly, Deborah noticed a shadow above, blotting off the stars. She heard the squeak of a foot pressing down on the wet sand, and a dark figure bent over her.

40

Deborah let out a cry and sat up, only to recognize one of Kassite's two servants. He motioned her to follow him. She did, walking carefully on her bandaged feet over the sand and across the short bridge.

Inside the house, Kassite was seated at the table, which was set for one person with a plate, a knife, an empty wooden goblet, and a corked clay jug. Deborah glanced at the jug, wondering whether it contained the Male Elixir, or good wine from Aphek to go with Kassite's dinner.

"There you are," he said. "I hear it's been an eventful day."

"Yes, Master."

He appraised her up and down. "No wonder your own husband could not tell you apart from the men."

"He hurt the guards and some of the slaves."

"That was the reason I sent you away from the gate when you first arrived. If no one knows you entered the tannery, no one can tell your husband."

She almost told him about One Eye but held her tongue, reluctant to give him any reason to change his mind and send her away.

"I think we are safe now," he said.

Knowing Seesya's violent nature and the depth of his rage at the humiliation she had repeatedly inflicted on him, Deborah didn't share his optimism.

"He isn't one to be fooled easily," she said.

Kassite touched the knife but didn't pick it up. "I heard a story in Aphek about a Hebrew girl defending a group of lepers from a gang of boys, scaring them off with surprisingly accurate stone-throwing. I took care to spread a rumor that the boys caught the girl later and tossed her in the river by the gorge, where she drowned, her body swept downstream by the fast current."

"Thank you," she said, though in her heart she doubted whether

Seesya would ever give up. "It was fortunate that you were absent when he arrived today."

"Fortune had nothing to do with it." Kassite chuckled. "Anticipating danger ahead of time allows for planning an effective defense, and sometimes the best defense is avoidance."

Deborah was too tired to follow his clever words. There was only one thing on her mind. "Have you found the ingredients for the Male Elixir?"

"Have you not suffered enough today to realize that a boy's life might be worse than that of a girl?"

She shook her head.

"In my experience, even grown men often break down on their first day as slaves in the tannery." He gestured at her hands and feet. "In fourteen years as a girl, have you ever been in such pain?"

"I have had blisters many times. They heal."

"This is only the beginning The process will be long and arduous."

"Three phases. I remember."

"That's right. Three phases. Today was only a small sample of the hardship to come."

"I'm ready for it."

Kassite looked at her at length. "Are you sure?"

In the window, against the faint glow of the stars, she saw a dark shape flying. It was a large bird, maybe a hawk or an eagle, its wings stretched out as it glided out of sight.

"Yes, Master," she said. "I'm sure."

"Very well." He unplugged the clay jug, poured its contents into the goblet, and used a twig to stir it. "This is what you came to me for – the Male Elixir."

Deborah shuddered with a mix of elation and dread. This was the point of no return.

"As I explained yesterday,' Kassite said, pronouncing each word with slow deliberation, "this will help you gain the physical strength and resilience of a young man."

"Yes, Master."

"Fortunately, I managed to obtain all the ingredients." He took out the twig and held it above the goblet. Dark drops trickled down. "It is a potent brew."

Deborah wondered what the ingredients were, but she dared not ask. It didn't matter.

He offered her the goblet.

Accepting it with both hands, Deborah brought the goblet to her lips, but paused when the sharp odor hit her nostrils. Putrid meat and rotten eggs!

"Something wrong?" His voice was even, but he was smiling.

"It smells."

"The path ahead will be much worse than stench. Much worse, in fact, than you can imagine."

Deborah peered into the goblet. The liquid was nearly black. On the surface, small bubbles popped while new ones emerged from below. It didn't look magical or powerful, but she knew it was both. Drinking it would put her on the path to achieving the transformation she longed for. But why did it have to reek so badly? Would it make her sick? Or cause her to collapse and writhe in pain?

"Having second thoughts?"

Deborah brought the goblet to her lips.

"Never say I did not warn you," he said.

Tilting the goblet, she made the mistake of breathing through her nose. The odor hit her again, stronger this time, and she shivered with disgust.

"You can still change your mind." Kassite reached for the goblet. "No shame in choosing wisely."

She moved the goblet out of his reach. "My mind is set."

"Fine. If you are certain."

The first mouthful stunned her with its overwhelming sourness. The elixir was pasty, its consistency uneven, speckled with small gooey chunks and granulated nuggets. She forced it down and winced.

"Go on," he said. "Better to do it quickly."

The smell was getting worse, with traces of sour milk and a whiff of an animal carcass that had been left in the sun for too long. She poured a little more into her mouth, swallowed, and gagged.

"What is the problem, girl? Don't you want to become a boy?"

She inhaled deeply, but this time only through her mouth.

"A boy," Kassite said, "would drink the whole thing in one shot, finished and done with."

His words angered her. He was wrong, because a boy would be as repulsed by this nasty odor as she was. Deborah brushed aside her revulsion and gulped the rest of the elixir without pause.

Her stomach heaved. She took quick breaths and pressed her hand to her chest.

He took the empty goblet, chuckling.

Deborah burped, tasting it again, and fought off a tide of nausea.

"Let out the vapors," he said, "but do not vomit."

She gulped, somehow keeping it down.

"Other than the queasiness, you will feel little effect at first." He gave the goblet to one of the servants, who left the room with it. "The elixir works slowly, from deep within your body and mind. Remember, it is only an accelerant."

She had no trouble understanding his halting, measured speech, but she didn't always catch his meaning. "What was the last word?"

"Accelerant. It speeds up the process, but you still have to do all the hard work."

"Imitate to mutate."

"Exactly."

Deborah rubbed her stomach. Other than the awkward belching and the foul aftertaste, she felt fine. There was no pain—not yet, anyway.

A servant returned with a large pot and spooned out chunks of meat and carrots in light sauce onto Kassite's plate. Steam rose from the stew. In contrast to the elixir, the smell was mouthwatering, even in her state of nausea. The other servant brought a jug of wine and a cup, which he filled up and set down next to the plate.

Raising the cup, Kassite said, "Good luck to you."

A surge of joy overwhelmed her. "I can't believe it. After all this time searching for you, and everything that happened to me along the way— I've just drunk the Male Elixir! I'm going to be a boy, a young man!"

He took a sip of wine. "Not to spoil your celebration, but as I told you yesterday, the process will be long and hard."

"But the women of Edom changed into men overnight, didn't they?"

"That was different." He took another sip. "Temporary transformation isn't the same as what you're seeking."

"How long will I have to work as a slave?"

"It depends on you." Kassite pointed at the door. "Good night."

"A week? A month?"

"No more questions."

"I only want to know—"

Kassite slammed down the cup, splashing red wine on the table. "Are you reneging on your vow of total obedience?"

Deborah was bursting with excitement and impatience, but the mention of the vow she had taken, invoking Yahweh's name, muzzled her. She took a deep breath, exhaled, and bowed her head.

"That's better," he said. "Now go to sleep in the pavilion with all the men. You're one of the slaves now. Work begins at sunrise."

"Yes, Master."

A servant opened the door, and she left Kassite's house.

Halfway to the pavilion, Deborah stopped and looked up at the dark sky. She searched for the great bird that had flown across Kassite's window earlier, but there was nothing up there.

Another burp escaped her lips, accompanied by the taste of the Male Elixir. How long would it take for her to complete the transformation and emerge as a young man?

It depended on her, Kassite had said, but she wasn't alone on this journey. In the words of the blacksmith in Shiloh: "When you pursue your True Calling, God provides the shortcuts." There was no doubt in her mind that she was pursuing her True Calling.

In the back of the pavilion, Deborah collected a straw mat. The floor was filled with rows of sleeping men. She found a spot near Petro and the other members of her group. One Eye slept nearby, snoring lightly.

Lying side-by-side with strange men felt abnormal, a violation of everything she was accustomed to, except that she was no longer the helpless orphan girl from Emanuel. She had become Borah, a young slave who belonged among the men, not in the women's quarters. And, in the morning, and every morning from now on, she would rise with the bell, work alongside these men, and imitate their manners, postures, and habits until she had mutated into one of them.

In her mind, Deborah could see her transformation complete, leaving this odorous tannery to fight the house of Zifron, win back Palm Homestead, and live freely on her ancestors' land while serving God, as her father had dreamt.

For the first time since the horror of Tamar's stoning, Deborah felt truly hopeful. She burped again, but this time, there was no sour taste in her mouth. Her lips curled in a smile, her eyes closed, and she fell asleep.

To be continued …

NOTE TO THE READER

Deborah's journey continues in the second book in the series – *Deborah Calling* (HarperCollins, 2017), which is available both as an E-book and in paperback.

But first, here is a brief background on how this story came about in the first place. During a family trip to Israel, my sister, Iris Davidovich, took us to see the archeological remains of the ancient city of Shiloh, located in the Samariah Hills (currently called the "West Bank"), about 25 miles east of Tel Aviv. The site brings to life the Holy Tabernacle, where the tribes of Israel had worshiped for three centuries (before King David moved the temple in Jerusalem). The tangible relics fired up my imagination and inspired me to fill an enigmatic gap in the dramatic story of the first woman to lead any nation in recorded human history: Deborah.

While the *Book of Judges* describes Deborah's stunning success as a prophet, a judge and a military leader, who liberated her people from Canaanite oppression, there is no information about her family, upbringing, and youth. How could a girl, growing up in a world controlled by men, rise to rule over them? What hardships feuled her tenacity? What setbacks steeled her resilience? What battles transformed her into a formidable leader? These are the fascinating mysteries I attempt to unravel by telling Deborah's story in this series of novels.

In researching Deborah's story, I consulted countless books and articles about the way people lived in the ancient Mideast. They are too many to list here, but I am particularly indebted to the scholarly works of William F. Albright, Yigael Yadin, Avraham Biran, Israel Finkelstein, Benjamin Mazar, Amihai Mazar, William G. Dever, Joyce Salisbury, Carol Meyers, Thomas E. Levi, George Hart, Bruce Routledge, Richard Elliot Friedman, Geraldine Harris, Richard Wilkinson, Boyd Seevers, Gale A. Yee, Brian Schmidt, Alan Dickin, Monroe Rosenthal, Isaac Mozenson, Diana Vikander Edelman, Hershel Shanks and Claudia Valentino.

The team at HarperCollins Publishers has been incredibly supportive and professional, including Hannah Rivera, who guided me during the initial stages, Anna Paustenbach, who steered the manuscript through its multiple stages with unfailing expertise, judicious counsel, and good humor, and copyeditor Kathy Reigstad, who made numerous improvements to the manuscript. Needless to say, the responsibility for any mistakes is mine alone.

We are blessed with wonderful friends and family members, who read my manuscripts at various stages, provide insightful observations and, most graciously, offer enthusiastic support. They include (in alphabetical order) Margie and Arie Adler, Sarai Azrieli, Talya, Ben, and Elan Azrieli, Hagit and Michael David, Rabbi Dr. Israel Drazin, Don Eddins, Monica and Prof. Michael Finkelthal, Risa and Dr. Opher Ganel, Rachel and Joel Glazer, Prof. Sharon Glazer and Tamas Karpati, Julie and Hanan Gur, Dr. Jennifer and Nir Margalit, Linda and Dr. Bernard Rosenbaum, Glenna Salisbury, Wendy and Avner Skolnik, Stephen J. Wall, Stephanie and Ernie Wechsler, and Carol Wilner.

As always, this novel would not have come to life without the tireless support of my wife, Fiona, a dedicated physician who finds time to read the first draft of every new novel and provides astute critique, perceptive comments, and inspiring encouragement. Fiona and our children fill my life with love and laughter, which sustain me daily.

Last but not least, I owe a debt of gratitude to you, my readers, for choosing to spend your precious time with my books, for recommending the books to your friends, and for posting thoughtful insights and reviews on social media. There is no greater joy for a writer than a supportive community of readers. Thank you!

ABOUT THE AUTHOR

Avraham Azrieli is the author of books and screenplays. His first novel was *The Masada Complex* (a political thriller), followed by Israeli spy novels *The Jerusalem Inception* and *The Jerusalem Assassin*, as well as *Christmas for Joshua* (an interfaith family drama), *The Mormon Candidate* (a political thriller), *Thump* (a courtroom drama featuring sexual harassment and racism), and *The Bootstrap Ultimatum* (a mystery involving the commercialization of Memorial Day). Most recently, he has written a series of novels inspired by the true story of the first woman to lead a nation in human history, starting with *Deborah Rising* and *Deborah Calling* (HarperCollins, 2016 and 2017), and continuing with *Deborah Slaying* and *Deborah Leading*.

Beside fiction, he has also authored *Your Lawyer on a Short Leash - a guide to dealing with lawyers* and *One Step Ahead – A Mother of Seven Escaping Hitler's Claws* (an acclaimed WWII true story, which inspired the musical By Wheel and by Wing).

While growing up in Israel, Avraham received extensive Talmudic education, before attending law school and serving as a law clerk at the Israeli Supreme Court in Jerusalem. He later earned an advanced law degree from Columbia University in New York City, served as a law clerk for the Federal District Court, and started his legal career with Davis Polk & Wardwell. He has represented clients in numerous complex court cases before trial and appellate courts, including the United States Supreme Court. He currently lives near Washington DC with his wife and children. Like Ben Teller, the protagonist in *The Mormon Candidate* and *The Bootstrap Ultimatum*, Avraham often rides his motorcycle in the mountainous forests of western Maryland. To learn more, please visit www.AzrieliBooks.com

BOOKS BY AVRAHAM AZRIELI

Fiction:

The Masada Complex
The Jerusalem Inception
The Jerusalem Assassin
Christmas for Joshua
The Mormon Candidate
The Bootstrap Ultimatum
Thump
Deborah Rising
Deborah Calling
Deborah Slaying
Deborah Leading
The Elixirist

Nonfiction:

Your Lawyer on a Short Leash – A Guide to Dealing with Lawyers
One Step Ahead – A Mother of Seven Escaping Hitler's Claws

Author Website:

www.AzrieliBooks.com